NOVELS
Chase in Shadow
Clear Water
Gambling Men: The Novel
The Locker Room
Sidecar
A Solid Core of Alpha
The Talker Collection (Anthology)

THE KEEPING PROMISE ROCK SERIES
Keeping Promise Rock
Making Promises
Living Promises

NOVELLAS
Bewitched by Bella's Brother
Christmas with Danny Fit
Hammer and Air
If I Must
It's Not Shakespeare
Puppy, Car, and Snow
Super Sock Man
Truth in the Dark
The Winter Courtship Rituals of Fur-Bearing Critters

GREEN'S HILL
Guarding the Vampire's Ghost
I love you, asshole!
Litha's Constant Whim

TALKER SERIES
Talker
Talker's Redemption
Talker's Graduation

Published by DREAMSPINNER PRESS
http://www.dreamspinnerpress.com

Sidecar
Amy Lane

Dreamspinner Press

Published by
Dreamspinner Press
382 NE 191st Street #88329
Miami, FL 33179-3899, USA
http://www.dreamspinnerpress.com/

Sidecar

Cover Art by Shobana Appavu bob@bob-artist.com

ISBN: 978-1-61372-568-9

Printed in the United States of America
First Edition
June 2012

eBook edition available
eBook ISBN: 978-1-61372-569-6

This is for men like my husband and father who believe parenthood is a sacrament and good works bring us closer to the good in the universe, for whom gentleness is not weakness and flaws are forgivable, who struggle daily between what is good and what is easy and very nearly land on the right side of that every single time.

Note from the Author

BACK when I used to teach high school, my students would come up to me and try to get me not just to *listen* to their music, but to *love* their music.

It was never going to happen.

Besides the fact that I was a die-hard Springsteen fan (which just sort of takes you out of all other music categories, favorite-wise!), my tastes ran completely counter to the popular music in the area in which I was teaching—but I told my kids that it didn't matter. In fact, I told them to embrace it.

"Okay—you guys, don't listen to what grown-ups say about your music, because the fact is, that music will help you time travel. You don't believe me? In twenty years when you're exhausted and you're worried about your job or your kids or politics or your spouse, and you feel like you've got the weight of the world on your shoulders, you will hear a song, and *BOOM!* There you'll be. Twenty years in the past, when you had the entire world before you!"

I've had kids come back and tell me that I was right, and that was true, and they thanked me, because I gave them permission to fly the way they wanted to without ever trying to be someone different than who I was.

Every chapter in this book is a song title. The two chapters set in the modern day were taken off of 2011 *Billboard* charts. However, Joe and Casey's story starts in 1987—and some years are more important to us than others. So I took every chapter title for the rest of the story from a list of the top 100 songs of 1987. Enjoy them. Think of them as your very own time machine, and travel back a little. For some of us (raises hand), 1987 was a *very* good year!

Someone Like You
~Casey

THE kid was cold. Casey could see that as Joe puttered past him in the tree-shaded twilight of Foresthill Road near Sugar Pine Lake. It was November and in the forties this time of night, and the lost thing on the side of the road was not dressed for the weather. He didn't look good at all. His lips were blue, his thin arms folded in front of him were paler than the grimy T-shirt, and his cheeks were hectically flushed.

And his eyes were dead.

Casey reached from under the fleece-lined leather lap robe that nestled him in the cozy sidecar (complete with a little space heater at his feet, because Joe took care of details like that) and tapped Joe's thigh, but he didn't need to bother. Joe was the same guy he'd been twenty-five years earlier. He could spot a miserable runaway a mile away.

They pulled the cycle over to the side of the road, and Casey took off his helmet—because he knew they looked scary when you were cold and alone on the side of a country road—and called out.

"Hey, kid!"

They'd passed the boy up, walking in the opposite direction, and Casey could see the kid's shoulders stiffen as they called out to him.

"Yeah?" he asked, like he was bracing himself for a blow.

Casey and Joe met eyes. Casey sighed and got out of the sidecar, then walked carefully to about five yards from the boy. A big enough distance so the kid could run away if he felt like he needed to, and close enough so he could see that Casey, at forty-one, was probably fit enough to catch him, and maybe mean enough to give chase.

"Kid, look. It's going to dip into freezing tonight. Can we take you anywhere?"

The kid narrowed his eyes, and he gave a convulsive shudder. "I...." He closed his eyes. "I don't got nowhere to go."

Casey nodded, because they'd known that. "We've got a spare bedroom," he said cautiously. "For the night. No strings. We've even got some food."

Oh, God. The eyes on this kid. Brown, deep, and terrified.

"I...." The kid shivered again. "I don't got no money, but I can"—he grabbed his crotch uncomfortably—"I can pay."

Casey wrinkled his nose. "You see that graying bastard on the back of that motorcycle?"

The kid looked up. Joe was sitting there, his comfortably wrinkling face sunk into what looked to be a habitual scowl but was really just a thoughtfulness almost out of place in this century. His gray-and-white ponytail was sticking out from under his helmet like a barely contained coal brush, and he had a fairly frightening Fu Manchu mustache with matching soul patch. He was easily six feet five inches tall, and his shoulders were (at least to a young man's eyes) as broad as a barn. He was one of those men who became thick with age in spite of the best efforts of diet and exercise, and he looked like one hammer swing from his fist would effectively dent the hood of a half-ton pickup.

The kid's eyes grew huge. "Yeah," he whispered, obviously scared of what came next.

"He keeps me plenty busy. And if I slept around, he'd kill me. And if he slept around, I'd geld him. I'd say you're safer in the spare bedroom of two old queers than you are almost anywhere else in the county." Casey lowered his voice. "Including, maybe, your own home."

The kid looked up, and something dropped from his eyes, and what was left was naked, feverish, and damned near to done. "I'll do anything," he begged.

"No worries," Casey said, keeping his voice low and soothing, like he would with a wild bear or a rabid chicken. "Here. We'll let you sit in the sidecar home. We've got a spare helmet; it's nice and warm. It'll be good. Trust me."

The kid cast a hunted look at Joe, who was watching the two of them with serene curiosity. "That guy—that guy's not gonna...." He shuddered.

Casey rolled his eyes. "Kid, you should be so lucky. But no. I worked too hard to make him mine, okay?"

The kid looked dubious, and Casey smiled to himself. Odds were good they'd take the kid home, give him a couple of warm meals, and find somewhere for him to go live. Maybe, if he was like some of the other strays they'd picked up, he'd stay a few months, or maybe a few years, but either way, the kid had nothing to worry about from Josiah Daniels. Joe was 100 percent decent—and 110 percent Casey's. But even if the kid *did* end up placed with them, and even lived with them for years, he probably would never hear the whole story. That story was for Casey and Joe alone.

The kid looked at the sidecar again, and the lines of his face, bitter and saturnine—even at what? Fifteen? Sixteen?—eased for a minute.

"Would I really get to ride in that?" he asked, and Casey got a glimpse of little kid in the bitter, tattered thing on the side of the road.

"Yeah!" Casey grinned at the kid and then looked at Joe with the same grin. Something in Joe's slightly weathered fiftyish features softened, and the kid looked quickly from Casey to Joe and back again.

"He really likes you," the kid whispered, and Casey shrugged.

"Yeah. Yeah, he really does." The kid didn't have to know how long it took Casey before Joe admitted to it. "So, kid, you want to use our spare room? We got a mother-in-law cottage. You can sleep there if you want."

The kid looked hungrily at the sidecar, with the fleece lap robe and the spare helmet Joe was casually pulling out from underneath the seat. Then Joe added the kicker—an extra peanut butter and jelly sandwich that they'd packed before they'd set out on the bike that afternoon. They'd ended up eating out at The Oar Cart anyway, but the sandwich had let them ride farther before they turned around. Casey could tell when the kid spotted the sandwich. His tongue must have smacked on his palate about six times. *Then* Joe pulled out the little takeout box from The Oar Cart, the one with half a pound of meat and sourdough bun in it, and Casey could smell the aroma of world-famous burger from where he was standing. He thought the kid was going to swoon.

"I don't care," the boy said, swallowing. "Maybe your house… just for a night."

Casey grinned again and held out his hand. "Casey," he said. "Casey Daniels." Somewhere out there was probably a birth certificate and a Social Security card and a thousand other things that proclaimed he'd been born with a different name, but he couldn't find them, and Joe didn't know where they were, and even Casey's driver's license said Casey Daniels now.

"Austin," the kid said earnestly. "Austin Harris." He had brown hair that looked like it had been hacked off in the back, sides, and front, and teeth that hadn't been brushed in too long. Casey reached out his hand again, and the kid shook it, tentatively.

"It's not clean," he said by way of apology, and Casey shrugged, wiggling his fingers.

"Skin washes," he said with quiet optimism. "Here. You eat on the way, and you can take a shower before you go to sleep, okay?"

The kid shivered all over and squeezed his eyes tight shut. "I think I have lice," he said, miserable, like this confession cost him everything.

Casey grimaced. "Well, thanks for warning us. We'll be sure to treat that helmet with the disinfectant shit when we get home." He pursed his lips. "I think we've got a lice comb and some mineral oil— or would you rather just shave it off?"

The kid shook his head. "I don't care," he said, shivering. "Food, a place to sleep, a door… shave me bald, I don't care."

Casey gestured toward the motorcycle. "Go get yourself settled in. Try not to spill too much on the lap robe. That was a present."

The kid didn't hear that last part. He was trotting toward the sidecar like it was a little slice of heaven. Casey followed more sedately, wondering if they were going to wake up with their throats slit and their television gone but thinking probably not. He knew this kid, knew what he wanted—had *been* this kid.

He got to the motorcycle and planted his hands easily on Josiah's strong shoulders, swung his leg around, and got his feet settled on the pegs.

"You know who that kid reminds me of?" Joe told him as they watched the kid fumble with the helmet strap and get settled under the lap robe, huddling down near the space heater using as much play as the seat belt would give him.

"Yeah, I know," Casey said, resting his cheek against Joe's back, careful of clunking the state-of-the-art bright turquoise helmet on his head against Joe's back, or against his no-nonsense-black helmet, with too much force. Joe could take it—the sonuvabitch was strong—but Casey wouldn't ever do anything to cause him pain.

"You only think you know," Josiah said softly. "You'll never know what it costs me, seeing you in them, again and again and again."

"But you take them in, every time," Casey reminded him, tightening his grip around Joe's waist.

"Yeah, well, what else would I do?"

"Not a damned thing."

The kid had overcome the adjustment shivers and was starting to plow through the food. They had about a half an hour before they got to their own little piece of Foresthill, so Joe didn't waste any time kick-starting the bike and roaring back onto the road.

He wouldn't do a damned thing different, and Casey wouldn't want him to. After twenty-five years, that was saying something.

Because Casey wouldn't change it either.

Livin' On a Prayer
~Casey

25 Years Earlier

FUCK, it was cold in the foothills. The truck driver had pulled off at some bizarre intersection on I-80 that proclaimed itself to be the exit for a place called Foresthill. He parked the rig (no payload, or he wouldn't have been able to pull off) in the parking lot of a Raley's supermarket with a McDonald's in the lower quadrant. He stopped to go get food, and when Casey asked if the guy could get him some, he was met with another round of *This Is Your Ass*.

"You gonna let me again?" the guy asked. He was a short, stocky guy with a thankfully midsized dick.

"I didn't let you the first six times," Casey snapped, tired of it all. "All I ever offered was a fucking blowjob, and you've fucked me six times in the last two days. I think I could get some goddamned food!"

The guy—Big Daddy (ugh!) or Glen or whateverthefuckhis namewas—was sitting on the far side of the truck, which meant that moving in to crack Casey across the face was awkward, which was good, because if he'd actually landed the blow he'd had planned, he would have knocked Casey unconscious. As it was, he laid open Casey's lip on his teeth and bloodied his nose, all in one casual crack of a closed fist.

Casey had been hit a lot in the last couple of months. He grunted and let his body go limp to absorb some of the pain.

"I'll be back in a few," the guy said like he hadn't just practically knocked Casey's teeth out. "Maybe I'll bring food."

Well, maybe "maybe" wasn't good enough. The thought was hard to get past Casey's ringing head and the pain blossom in his face, but still, he heard it loud and clear.

He opened the door and hissed—it was *fucking* cold, and the taste of snow was like the edge of bronze on his tongue—but that didn't stop his resolve any. He was still dizzy, so scrambling down from the big rig was hard, and he was damned grateful he didn't fall on his ass. He eventually made it to his own two feet, though, and tried to take stock. He walked to the edge of the parking lot, almost amused to see a sidewalk rounding this little corner of strip mall, and then saw the yellow sign across the street. It prohibited any vehicle over five tons from driving the granite-wall-lined road beyond.

Well thankyajebus, it looked like things were finally going his way.

He tucked his hands in the pockets of his dirty 501 jeans, pulled up the collar of his grungy, once-pink Izod shirt, and started walking down the side of the road.

For the first quarter mile, he was protected by the roughly cut granite walls, which blocked the wind, and he was grateful. Then the blind drop of the hill he was walking down ended, and he caught his breath.

He was going to cross *that*?

The road dipped down and then became a bridge—one of the tallest Casey had ever seen—spanning the gap between what looked to be two mountains. And as Casey was trying to catch his breath for the height of the bridge, his granite windbreak ended, and he was exposed to the force of the wind. It was sharp enough to bring tears to his eyes, but not once did he think of going back.

He plodded, grimly determined not to wander back up that hill to where Glen "Big Daddy" truck driver waited with his ready fist and hamster's libido. Glen hadn't been the first Big Daddy Casey had met in the last two months, and in this moment, walking toward that vast, tenuous space between everything that was safe, Casey felt like he was leaving Glen and all those other horrors behind. He was done with them. The wind grew stronger until, by the time he was actually on the bridge, on the little pedestrian walkway of the separated lane that was going east, it felt like it was actively trying to rip him off his feet and hurl him over the chest-high rail.

If it hadn't been for his piss-stubborn defiance to resist doing what the wind was trying to *make* him do, he might have simply climbed up and jumped off all on his own. As it was, that trip across the bridge—some twenty-five hundred feet, compared to the more than seven hundred foot drop below him—was the longest walk of his life.

But the bridge ended, like all things must end, and he wisely didn't stop and turn around to see what it was he'd just crossed. Most of him knew that until he could no longer see the bridge, the temptation to jump off of it might just break him.

The road after the bridge wound about, and the outside edge of it went from being on top of a low rise to being the crumbling edge of a steep cliff. Casey was beyond cold by this time, and beyond caring. His teeth were rattling around in his head, and his scalp itched to the point of misery, but he couldn't bring himself to worry. Somehow jumping off the edge of the road didn't have the same drama as jumping off the bridge. He was just going to keep walking until his body gave out, until the abused muscles in his thighs and ass cramped and he simply sank to his knees on the side of the road and fell asleep in the encroaching dusk.

He'd just tripped a second time when he heard the roar of a motorcycle behind him. It wasn't the first vehicle that had come his way, but it was the first vehicle that pulled up ahead and stopped.

The guy on the back of it was really terrifying.

For one thing, he was huge—well over six feet tall. He had a Fu Manchu mustache and a soul patch, both of them dark, silky brown, and a whole lot of dark brown hair pulled back in a ponytail under his helmet. His bike was something big, with a mildly extended front end and just enough chrome to be shiny, not enough to make it look gaudy. Proud but not a douche bag—that was Casey's first thought.

Then the guy took off his helmet, and Casey's second thought was that he was at least good-looking, unlike the parade of ass-fuckers who'd managed to get Casey from Bakersfield to wherever-the-fuck-he-was now. He had dark brown eyes and a short, square jaw; surprisingly pink lips that weren't too full and not too lean, either; and a nose that sloped solidly outward but wasn't too big. Pleasing. Under the handlebar mustache and the soul patch and the loosely swinging ponytail of shiny dark hair, he was actually really pretty. Casey would think later that maybe that was the reason for all the hair—the hair hid the prettiness—but that was not what he was thinking now.

Right now he was thinking that the guy was taking off his jacket on the side of the road, and Casey had damned near had enough.

"I'm not doing that," he snapped, pretty sure he'd rather die than do that one more goddamned time.

The guy looked up, unoffended. "I'm not asking you to," he said, his voice mild. "You're cold."

The jacket was leather, shiny and well cared for, with a fleece lining, and the big man with all the hair took it off, took a few steps forward, and set it down on the ground. He was wearing a hooded sweatshirt underneath, bright green, with an eyeball-searing CSUS emblazoned on the front in gold. The sweatshirt looked warm—warmer than what Casey had on—but it wouldn't be so warm when the guy got back on the bike. Casey looked at the jacket with longing. Was it his imagination, or was there steam rising up from the mysterious stranger's body heat?

Mysterious Stranger took a few steps back so Casey could walk up and claim the jacket, and Casey screwed his eyes tight against tears.

"Thanks," he said, caving. He trotted forward and picked up the jacket, then trotted back into his safety zone, sliding it over his shoulders. Oh God, it was still warm. It smelled good too, like sweat, but clean sweat; antiseptic; Old Spice deodorant; Irish Spring soap. He shivered and snuggled deep into it. The guy had a broad chest, powerful. It looked like he worked outside a lot, and the jacket went practically to Casey's midthigh. Casey scratched his head for a second and then put his hands in the pockets to keep them warm.

"There's money in the pocket," the stranger said, and Casey rooted through and found a twenty-dollar bill. He swallowed. That could buy nearly forty hamburgers, but this guy had been really decent about the jacket. He pulled the money out and was about to set it on the ground when the stranger said, "No, no—you can keep it if you want.

Or you can come home with me and use my spare room. I've got food.
You can shower."

Casey scowled at him. "What do I have to do in return?" he
asked, rightfully suspicious. He'd washed dishes at a little mom-and-
pop place once, spent the entire night cleaning up the kitchen of the
diner until his bones ached, and when he was done, he'd asked for the
food the owner had promised him and was told he had to do one more
favor first. He'd gotten fed, eventually, but he was good and sick of
favors.

The guy shrugged. "I've got some work I'm doing on my
property. You can help with that. But first, get you clean. Get you food.
Get you some sleep. You can decide on a fair price when that's done."

Later Casey would wonder why. He'd look deeply into this man's
heart and try to find the reason for this much kindness. Later he'd
berate himself for being seven kinds of fool for going with him, and
then berate himself for being seven kinds of fool for ever doubting him.
But that was later.

"Food?" he asked, his voice breaking. God. Big Daddy truck
driver had given him half a hamburger and some leftover fries the day
before, but his stomach was damned near cramping. The guy nodded,
then opened up the little seat compartment of his motorcycle. He pulled
out a granola bar—the real kind, not the kind with chocolate and shit on
it—and made a tentative throwing motion. Casey put his hands out in
front of him, and he threw it for real.

Casey scratched his scalp and then opened the package and
devoured the crunchy, dry thing with a ferocity he didn't know he had.
When he'd swallowed, he crumpled up the wrapper, and the guy said,
"Put it in your pocket. You can throw it away at my house."

Casey looked at him then and sighed. The guy had given him
food up front, and the jacket. He shifted uneasily in his jeans and itched
his crotch. "Thank you," he said. "I'll do *that* if you want now."

The guy shook his head. "*That's* not on the menu, kid. For one
thing, I think you've got crabs."

Casey scrunched up his face. "Oh, ew!"

The guy nodded sympathetically. "Yeah," he sighed. "I'm gonna have to dry-clean the jacket too."

Oh shit. Casey felt his face crumple. "Lice," he muttered, scratching at his scalp again. "Oh God. That's just so gross. You're going to have to shave my head and…." He felt tears threaten. It was stupid, but he liked his hair. It was brown now, but in the summer, it bleached this sort of honey color, and it was soft, and before he'd run away, he'd gotten it cut all fashionable like that guy on television who rode in the boat and had an alligator.

Mysterious Stranger took a couple of steps forward, so Casey could read his expression in the thickening twilight. "Naw, kid. I've got a lice comb and some Rid-X and all that shit. Even the Kwell for the crabs."

"You get crabs a lot?" Oh God. This could go south *so* many ways.

Mysterious Stranger laughed. "No. I take in strays a lot. And I work in a hospital, so there's always a danger of getting something from the sheets or something like that."

Casey nodded like that made sense, even though it didn't because nobody was that good a person. "You a doctor?" He looked awfully young. *Nobody* that young was a doctor, unless it was on television, and the guy shook his head.

"I'm a nurse."

Casey was shocked. "You're… you're… you're a *man!*"

The guy laughed dryly. He'd heard that one before. "So they tell me. Kid, it's getting cold. If I'm gonna save your life, we'd best get on the motorcycle soon."

Casey nodded, still unsure, and then his stomach growled, loudly and with prejudice. Well, hell. If the guy *was* still planning on taking Casey to his place and killing him, Casey could fight back better fed.

"Okay," he said, still uncertain, and Mysterious Stranger stuck out a hand.

"I'm Josiah Daniels. You can call me Joe."

Casey had to walk forward a bit before he could take that hand. "Casey," he said, not wanting to talk about his last name. His parents didn't want him; he didn't want them. Joe's hand was still out, and he held perfectly still until Casey grasped it, and then he shook slowly, carefully, letting Casey control the pressure. Casey was reassured somehow. That hand was warmer than his, and it was bigger, stronger, with calluses, but it didn't do anything it didn't have to do.

Joe gestured to the motorcycle and then got on first, which was good, because Casey needed to grab hold of his shoulders to swing his leg over. In spite of the fact that Casey was pretty sure his body stench was scaring off small animals, Joe didn't even flinch. He held very still until Casey's arms were around his waist, and then started the bike up again, pulled it up from its lean on the kickstand, and took off in one smooth motion.

Casey would remember that ride behind Joe forever.

The man's chest really was wide, and his waist was trim, and he had a way of moving his body to block the wind. The sky above them had turned the color of a girl's party dress, and the road was purple, like a bruise. The trees were all pine and fir here, and they lined the road like serene sentinels, gesturing the way toward that cotton-candy sky. Without the bite of the wind, the colors and the shadows of the chill of the Sierras were almost friendly, and Casey forgave the cold for trying to kill him a while ago, because he was snuggled deep inside Joe's jacket, and nothing could hurt him. Instead, Casey grasped that trim waist and tightened against him and closed his eyes, and between the whoosh of the air and the rumble of the bike, he might have fallen asleep if Joe hadn't felt his grip slacken and grabbed his hands and shaken them every so often.

It was the first peace Casey had felt in months. No one yelling at him, nobody wanting something from him—just this guy, this warm, big guy putting Casey's destiny in his big, rough hands. Casey sort of wished that ride could have gone on forever.

As it was, Josiah-call-me-Joe took a turn into a barely there road off of Foresthill and then another turn into what looked like a driveway. The driveway was at least a quarter of a mile long and freshly paved, which was a good thing, because the chopper didn't look like it was ready for the sort of off-roading this country seemed to lend itself to. At the end of the driveway was a little pathway of broken paving stones—

the round kind—that led to a ramshackle two-story house with a new roof and a desperate need for new siding. At present, the house was sided with silvering, splintered shingles that were rotting off seemingly as Casey looked. There was a garage on one side of the house, as well as a dilapidated carport on the other side with a plastic roof that was threatening to cave in the middle, and a shitload of new lumber and drywall tucked into the side of the carport.

Casey took a look around the whole thing with dull eyes, not sure he had the wherewithal to really take in all the damage.

"God, you weren't kidding about day labor," was what he did say, and he caught Joe's grin as the bigger man swung off the bike and then gave Casey a hand off himself.

"Nope. Just bought the place a couple of months ago."

"It's a wreck. Why bother?" Casey's mind boggled at the amount of work to be done, but Josiah Daniels didn't seem to be offended.

"Listen to that," he said, the smile on his face like one of those saints in a painting.

"Listen to what?"

"Do you hear the neighbors?"

"No."

"Do you hear the traffic?"

"No."

"Exactly." Joe moved toward the house before Casey could chew on that any longer, and Casey followed him, because there were at least two miles of cold black road between him and another human being, and he was done with the running.

Inside, it was simple and plain. The entryway opened up to a kitchen with a small dining table on the left, and a living room with a couch on the right. The carpet was plain light brown, old, and badly in need of stretching. Joe gestured to the table.

"Wash your hands in the kitchen sink, sit down, and I'll feed you. Then you can shower—I'll get you some night clothes, okay?"

Casey nodded, grateful that the food would come first, although just looking at the clean dinette set, the clean brown corduroy couch, and the clean white walls made him itch even more. As he used the sink—washing his hands several times with dish soap before he stopped seeing them brown and wrinkled with filth—Joe busied himself in the refrigerator. Casey sat down to a solid peanut butter and jelly sandwich and a microwaved bowl of chicken noodle soup.

It was heaven. He'd forgotten how much he liked peanut butter and jelly as a kid. He'd forgotten the saltiness and solidness of the peanut butter and the burst of sweetness as the jelly just sang on your tongue. He'd forgotten the solid earthiness of wheat bread and how the whole thing felt right and perfect in his stomach. Milk was a gift from the gods. The sandwich was gone, and he was literally licking the bowl that had held the chicken noodle soup when he felt Joe's hand on his shoulder and realized he'd lost a little bit of time from sitting down to scarfing down.

"Kid, I'm going to make you some more stuff, but first, we'll let that settle, okay?"

No! Food! More food now! Casey kept that back in his head with a whimper and stood up, reluctant to shed the wonderful jacket, even though Josiah had apparently started a fire while he'd been lost in food-land. "Okay," he whispered. "What now?" He knew. He'd known when he'd first taken the jacket. But he'd been fed, and now he didn't care so much.

"Shower, remember? C'mere."

The living room had a short hallway, and Casey's companion sighed as he led the way.

"Eventually, I'll have the loft upstairs all fixed up, and I'll be sleeping there. Right now, we're in the guest bedrooms, and they share a bathroom. We're lucky—I just put in a tub, so you can soak for a while before you stand up and rinse off. But first...."

Joe opened a door into a small bedroom. "Here, wait for a sec." He disappeared again, and Casey took off the jacket and laid it neatly on the plain queen-size bed. There was a generic tan bedspread on the top and what looked to be stolen hospital sheets underneath—and they didn't fit, either, because the one on the bottom was just sort of on top of the mattress, and the edges were bare flowered nylon. But it had pillows, and a single dresser next to the headboard. They were the only objects in the room, and Casey could appreciate that Joe maybe hadn't been as interested in decorating as he had been in simply making things serviceable.

He started taking off his clothes then, shuddering as they slid down into a puddle at his feet. He wanted to grab a sheet or something to hide himself, but he didn't want any of the things living on his skin to get on that too. In a sudden panic, he grabbed the jacket and held it up against his naked body, not even wanting to look at himself. He was skinny. When he'd left his parents' house with only the clothes on his back and a wallet two months earlier, he'd been developing a chest and some muscles—training for basketball did that to a guy.

Of course, getting caught blowing your center after practice when your parents came home early was what got you kicked out and on the streets, so maybe basketball wasn't such a great thing after all. He was only ever going to be five foot eight, tops, so it wasn't like he'd been bound for the pros.

He held the jacket up and shivered, a little surprised that there was a knock at the door before it swung open.

"Whoa!" Joe cried out, holding his full hands up to his eyes. "No! No, no, no—not for me to see. Shit." Carefully, keeping his back to Casey like he was some virgin girl, Joe edged over to the bed and put down a set of sea-green hospital scrubs.

"They're my old shit—gonna be really fucking big."

Casey almost laughed, the guy was so uncomfortable. For a minute, he wanted to point out that there was nothing there that random truckers and assholes hadn't been seeing for two months, but he had a sudden thought of the kindness and the warm jacket and the food, and he didn't. For a minute, he *really* didn't want Joe to know he was a slutty man-pussy, and everyone's meat. This guy had been treating him like he was worth something. Casey was going to let him keep his illusions.

"And here."

Casey looked, and Joe had put down a pharmacy squirt bottle, brown, on top of the clothes.

"What's that?"

"It's Kwell. You're going to want to rub it into your hair... uhm... *all* of your hair, even over your... you know...."

"Pubes?" It felt like he was being delicate, but Joe shook his head, and the back of his neck under his ponytail was getting redder by the second.

"Not just the pubes. Your asshole hair too."

"I've got hair on my asshole?" Jesus! Casey hadn't gotten that far or that intimate with anybody. It was usually just "Bend over, boy!" and that was the extent of it.

"Well, you might not, but a lot of guys do!" The irritation must have helped with the embarrassment, because his neck paled a little. "And you need to not get it on any open sores, because it will sting like a motherfucker."

Casey whimpered, and the sound must have been pretty naked, because Joe turned around.

"What?"

Casey shrugged. "Uhm, about my asshole...." He winced, and Joe winced, and then Joe sighed.

"Okay, look, kid. Use the Kwell on everything else, just wash that. We'll put the Kwell back on in a week, okay?"

Casey nodded. His eyes were watering, and he couldn't pinpoint why.

"Don't get anything in your eyes, okay? The bathroom has two doors—one to my room. I want you to lock that door whenever you're in there because I just don't want to walk in on you, okay? You lock that door, the only way in is through your door, right? So rub the shit in your hair, upstairs and downstairs, go get in the tub, soak off the dirt, and rinse the shit off your head. I'll go through it with a pick while you eat round two, and let's see if we can get you healthy, okay?"

Casey nodded, his vision blurring, and Joe turned to go. He stopped midstride and sighed, took a few steps forward, and then took Casey's chin in his fingers.

"It's going to be all right, okay, boy? I'll find you someplace to stay, we'll keep you safe, okay?"

Casey nodded, his jaw working. "Why?" he asked, unsure of where the question came from, and Joe shrugged and looked away.

"I was just always taught to do good works. I know... sounds like freaky hippy shit. But that's just what I learned growing up."

He turned around and left, and Casey didn't even get to say thank you. He was left there in the room, and after laying the jacket down carefully on the end table so it wouldn't get any cooties on the sheets, he went to work with the greasy white stuff in the bottle.

After he was done massaging it all in, he spent about an hour in the tub. He must have washed himself about five hundred times with the Irish Spring soap and the washcloth, and his hair could not be shampooed enough. It wasn't until the water got to be frigid—long after his fingers and toes got to be pruney—that he finally got out.

The water in the tub was brown, and he spent a few minutes washing the ring off the edges before going into the guest room and putting on the scrubs. Well, they were clean, they were comfy, and they seemed to be one-size-fits-all. What wasn't to like, right? He went commando, which was fine, because his pubes were still tingling from all of the chemical attention.

When he got into the living room, Casey saw the back of Joe's head where he sat on the couch, watching television, in a similar set of scrubs, a small plate with crumbs next to him on the end table. There was a plate of hamburgers, the kind made from the frozen patties and regular bread, on the table in the kitchen.

"Is that food for me?" he asked and was surprised when the big man on the couch startled.

"Wha? Yeah." Joe yawned. "Eat yourself stupid. Sorry. I just worked three twelves in a row—I'm sort of beat."

Casey started digging into the hamburgers—and they were no less heavenly than the PB&J. He was on his third, and not even thinking about slowing down, when Joe got up from the couch and came up behind him to touch his head.

And Casey spazzed out, throwing one arm back in defense and dropping the hamburger on the plate. His hand smacked Joe in the chin, and Joe grunted and took a step back.

"Sorry, kid," he said after an awkward moment, during which Casey picked up the hamburger out of sheer reflex. "I didn't mean to startle you. I'll remember to be more careful. I was just going to check your hair for nits."

Casey took a bite to mask his quickened breathing, and then swallowed. "While I'm eating?"

"You were looking pretty out of it. I thought I could get this done and you could go to sleep." There was a silence, and Casey took a quick look to the side and saw that Joe was looking sheepish. "Yeah, I guess that's sort of gross while you're eating."

Casey shrugged. Really? He was going to complain about gross after what he'd just washed off his body? "Knock yourself out," he said, trying to mask his embarrassment. "It would be good not to itch."

He made it through another hamburger before he pushed the plate away. Joe's fingers were gentle and firm on his scalp as he sectioned little locks of hair from each other and pulled the tiny nit comb through. Casey could hear the rasp of the teeth against the strands of his hair whenever Joe found something. The television was still on in the front room—a big set, but not a console type—it was playing a sitcom on low volume. Casey's head lowered to his hands, and above him, Joe started humming as he worked.

"I was born… six gun in my hand…"

It was old rock, nothing that Casey had on cassette tapes back home. Casey had George Michael and Boy George and Madonna, but still, he knew this song. He found himself humming along.

"Bad company, I can't deny…"

Joe let him, and Casey was still hearing that deep from-your-toes voice as he closed his eyes.

He wasn't sure when, but eventually Joe shook his shoulders gently. "C'mon, kid, you're too big to carry."

Casey wanted to say that he wasn't a kid. He'd lived through the last two months, right? But big warm hands were on his shoulders, and he stood up to be steered gently down the hall. Joe made him stop and turn at the bedroom, and then pulled down the sheets for him.

"Don't worry about getting up, kid. You sleep as long as you want. Remember, lock my side of the bathroom when you're in there, and I'll know not to come in."

Casey grunted, then looked up. "I'm not sleeping in your bed?"

"No, Goldilocks, this one here is just right."

That was really all Casey needed to know before he fell asleep for more than fifteen hours.

Brilliant Disguise
~Josiah

THE Quaker movement, or the Religious Society of Friends, was not as prevalent or as structured or as organized as it had been at the country's inception, but there were still pockets of Quakers throughout the northeast. Joe's parents had been raised Quakers in the relative quiet of upstate New York, in a tiny village not far from the Canadian border. They were both soft-spoken, sturdy people—his mother had been a nurse, his father a history teacher—and together they'd raised a quiet, happy family before they retired. Joe had three brothers and two sisters, all older than he was.

His older sister, the second oldest in the family, had loved him best of all. When he'd first come to California in the early eighties, everybody was talking about astrological signs, and Joe had learned that he was a Scorpio, because his birthday was November 19, and Jeannie had been a Virgo. Virgos and Scorpios adored each other—it was literally written in the stars.

Jeannie had loved him best, even though she'd been nearly fourteen years his senior. She had been the sister who held him most as a baby and who fed and dressed him as he grew older. In the mornings, she was the one who walked him to the neighbor's when their mother had a shift, and she had always secretly given him the biggest cupcake. Jeannie read him stories when he was little, about firemen and policemen and teachers, and when they went to church, and he sat through the simple service, she explained that working to make the world a better place was working for God.

Josiah had always had a sort of hazy idea about God. The God of the Quakers was a gentle sort, a forgiving sort, and Joe liked that fine, but it often seemed he was inactive about the things Joe thought he should be most active about. If God, whom everybody was supposed to have all this faith in, was so all-God-damned powerful, he should have been able to see through the despair of an eighteen-year-old girl, shouldn't he? He should have seen that Jeannie had been struggling, that the boy that she'd nursed a painful crush on through her senior year had showed her a whole bunch of attention and then just left her alone. He should have seen that her friends had been taunting her.

God should have been watching as Joe's older sister took her life in her hands and went to see a drunken doctor who would work under the table. He should have given her the strength to see that their parents would have forgiven her anything, and God should have told her not to go. He should have given her the immune system to fight a botched abortion.

God should have done something, and he didn't. God let Jeannie stumble home, bleeding, to die of a fever as Joe sat at her bedside and their mother cried. God let that happen when Jeannie had only ever sung his praises and taught Joe to do the same. At six, even before Josiah understood everything about what had happened to Jeannie Daniels, Joe was 'bout done with God. Besides, it seemed like serving the rest of the world was a better option—if that worked well, Joe shouldn't have to worry about God. Joe could take care of people just fine.

So that was what he grew up to do. But the growing up grew complicated.

Josiah was nine years old when Woodstock shook his little corner of the world. His parents' small town north of Bear Mountain was really nowhere near Bethel, New York, but everybody heard about it. Josiah was entranced by the idea. People gathered together to listen to music. Josiah adored music—"Simple Gifts" was his favorite song when he was nine. And even though those people weren't listening to "Simple Gifts," those people who gathered took care of each other and didn't listen to what God or teachers told them about rules? Right away, no matter *what* the music, Josiah was a fan!

When he was nineteen, the world was a more cynical place. The music, for one thing, was not as good. Josiah liked Bad Company,

Journey, Bruce Springsteen, and Kansas just fine, but he was not a fan of disco. In fact, that entire five years of the music scene had been incredibly painful for him. For one thing, he had no rhythm. He moved too slowly for any of that music. But power rock? That moved just right for him.

Joe graduated from high school and moved to California the year *Darkness on the Edge of Town* was released. He'd always loved that the album had been recorded not too far from where he lived. The pretext for moving to California was that he had a scholarship at a nursing school. This was true, but there were plenty of nursing schools in New York or New Jersey or Vermont. The truth was that he wanted to be somewhere nobody knew him.

Upstate New York was incredibly beautiful. National parks, Bear Mountain, acres of rural farmland. Josiah loved it; it was a part of his heart and bones. But after Jeannie's death, he looked at it and somehow saw only lines. County lines, township lines, lines that surrounded what a person should be. Maybe it was because he'd spent twelve years thinking about Jeannie and how ashamed she must have been about crossing lines, about being someone besides the good girl she'd tried so hard to be.

Maybe it was because he played percussion for the symphonic band, and one summer night, as he walked home from band practice, the lead trumpet player had taken him behind a stand of trees and kissed him on the mouth. Joe had returned the kiss—surprised, because it had been his first and he'd always assumed it would be with a girl— and then Tim had tilted Joe's head back and told him to look at the stars. Joe had, and Tim had proceeded to kiss down his throat, under his rucked-up shirt, and to the soft swell of his stomach. He'd bitten there, and suckled the flesh into his mouth, and before Joe could do more than groan in sudden want, Tim had unzipped his cut-off jeans and taken Joe's cock into his mouth.

Suddenly the stars were behind Joe's eyes as well as in front of them, and Tim pulled back and stroked Joe until he'd finished spurting into the leaf mold Tim was kneeling on. When Tim stood up, he'd kissed Joe again and said next time Joe could return the favor. Joe had. For an entire summer, they'd stopped in that stand of trees and simply explored each other, unhurriedly, without talking about a relationship or what they were doing or how it was wrong. When the summer was over, Tim told Joe he was going to ask out Kathy, a flute player, and Joe was okay with that.

Joe had dated her friend, Susan, for most of their junior year.

But when high school ended, Josiah didn't want to marry Susan. He didn't want to marry Tim, for that matter. He simply wanted to be somewhere... different. Somewhere without the little lines telling him that he *should* want to marry Susan instead of Tim. Somewhere a girl like Jeannie might not feel like she'd be better off putting her life at risk than facing her parents with the results of an accident in the back seat of a car after the Valentine's Day dance.

That being said, he could have been bitterly disappointed in California.

Yes, it was true. San Francisco State College was a *lot* different than upstate New York. There *were* no boundaries—either personal or moral—that Joe didn't get a chance to cross. It was a good thing Josiah was relatively bright, because he killed a *lot* of brain cells in college—and had learned to use a rubber right quick after his first dose of penicillin for the clap, because there wasn't much, both male and female, that he didn't do.

In spite of all that (and a harpy of an attending professor who thought that men shouldn't *be* nurses, and who butchered all of his papers to try and prove that point), Joe finished up his schooling with a bachelor's degree in nursing, which, in the early eighties, could get him a job about anywhere in the country.

But by then, Joe was tired of the city and *really* tired of having his personal boundaries overridden, especially by so many sweating, heaving bodies. Sex was okay, but he would rather have it be kept personal, thank you very much, and he would be just as glad to wait for the right persons to keep it that way.

Besides. He missed the quiet of the Adirondacks. He missed the way you could walk a mile from one house to the next without seeing anyone.

He looked around. At first he wanted farmland, but Bakersfield and Fresno held no appeal to him whatsoever, and he started looking into the Sierra Foothills.

He liked pretty much everything north of Rocklin, which, back then, was a flea speck of a town whose only claim to fame was Sierra Community College. He got a job at Auburn General and, after living in a rental for a little while, started looking for his own property.

Foresthill was about a twenty-mile commute, which wasn't bad, even on the bike, and like he said to Casey, you couldn't hear anything. Not a neighbor, not a car. Just the rush of the wind in the trees overhead and the occasional owl.

Of course, the morning after Casey arrived, there was the goddamned neighbor's dog, who wouldn't shut the fuck up, and Josiah groaned as he rolled out of bed.

Oh Jesus, couldn't that ornery old geezer feed his fucking Rottweiler? (Joe had learned to embrace swearing in college. It was, to his mind, even better than pot and beer, and he planned to keep that habit a lot longer than he'd kept pot and beer, too!) With a yawn and a stretch, he put on a jacket over his scrub top and put his feet into moccasins. He'd left the thermostat at sixty the night before, and it was damned cold in the house in the morning, but since he hadn't had time to insulate, he couldn't afford to heat it all the way when blankets would do just fine.

He'd showered the night before but hadn't dried his hair, and it was a frightful, kinky mess down his back as he padded toward the garage, but he didn't care. If the damned dog had woken Casey up to see him look like the bride of fucking Frankenstein, Casey would have let him know already.

Casey was not, in fact, his first rescue. His first rescue had been a pair of kids who'd been left on the side of the road like unwanted kittens. (He'd rescued a number of those too, and he remembered to put a giant scoop of cat food into the bowl by the door leading from the kitchen to the garage.) He'd taken them home, given them baths, fed them, and called social services the next day. Social services had come and gotten them, and Josiah had spent the next week picking cootie nits out of his hair because he hadn't been careful. He knew better now—

kept a gamut of medication for those sorts of things on his shelves, and the hospital had been an oblivious benefactor for his altruistic pursuits.

So the truth was, it didn't matter if Casey *did* see him looking like the Bride of Fucking Frankenstein and it scared him. As soon as Joe was done feeding Ira Kenby's fucking dog, he was going to call social services again, and Casey would be taken to a home that would be more appropriate for a runaway.

So really, Joe would say, they owed much of their lives together to a senile old man and a dog tortured by hunger to the point it didn't know better. (Casey would always reply that they would have met again, because there was just no way they could have lived without each other, but Joe's faith didn't run that deep. Casey would say that was because Joe didn't have a Josiah Daniels in his life, and Joe would shake his head and walk off, but that was later in their story.)

Joe's neighbor lived about a half a mile away by the dirt road that had brought the motorcycle to the garage the night before, but if you cut through the back, you could find the fence that divided the property (an anomaly in New York, but Joe had gotten used to them here in "free" California) about two hundred yards through the trees. Joe's property spanned about twenty acres, but Joe hadn't been that interested in those numbers when he'd been looking at it to buy. He'd mostly just seen the big batch of space between the two houses and been sold.

And the only time that space didn't seem to be a blessing was when he was scratching the hell out of his ankles on the underbrush as he walked the path he himself had worn between his house and the fence. Fucking Rufus. Damned dog *would* be eating Kenby out of house and home, but Joe had made the mistake of bringing home some kitchen scraps for him once—one lousy, fucking time—and the dog had lost his mind. Now, if old Kenby didn't dig deep enough into the gargantuan bag of kibble for the poor bastard, Rufus was howling at the fence, trying to get Joe's attention.

Except… oh, dammit. This time, of all moronic fucking things! Rufus was tangled in the bent pig fence, having chewed his way through the support post and leapt halfway over the fence before it twisted. Oh crap. It looked like the dog's leg was broken in one of the smaller gaps, and Joe resisted the urge to just turn around and call Ira and have him clean up his mess.

Rufus caught sight of him then and let loose with a howl, both pathetic and pitiful, and Joe sighed. Ira was too old to be living alone as it was.

"All right, Rufus. C'mon, big guy. You and me, we're going to have to work together, see? Now I'm just going to move the fence so—"

A howl punctuated the sudden quiet as Josiah shifted the fencing so that he could walk on top of it and get to the dog to help free him.

"Yeah, yeah—I'm sorry about that, big guy. Here. Here. See? Here I am, got my arm over your shoulder, I'm working the leg through, okay? And—*fuck!*" Oh, ouch, oh fuck, oh shit, oh holy fucking Moses in a bushel basket with cookies, ouch!

"Jesus, Rufus!" Joe fought back tears and the urge to look at his bicep, where the damned dog, in his fear and pain, had just sunk his big long fucking teeth through the denim jacket, the skin, and the muscle, right to the fucking bone. But Joe was this close to getting the dog's leg out, and the dog already had a hold of his arm—why the hell not finish the job?

Suddenly the leg came free, broken and bloody, and Joe let go of it, hoping that Rufus would let go of his arm.

Rufus did, and sank to the ground in a whimpering puddle, hurt and scared and probably embarrassed and sorry to boot.

Joe still didn't look at his arm. Instead, he knelt on the flattened pig wire and picked Rufus up—all one hundred pounds of him—and then walked over the pig wire back toward his house. It was an effort—his arm was bitching up a storm—but he carried Rufus to the back of the beat-to-shit Chevy Half-Ton that sat in the carport, next to the Harley.

He set Rufus inside and got some old blankets and tarps from the garage, covered the animal so he'd be okay when he went into shock, and then walked back into the house, looking at the clock on his brand-new microwave as he opened the door.

Oh shit! Was that the time? God, poor Rufus. The three twelve-hour shifts in a row had about knocked Joe on his ass. Usually he heard the dog barking at around eight in the morning, and it was already ten. Casey had been asleep since around seven the night before. Fuck. Fuck, fuck, fuck.

Joe closed his eyes and tried to put shit in order. Okay. Casey first, Rufus second. He brushed his arm against the doorframe and saw black. Scratch that. First aid first, Casey second, Rufus to the vet's third.

He stumbled to his bedroom and shed his jacket in the corner, not even wanting to look at the sleeve, then went into the bathroom for some antiseptic and bandages. Oh God—a dog's mouth. Those animals licked dead things, *then* licked their balls, *then* threw up and ate it. Joe got the bottle of rubbing alcohol out, braced his hurt arm on the sink, and, regardless of the mess, dumped half of it over the double jagged row of dripping, red bite marks. Each round hole was slightly torn, probably from when Rufus had jerked as Joe freed his leg, and Joe closed his eyes at the thought of infection and stitches. He put the rest of the alcohol away and pulled out a bottle of hydrogen peroxide, and then dumped that too, hissing as it bubbled. Oh God. The bite was pretty high up, and Joe fought off a mutter to himself. He was going to need help.

"Kid!" he called through the door. "Kid, you up yet?"

"Mmmffff...."

Poor baby. He probably hadn't slept in months—Joe hated to wake him up this way.

"Kid—*Casey!* Buddy, I need your help here. I hate to wake you up, but if you could, maybe, come in here and give me a hand here with something?"

Then, clear through the door, came the grumpy reply. "I thought you said I wouldn't have to do that."

Oh God. Really? Jesus, this kid didn't give an inch, did he? "Not *that*, dammit! I need to bandage my arm, and I can't fuckin' reach!"

There was some movement and the uneven padding of feet. The kid who opened the door was bleary and irritated—but he wasn't starving, freezing, or frightened, so maybe that was an improvement.

He wasn't a bad-looking kid—narrow chin and a heart-shaped face made him look almost girl-pretty. He had deep-set gray eyes, the kind that almost always looked sleepy or irritated unless he was actively trying to smile. Joe only imagined that last part. The kid hadn't had a lot to smile about since they met.

Those eyes widened when they saw Joe using a towel to gingerly dry off his arm.

"Holy shit!"

"How old are you?"

"I'll be sixteen on September fifteenth," the boy said, and Joe raised his eyebrows.

"It's November twelfth," he said, and he was unprepared for the terrible look of disappointment on Casey's face.

"Oh yeah... then I'm sixteen."

Joe grimaced and set about getting the antibiotic ointment out of the cabinet too. "How long since you knew what day it was?"

"September third," Casey said hoarsely. "Coach let practice out early, and me and Dillon got to my house early."

Joe sighed. He knew where this was going. The kid didn't have it tattooed on his ass, but then, he wouldn't need to wear his bandana in the right pocket in public to get laid, either. "What happened?" he prodded gently, dabbing the ointment on his arm and keeping his attention on Casey so he wouldn't have to think about the pain.

Casey couldn't seem to keep his eyes off of Joe's wound. "I started necking with Dillon, because, you know, we got bored, and we were talking about girls, and I started saying how my last blowjob almost made me queasy. He said him too. Maybe we should try with boys. So we did."

Joe almost laughed. God. Fifteen. It could be a fun age when that shit started happening. He'd always wondered what happened to Tim. But Joe and Tim's story had been over when the summer was over. Casey's story had just started.

"An-nd?" There was a tear on the underside of his arm, where shit got really sensitive, and that needed a lot of attention.

"And my folks caught us. And started screaming. And my dad said I wasn't his son. He rushed Dillon, and both of us ran out of there. Dillon went home and...." He swallowed.

"And you didn't."

"No."

"You talked to them since?"

Casey shook his head. "No."

Joe breathed out. "Kid, I'm going to have to call social services, you know that, right?"

Casey looked at him, just looked at him, those naturally guarded eyes open and limpid. "Please," he whispered. "It took me two months to get someplace I don't hate."

Joe was going to tell him no—or at least he was going to *try* to tell him no—but then his arm slipped off the sink and his vision got a little gray. Not gray enough to miss the total expression of triumph in Casey's eyes, though.

"You *can't* let me go!" he said excitedly, taking two steps into the bathroom and taking the gauze. "You *can't*. You need me!"

"Wash your hands," Joe said sharply, and Casey nodded like he should have known. Still, his hands were steady as he wrapped the gauze around Joe's arm again and again, until the roll was gone and there was nothing to do but tape the ends and then tape them to Joe's arm.

He did—in fact, he was good at it. For some reason, the pressure of the bandage and the lack of exposure to the air helped, and Joe nodded.

"Good. Thanks, kid. Let me get some Tylenol, 'kay? Then I've got to take the damned dog to the vet's."

"The dog that *bit* you?" Casey stepped back and looked at him like he was insane.

Joe sighed. Well, yeah. Maybe. "He was scared and hurt. Broke his leg in the fence because I was a dumbass and overslept. Now we got to get him fixed, or Mr. Kenby's going to come over here and fuckin' shoot me for hurting his dog. You good to stay here alone, kid? There's food, your clothes are in the dryer—"

"I was sort of hoping you burned them."

"Well, I don't know if any of them are left after three cycles in hot—that may still be an option. I can get you something after I take Rufus to the vet in town, but I gotta get a move on."

Casey looked down at his scrubs and then back at Joe. "Uhm, can I come with you? You're not looking too good."

Joe scowled. "You wouldn't look that great either, kid." He didn't want to see, but he risked a look in the mirror. He was pale and sweating and his hair was all over the place, and he swore. "All right. Tell you what. You come with me to keep me from driving off the road, and we can stop in town and get you some clothes."

Casey looked down, unaccountably shy. "I can't pay you," he said, his voice muffled. "Are you sure you don't want—"

"Oh Jesus, kid, give it a rest. You're fifteen—"

"Sixteen."

"Nah. You get a pass. No sixteenth birthday party, no sixteen. You're fifteen. If I caught anyone my age sniffing around you, I'd run 'em off with a shotgun. Now forget about sex for a minute and go into my room. There's another pair of moccasins in there that should fit— grab those and a couple of sweatshirts from the drawer. I'm gonna need help getting in mine, so make it big and loose, okay?"

Casey was already through the other door, and Joe was there in his plain little bathroom. He'd picked out dark-blue tile for it, because he liked it, and the towels were dark blue and dark yellow, but other than that, the walls were white, and so was the shower curtain. Well, one thing at a time. His big project had been getting the roof redone. Now he needed to fix up the carport, because the snows were going to crush it, and he didn't have much longer.

He heard the kid rooting around in his room and sighed. Well, help he might need, but he'd been planning on a work party with a bunch of people from work, not on recruiting slave labor from the side of the road. He'd sort of lied to Casey about that the night before. He would have done about anything to get that kid off the side of the road, because he hadn't looked like he'd make it one more day.

And Joe might still have the work party, and he might still let Casey help with the repairs on the house. He might still do that. But one thing was for sure: he wasn't going to be calling social services today.

Lean on Me
~Casey

JOE was a tough sonuvabitch, that was for certain. They drove the dog to the vet's, and since Joe had also taken him in for his rabies shots, they didn't have to kill the damned thing and dissect his brain. Joe seemed especially relieved about this, but Casey was sort of hoping he'd get to shoot the slobbering monster himself. The one guy to be nice to Casey in two months, and the dog damned near tore his arm off? Casey was not amused, and everything was *not* copacetic, and Casey was not forgiving.

Joe told him to take a deep breath and let it go. There was no use holding a creature's nature against him. It was like beating a child for spilling milk.

Casey had subsided then, although he'd made Joe go to the hospital before they went to get clothes. He was sweating buckets by the time they pulled into the tiny parking lot of Auburn General, and his breathing was strained with the effort of keeping back the pain.

The admissions nurse, a pretty woman with brown hair and freckles, knew him and took him into a cubicle to clean the wound. Casey knew he wasn't kin, knew he was just some stray off the street, but for some reason, when she went to pull the curtain to give him privacy, a sound came out of Casey's mouth a lot like the sound that had come out of Rufus's when Joe had picked him up out of the bed of the pickup truck.

"Let the boy stay," Joe said easily. "He doesn't like to be left alone."

The nurse glanced at Casey in his scrubs and moccasins, and Casey stared defiantly back. "Nice," she muttered. "Your nephew?"

And then Joe said a curious thing—something Casey would use a *lot* in the coming years as a reason to hope. "Friend of the family. C'mere, kid."

Casey did, sitting in the small chair by the head of the bed. The nurse checked out the wound, grunting, and then said, "Okay, the doc's probably going to want to give you a tetanus shot and a shot of antibiotics. It's all puncture wounds, and they've got scabs now—irrigating them is going to be a bitch, and they're probably going to get infected anyway, even with the shot, so you're in for a ride. You're sure this dog didn't have rabies?"

Joe pulled out the piece of paper he'd gotten from the vet, proving that he didn't have to go through the rabies course, and the nurse seemed satisfied.

"I'm doubting you'll be able to work for a couple of days. I'll trade out your shifts for a week, if that's okay."

Joe sighed. "Five days."

"A week."

"I'm going to be working on my carport the whole time. It feels like sort of a scam. Five days."

"God, you're stubborn. Five days it is. If you finish your carport, does that mean we're not having the work party?"

"I'm going to need some serious help." Joe nodded. "I'm saying the work party's still a go. Next week. My pizza, my beer, my hammers and nails."

"Good. I'll tell Jimmy and the guys. They're looking forward to it. You bought good beer when they helped with the roof."

Joe smiled a little and she left, and Casey watched as he plumped the pillow, adjusted the bed so it was sitting up, and then leaned back. "Might as well get comfy, kid. It's going to take a while."

Casey did, kicking back in the chair and leaning his head against the bed. They'd stopped at McDonald's after they'd taken Rufus to the vet's, so he wasn't hungry, but he couldn't help contrasting Joe's easy generosity—"What do you want? That all? I'll double it."—with the guy he'd run away from the last time he was there.

"You're nice," he said thoughtfully.

"Sometimes."

"No, you're really nice. My dad, he'd see someone like you, with all the hair, and the pickup truck, and he'd say mean shit about bikers and hippies, and then he'd find out you're a nurse and call you a fag—but you're nice."

Joe looked at him, and Casey reflected that his eyes were really large and really brown. "Is that the same dad who drove you out of the house?"

"Yeah."

"Maybe we don't think so much about the shit he used to say about other people, 'kay?"

"Even me?"

"Especially you."

God, it put paid to so much. Casey's dad wouldn't have liked Joe—wouldn't have liked his hair, or his bike, or his profession. And he would have been wrong, wrong about all of it. So maybe that shit, that horrible shit about being a worthless fag and a slut and an open asshole and anyone's meat, maybe that shit was wrong too. To his horror, Casey found his eyes were watering.

"You can't call social services," he whispered. "You can't. They won't tell me things like that."

"Kid, I can be an incredibly grumpy bastard."

"But you've got a spare room. I'll work for you, I will. I can help. I'll make your place real nice, I'll—"

"You'd have to go to school."

Casey looked away. "After all the shit I've done?"

Joe grunted. "Casey, from the looks of it, a lot of it wasn't what you'd done but what was done to you. And either way, that shit is yours to keep. You start school, however you do that, and you start over. You be a kid. You don't tell anyone."

Casey sucked in his breath, captivated by the thought. He'd been a jock, because his dad had thrown a ball at him since he was little, but suddenly, he didn't have to do that anymore. He'd been a cutup, a pain in the ass, a kid who'd rather play the fool than work at his grades. That was how he'd gotten attention. That was why Dillon had wanted to come home with him. That was how he'd gotten his dad to talk at the dinner table. That had been Casey.

But now? He didn't have to do that anymore. It was... it was like walking out of that semi and across the great canyon over the clean space had been walking out of the old Casey. He could do anything.

As long as he didn't have to go home.

"I don't want you to call social services," he said, and he must have been in his head for quite some time, because Joe grunted like he'd fallen asleep.

"Well," Joe conceded, his voice groggy, "it's not going to happen today."

There was a whooshing sound, and the doctor came to dress Joe's wound some more, and Casey took what he could get.

JOE took an injected painkiller instead of an oral one because he still had to drive home, and Casey thought that maybe a driver's license was something he'd want to get started on. He was sixteen, right? Excellent. He'd put it on his list of things for Joe to help him get. Not once did he think Joe wouldn't help him out. He'd wonder at that later—how arrogant the young were, and how easily they reaped the rewards of a faith they took for granted. Joe had fed him, clothed him, cleaned him, and spoken to him like he wasn't stupid or subhuman. Joe would take care of him.

Casey just had to be very, very good.

They stopped at a bank with a vacuum tube drive-through, and Joe pulled out some cash, then drove to a Ross department store not far from old-town Auburn. By now, Joe's pain meds had about worn off, and he was not looking so good.

He made a terrible whining sound when he pulled up on the chrome handle of the pickup, and Casey looked at him worriedly.

"Tell you what," he said, thinking that he really needed clothes. "How 'bout I go inside and get some clothes, and you rest in here."

Joe closed his eyes. "Not gonna find you on the side of the road again, am I?"

"Not if you promise not to call social services when you're better."

Joe grunted a little in pain. "Oh God, kid. Shit. Can I just promise not to do it without talking it over with you first?"

Yippee!

"I'll let that stand for now," Casey said, feeling generous.

Joe reached with an effort into his wallet and pulled out five twenties. Casey grimaced. One of the things he had liked about his past life had been the clothes. Mom had dropped him off at the mall anytime he asked, and given him a credit card. Sure, it wasn't his money, but that didn't mean he didn't see the amount.

A hundred dollars wasn't it.

"Keep it simple today," Joe said, his breath coming hard through the pain. "Two pairs of jeans, some T-shirts and underwear, a couple of basic sweatshirts. If you can wear scrubs to bed, you can get yourself some cheap tennis shoes and some socks. Will that do?"

Yeah, this guy just gave a kid who wasn't his a hundred dollars to buy clothes to live in. Casey decided that for the moment, he was over being a fashion plate. He also decided he really wanted a job of his own, but now was not the time.

"You want to take those pain pills?" he asked instead. He grabbed the pharmacy bag and pulled them out, then grabbed Joe's soda from McDonald's, because there was still half a cup left.

"Don't want to pass out on you, kid."

Casey didn't want to see him in pain. "Here. I'll wake you up when I'm done. It'll be an hour at least, right?"

Joe grunted, and he must really have been feeling it, because he took the pills and slumped back against the window. There was a gap between the seat and the back of the truck, and Casey searched it for a blanket, pleased to see that there was an old Army surplus wool thing back there, like he'd suspected. Joe seemed the type to come prepared. He covered Joe up and jogged across the parking lot to try to become a real boy.

It took him nearly exactly an hour, but part of that was because he was followed so closely by the security guy that it was a wonder the jerk-off didn't get an image of Glen "Big Daddy" going up Casey's tailpipe. It didn't matter. Casey kept the little basket in plain sight, and security guy had to concede that he bought everything he put there. When Casey was done, he walked up to the guy who was glaring at him in his hospital scrub bottoms and flip-flops, and gave him the sort of expression that adults usually saved for their own kids *when they* were screwing around.

"Did I pass inspection, chief?" he asked, and the guy scowled.

"I didn't see you steal nothin'."

"Bitchin'! Now that I got the tags and a receipt, are you going to give me shit if I go into the bathroom over there by customer service so I can change?"

The guy grunted again. "Why you want to change here?"

"Because it's fucking cold out there, and the scrubs are thin."

"What, those the only clothes you got?" The guy was squat, midfifties, with a crew cut. Casey hated him sort of on sight.

"Yeah. Yeah, they are. I ran away to my uncle's with the clothes on my back. Those about rotted off, and these are the only fucking clothes I got. Do you know enough about my life now? Can I go get dressed?" He glared at the guy, who held up his hands and backed down, and Casey went into the bathroom, rather amazed at his own chutzpah.

Who knew that being the guy with nothing to lose made it so much easier to win?

And God, didn't he feel human now that he was dressed. He'd spent that hundred dollars about down to the last two bucks, and was proud of that too. He even managed some baseball T-shirts with bands on them, even though one of the bands was Journey, and he thought that was probably more Joe's speed than his. Besides, hadn't they broken up? But he was warmer and cleaner and happier when he got back to the car to find Joe shivering under the blanket and trying hard to wake up.

Casey's new chutzpah hadn't all faded. He looked at the truck, saw that it was an automatic transmission, and tried to remember how to get to Joe's place. He realized that it wasn't that hard, really. Back to the freeway, off at that really big intersection called the Foresthill Exit, and hang a really big right.

He could do this.

"Here, Joe," he said, getting in on the driver's side after dumping all his bags on the passenger side. "Move over."

"What in the fuck?" Joe shivered hard on the word "fuck," and Casey patted his shoulder sympathetically, and then jerked back when Joe did. Shit. He'd hit the sore arm. God, he was a moron.

"Move over. I'm driving."

"You're *what*?" Joe sat up straight and glared at him, and Casey shrugged.

"How hard can it be? Every moron in California has a driver's license. Now scoot over and I'll take you home."

"Do you even know how to get there?"

"Yeah. Get to the freeway. Turn right at that big intersection exit with the McDonald's. After that it's sort of deep in the woods. I'll wake you up for that part."

Joe grunted. "It's twenty miles after the exit," he said, and Casey nodded. It had seemed shorter both times he'd been driven on it. Once he got in with Joe, everything was aces.

"C'mon, Joe. Scoot. Turn the ignition, put it into drive, gas on the right, brake on the left. I can do it. Move."

And Joe did, grumbling, "I may still have to call social services" in warning, and Casey nodded.

"I appreciate you being straight with me and all, but you need to get home to do that, and I don't see that happening right now. Now move your ass, old man!"

"'M twenty-seven."

Wow. Not thirty? Casey smiled and looked at him again. He'd seen the guy without a shirt, and he was pretty buff. He had a little tummy, yeah, but you could tell he spent his time working on his house or his property or running around saving strays—he was definitely not a sit-on-the-couch-with-a-beer guy, unless he was ready for bed, if his muscles had anything to say about it.

"Awesome. Maybe we *can* do that!"

"Oh *Christ*, no!"

Oh. That was disappointing. "Don't like guys?"

"Don't like *children*. The key's in the ignition, young'un. Now start the truck and prove to me we're not gonna die at your hands!"

Casey did, and he spent a few minutes in the almost-empty parking lot in front of Ross, driving slowly back and forth and getting the hang of things like brake time and acceleration. He decided that driving was okay—but a little overrated. As he eased the truck back onto the road and toward the freeway, he hardly had to step on the accelerator at all to get the car up to speed.

"God, this thing's faster than it looks," he muttered, but they were going up a pretty steep incline, so maybe that power was a good thing.

He hadn't counted on the pulse-pounding fear of driving a car on the single lane of the double bridge. There was a wall on either side, yes, but he'd walked on the pedestrian part of the bridge and looked down—he *knew* what was in store for them if he lost his mind and just drove the truck through the rail and off the side. What had seemed so appealing when he'd been lost and cold and starving didn't seem like so much fun now that he had a full belly and someplace to sleep without fear.

"Easy, kid," Joe said from the other side of the truck, and some of the tension cramping Casey's hands eased up. "Everyone hates this part."

"Yeah?"

"When all is said and done, we've really only got a narrow path to tread."

It sounded like crazy hippy shit, so Casey was relieved when Joe closed his eyes and started humming "Only the Young Can Say" under his breath. Casey liked that one. They'd determined on the way to town that the radio had no reception, and Joe didn't have tapes in the car, so Casey sang with him, and together they made it over the bridge.

JOE got home and slept until five o'clock. Casey slept too, but he woke up before Joe and raided the refrigerator and the cabinets, settling on some canned soup—he made enough for two, and Joe had some when he emerged from the bedroom to down some pain pills and sit on the couch and veg.

"Shit," Joe muttered, digging into the soup. "I was going to do so much today. I gotta get that carport done in the next week, before it starts to snow up here. Can't have the bike out in the elements, man, that just won't do."

Casey got up and went to the kitchen and pulled bread and butter out of the fridge. (He couldn't figure out why Joe kept the bread in the refrigerator. Joe told him later it was to keep it from going bad.) He buttered a slice and walked it to Joe, because he liked that in his soup, and Joe took it with an appreciative thanks.

"I could start clearing the debris out," Casey said after flopping back down on the couch.

"Kid—"

"Look, do you not want me here?"

Sigh. It shook the couch. "You've been damned useful so far."

"Then let me be useful. Maybe I can get a job in Foresthill, right? Pay rent—"

"You're a kid. No paying rent."

"Well, I can work for my keep—"

"Dammit, kid! The way you get to be a kid is to go to school while someone worries about rent for you! Jesus—you still need raising, Casey. You're still not grown. Don't you want to go back home and—"

"No." Casey tried to keep the break out of his voice and failed. "I don't want to go home. They didn't want me."

"Have you thought that maybe they've changed their minds now that you've been gone for two months?"

Casey thought about it and felt his throat swell. "No," he whispered. "Please don't make me go back and find out."

"Kid, no one's going to let you stay with a single man. They just—"

"But who's they? I've been on the streets for two months. Just take me to school, let me fill out the paperwork. I'll tell a few lies. You'll be a friend of the family, and I'll get my transcripts from my old school and—look, Joe, please?"

Joe slumped back against the couch, and Casey could tell he was about done, period. Odds were, his pain meds had kicked in. He'd been tired the night before and he'd already had one hell of a morning. It was obvious that he just didn't have the energy for this. "Kid, if I say we don't have to decide right now, will that be enough?"

Casey stood up and collected the dishes. Hell yes. It had gotten him from Auburn back to Joe's house, and his confidence wasn't shaken. They could do this. He was sure of it.

BETWEEN the two of them, they managed to clear the carport of refuse and get the frame set before the work party. Casey had wondered, at first, why not use the garage for the vehicles, and then he'd actually *seen* the garage and realized that Joe had sunk a lot of the spare money from the home loan into home improvement stuff, and although he'd seen some of it waiting to be used in the carport, the bulk of it was in the garage. Lumber, drywall, siding, paint—Joe had himself about four years of home improvement to do, which was awesome, because Casey had at least two years of growing up to do, and he figured he'd be along for the ride.

He and Joe worked well together. Joe gave concise instructions, and Casey found that when he wasn't trying to piss off the grown-up he was working with, he was actually pretty good at following orders. He tried to be considerate—he warned Joe when something was about to fall, and asked for help with stuff he didn't understand. For his part, Joe tried to keep a rein on his unexpected temper.

The temper was a surprise, but sort of a welcome one. Casey had started to think of Joe as someone all wise and all patient, and a little part of himself was all set to walk over the guy, because Joe would let him do anything, right?

But no. The first day, Casey was on the roof, throwing broken pieces of plastic down on the ground, and Joe called up to him to stay on the beams so he didn't fall through the plastic. But that didn't make sense, because Casey wasn't tall, and he was certainly not fat, and if he just took a step there—

He scrambled back and barely made it to the nearest beam before the plastic crumbled beneath his feet.

"Goddammit, Casey! Do what you're goddamned told!"

Casey had actually needed to brace himself against the roof of the house for a moment, because the snapped order made his heart pound like he was a criminal caught in the act. His father used to yell a lot. *Goddammit, kid, could you keep the fucking ball out of the house? Jesus, Casey, do you ever fucking think? Maybe if you stopped fucking up in class, I'd give a shit about your fucking ball games. I mean, it's not like you're first string or anything. God, the way you run? I'm surprised they let you on the fucking team!*

And for a minute, Casey had flashed back to that and had felt a totally familiar urge to hop off the roof and run into the forest, maybe take his chances on Rufus's property, now that the dumbass dog was wandering around in a doggy cast, hitting Joe up for food.

Then Casey looked down and saw Joe's bad-tempered expression and realized that in the middle of all that pissed off was a whole lot of concern.

"Yeah, Joe. Sorry 'bout that!"

"Jesus, kid. Don't scare me like that."

And Casey did his best not to. He did sometimes: banged his thumb with the hammer, accidentally bumped Joe's sore shoulder, yelled at the dog when the dog started whining for food. Mostly Joe was patient and mild, but that temper? Casey started to cherish it.

Joe went back to work after the five days, like he'd promised. Casey spent the first day knocking around the property, exploring the nooks and crannies. It was mostly forest land, lots of places to walk, although there were some areas that would have made good places for outbuildings, if Joe ever wanted to build one. When Joe got back, though, he made it clear that he expected Casey to spend his time better.

"What's this?" Casey looked curiously at the bakery box on the table.

"A birthday cake. We can have some after dinner."

Casey blinked at him, absurdly moved. "It's almost Thanksgiving."

"Well, like I said. You're not officially sixteen 'til you have a party."

"That's awesome. Thanks, Joe."

"I got you boring grown-up presents. Don't thank me yet."

Casey brightened, some of the hotness behind his eyes easing. "What'd you get me?"

"Clothes you won't look at with disdain, for one."

Casey *really* brightened. "Yeah?"

"Yeah. Sorry about the clothes—I threw some money at you, told you to stock up. You did real good, but I'm thinkin' you'd like something shinier."

Casey couldn't contain his grin. Even if the clothes turned out to be not his thing, it was nice to be thought of. "Anything else?"

"Yeah, but you'll get it after dinner. It's grown-up shit. Don't get excited."

But "grown-up shit" turned out to be the most exciting thing of all. "Grown-up shit" turned out to be an enrollment packet from the local continuation school, plus some books to read, some packets from the English class for him to fill out, and an algebra two workbook. Casey looked at the stuff with dawning comprehension and pushed his hair back from his face. (It was long and in his eyes now—it had been short and spiky in the front when he'd left home.)

"Hey…," he said, grinning up at Joe, the little birthday cake with the blown-out candles completely forgotten. "Does this mean I'm here to stay?"

Joe grimaced. "Don't get your panties in a twist, kid. We still have to fill that shit out, and you still have to get your transcripts. If we run into a social worker, this whole thing could be moot." He crossed his arms in front of him as he said this and stretched moodily at the muscles in his sore arm. Casey noticed he did that a lot, like he was struggling against limitations.

Casey turned anxious eyes toward him. "You want me to stay, right? I've been a good kid this week, right?"

Joe frowned at him. "You're a great kid. Never doubt it. Whether or not you stay here, that has nothing to do with what kind of kid you are. I'm a single man, Casey—not exactly father material."

"Ew. You are *not* my father. That's *not* why I want to stay."

Joe's eyes narrowed. "I'm not your boyfriend," he warned, and Casey nodded like he believed it.

"So, acid-wash jeans? And the jacket over them? Joe… that's amazing. Thank you!" He turned a shining smile to Joe, who gave a cautious one back, and Casey could have cursed himself, because it looked like Joe wasn't fooled for a minute.

THE work party was fun. Joe worked with fun people—orderlies, other nurses, supply people, clerks. At first Casey expected a lot of male doctors and female nurses, with people necking in every corner, but he quickly learned that was just in the television shows. Bitching about doctors was everybody's favorite hobby, and Casey learned to hate them too, just by proxy.

Joe introduced Casey as simply a friend who was staying, and no one seemed to think that was odd in the least, and everyone seemed comfortable with Casey being part of the "leadership team" when it came to building the carport. Casey, for his part, had become vested in the project. He'd spent a week on it already!

People started arriving at eight in the morning. By sunset, it was done: a sturdy three-sided building with a roof that sloped from the roof of the house, and enough space to fit three cars—more than enough to fit the motorcycle and the truck. The fifteen or so people—they were all between twenty-five and forty—who had come to help had gone inside to get warm and were eating Joe's pizza, drinking his beer, and, if Casey wasn't mistaken, toking a little weed. He'd seen Joe's stash box in the drawer under his pajama bottoms that first day when he'd been looking for sweatshirts. It had been a little dusty, but it didn't surprise Casey that some of Joe's friends were the type to get high. His own parents had a nice little collection of rolled-up dollar bills with white powder on one end, brought out once a month. That was just what people did.

Joe was sweeping up the last of the stuff on the concrete foundation and putting it in the big dustbin. (Casey had been appalled to find out that there was no trash pickup out here—Joe had to cart it all to a dump site in Roseville once a month, which explained why he was really big on reusing everything, from cardboard boxes to the little tie things on the ends of bread loaves.) He looked up and saw Casey admiring their handiwork, and grinned.

"Not a bad way to spend a Saturday, is it?"

Casey smiled at him, liking the way his eyes crinkled and the way the sun caught the red highlights in his otherwise dark-brown hair. It was pulled back in a ponytail today and trimmed evenly on the ends, and Casey had started to fantasize about what it would feel like if he touched it.

"It was great," he said after a pause that went on too long, and he could have kicked himself when Joe's smile turned to a grimace and his eyes went sad.

"Go inside, kid. Have some pizza. But do me a favor and just pass the joint if someone hands it to you, okay?"

"I get high!" Didn't everybody? *Just say no?* Seriously?

"Yeah, but not anymore. If I'm going to keep you, I gotta give it up. I gotta give it up, you gotta give it up, okay?"

Casey blinked. Were adults ever that honest? Well, he hadn't really been that excited about inhaling the nasty stuff anyway. It had made Dillon smile at him pretty, and that had been fun, but otherwise? Their aborted make-out session had been *way* better.

"Yeah. Fine. Whatever"—and he had to laugh when Joe wrinkled his nose.

"God, cursing used to be honest, you know? When did 'whatever' come to mean 'fuck you'?"

"You know, for a guy with a ponytail and a soul patch, you sound an awful lot like my grandmother."

"You know, for a kid who weighs ninety-eight pounds soaking wet, you sure got a mouth on you."

"Yeah, wanna know what I can do with it?"

Joe grimaced again. "Kid? You know what? I'm going in there, and I'm going to eat pizza and congratulate all my friends on a job well done. I'm going to have a beer, and I'm going to hope that maybe Sharon Rosenthal, the pretty girl with the long, blonde hair—"

"The one with the sweater that could fit me?"

"You should be so well-endowed. Yeah, her. I'm going to go make out with her. She might even spend the night. If that happens, you're going to sleep in my guest bedroom, do your English packet in the morning, and make plans to become a truly outstanding human being—in two or so years, okay?"

Casey shook his head, at a loss. "You know, I don't think I've met another human being so opposed to a blowjob before."

Joe rolled his eyes. "That's because you haven't offered one to the male half of the people in that room. And you're not going to. You go to school, find the other sixteen-year-old boys, and score all the tail you can manage. But you hit on me too hard and I'm going to knock you into the nearest foster home, you hear me? I don't do that. And as far as I remember, you must have said sixty thousand times that you didn't want to do that either!"

With that unexpected flare of temper, Joe slammed down the broom and went stalking into the house, and Casey watched him through the living room window as he slid his arm around Sharon

Rosenthal's slender waist and took a piece of pizza from her. He was looking at her like she held the answer to his prayers, and she leaned her head on his shoulder like he was everything she'd ever wanted.

Casey nursed a sudden ache in his heart.

"That's because I didn't know you yet," he said quietly, even though Joe was in his living room and well on the way to getting laid. "I was stupid. If I'd known you, I would have *made* you love me first."

But Joe didn't hear him, and eventually Casey had to go inside. He stayed in the living room for a while and talked to the people he'd worked with all day. They were decent people—hardworking, hard-drinking people, but not all obsessed with their tax portfolios like his parents' friends. They told raunchy jokes and talked about cars and going to motorcycle races and rock concerts, and Casey liked them. But Joe's arm never left Sharon's waist, and she didn't waste any opportunities to kiss his cheek or lean on his shoulder. She'd been kind to Casey as they were working, asking his opinion on what to do with things and generally acknowledging that Casey had been there on the project when she had not, and Casey had started out liking her very much.

She looked up at him from Joe's shoulder, smiling, and then looked surprised at something, and that was when he realized that he was glaring at a perfectly nice woman who hadn't done anything to Casey but... but....

But horn in on a man he wasn't old enough for.

That was when Casey cut out to his own room. The party was winding down anyway, dwindling to a few people who liked to play card games around the table, and normally, Casey would have been all over that (he'd loved doing it at his mom's parents' house, when they'd still been alive), but not tonight. Tonight, he was going to his room and reading *The Great Gatsby* and answering all sorts of questions about it so he could get a start on getting credits in eleventh grade English. Tonight, he was going to pretend this whole thing didn't rip his heart out, because in his head, he knew Joe was right and that he couldn't possibly trust the guy if Joe took him up on his crush. Tonight, he was going to remember what it was like to be a kid and sit at the kids' table, oh yes he was. He could do it. He'd survived two months on the streets, dammit, and this wasn't any different.

He fell asleep on his bed, thinking that Tom Buchanan was a royal douche bag and Daisy Buchanan wasn't much better, and woke up to a quiet house. Two people were passing his bedroom door from Joe's room.

"You sure you've got to go?" Joe was asking plaintively, and the low, sexy laugh on the other side of Casey's door was obviously Sharon.

"It was wonderful, sweetheart." Her murmur was a lot like Daisy Buchanan's, and Casey was too tired to kick himself for being an ass. "I want to do it again soon. But I don't think Casey will be too happy if I'm here in the morning."

"Casey?"

"Yeah—he just got you in his life, baby. Now's not the time to spring someone else on him. Give it some time. If we last at all, we can do sleepovers then, okay?"

There was a quiet, muffled sound, and Casey wanted to kick something. Damn her. *Damn* her, for being kind and reasonable. Because Joe wouldn't *be* with someone else, would he? Damn, damn, damn, damn…. Finally, the kiss broke off, and Sharon's next words were breathless.

"I gotta go, okay? I need to catch some sleep before my next shift." And with that, Joe walked her to the door. Casey heard him go back to his own room, and lay there in the dark, tormenting himself with horrible images of the two of them together. Had she gone down on him? Did she get to see him naked? Did she get to touch his skin? God…. Casey had done enough with girls—and just enough with Dillon—to have had a taste of that. He'd had enough done to *him* to know where that taste had been leading, if he'd been allowed to taste. Well, he *wanted* to taste, and now he wanted to taste Joe. He *needed* to taste Joe. It was *imperative.*

And that was what drove him out of his bed that night. Joe never locked his side of the bathroom door—why should he? Casey's worry in the last two weeks had all been about Joe coming over to see *him.* But now that Casey knew what he wanted, he figured all he had to do was reach for it. That was what people had done to him, wasn't it? *C'mere, boy, let me have you. C'mere, boy, suck my cock. C'mere, bend over. I want your ass.* Wasn't that the way it worked? Well, now maybe Casey could have him some of that.

Joe's room was almost as spartan as Casey's. It had a dresser with a mirror on it, and a small bookshelf, and a couple of framed prints by some guy named Steve Hanks that Casey thought were damned sentimental, but other than that, its main feature was the king-size bed in the center, with the big man sprawled out toward the middle. Joe didn't move when Casey padded into his room. He just lay there on his side, his head pillowed on his arms and his hair spread out around his shoulders like some sort of bloodsucking wild animal. (Casey loved Joe's hair, he was just always surprised by the sheer volume.) Casey, being a dumbass, didn't even bother to strip off his pants. He just slid under the sheets on his side of the bed, ignoring the smell of sex and the damp spots.

Like a rabbit burrowing into warmth, he scooted over to where Joe was sleeping, and wrapped his arms around Joe's waist, pressing the length of his young, slender body up against Joe's back.

He wasn't entirely sure how he ended up being kicked out of bed, but the thump of his ass hitting the floor shook the little house.

Joe was sitting up in bed, scowling at him. "Do this again, I'll call the social worker in the middle of the goddamned night!" he snarled, that temper flare lighting up the darkened room. "Jesus, kid. Go the fuck back to bed!"

Casey turned around and bolted, slammed his side of the bathroom door shut, and made sure it was locked from his room. He lay in his bed, shivering, until dawn, held awake by embarrassment and humiliation.

THE next morning, Joe greeted him with pancakes and a grunted good morning. He asked about Casey's schoolwork, and he asked for Casey's help making a shopping list for Thanksgiving dinner. He wanted to know if Casey wanted a haircut, since Joe was going into town, and he wanted Casey's opinion on how best to get his transcripts. He was kind, personal, and involved in Casey's life, just like he had been for the past two weeks.

He didn't once mention what he and Sharon had been doing in the room before she left, and he didn't once mention what Casey had done afterward. It was like it didn't happen.

Casey decided that, for the time being, he could live with that.

Shakedown
~Joe

THEY spent Christmas and Thanksgiving quietly enough. Casey helped Joe cook both dinners, and they both waited for the next morning to do cleanup. Joe bought Casey his own Walkman for Christmas and took him to town to buy music. (And then counted himself very virtuous indeed, because the kid's music? Really? George Michael and Madonna? Gross!)

The kid's little attempt at seduction was not even *discussed* between them. Joe thought it was better that way. He had to give the kid points for trying, but really? Sixteen? Joe had *some* standards.

And he had to admit, Casey met them. Yeah, he was feisty, and he tended to do shit without thinking, but by the time Christmas was over, not only had he taken to feeding the outside cats, he'd adopted a trio of kittens and brought them inside. After the first day of walking inside and seeing that kid cuddling a little orange fuzzball to his cheek and talking to it like it was human—"Hey, furr-burf, stop that. No, I don't want my nose bit. No. I said no. Yeah, well, licking's okay. Go ahead. Good for the pores. Who needs Clearasil when you've got kitten tongue? Oh yeah, right there, keep going. I'll go put some milk on my forehead, we'll clear that little blackhead problem right up!"—Joe went and bought a cat box for the bathroom, and suddenly the little fuckers couldn't run under his feet enough. (He also bought some Clearasil, for which Casey expressed profound gratitude.)

But that was okay. Between Casey and Nick, Jay, and Jordan (because, according to the kid, those were the only three characters he could stand from the damned book), the house was a little less lonely. (Although Joe did notice that Nick was a girl cat, like Jordan. When he asked Casey about this, Casey replied that he'd always figured Gatsby was giving it to Nick anyway—this way, the cats could do something about it. Joe was planning on getting the cats fixed, but he put it off when he heard this. Anything so Casey could see a happy ending.)

But eventually they did have to deal with the paperwork thing when enrolling Casey in school, and a social worker *did* need to get called in. Joe could hardly blame Casey, either—the kid had kept his nose clean, had worked hard, apparently had been a model prisoner at the continuation school. (Given what Casey said about his fellow inmates, this wasn't far off. He claimed to have spent a half an hour during a "science" class searching a local field for psilocybin mushrooms. He had a small baggie full of regular run-of-the-mill fungus to prove it.) But eventually the authorities figured out the bogus social security number *wasn't* his and that was how the transcripts he'd doctored to say Casey Daniels didn't pass muster.

So here Joe was, looking at the fortyish social worker with the newly minted tatas and the overly full lips and trying to explain why the kid should stay with him.

"See, the thing is," Joe said, smiling apologetically, "he doesn't want to go home, and I don't want him back out on the street. He almost didn't survive last time."

The woman had no eyebrows. Or she did, but they were penciled in, and those little pencil lines formed perfect semicircles when she made a little "oooh" movement with her red-lipsticked mouth.

"Oh, that's just so *sad*! And you brought him here and took care of him? Without a woman here? Oh, Mr. Daniels, that's just so *kind* of you."

Mrs. Cahill put a perfectly manicured set of bright red nails on Joe's sleeve. He looked at the hand, to her suddenly predatory eyes, to her hand again. He closed his eyes for a second and then looked at Casey, who was sitting across the table from him.

Casey scowled at the hand, and then met Joe's eyes, and then looked at Mrs. Cahill, who had told them straight off that they were probably going to have to change this living arrangement immediately.

Casey swallowed—Joe could see it from across the table. Joe pulled up a smile to cover the silence. "Well, ma'am, I do like helping people out."

"Oh, you *do*?" she cooed, leaning in further so Joe could see how low-cut her sweater really was and how very firm her recently purchased breasts were too. "Now, see, that's nice." She leaned even further forward, so those hard breasts were butting up against his arm. The nipples were very, very pointy against the cashmere of her sweater. "There are not many men who would do that for... for *anyone*, much less a young boy!"

Joe swallowed and met Casey's eyes. Casey was looking like he'd just sucked a lemon, but he sighed and nodded, like he was giving Joe permission to do whatever it took.

"Well, ma'am, I was taught to give back, you know what I mean?"

She was practically sitting in his lap, and, well, his lap had never really objected to a curvy set of anything pressed up against it, and was responding in kind. That wicked scarlet manicure dropped down to his thigh, brushing his semierect cock in his jeans.

"That's really rare," she breathed in his ear. "I think that maybe, if you were willing to demonstrate just how... how *deep* that commitment to *giving back* really was, we could see if maybe you and your young charge could continue on in peace."

Joe and Casey locked eyes one more time, and Joe was half-defiant—You *wanted this!*—and half-pleading—*Save me!* Casey's beseeching look back told Joe all he needed to know.

"Why sure, Mrs. Cahill. Whatever I can do to, uhm, deepen my commitment, right?" He turned and smiled at her, knowing that he had a nice one, with well-cared-for teeth and generous lips under his mustache and soul patch.

She was so close he could smell her cosmetics. "For one thing, you could call me Sandy."

Joe licked his lips. "Well, Sandy, how 'bout we go into the other room and talk while Casey goes and does his homework."

He looked up at Casey and rolled his eyes, while Casey mouthed "Thank you!" with almost desperate gratitude. Sure, the little bastard would thank him *now*! Where was he going to be when Joe had to 'fess up to Sharon, whom he had almost convinced to stay the night?

But it didn't matter. He had a condom in his pocket, and Mrs. "Call me Sandy!" the social worker was rubbing his thighs, and he had a job to do. Joe had to go take one for the team.

JOE got out of the shower and found that Casey had made hamburgers. He'd even cut up tomatoes, lettuce, and pickles on a little plate and toasted the bread. Joe smiled tiredly and wondered if it would be overkill to take another shower before he went to bed.

"Thank you," Casey said quietly as Joe sat down, and Joe nodded.

"She's going to be back in three months."

Casey grimaced. "I'm so sorry."

"I bleached the couch." He had a little spray bottle of Formula 409, which he used for the bathroom. The couch wasn't going to smell right for a week.

"I really appreciate it."

"I'm a shitty role model."

"No!" Casey shook his head adamantly, and Joe was surprised to see that his eyes were shiny. He stood up abruptly, and the chair behind him went flying backward, and he launched himself at Joe for a long, wordless hug. Joe held him tightly, for once not concerned with propriety or breaking the boundary he'd worked so hard to establish. Suddenly just the warm, nonjudgmental human contact of someone who wasn't going to hold that half hour of his life against him was really all he could ask for.

"You're a great role model," Casey whispered into his still damp hair. "You're great." He got hold of himself after a minute and went and sat down, and Joe missed him. Not in a sexual way—oh God, no!—but in a warm way. Still, he'd been raised to be honest, and he was about to correct Casey—what he'd done was easy. It was true, he wasn't a fan of rules, but that half an hour had broken a big one—and for no other reason than that Joe didn't want to deal with all of the other rule makers when what it came down to was that they were butting into how he lived his life in his house. Even more than that, he didn't want to deal with Casey's fear or his own ever-present fear that Casey would just turn around and bolt and run.

"I could have done something different," Joe muttered, and Casey shook his head.

"My dad," he said, and Joe grew very still. Two months— November, December, and now they were into January, and Casey hadn't so much as breathed a word about his folks.

"My dad," Casey repeated, breathing carefully, "snorted coke once a month—used to say it was his reward for being a good little corporate slave. So he voted for Reagan, and even has a picture of Nancy on his wall, and he's snorting coke once a month, and I'm pretty sure he's banging the secretary or someone, because Mom's been drinking an awful lot. And both of them have dinner parties, and they trot me out and talk about my sports and my grades, and the way my dad talks to teachers when I don't have the grades he wants?" Casey shivered and wiped his face with the back of his hand. "And it's my fault too. I was a shitty student. If someone didn't make me, I just didn't do it. And here—" Casey gestured with his hand. Here. Here it was different. He swallowed and then looked at Joe with an expression so damned grown-up, Joe's heart poinged a little. "Here what I do or say matters. You talk to me about the books, and they matter to you. You just did something a little wrong so I could stay. I'm so grateful, because the place I was from, that was a lot more wrong, okay?"

Joe nodded and looked at his hamburger. The kid had used ground beef instead of the frozen patties. He'd cut up little onions and peppers in it, like Joe had shown him. He'd still need that second shower, he thought, picking up the hamburger, but maybe he wouldn't need the wire brush.

He took a bite and swallowed and smiled at Casey. "This is really good," he said, and Casey smiled back a little.

"Thanks, Joe."

"You're welcome, kid."

IN JANUARY, not long after Joe soiled his morals and his pecker in
Mrs. Kindness-is-Frickin'-Deep Cahill's patoongie (and consequently
broke up with Sharon Rosenthal), Joe took Casey to get his driver's
permit. Two weeks later he took him to get his license, and the truck,
such as it was, was Casey's to drive to school. After two weeks of
working his ass off and catching up on his classes, Casey begged super
nicely and was allowed to get a job working at the McDonald's right up
at the Foresthill exit. Casey often called it "the place where it all
began," but Joe could never get him to explain that.

One night Casey was late enough back from his shift—which
ended at nine—that Joe began to pace, stalking from one end of the
yard to the other, his hands in the pockets of his lined leather jacket, his
booted feet crunching in the one or two inches of snow that had hit the
ground the night before. He heard the puttering whine of a motorcycle
with a small engine and a light frame about three minutes before the
shitty-looking UJM with the peeling electric-teal paint job on the tank
pulled up. Casey was on the back, and because there wasn't a bitch
seat, he was scooted forward so far his crotch must have been rubbing
the other kid's ass for the entire ride. His head was as bare as a baby's
ass, and he was shivering in the hooded sweatshirt he'd worn to school
that morning.

The kid on the front was in full regalia: a helmet with a
windscreen, leather jacket, leather riding gloves, and a scarf. Joe's jaw
tightened. Casey got off the back of the bike, blowing on his hands and
looking apologetically at Joe.

"I'm sorry," he chattered as he took a few awkward steps
forward. "The truck wouldn't start. I tried getting it jumped and
everything, and I d-d-d-idn't figure out what it was."

Joe closed his eyes and swore. Okay. That was forgivable. Then
he opened his eyes and narrowed them on the kid with the helmet.

"Take your helmet off," he snarled, and the kid did. Joe didn't
like him any better without it. He had a narrow face, with acne (it was
the age—Clearasil wasn't helping Casey none either), but he sported
about six hairs on his chin and five on his upper lip and was trying to
pass them off as a goatee. His eyes were nice—blue-green, lined with

dark lashes—but Joe was not going to be pacified by the thought that Casey's hormones allowed him to overcome his common sense.

Joe glared at the boy long enough to make him uncomfortable.

"Casey, I thought you said you didn't live with your dad?"

"C'mere," Joe snapped. The kid did, taking a few tentative steps in. Joe gave him a quick open-palmed smack on the side of the head.

"Hey!"

"That hurt?"

The kid just gaped at him, and Casey was screaming "*Joe!*" behind them.

"Did that hurt?"

"Yes!"

"What do you think a crash would feel like?"

The kid's mouth opened and closed, Casey shut up abruptly, and Joe nodded. "'Kay, I'll give you points. You were trying to do a good deed. Good for you. Points for good intentions. Do you see his head? Nice shape, right?"

The kid nodded, those pretty eyes wide and apprehensive, and his gaze raked Casey over. He stopped for a moment to make soft eye contact with Casey himself, who smiled encouragingly. Wonderful. "Yeah, I guess," he stammered.

"Glad you think so. Now I've ridden a bike in that canyon for a year, and I've flipped it twice, and I've been riding for fifteen years. What do you think would happen to that pretty melon you like so much if you flipped your fuckin' bike?"

To his credit, the kid let his jaw drop in fear, and he closed his mouth and swallowed. "Wouldn't be good," he muttered.

Joe nodded. "Yeah. Wouldn't be good. I've seen firsthand how it wouldn't be good." He shuddered, trying not to replay a slide show of the worst moments from his ER and ICU rotations. "Next time you have a friend on your bike, you either carry an extra or you go without, you hear me? That's the right thing to do."

The kid nodded, his cheeks going paler in the cold and those expressive eyes welling up and shiny under the full moon.

Joe sighed. "Go inside. There's coffee made if you want. You can warm up before you go home."

"Thanks," the kid whispered. He took some stiff-legged steps to the house, apparently planning to take Joe up on the offer, and Joe turned to Casey, who was looking embarrassed and still cold in the silver dark.

"Sorry, Joe," he muttered, not looking Joe in the eyes.

Joe took a few steps in and put an arm over his shoulders, as much to warm him up as to steer him inside. "Jesus fucking Christ, kid, you ever hear of a goddamned phone? Scared the shit out of me."

Casey's look was eloquent. "You were worried?"

"'Course I was. You've been a model prisoner—always on time, no stopping to screw around, and suddenly you're *late*? I would have come pick you up... not that you probably didn't enjoy this ride more," he said slyly.

They'd reached the porch, and Joe stepped back to let Casey go through first. Casey's cheeks were flushed, and he had the sort of complexion that would show that easily, so it was fun to watch.

"He's nice to me. But he goes to the regular high school."

Joe shrugged. "So?"

Casey looked sideways. "Don't think he's ever been kissed."

"Kid?"

Casey turned toward him, those defiant gray eyes of his trying their best to be hard. "Yeah?"

"You're still a kid. That shit you're worried about? You can tell him if you want, but mostly, that's yours to keep. As long as you use a rubber on your pecker when the time comes, it's no one's business unless you want it to be."

Casey frowned. "Why would I need a rubber on my peck—"

"Casey?" Motorcycle Boy was already in the kitchen, and Joe had to admit, he sure did know how to make himself at home.

"Yeah, Dev?"

"Uhm... do you have milk? And sugar? And maybe some chocolate? I really hate coffee."

Casey pulled his head back and screwed up one side of his mouth. "Well, why did you pour yourself some, you moron?"

"He said I should!" Dev peered around the partition that separated the kitchen from the entryway into the living room. His mouth made a perfectly round O when he saw Joe, and Joe tried very hard not to ruin the scary-man thing he apparently had going by laughing.

Casey grimaced and muttered something like "Dumber than diaper shit," and then pulled on a brittle, bright smile that Joe had never seen before. He walked into the kitchen and flashed that smile at Dev, then took the cup of coffee from him and set it on the counter. He started rummaging in the refrigerator while Dev stood by, looking at him helplessly. When Casey came out, he had a plastic gallon of milk, and he grabbed the sugar from the counter, reaching around Dev, and under his arms, and behind his back. When he finished, they were chest to chest, and Dev was blushing furiously, and Casey's obvious irritation had faded to a faintly predatory look.

Joe watched with interest, laughing softly to himself. God, the kid was resilient—a survivor of the first water. Joe loved him to death.

Dev licked his lips, the gesture innocent enough, but Joe saw his cue. He backed out of the kitchen slowly, just as Casey leaned forward for a kiss.

A half an hour later, he sat reading *The Talisman* by Stephen King (which he adored—it was his second reading, and he rarely reread a book) and was surprised by a soft knock on the door.

"Yeah?"

The door cracked open and Casey came in, looking lost. Joe was wearing a T-shirt and pajama bottoms. He used the book to gesture to the bottom of the bed, and Casey sat down, folding one leg under himself. He was still wearing his McDonald's uniform pants—charcoal gray—and the rugby shirt that topped them, and he smelled faintly of grease and cooking meat. Usually he liked to shower as soon as he got home, but apparently tonight he'd had other things to do. His brown-gold hair was a little greasy, and his button nose was shiny and about to break out, but he'd put on maybe twenty pounds, and Joe thought he looked a long way from the scrawny half-dead thing he'd had to delouse four months earlier. His mother, a perpetual feeder of strays, would be proud.

"I repeat, 'Yeah?'"

Casey grinned at him like he knew Joe was only trying to be grumpy and didn't really have the heart for it. "I kissed him."

Joe kept his smile gentle under his beard. "Yeah?"

"He'd been kissed before."

"By a boy?"

"No."

"How'd he take it?"

Casey laughed and looked down as his foot—covered in a slightly rank sweat sock—swung against the bottom of the bed frame. "He said he'd maybe like to do more of it."

Joe leaned forward and ruffled his hair, and Casey caught his hand.

"You think this is going to change the way I feel about you?" Casey asked, and Joe pulled his hand away and threw himself back against the pillow with a sigh.

"I'll take the bike to town tomorrow and fix the truck while you're in school. If nothing else, I've got a friend who can give you a ride—"

Casey shook his head too quickly. "All right," he said, brusquely, swallowing hard. "I get it. Off-limits. We'll get the car fixed, we keep our little household going, we don't talk about that." Suddenly he stopped moving and pinned Joe back to the bed with those remarkable gray eyes. "Someday, I'm going to be old enough, and you're going to have to deal with this—and *don't* tell me I'll have moved on by then. Even if I do, I don't want to hear it now. But right now, I'll be up and ready early, because you have to be at work at one, and I want you to have time to fix the truck and not have to hurry too fast, okay?"

Joe nodded and pretended his heart wasn't pattering in his ears in reaction to the sudden frightening prospect of fighting off Casey's advances in a very real way. It was a good thing the kid had a head on his shoulders, or their cozy little household of two would be very, very doomed.

"Yeah." The quiet in the bare room hung heavily, but Casey wasn't moving. Joe took a deep breath, not wanting to stop Casey from coming in and speaking his peace if he needed to. "You going to be doing more of it?" he asked.

Casey looked up from the spot of secret sauce that he'd been scratching off the knee of his twill uniform pants. "What?"

"Kissing Dev?"

Casey blushed. "Yeah."

"Good."

"Why?"

"Because he's sweet and stupid, and he likes you. You need some of that."

Casey's eyes slid sideways. "It's not going to stay all John Hughes forever, you know."

"John who?"

"God—when was the last time you went to the movies?"

Joe opened his mouth and shut it. "I—"

"You don't even have a VCR."

"Well, I've—"

"Look, after we fix the truck, let's get one. There's a rental place right in Foresthill. We don't even have to go to Auburn. We can watch movies when we have time, okay?"

"Yeah, kid, whatever you say. The twentieth century can move into the living room. I hear you."

Casey was abruptly the boy he needed to be and not the predatory, seductive man he'd been trying to be only moments before. "It's about fucking time," he said, pleased. He sobered for a moment and added, "Can I have Dev over to watch movies too?"

All of the tension Joe had been holding in his neck and shoulders dribbled out. "Yeah, kid. Yeah. That's fine. So, the kiss. It was okay?"

Casey paused for a minute, searching for words. "It was coffee with too much cream and sugar," he said eventually. He looked up at Joe, his grin a little bit evil. "And I like mine black."

Joe rolled his eyes, and they spoke for a few minutes more, and then Casey stood up and made to turn around. He paused at the bed, then whirled around and threw himself into Joe's arms for a purely platonic, purely joyful hug. Joe returned it, feeling proud. This kid was going to grow up, fall in love, have a life. Joe could say he had a part of that. It felt every bit as good as his parents' church services had said it would, and for a moment, as he watched Casey turn wordlessly and dart into the bathroom for his long-delayed shower, he almost believed, just like he had as a child, before his sister had died and his faith had been all sobbed out and bled away like his broken heart.

But then, life with Casey would tend to be that way for Joe—moments of gorgeous, shining faith and moments of agonizing, painful doubt. Joe was young in his way too. It would take him years before he recognized the ebb and flow of true love.

The Way It Is
~Casey

1988

CASEY remembered Joe's stash box from when Joe had been hurt and Casey had been rifling his drawers to find a sweatshirt. It didn't take a whole lot of resourcefulness to dig it out of Joe's underwear drawer now, an intricately carved wooden box that smelled of patchouli and pot.

Casey resolutely didn't think of how much he hadn't liked pot the first few times he'd tried it. Joe had had three cans of beer in the inside refrigerator—*had* being the operative word—and Casey thought that if he drank the other two cans in the garage refrigerator, he'd throw up. And they weren't working. They made him woozy and weird, but he was still pissed and hurt and sad, and if the beer didn't get rid of that shit, then maybe the pot would.

There was an art to rolling a number. Casey had never quite mastered it when he'd lived at home, but then, he'd never had his own stash. He had it now. Joe wasn't due home until midnight—another twelve-hour shift. Joe said they were great for the paycheck, and Casey could tell that working three or four twelves in a row could really free up the rest of his week, but they tired Joe out like nothing else. He usually spent his first day off sleeping. So this was his fourth in a row, and he wasn't due back until midnight, and Casey could safely abuse his body until he forgot about the thing that had set him off.

He sat at the couch and drunkenly rolled joints until he had a neat stack of dusty-smelling marijuana cigarettes in the little compartment, and then he took the handy-dandy lighter and lit up.

His choking scared the shit out of the cats. All three of the fuzzy orange furballs went hauling ass for the unused upstairs until he'd calmed down and mastered the art of breathing once again, but by then? By then his head was nice and floaty, perfectly detachable from the rest of his body, and he was far, far away.

He was still far, far away when Joe walked in less than an hour later. He was also down at least two joints, and the cats were all dizzily humping his leg and his arm and his ankle in an attempt to get even closer to that wonderful, unusual smell.

"Oh shit," Casey said, blinking watery eyes. It didn't stop him from taking his next toke, though. He really didn't want to lose this excellent feeling of not giving a perfectly round ripe shit about anything at all.

Joe took a cautious look around the house, saw the three beer cans lined up neatly on the table, and the open box of stash. He blinked a couple of times and then swallowed hard, like he was trying to swallow his temper. He took three deep breaths, started coughing, and walked to the kitchen.

He came back with a half a gallon of vanilla ice cream and a spoon. He handed it to Casey, and when Casey reached out for it, Joe took the joint from him and inhaled, grimacing when the smoke hit his throat.

"Oh Christ, kid. This is the worst weed in history."

Casey shoved a spoonful of ice cream in his mouth and actually shuddered, it tasted so good. "Thank God," he mumbled, trying to swallow and talk at the same time. "I thought the whole world was just nucking fucking futs, uhm, nuts, to be voluntarily doing that shit when it sucked this bad."

Joe sighed and plopped into the stuffed chair and propped his feet up on the end table. "Well, I reckon it's been about two years since I got this. It's old. It's not supposed to be this hard to get high. Sort of defeats the purpose."

Casey nodded, totally sinking into the absolute joy of the ice cream. "Yeah, well, the purpose was to get high. It worked."

Joe inhaled again and nodded, exhaling before he spoke. "Bitchin', kid. And helpful, since I'm not planning on buying any more of this shit. Can you tell me why we're smoking two-year-old weed?"

Casey swallowed and looked at him sorrowfully. "You weren't supposed to be home."

Joe nodded and grabbed the little alligator clip from the box so they could smoke the roach down to the last of the paper. "Yeah, well, they stopped me at eight hours. Said twelve was too much overtime this week, it was a new policy. So you didn't want me to see?"

Casey shook his head no, then took another bite, then held his palm to his eyeball in pain. "Fuck... fuck... ice cream headache... ouch, ouch, ouch, ouch...."

Joe was quiet until the explosion of cold in Casey's head went away. When Casey looked up, Joe had a glass of tepid water at his elbow, and Casey drank that, grateful to feel the last of the ice cream headache go away. Good. Casey wasn't finished wiping out the half gallon yet.

"So...?" Joe asked, and as high as Casey undoubtedly was, he wasn't high enough to forget the question. God, if only he could fucking forget *something*.

"So I wanted to be high and asleep when you got home," Casey said miserably, thinking that the ice cream, rich, creamy, full of milk and carbohydrates, might be the only thing that understood him.

Joe nodded and gently put the roach out in the ashtray Casey had been using. It didn't get a lot of service in Joe's house—Casey had been lucky to find it.

"So this was part of a *plan*," Joe prodded, and Casey took another bite, then swirled the melty ice cream around his mouth moodily before answering.

"Yes," he decided after a moment. "I *planned* to get high."

"And when did you *plan* to get high, Casey? I've got to say, after three months of stone-cold sobriety, I'm sort of wondering why this suddenly seemed like such a good plan."

Casey put the ice cream down dispiritedly. "I don't really like getting high," he confessed. "I didn't like it before, either. I just... people keep saying that you do it to forget shit. I wanted to forget something."

Joe laughed a little. "You mean like, I don't know, a magic potion?"

Casey nodded, not seeing any irony in it at all. "Yeah. I wanted a magic potion to make me forget."

"What did you want to forget so bad, Casey?" Joe asked, and Casey couldn't look at him.

"It's your fault, you know," he said, meaning it and seriously pissed off because it was true.

"What is?"

"You said you were mad at me because you gave a shit and I scared you. And I thought...." Casey squished his eyes shut so hard he saw stars. "I thought that meant they were worried about me."

Joe grunted, but Casey still couldn't open his eyes.

"So I called them up, right?" God. His hands had been shaking so hard on Joe's rotary dial phone. He'd had to try three times, and he'd been so surprised he remembered the number, even though they'd lived in that house his whole life.

"What'd they say?" Joe's voice was so soft, it was almost a whisper.

"It was Mom, right? And she... she sounded glad to hear from me at first, you know? Like she was so excited and almost in tears. And... I didn't know Dad would be home, which is stupid, because it was after six, you know? He's always home after six."

"So that's good, right?" Except Joe had a sound in his voice, like he knew what came next, and Casey snapped at him in irritation.

"Would I have gotten this high if it was good?"

"No."

"It was great! For a minute, I thought I could... I love it here, Joe, I do, but you keep telling me to be a kid, and I thought, you know, maybe—" He couldn't finish because it sounded so lame and so ungrateful. He'd been living a good life here, and the thought that he would leave it, willingly, just—

"You wanted to go home and be a kid again," Joe said softly. "It's okay, kid. I get it. You don't have to feel ashamed."

Casey nodded and wiped his face with the back of his hand, feeling worse now than he had at the beginning, when he'd gone through three rolling papers to make his first joint. "What the fuck ever," he mumbled. "I just thought it would be nice if they knew where I was, and for a minute, it was great. Mom wanted to know if I was okay and if I had a place to stay and if I was getting enough to eat, and I told her yeah, I was in school, and I had a job, and she'd be real proud of me, and she... she sounded like she used to. I'd come home with a good report card and she'd be happy for me, you know, before I hit high school and suddenly Dad had to just be there to fuck with everyone and make sure they all knew I was fucking perfect and everything."

There was a silence, and he looked up at Joe, only to find those fine, wide, brown eyes looking back at him with what seemed to be immeasurable patience. Casey knew it was only partly true. Joe could lose his nut like everyone else on the planet, but right here, right now, he was simply there, waiting, without judgment or hurry. Casey wiped his cheek again, with the flat of his hand this time.

"My dad started shouting," he said, hearing the sharpness, the anger, in the background all over again. "He told her to ask me if I was still a fag." Casey swallowed and looked at Joe helplessly. "I mean, I turned down a date with Dev to make this phone call, right? He's... he's getting damned good at the hand job... thought we might progress from there... and she's asking me if I'm still 'one of them' and I'm thinking, 'One of what? A boy? A high school student? What the hell am I one of?' and I say, 'I still like boys, Mom,' and suddenly Dad's got the phone and he's shouting at me that I didn't get to come home, ever, if I was still a sissy little—"

Joe didn't let him finish the sentence. Suddenly Joe wasn't on the big stuffed chair, he was on his knees in front of Casey and holding him so tight as Casey sobbed in his arms.

He cried hard, the pot and the beer loosening that thing in him that would have let him stop, and before he was done, he was all but sitting in Joe's lap and whimpering on his shoulder. Finally, finally he was down to whimpers and chin quivers and deep, shuddering heaves of breath, and that was when Joe finally said something.

"My sister," he said quietly, "she was something really special. She… she would make me these no-bake cookies, with oatmeal and cocoa powder, or frosting and graham crackers—every day, after she got home from school."

Casey nodded like he understood, content to let Joe's resonant voice wash over him and tell him a story.

"And she loved me. She was… she told me stories and sang to me. My older brother was maybe a little too old when he was born, but he's also sort of ornery—doesn't ever relax, I guess—but she and Peter never really got along. Paul and David were only about thirteen months apart; they played like twins, and Cheryl—well, she was jealous of me because she thought *she* should have been the baby. But Jeannie loved me. I was her favorite, and I thought the sun rose and set in her hair."

"She sounds wonderful," Casey said, thinking his mother hadn't loved him that much—even when he'd believed she loved him, she hadn't loved him that much.

"She *was* wonderful," Joe whispered. "She died when I was six."

Casey gasped and looked sideways and up at Joe and thought maybe the pot had done something to him too, because his eyes were really red and watery, just like Casey's felt.

"How?"

"She… she went out with a boy, and he talked sweet to her, and then, after the Valentine's dance, he didn't talk to her at all. He spread all these rumors, which were true, right, and he should know, because he was there too. And then she went to a drunk butcher with a fold-out table to try to take the baby out of her belly because she was so afraid… so afraid of letting us down."

Casey found he was patting Joe's shoulder and crying again, this time without the earth-shattering sobs. "I'm sorry. I'm so sorry."

"The thing is," Joe said, talking straight over Casey's shoulder like he was talking to air, "the thing is, she was so afraid of what we would say, that she... she *literally* got killed trying to hide who she was. And my folks—they would have been disappointed, sure. But they wouldn't have yelled at her, and they wouldn't have hurt her or kicked her out. I know that, sure as the sun would rise. But the thing is, she never asked. See, kid, as fucked up as your folks are, at least you had the courage to ask. You have the courage to ask, you have the courage to live your life, you see? So you got slapped down, and I'm sorry, but I'm so proud of you. God, kid. You've got so much heart."

Joe sounded wobbly, and for a wild minute, Casey hoped. Casey hoped that Joe would break down and sob too, so Casey wouldn't feel like such a pussy. But Joe really was older than he was, and instead, he pushed at Casey until Casey stood up and then turned and gave Joe a hand up.

"You go to bed, kid," Joe said fondly, his voice almost steady. "I'll clean up the ice cream."

"What are you gonna do with the pot?" Casey asked, looking fearfully at the last few joints, like someone was going to make him smoke them for punishment.

"Flush it down the garbage disposal with some baking soda."

Casey turned a shining smile at him. "God, Joe. You're the best man on the entire face of the planet. We really gotta get you a VCR."

Joe squinted at him. "That again? Why?"

"Because next time I feel like getting high, maybe I'll just watch a movie instead."

With that, Casey wandered off to bed. He woke up headachy and queasy the next morning, with a mouth that tasted like recycled pig shit, and a solid knowledge that getting high was really not his thing.

He got out of bed and showered first thing, because although he didn't have to work until later that evening and he wasn't scheduled to be in school that day, his BO could have knocked a shit bug into a dead coma. He padded out of the bathroom wearing scrubs because they were cheap, comfy, and Joe brought home plenty, and was surprised to see Joe sitting cross-legged in the front room with a rather hefty piece of metal and plastic on his lap. He was reading a set of directions with the patience of a hound dog waiting for spring by a winter's fire.

"What are you doing up?" Casey asked. Joe usually slept in after a run of twelves. "And what the hell is that?"

Joe squinted up at him, bleary-eyed. "I never went to bed," he confessed. "I cleaned the house, went upstairs and sanded the drywall some, and then went out to town first thing this morning." He looked down at the object in his lap. "I bought tapes for it," he said, almost disconsolate in his befuddlement, "but I can't figure out how to set it up."

Casey, who had still been a little tired after he got out of the shower, was now completely awake. "You bought a VCR?" The thought made him dizzy.

Joe looked back down at the mess of cables in his hand. "Don't get excited, junior. It's not like it's working yet."

God, Joe was exhausted. Casey had a sudden thought that Joe might seem like a grown-up, but coming home to find your sixteen-year-old ward high as a kite and breaking his heart must have been a new experience, even for Joe.

"Here," Casey said, keeping his voice soothing. "Tell you what. You go sleep for a couple of hours, and when you wake up, I'll have breakfast made and the damned thing set up, okay?"

Joe's relief almost had smell. "Really? Can I take a shower?" Or maybe that was Joe himself.

"Yeah, big guy. Go take a shower, put on some scrubs, be dead to the world, okay?"

Joe nodded. "Sounds good. I'll… I'll…." He wobbled for a moment, even as he sat. "I'll do something when I get up."

"You plan on that." He'd been awake for nearly thirty hours, by Casey's estimation. Casey wondered if he could get someone to sub for him at work, just so he could make sure Joe would be okay that night, and then shook off that thought. He'd go rent *The Breakfast Club* and see if maybe Joe could catch up on his pop culture education.

But first, he bent down and lifted the VCR off Joe's lap and put it on the couch, because it was frickin' heavy, and then gave Joe a hand up. Joe smiled beatifically, and Casey slung an arm over his shoulder to steer him down the hallway. He probably would have killed that same shit bug Casey had worried about when *he'd* woken up, but Casey didn't mind. There was a simple trust in him that Casey enjoyed. Joe was good people. It was okay.

And after he heard the water running, indicating a shower and (probably) a better sleep when Joe was out, Casey sat to figure out the VCR—which was not nearly as hard to him as it had been to a befuddled Joe—and managed to get it hooked up to the television. There was a bag full of used VHS tapes that came with it, and Casey's eyes watered just looking at them. *Splash, Ferris Bueller's Day Off, Footloose*—Joe might not know about it or even understand it, but he certainly got *Casey*, and if Casey wasn't so embarrassed from his cry the night before, he might have sat down and had another one.

As it was, he set up a roast and some potatoes and broth in the Crock-Pot and then sat down and watched *Footloose*, thinking both that Kevin Bacon was really hot and that Joe, in his quiet, patient way, had been right. Casey had had the courage to ask—and even if he'd been turned down, he at least knew, for certain and in his heart, that right here, on Joe's old couch, eating cold cereal in hospital scrubs, was exactly where Casey belonged.

A MONTH later, Casey lay on the couch in the dark, waiting to see if Joe would prove him right or make their entire time together a colossal lie.

He was on the couch because his room was being used, and his room was being used by a pretty girl named Stacia with a nice rack and hard eyes.

Stacia had offered Casey a blowjob when Casey had gotten off work, if only he'd give her some leftover food. She'd been wearing jeans—thin in the seat and the knees—and a sweater that was almost too warm for March weather. Her dirty blonde hair was ragged at the ends, like it had been cut to layer and perm but all the styling had come out.

Casey had told her that they'd compacted all the leftover food for the night, and then asked her if she wanted to come home with him to Joe's.

The invitation had been issued without thinking. Joe had taken Casey in, so Joe would probably take in other people. But as Casey had tried to explain Joe to her, her eyes had narrowed and her look had turned speculative.

"Just lets people stay in his house? Sounds like a sucker. Why haven't you taken him?"

Casey glared at her. "Because he's a nice guy. And if you try to take him, I'll kick your ass!"

Stacia rolled her eyes. "Don't get all snippy. It would just be nice not to have to turn tricks for food, right?"

Casey revised his hasty plan to kick her out as soon as he reached Foresthill proper, and tried to think like Joe. "How long have you been on the road?"

The sigh she gave was shuddery. "What is it, March?"

"Yeah. Almost April."

"I ran away with my boyfriend in September. Shit... shit didn't go well, you know?"

Casey sighed. "Yeah. Yeah, I know." God. Since September? He'd been on the streets for two months, and he'd been ready to die.

She looked at him speculatively. "Well, you seem to be doing okay. Your guy a pervert? He keeping you around like a toy?"

Casey shook his head, taking a deep breath as they crossed the Foresthill bridge. It always freaked him out, no matter how many times he drove the old pickup over it. The damned thing felt vast around him anyway, and the wheel felt like it was wider than his shoulders. Putting it between the lane lines and pressing the accelerator was always an act of faith that the ancient land yacht really wasn't as huge as it seemed.

"No," he said shortly, clenching his hands on the wheel. "He's a good guy. I'm not taking you with me if you keep bad-mouthing him. He doesn't deserve that. And if you hurt him or try to take from him, I'll kick your fucking ass." Maybe it was the stress of crossing the bridge that put something hard in his voice, but she seemed to take the threat seriously.

"Okay, okay! I'm just wondering. I got into a car with a strange man, geez!"

Casey looked at her sideways and shook his head. He knew this was a bad idea.

Joe apparently knew it was a bad idea too. Casey had given her some sandwiches and the Kwell and the speech about a bath, and a spare set of scrubs, and he'd put her clothes in the washer while she'd been soaking in the tub—but he'd also taken all his valuables and stashed them in Joe's room, and then made sure the bathroom door was locked from Joe's side too. Joe kept a stash of cash *literally* in the ceramic cookie jar shaped like a curled-up cat, and Casey debated whether or not to move *that* too. Finally he just left it and figured if Stacia was going to steal the cash, maybe she'd leave all the other stuff, like the VCR, which Casey was just enjoying the holy hell out of.

But when Joe got home and saw Stacia sitting at the table, on her third bowl of soup, the look he shot Casey was hesitant. Casey shrugged. "This is Stacia. She offered to blow me for food."

Joe gave a helpless, troubled laugh. "That *is* desperate. Yeah. Okay. So, Stacia?"

The girl looked up from her soup, and Casey tried to look at her face through Joe's eyes. She had wide, peasant cheekbones and unremarkable hazel eyes—once she got older, she would no longer be pretty, and if she didn't do something to ease the bitter lines around her mouth, she'd be pretty unappealing on a lot of levels. "Yeah?" she asked suspiciously.

"We can feed you and get you some clothes. How old are you?"

"Eighteen," she said, her voice sort of desperate, and Joe rolled his eyes.

"In how many years?"

She deflated. "Three."

"Good God. Okay. We can get you to social services in the morning, okay?"

Her mouth thinned and flattened. "I'm not going back home."

Joe nodded. "Well, okay. They might not make you go back, but the fact is, you can't stay here, okay?"

The girl looked sideways at Casey. "He does," she said suggestively, and Joe shook his head and walked to the cupboard where he kept the Tylenol.

"Yeah, but he's a special case," Joe muttered. "Special head case is more like it. Kid, I'm gonna feed the outside cats. Can we talk for a second?"

Casey looked sideways at Stacia and wondered if she'd figured out the thing about the cookie jar yet, but he followed Joe because that seemed prudent.

"I'm sorry." He winced when they got out to the garage. Joe gave a scoop of cat food to the feral cat and turned to him, leaning on the still cycling washer.

"Kid...." He shook his head again. "It's not like your heart wasn't in the right place, I get that. But... but...."

"It's what you did for me!" Casey said defensively, and Joe grimaced.

"You were different," Joe said flatly.

"How?"

"For one thing, you wouldn't have slit my throat to make a buck!"

Casey had to concede that was true. "But how did you know that? For all you knew I was some sort of baby serial killer!"

The old white washer was unbalanced, and it gave a thump behind Joe that made him turn around and glare. "Look, did I mention the heart? Being in the right place? Wasn't shitting about that. But Casey—you were special, and not just because you helped me after I got hurt, okay? She can't stay."

Casey nodded emphatically. "Oh thank God. I keep worrying about the cash in the kitchen, and I'm *not* going to sleep well tonight!"

Joe laughed. "The cash she can have. But next time you feel like bringing home strays, maybe stick with a dog?"

Casey brightened. "Can we get one? I'd really love a dog!" He'd been throwing sticks for Rufus over the fence. Now that the dog wasn't hurting Joe, he seemed pretty decent. Casey was a fan.

Joe patted the old washer, which continued to thump away. "Yeah, we'll see. Maybe if we live through the night, we'll celebrate by getting a dog."

They both grunted and straightened their shoulders. Yeah. But first they'd have to survive the night.

They ate and Joe went up to work on the upstairs some more. Normally Casey would have gone up to help him. The master bedroom needed everything from new carpet to drywall to new plumbing fixtures, and it had been their ongoing project since pretty much after Christmas. They'd put the drywall up in February, and Joe had been sanding drywall for a month to try to get the whole room to look seamless. Casey quite frankly wouldn't have given a shit about seams from the drywall, but it seemed to be something Joe took pride in, so sand they did. Casey's job lately had been pulling carpet staples out of the hardwood, and the two of them had been debating whether to replace the hardwood or just recarpet all over it, which seemed a shame, since the floor was original. (And didn't match the first floor wood at all. Casey had spent long hours wondering at the mental deformities of the complete assholes who had built this house.)

But without even talking about it, Casey had stayed downstairs to keep an eye on Stacia. Now that the girl had eaten, she seemed less predatory and more sleepy, and sure enough, she dozed off on the chair. Casey woke her up and steered her toward his bedroom to put her to sleep. It had posters of George Michael in it now, and a new blue bedspread, because that was his favorite color, and blue-and-brown sheets, not hospital sheets anymore, that he'd gotten for Christmas. He hated letting her lie down there, but he felt like he had no choice. He took a spare blanket from the hall closet and the extra pillow and went to sleep on the couch.

Joe came back down cautiously about an hour after he usually went to bed. "She asleep?" he asked from the stairway, and Casey looked up from his spot on the couch.

"Yeah. It's safe."

Joe grunted and rubbed the back of his neck. "Speak for yourself. I think we're going to *have* to get a dog if you plan on bringing any more humans home, kid. I'm not sleeping well tonight, that's for certain."

Casey refrained from pointing out that the most serious danger was from Stacia's speculative, overtly sexual glances in Joe's direction when they'd come in from the garage. If she was planning on a new sugar daddy, she had come to the wrong place—but that didn't mean she couldn't make trouble before she figured that out.

Joe ate a sandwich standing up, then ruffled Casey's hair and went off to his shower and to bed. That had been an hour ago. The hinges on Casey's door squeaked—not loudly, but Casey had been lightly dozing when they'd made their telltale little alarm, and his eyes had popped open. He lay, still and motionless on the couch, half expecting the ceramic clink of the cookie jar next.

He didn't hear anything for a moment, and then:

THUMP!

"Oh, ouch! You asshole!"

"Stay out of my bed! Jesus Christ, you fuckin' kids, you're gonna be the death of me!"

"But I was just gonna—"

"You were just gonna go back to your own goddamned bed! I'm calling social services right the fuck now!"

And to Casey's surprise, as Stacia's footsteps padded rapidly back to Casey's room, sure enough, he heard Joe's voice leaving a message for social services. Casey was mildly shocked—he hadn't realized Joe had the number by the phone.

But that was okay. Joe had never used it for Casey. They were a team. He liked that. He could live with that. It was okay.

Mandolin Rain
~Joe

THEY got a giant something dog. Joe had no idea what breed it was, but it was big and white with what looked like a black bandit's mask across its eyes. Casey didn't name it Bandit, though. He'd been watching lots and lots of movies with Joe, and *Raising Arizona* had been a favorite.

They named the dog Hi. Hi Huxtable, because Casey watched a lot of television too.

And Joe loved that dog almost as much as Casey did. It'd started out at about twenty pounds, and the damned dog could skid across the floor on his stomach and eat shoes like nobody's business. Casey's money, which Joe had been making him save for college and gas for the car, started paying for Frisbees, rubber toys, and replacement shoes as well. It was all right, though—Joe was glad Casey had found a calling. Apparently taking care of the dog gave him something that school and work did not, and Joe really liked that Casey wasn't alone on the big spread when Joe was working late.

So Hi Huxtable the dog was a wonderful addition to their family, and right now, at—Joe squinted at the clock radio—2:13 in the morning, he was barking his fool head off. Fuck.

"Hi! Hi, goddammit, what the fuck's wrong with you?" It was summer, which meant it got down to seventy degrees at night, so Joe left the windows open. The heater worked in the winter, but air-conditioning was not happening yet, so it was leave the windows open, turn on the fans, and dust like mad or everything would turn the rust color of the dirt on the ground outside.

The dog kept barking, so Joe hauled his body out of bed, pulled on some scrub bottoms, and looked out the window. Oh fuck.

Hi wasn't the only one barking. Rufus was over there in the backyard barking too. The two of them were playing like long-denied friends—which they were, since they usually just licked each other's ears across the fence line—but there was no reason for Rufus to be there unless Ira Kenby had left the gate open.

Fuck. Joe swore and pounded down the stairs, calling for Casey. He wasn't in the living room, which surprised Joe, because Dev's motorcycle was still outside, so if he'd thought about it, Joe *shouldn't* have been surprised by what he saw when he opened Casey's door and shot the light on, but he was.

Casey was naked, on his hands and knees, sideways to the door, and Dev was behind him, his cock fully sheathed in Casey's ass. Casey was gasping—with pleasure, Joe was pretty sure, but also with surprise, because this was clearly something he didn't have a lot of practice at, at least in the good way. The little jar of Vaseline from the medicine cabinet was next to them.

There wasn't a rubber in sight.

Joe blinked hard twice, and Casey jerked his head sideways.

Dev said, "Oh shit!", pulled out, and *literally* threw himself on the ground next to the bed and rolled over in the comforter, which was lying half on the floor.

Joe and Casey turned and looked after him in surprise, and then Joe's sense of humor asserted itself and he choked back a giggle. "Rufus, uhm—"

"*Rufus?*" Casey repeated incredulously, still looking at Dev.

"He's out, Casey. He's playing with your retarded dog, and the two of them already dumped Dev's motorcycle because they're stupid. I'm worried about Ira—I need you to put Hi in the garage so I can take Rufus back."

While Joe was talking, Casey had rolled off the bed and pulled on a pair of scrubs that had been lying on the chair by the end table, suddenly all responsible and on task. "Yeah, Joe, I got it."

Joe nodded, pleased. He was the last person to tell the kid that he couldn't get busy. He hadn't been prepared—next time, he'd be damned sure to knock.

"I'm, uhm, sorry 'bout...." Casey jerked his chin in Dev's direction.

Dev had pulled the comforter over his body and was huddling there, parallel to the base of the bed, his skinny shins and big feet sticking out at the end. He was pretending like they couldn't see him.

Casey grimaced and, *finally*, blushed. "I... uhm...." He stood up and slid on some moccasins the puppy hadn't chewed on. "I, well, you know...."

"Jesus, kid. You've been dating for months. I just didn't realize you'd finally gotten your thing on. C'mon. Let's leave so Dev can die in peace."

"Thanks," came Dev's muffled voice, and Joe finally started to like the kid, and then they had better things to do.

Joe grabbed two leashes from the garage worktable on his way out. He called Rufus and Casey called Hi. They put Hi into the garage, and Joe took Rufus toward the small gate he'd cut into the fencing after the whole biting incident. Casey caught up with him as he neared Ira's house, which was in even worse shape than Joe's had been when Joe moved in.

"Where's the dog?" Joe asked as Rufus started to whine and tug at his lead.

"I left him in the house with Dev."

"Isn't Dev afraid of him?"

"A little bit. Serves him right. I told him Vaseline would suck as lubricant." Casey executed a weird little pelvic wiggle. "God, that shit's gonna be in there for fucking ever."

Joe fought the temptation to bash his head into a tree just to get the image of Dev and Casey out of it. God, some things you did *not* want to know about a roommate. "Kid, there's a Raley's in the *parking lot* of McDonald's. Buy some fucking condoms and some fucking lube before you start fucking again, okay?"

"What is the whole condom thing about?" Casey asked irritably. "I'm pretty sure he's not going to knock me up!"

Rufus was pulling on Joe's arm, but Joe took a moment to stop still and turn to Casey, who was squinting at the dim path through the pine trees and red dirt. "Kid, have you not heard of VD? Did you think that's just for girls with itchy cooters?"

Casey's confusion was heartbreaking. "But Joe, you had me get all sorts of shots after the social worker said I could stay. One of those would have taken care of the clap, you think? And Dev's a... *was* a virgin. I mean, what's to worry?"

Joe closed his eyes, seeing the daily workweek that he kept from Casey flashing behind them. Curtained units, places where people wore hazard masks all day long and picked up extra pay to work. Skin with crackling lesions; haunted eyes, miserable with loneliness; and the patina of fear so thick it filled the nostrils with something even worse than hospital stink.

"Look," Joe said, knowing Rufus was getting more and more frantic with every passing moment, "you, me, and Dev, we've got to have a talk, okay? And it's not going to be one any of us is going to be comfy having, so just throw on your bulletproof Underoos and we'll have at it. But not now." And with that, he gave in to his inner stirrings of unease and trotted after Rufus as the poor dog whined and pulled his way to Ira's disintegrating cabin.

Apparently the cabin wasn't just disintegrating, it had *disintegrated*, with Ira in it. When they opened the front door—which no one ever locked—Ira called faintly to them. Rufus whimpered and ran through a plain living room decorated with piles of newspaper and old dusty furniture, and into the back bedroom.

Ira had been married. His bedroom was actually neat and clean, with little rugs on either side of the bed and a woman's vanity dresser, still laid out with a small mirror, comb, and matching brush, just like they'd been when Ira's wife had died. But past the bedroom was the bathroom, and Joe turned on the light and steeled himself for what he'd see next.

"Fuck me stupid!" Casey muttered, and Joe winced.

"Help me," Ira whimpered, but Joe wasn't sure he could.

The hallway floor under their feet felt creaky with dry rot, and Ira's bathroom had apparently had enough. It had given out under Ira's feet, and as Ira had flailed backward, his old bones had given out too. He lay there, scrawny, wrinkled, and naked, his bathrobe flopping around his skinny body, both of his legs obviously broken at the tibia and submerged in the subflooring of the bathroom.

"Oh fuck," Joe muttered. "We're gonna need some fucking help." Rufus was licking Ira's face in comfort, and Joe hoped that worked.

The first thing he did was call an ambulance, *and* the fire department, and then he got some blankets and made Ira more comfortable and less exposed. The old man wasn't particularly coherent, and he mumbled for Dotty, his late wife, as his gnarled hand dug itself into Rufus's ruff. His white hair—a bird's nest under the best of times—was lank and sweaty on his tanned forehead, and Joe made sure he had a pillow under his head as he wrapped blankets around his chest, waist, and upper legs.

Then he and Casey grimly analyzed the problem.

"We gotta move his feet up," Casey said, his voice husky. "Looking at it that way—it's just wrong."

And Joe feared that Ira having his legs bent like that around his fractured bones was more than wrong. The flesh was mottled and swollen—Ira could be bleeding internally at the fracture site from the way it looked. Besides, the paramedics couldn't care for him any better than Joe could when he was stuck halfway through his floor.

Joe sent Casey to his garage to bring back the circular saw and a dolly, and had the kid crawl under the house to support Ira's feet as he sawed around the cracked wood. At first he thought Casey was going to argue. The crawl space under the house was dark, especially in the middle of the night—dank, muddy, and there were spiders and other crawlies down there. Even if you weren't a girl in a pink dress, it still wasn't a picnic, and not everybody had the stomach for it. But Ira moaned in pain even as Casey was wrinkling his nose, and then the kid took an unhappy look at Joe and went to work.

He kept up a running monologue of "Ick! Crap! What's that! Oh, fucking ew! Jesus! Oh crap—is that a black widow? Oh gross! Oh God—something shit down here. I'm gonna need to sit in the bathtub for a fucking week!" but he did it, and he did it well. He never wavered while holding the dolly steady so Ira's bones didn't break through his skin, and he was gentle and steady as he pushed the dolly up so Joe could back Ira up and lay him flat, his legs lying on the piece of plywood, supported by the rolling wheels.

By the time the paramedics got there, Ira had gone into shock, and Joe backed off as they wrapped the old man's legs in pressure casts and administered fluids before dropping the gurney and lifting him on.

Joe knew one of the guys, and Derrick clapped him on the shoulder as they were wheeling Ira out.

"Nice work there—you want to do some ride-alongs?"

Joe rolled his eyes. "I just want to know the old guy's gonna be okay," he said sincerely, and Derrick grimaced.

"Gotta tell you, Joe, it's not looking great. Whatever happens, I don't think he's going to be able to come back here to live."

Joe looked around the place, with the floorboard popping up and the drywall falling down, and sighed. "He's got a son who lives in SoCal. I'll give Richard a call and see if he can come get him settled someplace else."

Derrick nodded. "That would probably be a good idea. He's going to be in the hospital for a while—if nothing else, he might like a visit."

"We'll visit him," said Casey, coming up behind them, and Joe turned and ruffled his hair.

"You're a good kid," he said, feeling tired. The sun had risen in the last couple of minutes, and he found himself squinting into the red light. The temperature had dropped too, and the shorts and T-shirt he'd worn to bed were suddenly not nearly enough.

Casey shrugged and grinned, and then a sudden look of panic crossed his face.

"Oh shit! Dev!" and without another word he whistled for Rufus and went trotting down the path that led to their houses.

Joe smiled a little. "D'you see that? Just took the dog, no questions asked. That's my boy."

Derrick was looking at him with considerable warmth. "That's the kid you took in, right?"

Joe nodded and smiled a little. And then blushed. Derrick had light-brown hair with reddish tints, especially in the russet light, and light-brown eyes. He was a little younger than Joe, and apparently, he swung that way on occasion too.

"Yeah," he mumbled. "We're sort of roommates."

Derrick's grin cranked up a notch. "Would your roommate mind if you took a night off for dinner?"

Joe blinked. He was not used to being come on to. Usually there was a gentle sort of waltz before he ended up having dinner. But Sharon had *not* taken the news of the social worker well *at all* and, after slapping his face (a surprise!) and yelling that Joe loved Casey more than he loved her (well, *duh!*), had marched off into the sunset. She'd actually quit the floor at Auburn and was currently working at the railroad as their on-call nurse, just to get away from him. It had been a long time since someone had shown Joe the sort of interest looking out from Derrick's eyes right now.

"Uhm, okay," he said, feeling awkward. "You... uhm, I think you took my number when your partner was getting my info. Give me a call."

Derrick winked and promised he would, then hopped into the ambulance. The bus rattled down Ira's road, which was as out of repair as the rest of the house, and Joe wandered back down the path between the trees, thinking that he was going to need a couple of hours of sleep before he got up to go to work.

Then he saw Casey and Dev cozying up in front of Dev's little four-banger motorbike, and he sighed. One more thing to do before he slept.

He walked up to them and rolled his eyes when Dev turned bright red and buried his face in Casey's shoulder.

"Very cute," Joe said dryly. "But ineffective. You two—tomorrow's my day off. We're gonna take a little field trip and have ourselves a little discussion. No sex until then, okay? You hear me?"

"Yes, Mr. Daniels," Dev said, his face still tucked into Casey's shoulder. Casey put his hand protectively on the back of Dev's head and rolled his eyes at Joe.

"You done intimidating him?" Casey asked mildly, and Joe grinned at him.

"Nowhere near. Now I gotta go call Ira's son and let him know what happened. I work today and tomorrow we've got a date, but I've got a feeling we're spending the rest of our spare time up at Ira's place, getting his shit in order, so don't make any plans, okay?"

Casey nodded. "Yeah, I got it. We keeping Rufus?"

Joe's lips quirked. "I'd lay odds. Let's act like we're gonna, okay? He's going to be confused enough as it is."

And with that, he left the babes in boyland to have their sweet nothings while he dialed the number he'd gotten from Ira's drawer while he'd been waiting for the paramedics to wheel Ira out. An hour later, after a conversation that involved Joe listening to Richard yell at his wife a lot for his suitcases and then complain bitterly about time he couldn't afford to lose from work, Joe tramped back up his own stairs for a little shut-eye.

God, tomorrow was going to suck.

First he cleared it with his supervisor at work, who had looked at him with a combination of admiration and revulsion. "The kid's getting it on with his *boyfriend*, and this is your idea of an intervention?"

"I just want him to remember to use a rubber, okay?"

"You can't make him remember to screw girls?"

"Hell, I couldn't remember that half the time in college!"

A digestive silence while Donna, his supervisor, rearranged what she was about to say. Joe watched her do it, gave her time, and when she finally looked up, she had a serene smile on her face as she tried to convince them both that she wasn't about to say something really bitchy.

"Well, thank heavens you've seen the light," she tried. She had a broad face, the kind that blotched easily, with cheeks the texture of risen dough.

He just looked at her levelly without saying a thing until those cheeks blushed a patchy scarlet, and he walked away. He didn't *have* to tell her he swung both ways, but holy God was it ever satisfying.

It didn't matter. Donna gave it her approval, and Debbie… well, Debbie was so lonely, he didn't see her *not* wanting visitors.

It turned out he was right.

He took Casey and Dev out to eat first at The Oar Cart, because they grilled a hell of a burger and because he wasn't sure they would want to eat later. They talked like kids—car phones and how amazing it would be to have one, movies and which one they *really* wanted to see, movie stars and which one they *really* wanted to kiss. Tom Cruise from that fighter pilot movie Joe and Casey had watched on the VCR was a big favorite, closely followed by the blond guy from *The Princess Bride*. Casey considered, though, after Dev threw out that choice.

"I don't know," he said, throwing Joe an inscrutable look. "I kind of liked that Inigo Montoya guy. I thought he was pretty hot."

"Yeah, but he's old!" Dev complained, and Casey kept his eyes on Joe.

"Not that old. Only a few years older than Joe."

Joe raised an eyebrow and Casey went back to playing the game with Dev, but the moment sat heavy. The problem with those moments was that although they were few and far between, Casey seemed to mean them wholeheartedly whenever they occurred. The kid was not forgetting his first crush, nor was he apparently *ever* forgetting that he would eventually be old enough for it to mean something.

But they finished their burgers happily, and Joe took them to Auburn General through the front door, and not the employee entrance that he usually used. He walked them down the gently colored taupe corridors with the muted red lines that gave directions, and made a sharp left into a unit marked ICU.

In the future, patients like the one they were about to visit would change the face of the intensive care unit. In the future, every ICU patient would have his own cubicle with clear Plexiglas partitions that would give doctors a view of the goings-on but also give patients privacy. In the future, there would be a station for nonlatex gloves and a sink in every cubicle, as well as hand sanitizer with moisturizer so the medical staff didn't spend their lives with cracked, bleeding fingers. In the future, there would be a special box for needles or any other object that had touched blood and that people worried about and a place for face masks, should they be necessary. But that was in the future.

At the moment, there were four tiny cubicles in a row, each one big enough for the bed and a couple of people, all of them divided by the big sheets on rollers that had been used in the ER. There was no sink, no privacy screen, and no chairs or real room for a visitor to sit. There was just a bare floor, a floating cloth wall, and the smallish woman lying in the center of the bed.

Joe had actually been there on the day Debbie had first walked into the hospital, about two months before he'd seen Casey on the side of the road. She'd wanted to get rid of the Karposi's sarcoma lesion that had developed on the side of her face. She'd been tall and chesty and a little bit plump, especially in the ass and thighs, but Joe had always been an ass and thigh man, so he'd thought she was damned attractive. She'd had toffee-brown hair and big brown eyes that had laugh wrinkles at the corners. And she'd had a full mouth that she'd tried not to press together in worry.

She'd gotten the lesion on her temple removed and had some blood work done, and that had been a year ago.

Joe had seen a lot of her since then.

They'd stopped removing the lesions when her recurring bouts of diarrhea got bad and every incision they made for the sarcoma got infected. At the moment, cervical cancer was the thing that was killing her.

Sort of.

The thing that was really killing her was AIDS.

Her pretty toffee-brown hair had mostly fallen out as her skin became a nightmare of flaky, cracked lesions. Her mouth was a mess of herpes sores. She weighed around ninety-five pounds. The only thing left of the pretty woman who had walked into the hospital was the big expressive brown eyes, but now they were clouded with fear, with pain, and with loneliness.

Nobody visited patients in this end of the ICU.

Those eyes lit up when she saw Joe, though, and then blinked at Casey and Dev, who were cowering back near the curtain.

"Hey, Joe," she said, his name coming out like a sigh of blessing. "These your humping bunnies?"

"Oh God," Dev whimpered from behind them. "You *told* her?"

Joe spared a glance for Casey's boyfriend, who was so pale his blemishes and freckles stood out in blotchy relief, and his narrow face looked like an eel's.

"Deb is about to give you guys some very private info, Mr. I-don't-need-a-fucking-condom, so you'd better put on your smoking jacket, grab your pipe and slippers, and sit down and pretend to be a grown-up, okay?"

A dry, husking laugh sounded from the bed. "Oh Joey-angel, keep your pantyhose on. They're babies. You remember what it was like to be a baby?"

Joe remembered Tim's body, smooth and willing beneath his in the moonlight on the way home from band practice, the way the little bottle of vegetable oil that he'd tucked in his backpack had come in mighty handy once they'd progressed that far. There hadn't been any fear then, not in 1973, and he wished bitterly that Casey had grown up then instead of now.

"I want them to stay babies, Deb," he said softly, pulling a folding chair from the wall and sitting down next to her. Quite naturally, he took her hand. She closed her eyes, and not because her skin was tender and sore, either. Nobody touched people in this wing; nobody hugged them or kissed them on the cheek. But Joe had been brought up to believe that human touch was part of healing and that you could not ease the body without easing the spirit. Just because he didn't expect God to show up and make it all better didn't mean he believed simple human contact wasn't a gift Joe had in his power to bestow.

"They can't stay babies when their bodies are rotting from the inside out."

Deb closed her eyes again and nodded. "Yeah, I get it. You want to keep them safe. You're a good man, Angel." She looked over at

Casey and Dev in the corner. "Kids, you know this man's the best, right? Lots of evil motherfuckers out there. I almost died thinking every man out in the world was a dick and every girl's a bitch, but Joey—he made it better. I'm gonna die thinking there's good people in the world, and maybe I'm one."

"It's the truth," Joe said softly. "You up to this?"

"Yeah, Joe," Deb said, smiling at him. Something in her smile, the way her eyes grew bright, and the vision of what she'd looked like that late-summer day, walking in through the front door of the hospital as Joe was walking out, superimposed itself on the disintegrating shell of fractured skin and rotting organs that lay on the bed. For a moment, she was a pretty girl, worried about appearing vain, but gorgeous, shaking back thick hair in the sun. "I'll do anything you need me to," she was saying softly, and Joe closed his eyes and kept that vision there, knowing she'd love to appear beautiful, even in his mind.

"I just need you to talk to them honest," Joe said, eyes still closed. "I need you to tell them shit you wish someone had told you." He opened his eyes and still saw her, a beautiful woman with a charming smile.

"Yeah, Angel. I'll do anything for you." Joe went to stand up so Casey could move closer, and Deb gave a little hurt whine, her hand clenching on his. The skin on the back crackled and bled, and Joe sat down again.

"Casey, do me a favor?"

"Yeah, Joe?"

"Look in that cupboard over there in the corner—you see that?"

He did, and Joe had Casey pull out a box of disposable latex gloves, the kind that made some people's hands itch, and put on a pair.

"I'm gonna get up, Deb, okay? But Casey's gonna hold your hand, is that all right?"

Deb's eyes grew limpid and sorrowful. "He's not gonna want to hold my hand, Joe. I'm scary."

Joe shook his head and glared at Casey, daring him to contradict. "You're beautiful, sweetheart. Did I ever tell you that? That first day I saw you, walking out of the hospital while I came on shift? I swear to

God, I almost hit on you right there." He stood up and gestured for Casey to sit down. "You had the greatest smile—and your eyes. Oh God, you've got the most beautiful brown eyes I've ever seen. I look in those eyes, and I think happy summer days, probably for the rest of my life, okay?" Her hand was all bones and dry, cracking skin, but he gently put it in Casey's, and Casey took a deep breath and clasped his hand over it.

Debbie was smiling at him, and Casey managed a shy smile back, like Joe, looking at her eyes and not at the rest of her body, racked with weeping sores.

"A little firmer, baby," she rasped. "I'm already broken. It takes some pressure for me to know you're there."

Casey's hand grew a little tighter, and Deb sighed and relaxed.

"So here it is," she said softly. "The whole true story about how Debbie Lightner went from chubby brunette to horror show extra. Are you ready?"

"Did it have something to do with not using a condom?" Casey asked, and she laughed dryly.

"You're quick, kid. But it's more than that. See, I had this boyfriend, and I loved the holy fucking shit out of him. You ever love someone like that?"

Casey's eyes darted sideways—not to Dev, who had crept forward and was standing on his left, but to Joe, who had moved a little down the bed. "Yeah," he said.

Joe sighed and grimaced and then started to move unobtrusively to the back of the room. He wanted to move to the *other* curtained cubicle, because *that* one had a sink, so he could wash and sanitize his hands, but he had to get there first without interrupting Deb. He moved toward the curtain quietly, pausing to look at Casey occasionally, but listening to Debbie's story all the way.

"Yeah. Me too. So I loved the holy fucking shit out of this guy, and I think he loved me too. In fact, I *know* he loved me too, but he also loved dick, and that was a problem."

"Wait!" Dev said, sounding surprised. "Who the hell is Dick?"

Casey and Deb met eyes then—Joe saw it. They met eyes, and Deb started to giggle, and so did Casey, and Casey shook his head. "Not Dick-Richard, moron! He was *gay!*"

Dev opened his mouth and closed it again. "But if he was gay, why was he sleeping with you?"

"Because," Casey said, looking at Debbie and grimacing. "Because sometimes when you tell your parents you're gay, they don't go out and get a membership in PFLAG, you lucky fucker. Sometimes they kick you out of the fucking house and let you live on the streets."

"Oh, baby," she said, her voice raw. "Did that happen to you?"

Joe grimaced and looked over his shoulder in time to meet Casey's eyes. "Yeah," Casey muttered, staring Joe down like he was pulling Joe's strength through the air. "Yeah. Joe found me."

"Mmm… so he's your angel too."

"Yeah. What happened to Dick-Richard, Debbie?" Casey looked back down at her, and for a minute, Joe gave in and prayed. *Please let him see her pretty, God. She wants him to see her pretty.*

"He wasn't a bad guy, you know?" she said like she was begging him to understand. "But I got this thing taken off my face, and he… he got freaked out, so he went and got tested. And… yeah. Yeah, he'd been fooling around in all the wrong places, and he gave me fucking AIDS, you know?"

"I'm sorry," Casey murmured, and Joe finally broke eye contact to move through the curtain, careful not to disturb Vince, who was in the bed next door. Vince didn't have long to go. He was out of it most of the time, and he was asleep now, grunting quietly in pain. Joe hurried to the sink and washed his hands in hot water, cursing his lapse. Glove protocols had just become stringent in the past year, and when you were talking to a patient like a friend, it got hard to remember, even when her blood was as lethal as a weapon. Joe washed with the harsh, powdered soap and then dried off. He grabbed a couple of gloves from the counter for good measure. He laid a soft hand on Vince's shoulder to quiet him before sneaking back behind the curtain gap to hear the rest of Debbie's story.

He'd heard it before, several times. Deb was pretty lucid right now, but not always. She rambled. Steve, her boyfriend, had been the love of her life. He'd been her first sex and her first love, and she would love him until she died.

Even though he'd died six months ago in a hotel room with a revolver in his mouth.

"I'm so sorry," Casey was saying again as Joe came back in the room.

"Aw, honey, don't be," Deb said, her voice surprisingly steady. "It's just... I think Joe wanted you to know. He wanted you to know that even real love ain't always enough. That it ain't always real enough to last. You need to protect yourself until you're sure. And you need to protect the people you're with too."

Joe saw Casey turn white, and he moved quickly behind the kid and bent down to whisper, "We'll make sure," in his ear before squeezing his shoulder.

"Thanks, Deb," Casey said softly after shivering a little. "We'll be careful."

"Good." Deb's eyes were fluttering shut. She'd been awake around half an hour now, and it was pretty exhausting for her. "Joe really loves you, you know? It would kill him if you got sick."

Casey sat up a little straighter and put his free hand on top of Joe's. "Well, he's my angel too. I'll try and make him happy."

They left shortly after that. Joe had Casey dispose of the latex gloves in the little trash can, and then bent down and kissed Debbie softly on top of what was left of her hair.

"I'll see you tomorrow, beautiful," he said softly, and she nodded, her eyes closed.

"I'll live for it, Joey-angel," she told him, and he made sure the lights were down before they slipped past the gap in the curtain and slid out. He kept his arm anchored securely around both Casey's and Dev's shoulders as they went through the hallway. Both kids were shaking so badly he was surprised they could still stand up.

He steered them to the cafeteria, where he got them both ice cream and watched as they ate automatically, their almost-seventeen-year-old metabolisms kicking in when their complete upset might have overridden the need for sweets. He waited until their hands stopped shaking, and then said, "Okay, guys. Any thoughts?"

"Condoms," Dev mumbled, wiping his cheek with the back of his hand. "Condoms forever and ever and fucking ever."

Casey patted his hand softly, then looked up and met Joe's eyes. "Testing," he said quietly. "I need to be tested."

Joe grimaced. Yeah. "Yeah," he said softly. "I didn't think of it when I found you. I should have. I'm sorry. I should have. But last year, this shit was just really starting to hit. We're still not prepared. No one's thinking it through yet. It's not part of the way we just... you know, behave. It's not part of who we are yet. But you're right. You need to be tested."

"What about me?" Dev asked, his voice breaking, and Joe grabbed his hand too. Casey's was dry and steady as a rock, but Dev's was clammy and shaking.

"We'll wait until Casey gets his results back, okay? If they're negative, we'll talk about one thing. If they're positive, we'll talk about another. Are we okay?"

"I'm not old enough for this!" Dev said, his voice sharp. "I'm not old enough to end up here. I'm not old enough to test for AIDS, I'm not, I'm not—"

"The hell you're not!" Joe hissed, because the boy's voice was rising and breaking. "You're old enough to have sex, you're old enough to think about this. Yeah, I know—you used to be able to fuck and all you had to worry about was crabs or knocking a girl up. We can't do that anymore, and we can't go back. If you can't look yourself in the mirror and say 'I'm gonna get laid tonight, and I need some fucking condoms', you're not old enough to do it. But once you start putting your peter some place besides your pants, you've got to cowboy up, do you hear me?"

"I... I... how do I even buy condoms?" Dev asked, his voice cracking again, and Casey reached across the table and whapped the top of his head.

"You walk into Raley's, find the family planning section, and get them," he snapped, out of patience. "If a teenaged girl can get a pregnancy test, you sure as shit can get a rubber and some goddamned lube!"

Joe shot Casey a droll look, and Casey grimaced and flushed.

"You talk to a lot of girls who get pregnancy tests?" Joe asked, trying to lighten things up just a little.

"It's a continuation school," Casey muttered. "Ninety percent of the girls there are mommies."

Joe blinked. He hadn't thought about that, and didn't he feel hella stupid?

"Well, you can learn all sorts of things at school, can't you?"

Casey snickered, and then Dev giggled, and both boys took a bite of ice cream.

They both calmed down, and that was good, but so was the fact that they thought it was real. Meeting Debbie wasn't like health class, where you could blow off the teacher because she was old and clueless and wore polyester suits. This was like real, where someone who had just become a friend was going to die, and nothing was going to change that.

THEY got Casey tested that day, and the results were back in two weeks. In the time between, when they weren't helping Ira's son clean out the old house and get it ready for sale, Casey asked to go back and visit Deb, and Joe took him to work for a day. Casey hung out with a book for most of it, but for an hour, he sat quietly and told Deb about cleaning out old Ira's place so they could sell the property and get Ira a good old age home. He talked about Hi and Rufus, and how the fool dogs could run around in circles and circles and then collapse, panting and happy, at Joe's feet. Joe came in and out for that hour, listening to Casey just talk to her like she was a friend and they'd have a chance to go do things together in the future.

Deb's parents hadn't come to visit once. Her boyfriend had killed himself before she'd even had to be hospitalized. She had a sister in Sacramento who wouldn't open her letters because she was afraid of contamination. Joe heard her voice, sometimes coherent and sometimes dreamy and unfocused, and knew that this hour right here, like the hours Joe had spent with her, was the bright moment, the moment she lived for, the thing that made death hopeful.

They got the test results five days later.

Negative. Casey just sat and looked at the little piece of paper for half an hour, his hands shaking. When he was done, he looked up at Joe with a furrow between his deep brows.

"It's a do-over," he said, his voice unsteady. "It's just like you said. I got do-overs. You gave me one. God gave me another."

Joe wanted to bite back on that. He wanted to say, "God didn't give you shit!" but he couldn't. Because although he hadn't realized it until Casey had opened the piece of paper in the mail, Joe had been thinking, *Oh please, please, please, please, please, please* the whole time. If he didn't believe the Big Guy gave you a break sometimes, who'd he been asking "please?"

"Okay," he said out loud. "Okay. You got a do-over. You've been doing it right so far, kid. You just keep on keeping on, okay?"

Casey nodded and wiped his mouth with a shaking palm. "Okay. Can I go visit Debbie again? I'd like to tell her myself."

Joe said yeah, and he went by her bed to check on his way out of work that night.

She wasn't there.

He got home that night and woke Casey up. He knocked first, but he really didn't need to. Dev had taken the news that Casey was negative quietly, but he was still a little freaked out. Casey didn't have to say anything, but Joe recognized all the signs of taking a little time-out when Dev didn't come over for a couple of days.

"Casey?"

"Come in."

Casey was reading one of Joe's books—this time it was *The Stand*, and Joe would have told him not to read that *now*, but he figured if Casey scared the piss out of himself some more, that could only work for the best.

Slowly, feeling truly old and not just old in comparison, Joe took a couple of steps to the bed and sat down heavily.

"Joe?" Casey said quietly, and Joe sighed.

"Kid, you won't be able to visit Debbie tomorrow."

Casey looked stricken, and his lower lip started to wobble. "No?"

"No."

Casey nodded like he was going to be stoic for a minute, and Joe opened his arms, because no one should be stoic for things like that. Casey cried in his arms like a baby, and Joe cried with him, and Joe actually said thank you to God in real words this time, because this was the worst pain Casey would know right now, and it was bad enough.

Land of Confusion

~Casey

1989

MAYBE it was that Dev's horniness won out over his fear, or maybe it was Dev's reluctance to start school without an ally on his side, even one who went to another school and whom all of his bound-for-college buddies would probably despise. Either way, Casey called him for Debbie's funeral, and three days later Casey, Joe, and Dev all squeezed into the pickup truck on the way to a tiny crematorium where a perfunctory service was held for them and them alone.

Because they were the only ones there, Casey figured that for Dev the realization might have been that everyone died and it would be nice not to die alone. Melodramatic? Oh yeah—but Dev was very young that way. No matter how it happened, though, Casey and Dev were back together by the time school started, which was nice, because that year it meant Casey had a boyfriend for his seventeenth birthday.

Joe took them out to dinner at the Sizzler and then to ice cream at Leatherby's, where he dared Casey to eat the giant sundae. Casey and Dev managed to eat the whole thing together, and Joe took a Polaroid of the two of them—faces covered in fudge sauce, smiling greenly at the camera—that stayed on their refrigerator for years.

Dev didn't stay that night—they both had school the next day—although they had sleepovers on the weekends, when the job and the extracurricular activities didn't get in the way. Joe was good about treating Casey like an adult in that department, and Casey appreciated it.

He especially appreciated it when he made another attempt to sneak into Joe's bed the night of his seventeenth birthday. He wound up on his ass on the floor, of course, but this time he was expecting it, and as Joe swore up a storm above him, he stood up and giggled his way back downstairs to his room.

Of course he wasn't giggling that November, when Joe's newest rescue—a very beautiful, very broken boy with corn silk hair and pale eyes, and whom Joe called Sunshine since he wouldn't give his name—tried the same trick.

Sunshine ended up being walked gently back to his room, and Joe asked Casey to sit with him until he fell asleep.

"Why doesn't he want me?" Sunshine said softly, lying in the dark.

Casey smoothed his hair back from his face like he would a little kid. "He doesn't want... doesn't want you to think that love has to mean sex," Casey said, mostly because he'd figured this out for himself.

"But... but how will I make him *keep* me, if he doesn't want that?" Sunshine was honest-to-God crying now, and Casey sighed. He and Dev had been bickering back and forth for a month. Casey didn't think they were going to break up immediately, but he could see the end coming. Dev wasn't that bright, but he got real good grades. A part of him bought into the snobbery that because Casey wasn't graduating from a real school, he wasn't real smart. Casey had tried to correct this idea, but it didn't stop Dev from talking down to Casey, or Casey from saying shit that Dev didn't understand and then not explaining it just so Casey could laugh at him.

"Sex can't be all you're staking your claim on," Casey said, his voice echoing in Joe's old room. Joe had let him paint the walls a nice sailor blue once he'd moved upstairs. Casey had painted his own room sort of a sky blue, with white and lavender trim. Yeah, it looked gay, but then, so was Casey, and Joe didn't seem to give a ripe shit.

"It's all I have," the boy said. God, what was he? Thirteen?

"You've got so much more," Casey told him, still stroking that hair. Casey had helped pick the nits out of it for three nights running, until they'd Kwell-treated him again. The boy's scalp had been a mess of bleeding sores, but he hadn't even scratched. He'd just looked at Joe and Casey with that passive, expectant look, waiting for the "thing" to happen, the one that meant he could eat some more or have a place to sleep. Unlike with Stacia, Casey hadn't been excited about watching Sunshine fail in his little trip to Joe's room. He'd known, just like Joe had, that Sunshine had to be treated like thin, untempered glass.

"I thought it was all I had too, once." Casey kept talking, wondering if his voice was helping or not. "But I'm going to graduate and go to college. I'm going to travel—there's like, whole other *countries* I haven't even *heard of* yet that I'm going to see. Sex is good—but there's music and movies and books and—"

"It's all I have," Sunshine repeated.

Casey kept talking to him, telling him about all the places he could go, the things he could see and do, and for a little while, Sunshine lived there and he did okay. Joe had gotten chickens over the summer because he liked the fresh eggs, and Sunshine took it upon himself to feed them and take care of them. For a couple of weeks it worked, and then Casey got home one day and found Joe's firewood axe, covered in blood, in the middle of the coop, and the remains of the rooster next to it. Sunshine was crouched, feral and weeping, in the back of the chicken coop, and Casey left him there and called Joe.

The social worker (a different one than the recently divorced Mrs. Cahill) had come with an ambulance then, and taken the boy away to Chana, the medical institution, not Casey's continuation school. Mr. Petty was a tall man, almost completely bald except for a fringe of gray hair around the edge of his head, like a watermelon in a hula skirt. He told Casey that they were damned lucky it hadn't been one of them lying mutilated in the chicken coop and that Joe needed to be careful whom he took into his home.

For his part, by the time Joe had gotten home, he'd been pale, sweaty, and shaking. The ambulance had gone, and Casey had been in the kitchen, making himself an egg sandwich, when Joe stomped into the kitchen and wrapped his arms around Casey, shaking so hard Casey sat him down so he didn't just collapse on the kitchen floor.

"I'm sorry," Joe muttered. "So sorry. I didn't know... God, I didn't know he was that damaged. He could have *hurt you.*"

Casey shook his head, not even seeing what all the fuss was about. "He wouldn't have hurt us," he said confidently. "It was all about that rooster chasing the damned hens around. I think...." Casey's voice dropped, and he looked at Joe carefully, uncertain how to put this into words. "I think, maybe, not sleeping with the kids you pick up— maybe it's a good idea, though. I think maybe that's why he didn't go after you with an axe too. Or me neither."

Joe just shuddered and held him closer, a big man who smelled like antiseptic and sweat, and Casey held Joe's head against his stomach and stroked his long hair back from his face while his egg sandwich burned behind him. He wondered how long, exactly, he was going to wait until he understood everything about love.

Sunshine was out of the mental institution and into a halfway house with a security lock by the time Casey graduated from high school. He and Joe sent the boy letters religiously, and they were both grateful, for once, for the social worker. For his part, Mr. Petty had determined in one visit that Casey was old enough to run away from any home they placed him in, and he seemed to be doing okay at Joe's. Joe was so grateful, he actually forgave Casey for making him sleep with Mrs. Cahill. Casey was so grateful, he actually felt bad that Joe had to break up with his girlfriend in order to do that.

Joe had a paramedic trying to get him into bed now. Casey didn't know Derrick that well, but he approved on general principle. If it was a guy, someday Casey might have a chance.

And time went on. As the year after Debbie's funeral progressed, Joe and Casey helped to clean up Ira's place—and Joe and Ira insisted that Ira's stiff-necked, venal prick of a son pay Casey for his time. The son sold the property for a *fortune* to a developer who turned the parcel of land into five different lots and built big houses on them. In spite of the fact that Ira had given them *both* an unexpected cut of the profits (probably because he knew in his bones who would be visiting him in the old age home—and they had), Joe hated it, at first. He complained about it for most of a year, bitterly, even when he spent the money on new siding for the house. He hated the construction noises, he hated the idea that big business won, and he *loathed* the fact that what used to be twenty acres of mostly wilderness was now twenty acres of residential area with *really big* backyards.

But the zoning laws were strict, at least. A family every four acres was really not bad. In early August, before Casey's *eighteenth* birthday, Casey stood outside, throwing a ball to Hi and Rufus, trying not to get it in the chicken coop because that way lay disaster, and watching Joe ride up the drive after work.

When the engine noise faded to echoes, Casey called out to him. "Here, Joe. Listen."

Joe stood out in the long shadows of late August afternoon, pulled off his helmet, and listened.

There was a pickup game at one of the houses, the one that had been built on Ira's old lot, and what sounded like a family—Mom, Dad, and four kids—was playing basketball on a driveway court. It was a good sound, lots of squeals from the girls and hoots of triumph from the boys, and the noises were distant, not up close and personal. Joe listened for a minute and then sighed and rolled his eyes.

"Yeah, well, it's not silence," he muttered, but under the Fu Manchu mustache and soul patch, his lips were quirking up.

"If you'd wanted silence, you wouldn't have kept me," Casey said smugly, and Joe socked him in the arm, then stumped inside to fix dinner. Casey laughed softly to himself because Joe didn't have to fix dinner—Casey had done it—and continued to throw the ball to the dogs until they were too tired to move.

It was a month before his eighteenth birthday, and in the meantime, he'd held his job, done his schoolwork, and graduated from continuation school early, in a little ceremony in January. He might not have had a cap and gown, but his diploma was just as good as anyone else's, and he hadn't objected when it had appeared on his wall in a frame. Joe had taken him and Dev out to eat again and given him the keys to an actual car—used, but sound—as a gift. He would be responsible for insurance and gas, but he'd about cried when he'd seen the almost stately Taurus sedan sitting outside the restaurant, where Joe'd had a friend park it.

A future—a real future—that was his for the taking. But mostly because Joe had given it to him.

Casey had gotten home from work early that day with the mixings of chicken casserole, the kind with the mayonnaise and the potato chips on the top and the cheese and pimentos. It was his favorite, after Joe had made it for him in Casey's first month there, and Casey didn't even mind that Joe said it was too fattening for him now. Casey liked Joe's solid body—there was plenty of heavy muscle, and still that adorable little tummy that Casey got to see in the summer when they went swimming at Sugar Pine or Joe slept without his shirt.

"What's the occasion, kid?" Joe asked as he set the table. Casey had put a cassette in the boom box Joe had bought him for his birthday the year before, and U2's *Rattle and Hum* was playing in the background. U2 and INXS were two bands that Joe and Casey could agree on, and they played a lot of them. Joe was trying to get Casey to like Guns N' Roses, and Casey was almost a convert, which meant that maybe they'd hear a little less Madonna, which was always something for Joe to look forward to. That made Casey happy too.

Casey grinned. "Dev's coming over for dinner, and your mother called."

Joe grunted. "What'd she say?"

Joe's mother had called periodically, maybe once a month, since Casey had come to live there and probably before that. She seemed like a nice woman, and she'd always been kind and interested in Casey's life. For two Christmases in a row, she'd sent him a gift certificate to Sears, and given the fact that he still hadn't lost his taste for spiffy clothes, he'd been grateful.

"Your sister had another baby."

"Sister or sister-in-law?"

"Your sister. Cheryl."

Joe grunted again. "I already sent her a gift and a card—did she have another one in the last week?"

Casey shook his head. "No, but your mom seemed pretty insistent that you call her too. She said you were becoming like your Great-Uncle Oscar—just a name on a tag with a really good present from nowhere."

Joe grunted again. "Cheryl's a priss. She's more comfortable with me being Great-Uncle Oscar. It makes her happier than having to deal with Josiah Daniels. Did my mom say anything else?"

Casey laughed. "She said you should take me out there for Christmas this year."

Joe tilted his head back. "Really? Did she *really* say that?"

"Yeah. She says I'm the closest thing to a grandkid you're ever going to give her."

Joe put his face in his arms. "Oh Jesus. Is she talking about grandkids *again*? She's got *ten*. And you're not my *son*, you're my *friend*. You're like a cousin something—"

"Yeah?" Casey looked at him hopefully. Cousin was *so* much more doable than surrogate son. Excellent. Him and Joe—it could happen! But first, there was Dev for dinner.

Joe was oblivious to the undercurrents of Casey's happiness, still lost in the vagaries of family drama. "God, what's it going to take to get her off my back?"

"You could show up with Derrick and sleep in the same bedroom," Casey said gaily, and Joe groaned some more.

"He's *so* persistent!"

"Yeah! He likes you! Why don't you put out for him?"

Joe covered his face with his hands. "Because the waitress from The Oar Cart keeps hitting on me too. I need to choose one of them."

"Lynnie? Really? She's hot, if I went for that sort of thing."

"You mean with breasts?"

"Yeah. *That* sort of thing."

"Well, I do and she is." Joe sighed. "And, let's face it, she'd be easier to talk about to Mom."

Casey pulled out the hot pads and paused as he was opening the stove. "You mean your mom doesn't know?"

Joe raised his eyebrows and straightened up over the table. "I don't know what you've been watching on daytime television, but not all mothers are thrilled to hear the sexual revolution was quite so successful."

Casey raised his eyebrows, and Joe blushed and shrugged. "If I end up in a long-term relationship with a man, Mom will know. As it is, I'm not in a long-term relationship with *anyone*, and she's pretty sure I'm not celibate. We don't all talk to our authority figures about sex, Casey. Can you live with that?"

Casey just shrugged, feeling an unexpected lump of disappointment. "Are you ashamed that you sleep with men sometimes?"

Joe sighed. "No." He sighed again. "Some of the best moments of my life have been with another man." For a moment, Casey's world was golden. "And some of the best moments have been with a woman too." And the world was back to regular old color TV. "I don't want my parents to… to *label* me, or what I do, or what sort of person I'm going to bring home before I know myself, okay?"

Casey digested this in silence and then bent and pulled the casserole out, using the quilted hot pads carefully as he took it to the table. He'd chopped up lettuce for a salad and put it in their one wooden salad bowl. Joe, sensing the occasion, whether Casey would admit to one or no, got out the good glasses—cut crystal—and put them at all three settings.

"So," Joe said, his voice a little less defensive, "are you going to tell me what the occasion is, really?"

Casey smiled at him, realizing that he wasn't disappointed after all. Joe was only human. The things that made him such an outstanding refuge to people just exactly like Casey were the same things that wouldn't want to cause a fuss about a significant other until there was a fuss to be had. "I took my placement exams at Sierra today. I see my counselor in a week, and I can register for classes."

Joe's beautiful, even grin split his face, white in the dark hair of his mustache and soul patch. "That's *awesome*, Casey! I'm so proud of you!"

He stood up and gave Casey a massive hug that Casey returned, closing his eyes and sinking into Joe's solidness with something close to desperation. *God, Joe. I love you so much, and I don't think it's the way you want me to, and I don't think I can change it.* Joe's arms were strong around his shoulders right then, though, and Casey wouldn't fuck up this moment, this pride, for anything on the planet, even the raging going on in his head.

There was a knock at the door right then, and Joe backed up and ruffled his hair, then went and opened the door for Dev.

Derrick was right behind him.

Joe's smile at Derrick was... troubled, to say the least, Casey thought. But Joe had some old-world manners, in spite of the motorcycle and the facial hair and the constantly ripped jeans. He fixed his smile and reached out a hand, shaking Derrick's hand heartily. Derrick's rectangular, pretty face looked bemused, a reddish-brown eyebrow arched skeptically, as though this hadn't been the greeting he'd expected, and Casey wondered meanly if he'd thought Joe would simper and kiss his cheek.

"Come on in, man! Casey cooked up a storm—he's sort of celebrating his entrance into junior college, you know?"

"'Cause that's so hard?" Dev asked, rolling his eyes and moving past them to kiss Casey on the cheek.

Casey looked at him levelly. "My SATs were higher than yours, rich boy," he said, his voice and face pleasant, and he was gratified when Dev flushed.

Dev smiled, somewhat ingratiatingly, and Casey thought that he might mean well, and moved in for a kiss. Dev opened his mouth with satisfying eagerness, but that didn't stop the unease in Casey's gut. This relationship was nice, but it wasn't going to be happy ever after— he'd be lucky if it was sex for the night. (They'd gotten sort of good at it, lately, and Dev had quit bitching about the condom about a month after Debbie's funeral. Sometimes Casey thought that might be because he was cheating, but since Casey was dating him while still being in love with Joe, he figured it was only fair.) Their relationship really was that tenuous, and sometimes he wasn't sure who couldn't stand who the most.

But this night—this night it didn't matter. Casey felt proud of himself, of where his life was going, and Joe was proud of him too. They sat, they ate, Joe pulled ice cream out of the freezer, and they had dessert. They watched *Terminator*, although Casey was *dying* for *Batman* to come out on video.

"We saw it in the theaters!" Joe protested good-naturedly, and Dev looked at Casey funny.

"I asked you to see that movie. You said no!"

Casey flushed and grabbed a handful of popcorn over Jay's fuzzy orange head. The cats tended to sprawl out on Joe and Casey's laps when they watched television, and the dogs slept on special pillows in the kitchen by the garage door. Casey had tuckered them out tonight, which was good, because Rufus tended to beg for popcorn. Joe had an air popper, and when you added garlic salt to the butter, it was *so* good. "Yeah," Casey answered to Dev's whine about *Batman*, "but that's because Joe and I had been talking about seeing it for a month. We had a day set out special and everything. I didn't want to blow that."

"I haven't seen it yet," Dev said, his voice pitching, and Casey pulled back on his temper.

"It's still at the theater in Auburn—we can go this week."

"Yeah, but...." Dev scowled at him. "Jesus, Casey. You made me watch *Ghostbusters II*—that movie *sucked*!"

Casey remembered what else had sucked that night, and he grinned at Dev and arched his eyebrows wickedly. Dev blushed and grinned and the discussion was effectively tabled, but Casey had to sigh inwardly. It was true—and maybe one of those things that made their relationship so tenuous—Casey did save the best parts of himself for Joe.

The movie ended, and Dev tugged gently on Casey's hand. Time to go to bed. Casey stood up reluctantly. It had been an epic action-adventure movie, but at the same time it had left him vaguely unsettled. Nuclear Armageddon seemed very close sometimes. This was the sort of thing he talked to Joe about, the sort of thing Joe managed to make him not feel so stupid about. Joe would show him a *Bloom County* cartoon or talk about all the many ways the Bible had been misinterpreted, and Casey would manage to get to sleep without waking up in a cold sweat. He couldn't do that with Dev there—he just couldn't. With Dev he had to put on a face that the whole world was all okay. Joe knew that Casey had seen the world when it hadn't been okay at all. Joe knew that, sometimes, he still saw it that way.

But Joe was standing up and stretching, and Derrick was looking at his exposed tummy with hooded eyes, like he wanted to get him some of that. The two of them had sat at opposite ends of the couch while Casey and Dev had sat between them on the floor, and not once had they even tried to hold hands, although Casey and Dev had been practically on top of each other. Casey knew the signs, though. He remembered when Joe had dated Sharon. He knew the deferential silence, the offers to go get popcorn. There was something brewing between them.

Casey let Dev pull him toward his bedroom, though, and Joe gave a sleepy, innocent grin as they disappeared down the hallway.

"Good night!"

You don't want him, Joe. He's sort of fast and slutty, and he just barged his way in here and—

"Casey, you coming?" Dev asked impatiently, and Casey sighed.

"Good night," Casey said wistfully, turning toward Dev and what was likely to be some decent, if silent, sex.

He never did see what Joe's expression was. For years, he thought it was probably indifferent, but eventually, eventually, he began to suspect it might have been as reluctant as his own.

HE SLEPT badly—bad dreams that Dev was not very patient with, usually elbowing him in the side with a "Jesus, what's wrong!"—and therefore woke up when Joe was in the shower. They'd managed to install an upstairs shower directly above the downstairs shower, but something about the homemade plumbing job caused the pipes to groan terribly with the water pressure it took to force the water up. The sound was so bad that Joe still frequently took his showers downstairs. The fact that he didn't on this morning told Casey way too clearly how the night had gone.

Casey groaned and rolled over, but Dev wasn't there. Casey blinked hard and took a breath and registered that his shower had been used recently. Dev brought his own aftershave from home when he stayed over, and it was *really* strong.

Oh God. Who could shower this early in the morning? Casey needed his coffee first, and with any luck *someone* had made coffee when they'd gotten up.

He rolled out of bed, pulled on some scrubs (because they still spelled comfort to him, even after nearly two years), and made his way out his bedroom door with his eyes half-closed. He *literally* almost collided with Joe as Joe came down the stairs, wearing his own scrubs as pajama bottoms and still pulling a brush through the wet, tangled hair that fell halfway down his back.

"Hey, Derrick!" he called as the two of them righted themselves and stumbled, half-laughing, around the corner of the living room. "Could you make us some coffee while you're down... there...."

"Are you shitting me?" Casey asked, looking blankly to the little dinette set where they'd eaten dinner the night before.

"Oh... for fuck's sake." Joe's voice was equally dispassionate, and Dev looked up from his place, bent over the table, Derrick behind him, in a reversal of the pose Casey knew intimately from the night before.

"Dev, you said you wouldn't bottom!"

"For fuck's sake, Derrick, are you even wearing a *fucking condom?*"

Derrick stopped pumping his cock into Dev's ass and caught his breath. "Joe... I'm sorry, he was totally asking for—"

Joe hit him.

Casey had never seen Joe move that fast, but sure enough, he lunged and threw a beauty of a haymaker in one fluid motion that had more to do with Joe being almost constantly active than with him being a born fighter.

Derrick went over backward, smacking his back on the wall of the small dinette space, and Dev fell off the table, naked and pathetic, his erection shriveling on his thighs as he fell down hard on his elbow.

Derrick sat down hard, rubbing his jaw gingerly and looking at Joe with an almost sheepish expression. "No second date?" he said hopefully.

"Remember the weed you offered me?" Joe said, his voice cold and grim.

"You want some *now*?" Derrick's shock seemed misplaced somehow.

"Leave it on the dresser when you get your shit," Joe said. He looked at the microwave clock. "You've got five minutes."

Derrick scrambled up without looking back, pulling his jeans up and buttoning them as he went.

"Devin?" Joe said, and Dev made an effort to push himself up. "You okay?"

"Yessir."

"Did he force you?"

Dev didn't meet Casey's eyes. "No, sir," he said quietly.

"Then I need you to leave. For pretty much fucking ever. Casey, you got a problem with that?"

"No, sir," Casey said grimly, shaking his head at Dev. Jesus. He'd known. He'd seen it fucking coming. But it was one thing to fuck around on Casey with his high school friends, the ones in all the academic clubs, because they were handy or because Dev had the morals of a hamster, but to do this in Joe's house? Under Joe's roof? Joe had been pretty fucking decent to Dev—screwing his date in the breakfast nook was pretty low.

Dev stood up and buttoned his acid-washed 501s, then scurried for Casey's room. "Sorry, Casey," he said, but he kept his pretty oval-shaped face turned away.

"Yeah, whatever."

Joe didn't say anything for a moment, and Casey watched him numbly as he walked into the kitchen and checked the coffee.

"Oh Jesus," he muttered. "All that and the guy can't even make a decent cup of fucking coffee." A deep, hearty funk sank over the room, and Casey didn't feel inclined to break it as he set one of the chairs that had been knocked over upright and then fed the cats, who, mindless of all the human fuss, were still fat and spoiled and wanted their morning kibble.

Derrick came thundering down the stairs as Casey opened the door to the garage so he could give the dogs their food and let them out, and Casey paused long enough to hear Joe bark, "Leave the weed!" at him before they both heard the door slam.

"Why leave the weed?" Casey asked, only semicurious. His insides were busy sorting shit out. Pain? Betrayal? Anger? Yeah... but also sort of a curious resignation. He'd seen this coming. Hell, he might have encouraged a little bit of it himself.

"Because we don't have any beer," Joe said, like that made sense.

"Why would we want—" Casey stopped, and looked at Joe, and heard the catch in his voice, and wanted to kick himself.

Yeah, sure, Casey might have been on the verge of breaking up with Dev for months. But Joe had *just* opened himself up enough to sleeping with Derrick. God, in two years, that made three lovers for Joe—and one of those was the social worker. Casey had given him shit for not wanting to commit to a man because of what he'd have to say to his mother, and now, looking at the crumpled iron of Joe's face, Casey realized that Joe had been 100 percent honest. He hadn't wanted to commit to *anyone* unless he was sure. Joe might have been a player in college, but that was a different Joe. This Joe was looking for somebody, somebody special. This Joe was as earnest in looking for a lover as he was in helping the lost or the needy. This was the Joe that Casey had fallen in love with at sixteen and might possibly love for his entire life.

"I ain't got nothin' doin' today," Casey drawled past the lump in his chest. Devin came pattering around the corner, pulling on his bright and spiffy leather boots and leather jacket. "Except maybe going to see *Batman* again," Casey added, and Joe gave him a sour grin.

"It's a deal. *Then* we'll come home and get high."

"Thought you didn't *get* high, Casey!" Dev sneered, and Casey sneered back.

"I thought you didn't bottom."

Dev blushed and ran away. The putt-putt of his little barely street-legal motorcycle echoed through their little valley as he went.

Casey felt an ache then, square in the middle of his chest, that said, in spite of the resignation and the feelings for Joe, in spite of Dev's snobbery and his condescension, he was still going to leave a hole.

"Joe," Casey said, then swallowed hard, "you know I was lying about *Batman.*"

Joe's back shivered for a second as he started rooting through the refrigerator, like he was fighting something down inside that was threatening to let loose. "I hear you, kid. Let me fix breakfast first. We're going to need more than potato chips to fight the munchies."

Casey nodded and then went out to feed the dogs. He shuffled to the shower after that and found that he was crying with the release of the hot water. In a way, he sort of wanted Joe to hold him, but as he shuddered out the last of the tears and got himself a towel, he realized that it wasn't necessary. What mattered in the grand scheme of things was that Joe was there to *catch* him, and for the moment, in spite of the feelings that didn't seem to be going anywhere, that was more than enough.

Who Will You Run To?
~Joe

1992

JOE heard the phone ring and groaned. For a minute he hoped Casey would get it, and then he remembered that Casey didn't live there anymore, hadn't lived there for six months, and he groaned again. Aw, goddammit. Goddammit all to fuck. If nothing else, he should get a phone line to the upstairs room just so he wouldn't have that god-awful realization on mornings like this, when he wasn't quite awake enough to remember. He couldn't even think about answering the phone without that horrible sucker punched feeling, that hole in his chest where the kid used to be but was only a vague, awful sort of loneliness now.

The kid didn't have to leave like that. He really didn't.

There was a soft voice downstairs, and Joe had a moment of relief. Lynnie had it. He'd forgotten she was staying in the guest bedroom. He rolled and yawned and stretched and tried to wake up. Hospital policy had changed once again, and he'd worked four twelves in a row, because that was his drug now. He would have resorted to weed or beer, and the day after Casey had moved out, he'd tried both. But he was thirty-three now, and he didn't recover from that like he used to. He still loved his job, and he had the dogs and the cats and the chickens to depend on him, but that wasn't why he didn't drink or smoke himself to sleep every night.

He just couldn't believe that Casey was gone for good. It was so fucking unfair.

"Joe?" Lynnie called from downstairs. "Joe? It's for Casey."

"He doesn't live here anymore," Joe called down, hauling himself down the stairs groggily. He and Casey had carpeted them in cream-colored short pile carpet the autumn after that horrible debacle with their respective boyfriends, and he was grateful. It felt so much less painful to stumble down carpeted stairs.

"Yeah, but the woman says she's his mother. She says this is the last number she has for him. She needs to get hold of him!"

"Ask her where the fuck she's been the last six years!" Joe snarled. God, it really was six years—it was late fall. Casey had left in early summer, but that didn't mean he wouldn't have appreciated the phone call from his mother.

But by now, Joe was at the bottom of the stairs and to the kitchen, and Lynnie was there, wearing a flannel nightgown, clutching the bathrobe to her five-month-along belly, her long brown hair hanging, tangled, down her back. God, his life would have been so much easier if he hadn't broken up with her right after Casey left. That baby would be his, and he could have married her and started a family, and he could pretend that some of the shit Casey had shouted at him on the way out wasn't true.

"Yeah?" he snapped into the phone.

Lynnie raised her eyebrows at him, because even when she'd come to him, looking for a place to stay after her replacement-for-Joe had smacked her around, kicked her out, and then refused to admit that the kid was his, Joe hadn't spoken to her quite so rudely.

"I'm... uhm... are you Josiah Daniels?"

"Yeah, lady, and I just worked four twelve-hour shifts in a row, and I'm sort of pissed off. Can we get to the point?"

"Doesn't Casey live there anymore?"

"He moved out in May, right after he graduated from Sierra."

"He graduated?"

"From junior college, yeah. He's going to Sac State now, not that you care."

There was a grunt then, and he realized that maybe the woman *did* care, and that he'd just hurt her needlessly. Well then, good for her.

This whole interlude in Joe's life seemed to be hurting needlessly; he was just glad to share.

"He's doing well, then?"

"Yeah," Joe muttered roughly. "He's doing good." Joe would have liked to say he didn't know. That Casey had moved out of his house and out of his life, and that was the end of that. But it wasn't true. Joe had fed him, cared for him, watched over him for five and a half years. You just didn't quit *caring* after that, even if the guy had shoved a knife in your chest and twisted the handle two, three, six times before he left. No. Joe knew where Casey was staying, and had gone by the place about twice a month since Casey had moved out. A couple of times he'd seen that Casey's car had been out of the driveway and had stopped to talk—first to Casey's boyfriend, who had been less than friendly, and then to Casey's roommate, who had been more than accommodating. It had been hard. Casey was both doing okay and he wasn't. He was waiting tables and making money, and he was making it to his classes, but it was all so skin of the teeth. His boyfriend had left him in the first two months after promising to be there, and Joe remembered their little pity party when Dev left, and knew that Casey had needed to have one when Robbie took off, and Joe hadn't been there. But he was still going to school, and he was still not talking to Joe. He hadn't called, and Joe hadn't called either, because Casey had been the one who'd told Joe to fuck off, and it was sort of on Casey's shoulders to take that back. He was apparently eating on occasion, although the roommate did confess that a lot of it was free french fries from the restaurant where Casey worked, and basically, he was doing the starving student thing, which was both fine with Joe and.... Joe refused to think about how that sentence ended.

"He's doing fine," Joe repeated now, more to reassure himself than this stranger on the phone. "Why are you trying to contact him now?"

"His...." The woman's voice broke, and Joe started to feel a little bad. She sounded more wrecked than he did, and he was only occasionally an asshole. "His father died," she said through her tears. "It... I wanted to tell him when the service would be."

"Aw, fuck," Joe muttered. "Fuck. Yeah. Here." He reached for the pen drawer—every house has one—and sorted through the dead batteries, old key sets, and assorted pairs of scissors for a pen. "Here. Give me the details. Yeah, we'll find it. Fucking Bakersfield, right?"

It was in Bakersfield, and Joe took down the address and the directions.

"You... you promise he'll be there?" the woman asked, her voice hesitant, and Joe grunted.

"I promise I'll tell him," Joe said with a sigh. "Beyond that, it's anyone's guess. His trip up here wasn't a picnic; he may not feel like making the trip back."

"I... is he still... you know...?"

"Gay?" Joe's disbelief flooded under his new vow of kindness. "Yeah, lady, last I heard, all cures for gay were a hoax. Does it matter?"

"He's my son. Of course it matters. I want to let him come back home."

"Well it's good to want things," Joe snapped bitterly, knowing he was talking more to himself than to her. "I'll let him know."

He hung the phone up on its cradle on the counter and then turned around and slid down his battered cabinets, thrilled that his body didn't ache when his ass hit the floor. Jordan padded up and shoved her fuzzy orange face up into his and started licking his nose. He forced a smile and set her on his stomach, then petted her dispiritedly while he swallowed hard against the tightness in his throat, his face, behind his eyes.

Lynnie watched him for a moment and then grabbed a chair from the dinette table and moved it to the middle of the kitchen so she could sit on it. She'd put on some weight in the last four months—sitting on the floor was probably not an option for her. "Joe?" she said quietly, and he sighed, wishing he could look at her.

"His dad died. I'm going to have to tell his roommate that his dad died, and then hope he forgives me enough to let me hold him."

"Forgives you?" she asked, her voice shrilling with attitude. "Forgives you for *what*?"

"For being stupid," Joe murmured, and Jordan kept up her licking. Nick and Jay were curled up on the couch. Like a rapidly aging Rufus and a depressed Hi, they were probably blaming him for Casey's absence too.

Joe certainly was blaming himself—although, when things had gone south, he'd thought he was doing the right thing.

THE day they'd gotten stoned on Derrick's weed, Joe had confessed something to Casey that he thought he should probably regret, but didn't.

They actually *had* gone to see a movie that night (*Say Anything*— a movie Joe still loved), after the high had worn off, and the high itself had been a temporary thing, soon washed out of their hair and munched away with breakfast. But the melancholy, the betrayal, the nasty, sticky residue of coming out of a night of sex—the good kind, where two people felt connected and caring—only to find out you were another body in bed, that had settled in for the both of them.

"I probably should have known," Casey said glumly on the way to the movie theater. "I mean… he just always thought he was so much better than me."

Joe looked at him protectively. "That's bullshit. Why would he feel like that?"

Casey's shrug wasn't a teenager's shrug anymore. He had his hands in his pockets, and his gray eyes, deep-set and narrow, were mild and introspective. This shrug was an adult's shrug, a twitch of the shoulders and not too much passion. "Same reason I felt that way when I lived with my folks, I guess. I was spoiled. He was spoiled. He'll learn."

Joe looked at him for a long moment as they stood in line then, with the dawning comprehension that Casey really didn't need him anymore. It was both gratifying and terrifying. If Casey didn't need him, why would he stick around?

Joe swallowed against that fear, managed to tamp it down in the pit of his stomach for the next two or so years, but it was there, growing, along with an awareness that Casey was as tall as he was ever going to get at five eight, and that his lean face and high cheekbones were pretty, and the deep-set eyes and power brow didn't change that but only made it deeper.

They talked about the movie on the way home, about the likelihood of finding the love of your life at nineteen. Joe said it was possible, yes, but he didn't want to bet anyone's life on it.

"I certainly don't want to bet yours!" he protested, and Casey snorted.

"That's just because you don't want to see me as an adult," he muttered, and Joe sighed. The tall trees on either side of the highway were outlined against the bright stars, and he looked at that ribbon of stars in front of them and wished them for Casey.

"You're right," Joe said, wanting to close his eyes against the beauty there, but he couldn't. He was driving. He focused on the road instead, which was better, because possum, skunk, and deer often made appearances in the darkness, and he didn't want to kill another critter *or* him and Casey. It was much safer that way, but not as wonderful.

"Why not?" It had been a long day, and Casey's voice was close enough to a whine to make Joe chuckle.

"It's scary," Joe said softly. "It's scary. If you're a kid, you need me. I grew up, I left the house, I haven't returned. I love my folks, and I miss them, and as much as I whine about my mom's phone calls, you know I make it a point to be there."

"You write letters," Casey interjected, and Joe still couldn't believe how blown away Casey had been by something that simple.

Joe shrugged. "Yeah. But... but my folks don't know about me, don't know about life out here. It's a lot easier to let them think I'm looking for *Mizz* Right instead of *Mr. slash Mizz* Right. And in a way, I'm sort of hoping it *is* Ms. Right—"

"Why?" Casey asked, his voice quick and a little angry.

But Joe figured Casey had seen him as a human being today, from stoned and angry to vulnerable and melancholy. Maybe he should know the truth about Joe—about all of him. "'Cause I want kids," he said baldly. "I mean, I can live without 'em, and if I'm in love enough with a man, I'll do that. But I can't lie to myself, say it's all right, that it won't hurt to give that up. That'll just confuse the whole thing."

Casey's voice throbbed with sadness in the dark. "You'd be a really, really good father," he said, like the admission cost him.

"Thanks. From you, Casey, that means a lot."

They'd gone to sleep that night sad, but happy too. Joe knew he'd been content to be Casey's friend, his older mentor, someone he could depend on in an uncertain world. But those words, that idea, that Joe was looking for a family, not just a mate—that seemed to lay between them.

Casey had tried to climb into his bed when he turned eighteen—but it was more as a joke than anything else. It was pretty obvious from the fact that the kid had lined the floor with pillows so it wouldn't hurt so bad when his ass hit the floor, and they'd both been laughing as he'd trundled off to his own bed. A few weeks later, Lynnie had done more than smile shyly at Joe when they went in to eat at The Oar Cart, like they did about twice a month, and had asked him for a date instead.

Joe had taken her to a movie—something he wouldn't have done before he met Casey—and then for a moonlit walk of his property. Somewhere between the chicken coop and the little mother-in-law cottage he was building, she'd turned to him in the moonlight and kissed him, and he'd kissed her back.

Making love that night had felt... blessed, and the look of sadness, almost of recrimination, in Casey's eyes the next morning as he'd kissed her good-bye had hurt.

"It's not just because she's a she," he said as the echoes from her little Toyota's engine died out.

"She's only twenty-three."

"Twenty-three isn't eighteen."

"When's it get to be old enough, Joe? When do I even get consideration before you bring someone else home?"

"When you're old enough to drink!" Joe snapped, and Casey sneered at him. It wasn't attractive, and it was the first time Joe had ever felt... less, in Casey's estimation.

"Stop bringing me home beer, then, oh child of the seventies, or that doesn't count."

Joe flushed. "Casey—why does this have to be hard? She's a pretty girl. We're dating. You've seen me date both—I'm happy with either. Why does this have to be ugly?"

Casey scowled at him. "Because she's your chance at breeding, and I may get it, but I don't have a uterus, so I'm not going to like it!"

"*I'm not dating her to breed!*" Joe roared, his sudden temper taking even *him* by surprise. "I'm dating her because she's a pretty girl! That's the definition of bisexual, Casey—pretty girls and pretty boys, it's like an all-you-can-fuck buffet!"

Casey's sudden snicker lightened the moment—and made Joe crack a reluctant smile—but that moment was just the first skirmish in what became an all-out war.

Casey was never rude to Lynnie; Joe had to give him credit for that. But Joe's preparation for every date was peppered with snide remarks; every sleepover was a stomach-sinking dread of what was coming out of Casey's mouth when Lynnie left. When she was there for dinner or a movie, Casey found more and more reasons to be gone, and when he was there, he frequently retreated to his room. It was like all of the dreaded symptoms of adolescence that Joe thought Casey had bypassed in high school came back to visit for those two years of junior college—but only when Lynnie was in the picture. More than once Joe contemplated breaking up with Lynnie just because spending time with Casey on any *other* day was really his favorite thing to do.

Casey had dates too. He didn't bring a lot of them home, and he only rarely slept over, and not without a phone call to Joe that he was going to be gone, but there were young men in his life. At first Joe was happy; it meant the kid wasn't there when Joe was dating Lynnie, and their friendship, however ill-defined it may have been, was intact.

And it was wonderful. They spent three more Christmases together, where they attempted to share music and videos and good deeds, like when Joe detailed Casey's car or when Casey stenciled the hallway and the living room so that they didn't look quite so spartan. They spent three more New Year's Eves watching the ball drop together, talking about Dick Clark and the picture of Dorian Grey he must have somewhere in his condo, and how Oscar Wilde was one fantastic writer for a flaming old 'mo. (Casey used that as a dig to Joe to maybe give up on girls altogether. Joe used it as a dig to Casey to strive to do great things.)

Joe watched Casey turn eighteen, then nineteen, then twenty, and gave thanks every morning that he'd get to see his friend: the constant sarcastic, funny voice in the morning, who grounded him and made the sun through the trees a thing to turn your face to and not to hide away from. They both worked, and Casey went to school, but their time off was very often together. When there were no dates with other people, they played with the dogs or went swimming at Sugar Pine or Lake Clementine and went to movies. They shared books—Joe hadn't gotten to read nearly as many classics when going through nursing school as Casey did going after a liberal studies degree. Casey's feistiness, his spirit—it grew brighter, more sure, more beautiful every day. Sometimes Joe would look at him and be reminded of something great and powerful and tenuous, something that should have been familiar but wasn't.

It wasn't until Casey brought Robbie home that Joe remembered where he'd first had that feeling, where the heart was too big for the chest, where the breath caught and the eyes teared up because looking at this person, this one perfect person, was so bright, so golden, that they had no choice.

Joe remembered the moment.

Lynnie was cooking that night, and she cooked lovely, delicate things—angel-hair pasta with cream pesto sauce, hummus and pita sandwiches, braised lamb with slivered shallots—things that tasted good but always left Casey and Joe quietly raiding the refrigerator together at two in the morning when she was either gone or asleep in Joe's bed.

The table was set, and Casey's car drove up, Ford white and serviceable. Casey took good care of it—Joe was proud. Joe stopped and went to the living room to look outside. It was his first glimpse of Robbie, the one guy in the past few months that Casey deemed worth bringing home, and Joe wanted a look at him before he was in Joe's house. Neither of them wanted a repeat of the whole Derrick/Devin thing—if Casey was introducing this guy to Joe, it was going to be important.

Joe watched them get out, and for a moment, yes, he checked Robbie out. Robbie was as small as Casey, slightly built, dark hair, dark eyes, wearing jeans and a plaid shirt. A lot of kids were wearing those these days—something about Pearl Jam, and since Joe could get into both the band and the fashion statement, he was impressed. He was not so impressed by the jeans that could seat three, and he laughed a little to himself as Robbie pulled the crotch of his jeans up so he could walk, and he looked to Casey to see what Casey thought.

Casey was leaning over the top of the car, his door open, and he was laughing. His head was tilted back, and his brownish-blond hair was turning gold in the May sunshine. It was longish now, hanging from a part in the center of his head, feathering back a little, and his gray eyes were half-closed as he smiled. His snub little nose was tilted to the sun, and the bridge was almost transparent. Joe knew if he was closer, he could see the faint—very faint, now—freckles right under Casey's eyes. Casey's cheeks grooved with his smile, but not too deeply—it was a gentle smile, not an all-out laugh. When Casey was laughing until he fell off the couch, he actually closed his eyes, and his smile carved his cheeks with wreaths.

But not now. Now it was gentle, and the sun was kissing him, like Joe… like Joe….

Joe swallowed. His chest swelled in that faintly familiar breath-stopping, overwhelming way, and he made a faint sound, a gasp really, as he remembered the last time he'd felt that, and knew with total assurance what it was.

It was when Jeannie had held his hand in church, when he was six and love was so simple, and so uncomplicated, and God was the reason you loved until you cried.

For the first time in twenty-seven years, Joe felt the existence of God. He was in Casey's smile, his eyes, the way he looked at his lover, the way he greeted the dogs. God was there, in the sunshine brushing Casey's hair, and warming his skin, and Joe….

Joe wanted to touch him.

For a moment, when there was no air in the room and the world was entombed in ice, Joe remembered swimming at Clementine the week before. The water had been cold, and the dogs had been about played out when Casey had started to swim, shivering, toward a place the sun had been hitting all day.

"Here!" he cried. "Joe, it's warm here! I swear! Come on out, please?"

And Joe had, because Casey had asked, and he'd been so sincere. And sure enough, it was warmer there, shallower, just barely chest level. They swam for a bit and then treaded water and talked, laughing as the dogs paced the shoreline, not happy about their humans in the water without them but reluctant to get wet again.

That moment had been so perfect, so golden, but Joe had been itchy, somehow, shaking with a need he couldn't name, a need that had something to do with Casey's tanned skin, the gold in his hair, the faint stubble glinting in the late spring sunshine. The narrow span of Casey's chest—still hairless—made Joe squirm, and the definition in his arms and abdomen made that discomfort worse. When Casey had gotten out before him in order to comfort the dogs, Joe had watched his bottom in cut-off jeans and realized that all of the walking and working on the property they did made his legs muscular in the right places, and his calves tight and hard. He'd shivered, then swam out to the coldest part of the lake to get over this sudden discomfort with Casey's body and the beauty Joe had always known about but never really seen for himself.

Now, watching Casey laugh at his boyfriend, Joe identified that itchiness, that restless squirm. He wanted to touch.

The thought was alien, alien and almost forbidden, and Joe shivered in the world that had been frozen with the thought. It was a betrayal, wasn't it? Of all he'd tried to do for Casey, of all he'd tried to be?

But you never said he was like a son to you, because he never was. You never said he was like blood and meant it, because he wasn't, and you knew that. You only promised to protect him, not to look at him like a wax mannequin, perfect and beautiful but not warm to the touch.

The moment started moving, thick and painful, sweet like honey, and Casey closed the door to his car and walked around it, spotting Joe in the window.

For a moment he waved and smiled, as natural as the two of them had been over the past six years, and then he stopped. He looked directly at Joe, his eyes narrowing as he tried to figure out what was different, what was wrong, and Joe was simply caught in the moment, a fly caught in honey, and Casey sighted him and looked him in the eyes...

And knew him.

Joe flushed, feeling young and vulnerable, and the smile that played at the corners of Casey's mouth was... was not saintly in the least. His eyes were narrow, and one corner of his mouth was higher than the other; his easy slouch straightened up, and he moved sinuously, arrogantly, like one of the cats who knew that rat in the chicken feed was his for the taking.

Joe just sat there, still caught, not sure what to do with this sight of Casey as adult, and beautiful, making his blood sing under his skin, making him shiver, making him ache, just by smiling in the sun.

"Joe?" Lynnie's voice washed over him, chill and tinkling, and Joe turned and looked at her, trying to find his footing, catch his breath, live in the moment like it was now and not something solid in time.

"Yeah?"

"Are they here? I thought I heard Casey's car?"

God, Lynnie was sweet. She had a little elfin face, with a pointed chin and an upturned nose and long, toffee-brown hair like the girls in the movies. She was kind, and she tried so very hard to mother them both. Joe summoned a smile for her, thinking that, as wonderful as she was, as sweet as their time in bed had become, nothing about her made time stop or made his breath come in gasps just from looking.

"Yeah," he said. "Yeah. They're here. In fact—"

And at that moment, Casey opened the door, and dinner and company began.

That night Joe and Casey washed dishes, and Casey asked casually if Lynnie was staying the night.

"She didn't bring clothes," he said, not sure why she hadn't. "I'm not sure. I should ask her. Robbie?"

"Mm… no," Casey said meditatively, as though he had just made up his mind. "I don't think so. We're almost there, but not yet."

Joe smiled, pretty sure it didn't reach his eyes. "You're very wise," he said quietly, moving to dry his hands.

"You're not," Casey said boldly, and Joe was too overwhelmed to answer cagily or to lie. He was leveled, destroyed, made new—not only by that moment of looking at Casey through the window but by standing shoulder to shoulder with him and noting the way he smelled faintly of sweat and deodorant and dog. And of adult male, something Joe hadn't buried his nose in for nearly three years and now missed with all his heart.

"I know it," he said quietly. "I am sometimes tremendously foolish. A big scary guy on a motorcycle with *way* too much hair. I'm well aware of my shortcomings, Casey. You don't need to remind me."

Suddenly Casey was right behind him, his hands on Joe's hips, just like he'd been that first night when he was no more than a kid, starving and filthy and reeking. But that wasn't the Casey who was standing on his tiptoes to whisper in Joe's ear. This Casey was the strong, confident adult that Joe had been so proud of, and was now just giving himself to Joe—if only Joe would reach out and take him.

"You're only foolish if you don't see why I would want you," Casey said softly, and then, as though they would both forget that moment of bravery, he lowered himself to his flat feet and turned toward the living room, while Joe went to the bathroom and tried to control his instant, painful erection.

LYNNIE drove back to Roseville that night—she actually lived in Auburn but had promised a girlfriend a late-night sleepover and a shopping trip in the morning. Robbie had a little duplex near the railroad tracks, and Casey asked Lynn to drop him off there. Robbie had been funny all night. Casey's new friend with the longish dark hair and limpid brown eyes had apparently won the vote for class clown in high school, and he lived up to it at dinner. He'd cracked jokes constantly—punny ones, and he was mostly antic, motor-mouthed, and entertaining—but he looked decidedly disappointed when Casey asked. Casey had excused himself then, and gone and talked to the boy, and when the two of them left, Robbie seemed mollified, like a kid who wasn't going to get cookies with lunch but who had been promised ice cream after dinner.

"He could have stayed," Joe said, yawning. He was legitimately tired: today was his first day off after three twelves and an eight, and his whole body felt creaky and thin. "I'm not going to be much fun tonight."

Casey shook his head. "He asked me to move in with him," he said softly, and Joe's eyes shot open. He was suddenly, shockingly awake. "I wanted to know what you thought of that."

Breathe. Breathe in. Breathe out. Remember that all kids moved out. He had moved out of his parents' house; Casey would want to move out of—*You're not his parent. You don't want to be. You never wanted to be.*

"Can you afford rent?" he asked, buying time before he was pulled underwater with the sudden fear.

"Barely," Casey admitted, quirking his mouth. "But I start Sac State in September, and Roseville is a helluvalot closer."

Joe nodded. "I hear they're opening classes in Auburn," he admitted, "but not right now."

Casey nodded and pursed his lips, his face shadowed in the hallway. Joe was standing by the stairs with the light on, and he was painfully aware that his every expression, every terrible realization, was on parade for Casey to make of what he would.

"Besides that, what do you think?" Casey prodded, and Joe had to remember that he was always honest, had always been honest, and had built his life on his heart being exactly what he wore on his face.

"I think I'd miss you," he said rawly. "But I think I should have been expecting this, and it shouldn't be quite such a surprise."

Casey nodded and then smiled that sharp-edged, slightly carnivorous smile. "Can you think of a reason for me to stay?"

I want you. I want to hold you. I'm suddenly, terrifyingly, overwhelmingly possessed with the idea of what your mouth would taste like under mine, and I don't know how to say it or even to think it.

Joe closed his eyes tightly and breathed very, very carefully. "Nothing I can put words to," he said. "Let me know what you decide."

He must have opened his eyes then, because he hadn't walked up the stairs to his bedroom—thoughtfully stenciled in black Celtic knotting by Casey that Christmas—without opening his eyes. He must have. But his vision had been so blurred, he couldn't remember how.

SO ALL things considered, he should have been expecting Casey to try it one more time that night, but somehow he wasn't.

He was curled into a miserable, self-protective ball of sleep and denial under the covers when warm hands started to massage his bare back. It was so late it was early. The air coming in through the screen over his open window was chilly, but there was the hint of heat, because the next day was June, and Foresthill got hot in the summer, just like the valley sometimes. So those hands, warm and hard—man's hands—felt good, and he straightened a little and stretched underneath their kindness.

"Mm...." He wasn't up to words yet. He didn't ask, "Who's that?" because the touch was so familiar, so intimate, he would have felt foolish for asking. He should *know* who this was—this was *his* person, and he knew it. He just didn't have the name straight in his head.

The hands on his shoulders stopped, and a strong arm went around his middle, rubbing his stomach, the furry trail down his lower abdomen, the embarrassing amount of hair on his chest. He insinuated his body into that touch, savoring it, because there was something in it that he'd missed for a while, and when an adventurous forefinger and thumb pinched his nipple, he shook them off. "Don't like that," he mumbled. "You know I don't."

"How am I supposed to know that?" Casey whispered sardonically in his ear. "We've never done this before."

Joe rolled over so quickly he almost nailed Casey in the head with his elbow. Oh God. He so hadn't been expecting this—not tonight. Not when everything he'd ever felt for Casey was suddenly shifted in its tracks, askew like the cracked foundation of a house schismed in an earthquake. Suddenly he was face to face with Casey, the moonlight coming through the window outlining every edge of the features he'd hungered for that afternoon, and Casey was looking at him with a plump, open mouth and eyes that knew *exactly* what they were doing.

For a moment, Joe caved.

For a moment, his lips touched Casey's, and he tasted. Casey's mouth opened under his eagerly, and Casey groaned, pulling Joe close and closer, and Joe plundered him. Oh God... the taste of his mouth, the feel of his jaw under Joe's hands, the feeling of his hard, tight body, lithe and pliant against Joe's heavier mass... it was heaven. It was perfect. Joe's aching erection was suddenly grinding up against Casey's groin, and Casey was hard and thrusting back.

And that was when Joe grew truly awake.

He didn't kick Casey out of bed this time; this time, he scrambled back himself, panting for breath. "No!" he said, feeling like the skin had peeled from his lips when he'd torn their mouths apart.

"Why no?" Casey demanded, sitting up in bed. He was wearing soft cotton shorts with boxers underneath, oh thank heavens, because the thought of him rubbing against Joe naked...

Might make Joe come without touching himself, for one.

"Because... oh God. Because—"

"You wanted it!" Casey accused, not giving an inch, and Joe had to concede.

"Of *course* I wanted it!" Oh God, so badly. "You're beautiful, Casey—your body is tight and perfect. Do you think I wouldn't want you?"

"Then why not? Dammit, for years, I was too young, but I'm not too young now, am I? You *wanted* me, and you wanted me *bad*. Tell me you want Lynnie that way! Tell me you groan and beg and tell her what you want and what you don't. I *live* in this house, Joe, and I've heard your noises at night. God! I've jacked off to them for the last three years, and *nothing* I've heard, *nothing*, sounds like what you just begged from me right now!"

Joe wrapped his arms around himself, feeling suddenly, unaccountably violated. He'd been living with Casey-the-kid, but Casey-the-adult had apparently been pursuing him with a subtle possession that Joe had completely overlooked.

"Adults don't sneak into someone else's bed, Casey." His voice was not even. It was barely steady enough to hear. "Grown-ups ask. Grown-ups go on dates. Grown-ups are up front about it. They don't... don't take advantage of someone when they're vulnerable. Oh God...." And for a minute, his voice really did crack. "Don't you see? That's what I've been trying not to do to you for the last three years?"

Casey's face crumpled for a moment as he was filled with self-doubt, filled with the possibility that he'd humiliated himself and that he'd hurt Joe and that he'd gone about this all wrong. In that moment, Joe thought maybe they could fix this, they could salvage this moment, Casey could apologize and back off and maybe give Joe some time to get used to the new levels on the floor and the odd shape of the roof, now that his entire world had tilted and the house he'd made a home had become something else entirely.

Joe saw the exact moment when Casey's youth and arrogance overcame him. His face twisted, and he dashed his hand across his cheeks, and he scrambled out of bed.

"That's an *excuse!*" he snarled. "You just want an *excuse* not to want me! You think that going out with Lynnie is going to make you straight, so you don't even have to *think* about wanting me, don't you?"

"No!" Joe denied, stung. "I care about Lynnie, just not—"

"Not like you care for me!" Casey cried, and he wiped his face again. "I *know* you love me, Joe, I feel it right here!" He pounded his chest then, and Joe closed his eyes, because it was true. Joe's whole body was shaking, most of it from the wanting and the denying—but that didn't mean he was going to just change his entire locomotive in its tracks after one curve.

"Of course I love you!" Joe shouted. "I've cared for you for six years—"

"But I'm not that kid! You love me this way!" Casey grabbed his crotch, and Joe grimaced.

"What if I do? Yeah? What if I *do* want you like that? What if it just crashed on my head like a waterfall, and suddenly I do? You think crawling in my bed is going to make me change my shit just right now? Give me a goddamned minute, Casey—"

"You've had three years," Casey muttered. He ran for the stairs and put his hand on the rail. "If you haven't figured it out in three years, it's because you're so busy looking for a breeder, you don't see the man who loves you right here."

"Casey—"

But he knew it was useless. Casey had run down the stairs and was thrashing around in his room. By the time Joe got on a pair of jeans and a T-shirt, Casey had thrown most of his clothes in his car.

"I'll be at Robbie's," he snarled, and Joe gave thanks that he had Robbie's phone number and address, just because Casey had been considerate like that.

"'Til when?" Joe asked, alarmed at the giant pile of clothes in the backseat of the Taurus.

"'Til forever!" Casey ran back inside for another pile and his boom box and cassettes from the kitchen counter, and he threw them in the backseat too.

"Casey," Joe begged, wishing he'd be reasonable, give Joe a day or, fuckitall, a fucking hour, but apparently the three years Joe had been watching him grow up all counted against him now. "God, Casey, don't do this."

Casey opened the driver's side door and glared at Joe, his face a misery of tears and anger and embarrassment. "Why not?" he asked, so angry Joe could hear his voice shake. "You said it yourself, Joe. You should have expected this. Well, here it is. It's my decision, just like you said. Aren't you proud of me?"

"Always," Joe whispered, willing him to hear.

But Casey slammed the door and peeled out of the driveway, leaving Joe alone under a graying sky, emptied of a full moon that had already set.

With or Without You
~Casey

CASEY woke up with Alvin pounding on his door. Oh fuck… was he late for class? Was Robbie's dad there to collect the rent? God knew since Robbie had moved out of the little duplex and back home that Daddy dear hadn't cut Casey a fucking break! Like it was Casey's fault Dad hadn't known his son was gay and moving in with his boyfriend and *not* his roommate until he'd stopped by unannounced?

But Casey had signed the lease, and it was all very legal, and he was pretty sure he had one more month before he was out on his ass, looking for an apartment—probably with Alvin, the world's horniest straight nerd boy, at his heels. God. Fuck. Whatever.

"What the fuck, Alvin!" he called out, looking at the neat piles of dirty laundry in the corner and wondering if he could find change in the bottom of the Taurus to go to the Laundromat. They'd *had* a working washer and drier until Robbie had chosen the straight life and a paid education over Casey and moved out, taking his appliances with him. Fortunately, Casey had had a friend at school getting rid of a refrigerator, or he'd be drinking sour milk out of an ice chest. "It's my fucking day off!"

"Look, Casey, I know you worked late, man, but there's that guy at the door. You know…." Alvin's voice dropped. "The scary dude who keeps bringing you eggs and vegetables?"

Casey shot up in bed. "Joe?" he asked, and his voice cracked a little, and he had to say it again. "*Joe* is here?"

"Yeah—and he's waiting outside in the fucking rain, man, and he looks sad as hell."

Oh no. One of the dogs! A cat! Joe was here to tell him something had happened to Hi, or Rufus—God knew Rufus was getting old. Oh shit! Casey scrambled up out of bed, threw on a pair of scrub bottoms and skipped finding the top, and rushed out the door so fast he almost hit Alvin with it when he shoved it open.

"*Jesus*, Casey—"

"You just let him *stand* there? In the rain?" Oh God. Casey had thought a hundred times that he should go back home. A thousand times. A day. A fucking *minute*. He'd heard Joe as he'd pulled out. *Aren't you proud of me? Always.* God, the fucking things Casey had said, and Joe could still say that? But Casey had made a stand, and he had to stick to it. What kind of grown-up was he if he couldn't make it out on his own for a day, a week, a month? Six months. Six lonely, aching months where he missed the red dirt and blue sky of his home with everything in him?

But… *Joe.*

Casey slowed down before he got to the door, remembering the groceries that had ended up in the refrigerator when he knew neither he nor Alvin had money with which to buy them. Besides, he knew what farm-fresh brown eggs looked like, and homegrown squash from their little garden next to the chicken coop, and thick bacon that Joe bartered their eggs for at the little store in town. He knew how that food ended up in his shitty little duplex and how carefully Joe must have worked at not being seen. Robbie had been contemptuous of the old biker dude and his shit for food, but Casey had made him squash, tomatoes, and cheese one night, and he'd pretty much shut up about it. Alvin was kinder, always answering Casey's unanswered questions courteously. *Yeah, Casey. He looked good. No, the girlfriend wasn't with him. It was just him. You know, it's just up the hill. It's not like you don't know the number.*

But something horrible, horrible and angry, had blocked up in his chest when it had been time to do just that. He'd been… God. He'd been *in the man's bed*, and Joe had been *hard and wanting*, and he'd just… just….

Adults don't sneak into someone else's bed, Casey.... Don't you see? That's what I've been trying not to do to you for the last three years?

Oh fuck. Holy mother of fuck. Could a grown person really die of shame? Whatever it had been, Casey hadn't been able to face it. He'd counted—as he'd so often counted—on Joe to be the better man. And Joe had been, and that had just made it harder.

Casey took three deep breaths and closed his eyes. In the dark he saw Joe playing with the dogs, working on the chicken coop, digging in the garden. Saw him in the morning, bare-chested, sleepy and unaware of how shy his smile was when he wasn't wide awake. Saw that curtain of hair, long and glossy and well cared for, coming over what was really a thin face, thin and... oh God. Young. Casey had been to bars in the past months—hadn't brought anyone home, really, because even a pocket full of condoms didn't make him want to take that risk for someone he'd just met—but he'd seen fortysomethings hitting on twentysomethings, the eyes of the older men hard and greedy, their sneers barely hidden in masks of carefully groomed pretty. Joe would never look like that. Joe would only always be plain and honest, as simple as oatmeal, or squash and tomatoes and cheese. A big Rottweiler of a man, but sweeter, more trusting, more hopeful of a bone or a pet or a hug coming his way than even Rufus, because Joe would never, *had* never, bitten, even when, Casey had to admit, he'd been in pain.

He took another breath and opened up the door.

"Hi," he said, his face hot and uncomfortable, even in the humid, frigid air coming from the doorway. "What's up?"

Joe had been standing at the porch, staring out into the fairly constant late November rain. Last week had been Thanksgiving, and Joe had left a small precooked turkey breast and stuffing. Alvin had fixed it up for the two of them, and Casey had been grateful.

But it hadn't been the big turkey and potatoes that Joe had done for him for the past five years. Not by a long shot.

Joe turned when he heard Casey at the door, and gave a weak smile. "You're thinner," he said critically. He swallowed. "Starving college student. It ain't just an expression, right?"

Casey shook his head, thinking that he'd been starving more for the sight of Joe than for food. "I, uhm… do you want to come in?"

Joe nodded. "Thanks. You, uhm… you may want to sit down. I've got some news."

"How's Lynnie?" Casey blurted, closing the door behind Joe as he came in. He smelled like wet leather, wet man—Joe. And Casey really didn't want to hear bad news. Right now, he'd rather actually hear about Joe's girlfriend than something that would suck.

"Pregnant," Joe said. Then, before Casey's heart could fail, he added, "It's not mine. I, uhm, broke up with her pretty much after you left."

Casey had to put his hand up against the wall, because there were spots dancing in front of his eyes. "Why?" he asked, not even trying to be subtle.

"Casey, we can't do this right now," Joe said softly, and Casey blinked and tried to put his head on right. Bad news. That was what had brought Joe to his doorstep, but still, God, there were some things he had to know.

"Where is she now?" he asked deliberately, and Joe looked at him from the middle of their crappy living room and sighed.

"The guest bedroom. Are you happy?"

"I think I could be," he answered with utmost sincerity. Stupid and juvenile, maybe, but Joe sounded like he was still up for grabs.

Then Casey sobered. Joe looked *really* uncomfortable—and he also looked cold. He used to come inside from riding his motorcycle when it was raining or snowy outside, and wear his leathers until the chills stopped. Casey walked over to him and handed him an afghan.

"If you give me your jacket, this'll keep you warmer," he said quietly, and Joe shook his head and worked hard at keeping his teeth from chattering.

"Kid—I mean, Casey, just sit down, okay?"

Joe sat carefully on an orange plaid, stuffed corner chair that Alvin had found on the side of the freeway, so Casey took their other piece of furniture, a red velour love seat that someone had left in front of their house for the trash pickup to get. The love seat was broken—

anyone who sat on the far left ended up falling into a hole made not just by the broken bottom but also by the arm of the love seat, which had detached from the rest of the body. Hugging the afghan to himself, Casey sat in the love seat, looking anxiously at Joe, who looked tired, and thin, and sad.

"Your mom called this morning," Joe said quietly. "Your dad passed away—I didn't ask how, but I looked up his obituary, and...." Joe grimaced. "I think it was something he did himself."

Casey just gaped at him, opening and closing his mouth, trying to figure out what he was supposed to do with this information.

Joe looked at him and nodded like that was about what he'd expected, and added, "The service is tomorrow."

Casey blinked. "My car can't make it," he said nakedly. "I... I blew a gasket because I changed my own oil and I added too much." He grimaced again. "I'm sorry, Joe. It barely makes it to school and back."

Joe's smile was dry. "You were trying. Forget about it. I'll take you, if you like."

Casey closed his eyes. "You don't have to," he said, wanting so badly to be in the car with Joe, just to talk, just to make things right, that he was almost glad his dad was dead.

"Of course I do." Casey felt a hand—cold and still shivering—on his knee.

"I'm sorry." Casey shuddered and covered that hand with his own, trying to warm it up while it warmed him. "I'm sorry you're always cleaning up their messes. You haven't even met them and they've fucked up your life—"

"Bullshit," Joe said firmly, and Casey looked up into his eyes.

"Bullshit?"

"Yeah. Bullshit. In fact, I owe them, kid—don't ever think I don't."

"Yeah, for fuckin' what?"

"For you."

Casey managed a smile, and his grip on Joe's hand tightened. He kept searching himself inside, wondering at the open blank spot where his father used to be. He couldn't find anything else—no strings, no nerves, no tender places. Was that normal?

Joe opened his mouth to say something, and at that moment, Alvin came in, his short-sleeved button-up shirt untucked from his corduroys and his mullet (seriously, a mullet? Like in high school?) in total disarray at the back.

"Casey, we've got school in, like, forty-five minutes. Are you coming? Because your car is the only one that works!"

"Yeah, in a minute," Casey called, and when Joe tried to pull his hand away, he held it tighter. "Do you work today?" he asked quietly, and Joe shook his head.

"No, but I've got to go in anyway so I can get the next couple of days off."

"Why the next couple of days?"

Joe's look from those dark-brown eyes was inscrutable. "Because I think it's going to take that long."

Casey nodded. "I'll... I guess I'll be ready tomorrow." Oh God. Laundry?

"Service is at two, so let's leave at seven thirty so we can stop and eat. Do you need me to do some laundry for you?"

Casey grimaced. Joe had always been so good at anticipating every need. Casey was tempted to say no, but, God. As much as he had his pride in front of Joe, he thought maybe his pride not to make Joe look bad might be just a little bit stronger.

"Yeah," he sighed. "I've got some slacks and shit, and I think they need to be dry-cleaned, and I don't really have any clean underwear." He didn't add that he'd been washing his hair with dish soap and hoping like hell he didn't get any in his eyes, because that shit *stung* in the eyes, and it wasn't much fun in the privates, either. Well, at least he didn't have lice, right?

"Great," said Joe, one corner of his mouth turned up like he was hearing the subtext. "I'll be here at six thirty, then, with your clothes."

Casey's hand convulsed in Joe's. "I wanted to see you when I was perfect," he admitted. "I wanted to see you when I was a grown-up." His voice dropped to a whisper, and now Joe's hand tightened in his.

"Hell, Casey, do you think you're the only college student who recycled his underwear?"

Casey looked up and saw that reassuring grin splitting between the mustache and the soul patch, and he swallowed and nodded. Joe always saw the best in him. These last six months, missing this man like a hole in his soul, how could he have forgotten that Joe saw the best in him?

"I'll—"

"Casey!"

Casey took a deep breath for patience and rolled his eyes. "I'll be ready tomorrow," he said quietly, and Joe smiled and stood up. He started fishing his motorcycle gloves out of his pocket, and Casey winced. "God, Joe—it's still pouring outside. Are you sure you don't want to stay?"

Joe grimaced. "Kid, I stay here much longer and I'll be tempted to clean, and you would never fucking forgive me. Now get me your clothes in a duffel or something so I can strap them to the back of the bike."

He was gone in a few minutes, and Casey's chest ached as he watched him drive off in the rain. He'd managed to put on some passable jeans and a hooded sweatshirt, but he felt... unkempt, rank, and young. Of course, he thought bitterly, nothing near as young as the night he'd climbed into the man's bed and tried to seduce him as he slept.

"So that was him?" Alvin asked, coming up behind Casey with Casey's backpack and the keys to the car. "The guy you were afraid to talk to because you were too humiliated for words?"

In spite of their poverty, Alvin was maybe one of the most decent things about Casey's living situation so far. He was hopelessly geeky, decidedly straight, and willing to stay up until the dark hours of the night eating pizza and talking about anything at all. Of course, Casey was never sure if the resulting crankiness was because he didn't get enough sleep or he didn't get enough time to beat off, but, well, it didn't seem to matter. Alvin was good people, and after Robbie had bailed, he'd taken the roommate opportunity quickly and without fuss, even though he was as perpetually broke as Casey.

"I didn't say it was rational," Casey said wistfully.

"God. He's like... like *terminally* laid-back. You said he's a *nurse?*"

Casey laughed a little, remembering his few glimpses of Joe at work: competent, low-key, talking quietly with the patients, that surprising smile always at the ready.

"He's really good at it." God, his throat ached, and his chest too. Every time he thought it was from seeing Joe, he remembered that his father was dead and that there were larger things to think about, but that was not what his body was telling him. His body was telling him that there was only one thing that mattered, and he'd just motored away with Casey's dry-cleaning strapped on the bitch seat.

"Casey," Alvin said tentatively, "should I start looking for another roommate?"

Casey looked at him and smiled reassuringly. "If it comes to that, buddy, I'll give you time, okay? I swear, no bailing."

Alvin nodded equably, and they went to school. Casey sat through his classes, took notes on his lectures, and reviewed his homework. Sometimes, a vague sort of gunshot would startle his thoughts, and he'd think *My father is dead*, but that part of him was still sitting on the couch at home, trying to decide how it felt about that.

Most of the time, though, while he struggled to concentrate on his physics class and his advanced trig and his graphic art, what was thrumming under his skin was *Joe, Joe, Joe, Joe....*

JOE was there a little before six thirty, which meant he had with him a new razor, some shaving cream, baby shampoo, a clean washcloth, and a whole brand-new package of socks and underwear, because the whole point of him arriving early was to take care of Casey.

It meant Casey could shower like a human being and his underwear wouldn't chafe either. Joe was looking good in a dark suit and a trench coat that Casey didn't even know he had, and he surprised Casey with a trench coat to go with the newly pressed slacks, shirt, and tie that Joe had given him to wear when he graduated from junior college.

Casey got out of the bathroom smelling like real body soap and feeling all soft and pretty, and found everything laid out on his bed, as well as three new clothes baskets in the corner with his laundry sorted into dark, light, and towels. He chuckled a little as he got dressed. Joe. Joe would probably have done all this for him if Casey had moved in sanely, like a grown-up, and he would have done it just this unobtrusively, with just as much quiet competence, the same way he'd brought Casey into his home.

Casey put on his clothes thoughtfully, suddenly wondering at his hubris. This whole time he'd been humiliated but angry too, because he thought that Joe was just denying everything he felt because of some stupid mind block about their ages, about Joe's role in his life.

It suddenly occurred to him that maybe, just maybe, Joe really was this nice to everyone. Maybe Casey had been young, and stupid, and arrogant. Maybe he'd made assumptions based on things he knew about Joe's sexuality, about Joe's desire for children—oh Jesus, all of those horrible things he'd said to Joe, and really, how wrong could he have been?

But that didn't matter, he realized as he came out of his room to where Joe waited. Joe's hair was back in a braid, and he hadn't taken off his trench coat. He was standing, quiet and still, in the front room, looking outside the dusty, colorless curtains into another day the color of wet concrete. It didn't matter, because Joe was here, in whatever capacity, and what he felt for Casey—*whatever* he felt for Casey—hadn't gone away.

Joe looked up at him as he walked out into the living room, and smiled. "Don't you look pretty," he teased, and Casey blushed.

"You clean up pretty good yourself."

Joe nodded decisively. "Well then, let's get this show on the road."

"Whose car is this?" It was a little Ford Escort sedan, and Joe grimaced.

"Lynnie lent hers to me, since the truck just guzzles gas. I hope it's okay."

Casey looked at him and rolled his eyes. "You're the one who's going to get his legs cramped. It's fine with me."

Joe grinned. "Yeah, well, after we stop for lunch, you can drive."

Casey was suddenly reassured. Whatever it was, however he felt, Joe was still his. Six months of living without had maybe done their job and taught Casey that any Joe was better than none.

Lynnie had a cassette player in her car, so as soon as they passed Sacramento's range for radio, they put in one of the cassettes from the box Joe had brought. Journey started playing, sounding sentimental and old, and definitely not enough to cover the space between them. They could either actually talk to each other or listen to the car bump over the music. Looking out the window was a whole lot of flat gray-green nothin' but cows, so they chose to talk. It was pretty easy, especially when Casey broke the ice.

"So, Lynnie's living in your guest room?"

He heard about it then, about Joe's breakup, about Lynnie's shitty choice in rebound guys and Joe taking her in with a split lip, a black eye, and a baby in her belly.

"Is she just gonna stay there?" Casey asked, and Joe looked sad.

"Naw. Her parents live in Oregon. In about two months, she's going to fly up there and have the baby and get a new start." Joe sighed, and Casey felt the weight of the thing Joe was giving up.

"You offered to marry her, didn't you?" he asked, knowing it would hurt but needing to know anyway.

"No," Joe said quietly, and then he smiled a little anyway. "But I did offer to keep the baby."

Casey looked at him, surprised. "Why didn't you marry her? You wouldn't have cared, would you?"

Joe shook his head. No. Of course not. Not Joe. "No. No, I wouldn't have. But...." He swallowed. "I didn't love her enough for forever. You were right about that. You just were."

Casey looked out the window at the gray expanse of cows, cow shit, and mud, and sighed. For the first time in his life, he felt enough outside of himself to realize that sometimes it sucked to be right, even if it meant you got the thing you most wanted in the world.

"I'm sorry about the baby," he said quietly, and he meant it.

Joe shrugged. "Yeah, well, so am I. But my life ain't over yet, is it? Still got time."

"I'd like to see that," Casey said softly, thinking about big Joe with a tiny, helpless pink thing in his massive arms. "That baby would feel so safe with you. You'd hold it, and love it, and you'd never hurt it or throw it out on its ass because...." Casey's voice trailed off, and he looked out into the shitty day.

"I guess I can't hate him anymore for that," Casey said, hearing that gunshot again.

"Sure you can," Joe said grimly. "But it might be better off if you forgave him for it instead."

"How did he die?"

Joe sighed heavily. "I, uhm, called your mother again after reading the paper," he said apologetically. "I asked so I could tell you myself."

"He shot himself, didn't he?"

Joe's eyes flickered from the nightmare ruler that was Interstate 5. "How'd you know that?"

Casey shook his head. "Just did. It was quick, it would work, and he wouldn't be there to clean up the mess. Let's just say it was sort of how he did things. No time to smoke weed, let's do blow instead, right?"

Joe grunted. "That right there makes the man a damned fool."

Casey laughed a little, thinking of the two times he and Joe had floated together. No, weed was not really something you wanted to do a lot of, but if you were going to get all drifty and floaty, wanted to be out of your body and be somebody else, Joe was the person to do it with, because he'd accept you no matter who you were.

"You've got to have some good memories of him," Joe said softly, and Casey reached for them and found only blankness. Something in him got a little desperate then, needy.

"Probably."

Joe grunted again. "You let me know when it's time to remember them, okay?"

"Yeah. Joe?"

"Yeah?"

"You said you didn't love Lynnie in a forever way."

"Yeah."

"How do you love me?"

Joe sighed. "Can we talk about this later, Casey? I mean… in a good way, but I don't want to have this conversation on a trip to a funeral in fucking Bakersfield."

"In a good way?"

Joe risked another look off the road. "I'm here, aren't I?"

Casey looked down at the little black console of the tiny car. "Yeah. But you're a good guy. You'd be here for anybody."

"No. Not just anybody." There was a pause, and Casey dared to hope, and then Joe gave a sigh. "Oh good, there it is. The turnoff on the map. We're going to be a little early."

"Fuck."

"Yeah, well, it's a six-hour drive—early's better than late."

"Not if you're me."

LOTS of pretty people in black. That was Casey's first impression, and it didn't go away. The grounds were beautiful—lots of ponds with orange fish inside, surrounded by trees, and flat headstones in neat little rows, flush with the lawn.

Bakersfield town proper had a central city and some extensive suburbs around it. The cemetery was in the central city, with an imposing two-story brick building in the front, as well as a little chapel to the side for funerals. Casey didn't know what the big brick building was, but Joe said he supposed it was where people stored the ashes of their loved ones in little boxes, like at a bank vault, and Casey blessed him for that. He tuned out the entire service in the chapel, wondering what aliens would say if they landed on earth and saw that great building that held nothing but boxes of ash.

He was at the point in his fantasy where the aliens figured out how to recombine all of the elements that made a human being and resurrected boxloads of zombies when the service in the chapel ended and everybody migrated outside.

Everyone stood there with their black umbrellas in their black trench coats, and even though Joe planned for most things, he seemed to have forgotten the umbrella, so they stood back away from the crowd, under a tree, where the rain wasn't quite as persistent.

"Do you know anyone?" Joe asked, and Casey finally found himself focusing on the people there.

"The blonde woman in the front who won't stop blowing her nose is my mother, Vivian."

"Okay. Who's the woman next to her?"

"The one with the gray hair that looks like a helmet? That's my dad's mom. They hate each other."

Joe choked back a laugh. "They seem to be leaning on each other now."

"Yeah, well, look at Grandma Spencer. She's telling my mom that there aren't enough people there and they should have had warm snacks at the house and that the mourners aren't well enough organized by the grave site and she would have done better if she'd gone to another cemetery."

Joe grimaced. "People shop around for that sort of thing?"

Casey looked with distaste at the woman in the flawless Chanel suit with the perfectly stylish black pumps and even *jewelry* that seemed accessorized for mourning. "If anyone does, my dad's mom does. My mom would just pick the most expensive and assume that was the best."

Joe grunted. "What would your dad do?"

Casey didn't have to think about it to answer, which was probably why he told the bold truth. "It wouldn't matter—he'd let someone else do it and then bitch about how they fucked up."

"What would he think about all of this?"

Casey looked around and saw a lot of elegant middle-aged people with sober faces and no real expressions. One woman, very beautiful and about Joe's age, was distraught, but she was hanging in the back, with no one to comfort her.

"He'd think they were a bunch of phonies," Casey said roughly, wondering if his father had made any provision for the mistress at all or if he'd just left her there to grieve without even a shoulder to cry on. "He'd say they were just here because they didn't want the world to know they don't give a shit. He used to talk such horrible trash behind people's backs, you know?"

"You don't do that," Joe said, and Casey felt his hand, warm and reassuring in the motorcycle glove, at the small of his back. It was a curiously intimate gesture, and Casey felt some warmth and humanity creeping up his spine and toward his chest. It hurt like hell, and Casey kept talking just so he didn't have to acknowledge the hurt.

"No. No, I don't. I always wondered what it was he said about me. When I left, I wondered if they ever talked about me or what they told the neighbors—was I at reform school, did they send me away to some sort of place that would cure me?" Casey's voice was quiet, and something about the dripping of the trees and the patter of the rain made it seem like he was disappearing. "My mom used to come to my room at night and kiss me good night. Maybe she missed me then— we'd talk about school and grades and stuff, you know, like you and me did over dinner. But I never watched movies with them or went out and shit. My dad might have missed me at the dinner table, but I never really talked there. And still, as stupid as it is, I wonder—would he have missed me? I don't know if I'm going to miss him. I had that same sort of fantasy, you know? That one day I'd see him, and I'd be all college graduate and super successful, and he'd have to respect me or even maybe fear me because he was in real estate, and I don't think he had a college degree. I wanted to say, 'See! Here I am! I'm everything you said I couldn't be, now fuck off!' And now I don't even get to do that, I don't even get to tell him to fuck off, because he told us all to fuck off...."

Casey's face was hot, even in the icy rain, and his chest was full and hot, and Joe's hand on the small of his back was his anchor, and suddenly he was adrift in pain without definition. It wasn't anger or bitterness or mourning; it was just loss, loss for all sorts of things that never really were. He took a deep breath and let it out on a sob, and then another one, and a third, and then Joe's arm went around his shoulders and he wrapped his arms around Joe's solid waist and cried honest tears in the rain.

He was still shuddering the tears out when the graveside service ended and the mourners walked to the pathway next to them. Joe put his hand up on Casey's face to shield him from the strangers, and Casey was grateful until two sets of black-heeled pumps intruded on his vision and he looked up at his mother and grandmother, both of them looking back at him with scowls on their faces.

"You came," his mother said, and Joe let go of his shoulder and grabbed his hand instead.

"It seemed the decent thing to do," Casey mumbled, and he was not surprised at his grandmother's venom.

"If you were going to be decent, you would have come alone."

"Don't you mean die alone?" Joe asked, his voice hard. "Because that's what you left him to do in the first place."

"We couldn't let him live in the house," Vivian Spencer said, her voice tremulous, and Casey looked at his mother without understanding.

"Why not, Mom? I was still the same kid."

"But what you were doing—"

"Was my business. I didn't break in on you and dad having sex. I wasn't going to make you watch."

Without warning, Casey's grandmother's black-gloved hand shot out and smacked Casey's cheek, hard. "You speak with *respect* of your father, young man."

Casey blinked at her, not even bothering to rub his cheek. She hadn't hit hard, but Joe angled his body more protectively. His hand on Casey's back was vibrating with anger.

"I just paid respects to him, ma'am. That was the last respect I think I have left." He looked at his mom. "Thanks for telling me. It was almost human of you. Come on, Joe. I want to go home and see the dogs."

"Wait!"

Casey stopped then and turned to his mother.

"Weren't you a little bit sad?"

Casey swallowed and huddled more into Joe's warmth, basking in the physical closeness that Joe had rarely given, because he'd always seemed to respect Casey's personal boundaries with absolute reverence. Casey appreciated the contact so much now, when those boundaries seemed to have disappeared. "I was, yeah. That's why I cried."

"I mean when you left. Weren't you a little sad to leave us?"

"Yeah, Mom, when I was starving and freezing and willing to get fucked in a bathroom so I could have someplace to sleep, I was a little fucking sad to leave you. But I won't be sad this time. This time I can take pretty good care of myself, and when I can't, Joe fills in the gaps. This time, I'll be just fine, so don't you worry about me."

Joe's arm tightened around his waist, and he leaned his head on Joe's shoulder. He didn't care if they thought he and Joe were lovers. He didn't care what they thought at all.

"Come on, Joe," he said softly. "I'm glad we came, but we're done now."

Joe leaned over and dropped a kiss on his hair, and it felt personal. Casey leaned into him for some more strength, and because he could.

"Yeah, no problem." But he wasn't moving.

Casey looked up and saw that Joe was giving Vivian and Grandma Spencer a measured look.

"He's mine after this. You want to talk to him, you talk to me first. You want to see him, you'll have to see me. He was a class act, showing up here today. You don't deserve that sort of class." He turned away then, Casey tucked under his arm, and paused to look back over his shoulder. "And for the record? Kicking him out might have been the best thing you ever did for him."

Then Joe steered him toward their little car in the parking lot by the chapel. Casey clung to his waist and shivered and wished desperately for their house, and their dogs, and a warm blanket and a chance to talk, and a little bit of peace.

Big Love
~Joe

JOE was shaking, he was so angry. He and Casey had spent six years feeling out how to do the right thing, and there they were, doing the right thing, and that bitch had *slapped* him! *Slapped* Joe's Casey. And Joe, with his size and intimidation, hadn't done anything about it.

They'd stopped for gas on the way into town, which was good because it meant Joe had nothing to do but drive after he sat in the car and roared out of the cemetery. He zigzagged out of town on sheer instinct. They had been in the car for about twenty minutes when Casey actually said something.

"Joe?"

"Yeah?"

"Thanks."

"I'm sorry."

"For what?"

"Those people hurt you. I... I didn't bring you there for those people to hurt you, you know?"

Casey sighed and shifted and leaned back against the seat rest, closing his eyes a little. "It's not your fault I was born," he said, a little bit of humor in his voice.

Joe's mouth quirked up. "Yeah, but I sure am glad I know you now."

The kid shifted in his seat, and Joe felt a hand on his knee. "I'm glad you know me now too. The grown-up me, mostly. More grown-up than six months ago, anyway."

Joe winced. "Yeah?"

"Yeah. I never apologized. You showed up, gave me shit news, took care of me—I never apologized. I acted badly—really, really badly. I... I guess I knew Robbie wasn't really who I wanted. I mean, it's always been you. As far as I know, it always will be. But I wanted you to... I don't know, give me a reason to say no. To tell him no. That's why I got impatient and crawled into your bed. It was... it was stupid. I was stupid. And the things I said...." Casey trailed off, and Joe, confident that they were going to be in fourth gear for a while and he wouldn't have to shift, grabbed his hand.

Casey turned his palm up and squeezed his fingers.

"Maybe," Joe said gruffly, "all I needed was a little bit of time. You think of that?"

"I hoped," Casey whispered. "But these last six months, when I couldn't even see you, it really fucking hurt to hope."

Joe felt a smile start at the corners of his mouth and spread. He took a careful look at Casey, who was looking at Joe's face with hungry eyes and a pucker between his dark brows.

"Don't let it hurt anymore, okay? Hope shouldn't hurt."

Another glance, and he saw the slow smile on Casey's high-cheekboned face. It was a slash of the lips, really, and then a curve. Casey had a lean mouth, and that full-out, shining smile made the grooves in his cheeks pop out. "I won't. How long am I going to have to hope? A time line would make it hurt even less."

Joe felt the blush burning up from his stomach. At odd times over the last six months, he'd relived that kiss. At first it had felt dirty, shameful, to think that he'd let himself be taken advantage of that way, and then he'd felt worse, because dammit, Casey was so much younger than he was. But Casey had turned twenty-one in the time between, and Joe was wondering how long he'd have to wait before that didn't matter anymore. Did he say twenty-five? Joe's parents had had two kids by the time they were twenty-five, and they still, as far as Joe knew, looked at each other with secret smiles when they thought no one was looking. Did he make Casey date other people until he was thirty? God, Joe would be forty-two—and as much as Casey would think four years was forever, nine years seemed like forever to Joe.

Casey's hand was warming up in Joe's grip, and he suddenly pulled it away and squeezed Joe's thigh. Joe gasped and his skin tingled in his thighs, in his groin, and he risked another look at Casey and thought that even with the longer rock-star hair and the lean mouth, he looked beautiful, and he looked grown. If Joe hadn't known him when he was sixteen, he wouldn't see any of the boy in him now.

"Maybe wait until we get home," Joe said breathily and shivered, the unfamiliar fabric of his best suit chafing the creases of his arms and his thighs.

Casey grunted and squeezed his thigh some more. Joe shuddered, six months of pent-up frustration, of yearning, suddenly assaulting his skin. He started looking for a turnoff so he could go get a soda and go to the bathroom and maybe get away from the steamy closeness inside this tiny car.

"I'm done with hoping," Casey said tightly. "I want *now!*"

Casey had large hands for such a slight body, and right now the one on Joe's leg spanned from a few inches above his knee, where his thumb rested, to the aching tip of Joe's sudden erection, where his small finger twitched. Joe shifted, not sure if he wanted the contact or wanted to move away from the contact. It didn't matter—it was a small car, and that tiny brush against the fabric *near* his erection was enough to make him gasp.

He reached down and grabbed Casey's hand, moved it back to his knee, and tried to catch his breath. He scowled and focused on the road. He didn't want to accidentally take the I-580 turnoff that led to San Francisco—it was notoriously hard to spot. A sign for a filling station at the next exit popped up, and Joe snatched his hand back so he could jerk the wheel to the right and make the exit. He couldn't even look at Casey as he was negotiating the turn, and when he pulled up at an ampm and parked in the little secluded spot on the side, he muttered, "Thirsty," and then tried to get out of the car.

Casey didn't let him.

"Wait," he said, his voice a little desperate. "Wait!"

Joe stopped and looked at him, trying to put his customary smile on his face, the one that said he was patient and everything was okay.

Casey knew that smile, and he wasn't buying it. His eyes were narrowed and his mouth was compressed in a scowl.

"What?" Joe asked, his smile slipping even as he spoke.

"Make me hope," Casey begged. "I can wait—I'm not sixteen anymore—but make me hope."

Joe closed his eyes, feeling totally vulnerable, but there had never, ever been a time when he could refuse to make Casey happy.

He didn't kiss by halves. He seized Casey's small face in his big hands and shoved his fingers through that straight sandy-blond hair, and liked the texture so much he did it again. Casey's narrow, streetwise eyes grew wide and shiny and his flat mouth puffed up because his teeth worried it in anticipation. Then Joe framed his face, holding him just so, tilted his head, and lowered his mouth with force and decision.

Casey groaned and opened his mouth at the first touch of lips, and Joe took command. He liked kissing that was hard, with lots of tongue, and he started by tasting the inside of Casey's mouth and *forcing* his tongue to engage. Casey got the hang of it in a moment and brought his own hand up to the nape of Joe's neck, digging his fingers into Joe's neat braid and hanging on for dear life.

Ahhh... kissing Casey this way was *glorious*. He kissed back hard, rapacious, demanding more and more and harder. Their teeth clashed for a moment, and Joe pulled back so he could kiss the groove of Casey's cheek and then the sharp angle of his jaw below his ear. He pulled a pierced earlobe into his mouth and toyed with the stud there, suckling the soft flesh until Casey's hand tightened in his hair and he whimpered. Joe let go of it reluctantly and then breathed softly into Casey's ear, close enough that he knew his mustache would tickle and his breath would sound like the roar of the wind.

"Is this hopeful enough?"

Casey pulled back and glowered at him. "More!" he demanded, and Joe took his mouth—swollen now, open, ready—and answered him.

Casey groaned, and Joe clenched both hands in his hair and held him still. The space of the little Escort was small, the black interior humid, and the rain outside wasn't doing anything to cool their overheated bodies in the unfamiliar wool clothes. Casey's hand, cool and trembling, was an urgent relief as it snuck under Joe's suit jacket and smoothed across his stomach. Joe sucked it in, self-conscious about the slight softness there in spite of the heavy muscle on his ribs and his chest, but Casey made a purring sound as he slid his hand between the buttons of Joe's shirt and under his T-shirt and kneaded the tender, slightly furry skin he found.

For a moment, Joe was torn. For a moment, Joe wanted to keep kissing as badly as he wanted to pull back, button his shirt, mask his vulnerability. Then Casey made that sound again, that wonderful, purring sex sound, and Joe swallowed it with another hard, tenderizing kiss.

He moved one of his hands to Casey's back and scrunched the stiff white shirt in his hand, pulling at it until he found the soft, sleek skin right above his belt. He spanned his hand across it, then delved into the backside of Casey's slacks, warming himself on the softer skin there.

Now it was Casey who pulled back, begging. "God, Joe… now… please?"

Joe pulled back, bumping the steering wheel with his elbow and trying not to throw the car into neutral, because it didn't always take the clutch. As he pulled back, his knees knocked the keys from the ignition, and Joe took three deep breaths and leaned forward, rested his forehead on the steering wheel, and laughed softly.

Casey groaned comically and thrust his hips up a little like he was seeking relief.

"Kid, I'll do anything for you, I swear to God I will, but if you make me fuck you in a Ford Escort, I'll never forgive you."

Casey started to laugh breathily, and Joe took heart.

"Besides," he added, "you said you needed hope. Now all you have to hope for is that it'll be worth the trip back home."

Casey turned toward him, his eyes still half-hooded, his lips parted and swollen, with razor burn on the fair skin of this neck. "Damn. Damn. I don't have to guess *that*. I *know*." He took a deep breath. "Now go get us some coffee, and I'll hit the head, and then I can drive us home, okay? You need to rest up. I've got us some plans."

THEY were both cranky and achy by the time they got to Foresthill. They'd stopped once for dinner at a fast-food place and stretched out, but by the time Joe, who was driving again, pulled Lynnie's car down the wide, flat space that doubled as a driveway, he felt like if he didn't lie down, he'd die.

He unfolded his long, wide body from the car and stretched his fingers to the stars, growling as he did so to help release some of the tension, and he watched as Casey did the same. They'd listened to Tesla and Pearl Jam almost the whole way up—when Casey was still in high school, Joe had taken him to a Night Ranger concert at Cal Expo, and Tesla had blown the snot out of Night Ranger as the opening band. Casey might still have liked Madonna, but Tesla was from their home turf, and it was a sentimental favorite. The result was that in spite of the cranky, achy part of traveling, he was in a good mood, and the tension, the worry of what they were going to be like together, had melted more with every mile.

So, after stretching easy in the moonlight, he reached in and grabbed their coats from the back and threw them over his arm. "I'm going to go put some jeans on and let the dogs out," he said, stifling a yawn. "I need to move a little before we go inside, okay?"

Casey nodded and turned his face up to the crystalline sky. It was cold and looking like snow up here, but unlike the valley and the flatlands, it wasn't raining. "Could you bring out a sweatshirt for me?" he asked. His clothes were still back at the duplex, and Joe knew they'd probably be there for a while. Casey had made it very clear that he had to honor his commitment with Alvin, and Joe understood. They would make time. They would date.

But first they'd make love, and Joe would make it everything.

He had a pretty good idea of how many lovers Casey'd had since he'd arrived on Joe's doorstep, and as unfair as it was, he wanted Casey to forget them *all*. If Casey had been saving the best of himself for Joe, then Joe wasn't going to make him sorry.

He walked into the house quietly, not wanting to disturb Lynnie, and found her awake on the couch, fully dressed, looking moodily out the window. The dogs clattered up to greet him, Hi's tail thumping on the walls and floors as he and Rufus vied for the honor of licking him to death, and he patted them on the head before giving them their heart's desire and letting them out to see Casey.

He looked back at Lynnie and saw that she was standing up and that her three suitcases of clothes were packed up on the floor next to her.

"Lynnie?"

"I'm going to stay with Stacy," she said quietly. "I'll be there until I fly to my folks'. You can forward my mail if you want, but I think I called everyone today."

Joe looked at her unhappily. She was so tiny. He hadn't told her, but the day after she'd shown up on his doorstep, he'd shown up on Brad's. Brad had looked worse than Lynnie by the time Joe was done, and he'd worn his newly battered face to jail when Joe had placed an anonymous call to the cops about the five baggies of rock on the coffee table. Lynnie hadn't done the drugs—she swore up and down that she hadn't—but her respiration had been elevated and her pupils dilated just from being *around* them. When she'd told Joe a month later that she was pregnant, Joe had thanked God—quite literally—that the baby in her belly wouldn't be like the too-thin, too-angry children he had been caring for in the NICU lately. He held them every night and closed his eyes and wished that the power of touch, a thing he'd held sacred all his life, didn't seem to hurt them quite so much.

And now as he looked at her, he knew that any move he made, any attempt to hug or to say good-bye, would do the same thing.

"Are you sure? You know you have a place here," he said quietly.

"Look at him," Lynnie said, her voice troubled. Casey was greeting the dogs with hugs and pets and excited jumping, and Joe felt his entire face glow. "He's so happy."

"Yeah."

"You know, you told me when we first started going out that you swung both ways." She laughed humorlessly. "I thought it was *very* progressive, you know. Sexy. You didn't give a fuck what anyone thought, you'd be with whoever you wanted."

Joe blushed, even in the dark. "I was not aware," he said dryly.

"Yeah, well, it turned my key," she said, her voice just as dry, and Joe laughed a little. They'd done that—been ironic with each other, teased without hardly inflecting their voices. It had been one of the reasons Joe had loved being with her. "It did," she repeated, her voice sinking. Neither one of them had moved to turn on a light, but there was enough moonlight coming in through the window to make her pale face vulnerable and cold. "I never, ever in a million years thought you'd choose him over me."

Joe pulled in a breath. "I never thought it would be a choice," he admitted painfully. "My whole... my whole goal was to get him grown, for him to be whole and well and independent. When I met you—"

"You were pining for him without knowing it," she said, and she wasn't smiling at all. "I'd love to stay here and have my baby, Joe. But the thing is, you'd want that baby so bad, watching me leave with it would kill you. I'll go now, before you get attached. You and him"— she smiled just a little—"you and him, you're going to have to find your own baby. Don't worry. I'm sure he's out there. But my mistakes are mine to keep."

She bent down then like she was going to grab her suitcases, but Joe beat her to it.

"I'll help you," he said quietly, and he took the two big ones. "We filled the car up as we got it up here. I'd like to have it serviced for you, with the trip and all."

"Not necessary," she said. She swung her purse over her hip, grunting. The tight jeans she had, the ones that circled her tiny waist and pegged at the ankles, didn't give her a lot of room with the five months of baby, and she was going to have to stop wearing them soon, but her oversized shirt would probably accommodate her until she was due. "I'd...." She sighed. One of the dogs barked, and they both looked outside to see Casey throwing a stick into the dark beyond the porch light. God, his body was lithe and tight, small muscles, small frame. He probably could have worked out and bulked up, but Joe liked him small, small and sturdy. They'd built the garage and remodeled the top floor and built the chicken coop and gardened together. Joe had no worries about Casey's strength.

"You don't have to do this," he said, not wanting to see her go. They'd lived in an uneasy peace these last few months. She'd cooked and cleaned, and he'd told her not to because he was used to doing it himself or taking turns with Casey. It hadn't been a good system, but it had worked for them.

"I really do," she said, not looking at him. "Because once he stays here tonight, I'll have a constant reminder that you picked him and not me, and you did it before you even knew you could have him."

He grimaced. "It was a near thing," he told her, thinking about how pretty she'd looked in the sunshine and how cold she looked now.

"Only because I could have your babies, Joe. And I still lost by a mile. C'mon."

So he helped her out and loaded her car while Casey looked on from the edge of the shadows. Joe hadn't had time to get that sweatshirt, so as Lynnie backed up and turned around to leave, Casey came up close to him, shivering.

Joe put a warming arm around his shoulders and pulled him close. God, even that shivering body next to his was a luxury. Casey's teeth chattered, and Joe pulled him flush up against his front, and shuddered.

"You feel so right," he murmured, and Casey burrowed closer.

"Why'd she leave?" Casey was looking up into his eyes, and Joe realized how far down he had to bend to kiss him—and didn't mind that much at all.

"Because she didn't want to see this."

Casey's lips were cold and the inside of his mouth was hot, and Joe sank into him like he was a down mattress top. Casey reached up and grabbed around his neck, gave a little hop, and then climbed Joe like a tree. He wrapped his legs around Joe's hips, grinding their groins together and kissing Joe back.

Joe cupped his big hands under Casey's ass and kept kissing and walking, grateful for the summer they'd spent laying the carefully flat paving stones and installing the big light that made their little property not look so vast. He'd worked out his muscles helping Lynnie, and now all he wanted was Casey, who was wrapped around him so tight he was almost a second skin.

Joe made it through the front door, still holding Casey, still tasting him, and he shut the door behind them, knowing the dogs would hang out in their big wooden house by the garage if no one came to get them. The dogs would be okay, but Joe wouldn't be if he had to let go of Casey. The stairs were tricky, though, and Casey slid down his body then. They parted reluctantly when his feet hit the first step, and then he turned around and tore up the stairs with Joe at his heels.

Joe caught him before he hit the bed and pressed Casey back against the wall, holding his hands together over his head with one hand and shoving his other hand under the double layer of T-shirt and dress shirt. He felt that smooth skin under his palm and flicked Casey's nipples, which were extraordinarily sensitive. Casey shivered and thrashed around, and Joe pulled back from that devouring kiss.

"Stop that," he rumbled, and Casey went absolutely still. Joe pinched one of those wonderful nipples, watching as Casey whimpered—but didn't move. He looked directly into Casey's wide gray eyes, wondering if Casey knew what he was giving. Casey whimpered again and thrust his groin up at Joe's thigh, and Joe figured that maybe he did.

Joe released Casey's hands, as they were over Casey's head, and said, "Stay there," experimentally, and sure enough, Casey stayed right there. Joe smiled a little and parted the halves of the shirt and then pushed under the T-shirt, shoving the whole works up and over Casey's hands, leaving him bare-chested and leaning against the wall. Then Joe kissed that vulnerable, pale neck, and then that exquisitely sensitive chest, and then down, going heavily to his knees to kiss Casey's hard, tight little stomach and tease the soft skin there with his teeth. Casey's head thunked back against the wall, and he groaned.

His hands came down and started rooting in Joe's hair, and Joe was busy with Casey's belt and the hook-and-eye fly of the slacks, so he wasn't going to argue. He dragged the pants and brand-new underwear down, holding Casey's weight as he slid pants and shoes and socks and underwear over his feet, and now Casey was naked, his cock and testicles large between his legs.

"God," he said reverently, nuzzling Casey's length with his nose and cheeks. Casey shuddered, because Joe's mustache probably tickled and aroused at the same time. "You're so perfect."

Casey found his hair again, and he had the presence of mind to pull the elastic from the tail so he could finger comb it while Joe used his fingertips and bare lips alone to explore Casey's most sensitive bits. He stuck out his tongue and traced a path from pubes to tip, enjoying the shudder of Casey's hands in his hair. He licked a path around the crown and then teased the little slit, loving the symphony of grunts and whimpers Casey made, the pleading noises in his throat, the increasingly urgent tugs he made on Joe's hair.

"Ah, God... Joe, please! Please... oh God...."

Joe opened his mouth and pulled him all in, relaxing his throat and then swallowing, fondling his balls, tugging on them gently until Casey's scrabbling in his hair became painful and his collapsing knees kept threatening to give out on him. Joe pulled back and wrapped a strong hand around Casey's surprisingly long, thick erection. "Stand up," he commanded gently, and Casey nodded, willing—as he always had been—to do whatever Joe asked, because Joe asked him to do stuff for a reason. Casey shored up his knees and Joe went back to swallowing him, taking him as deep into his throat as he could, heedless of the mess of spit and precome that was glazing his lips and dripping down his mustache.

"God, Joe, I'm going to come... condoms...."

Joe pulled back, smiling a little. "Did you get tested after Robbie?"

Casey nodded and swallowed, obviously trying to think against the odds. "He was my last guy—I'm still at baseline."

Good boy. "I got tested after Derrick, and Lynnie's totally clear," he said, because they were testing for that now, when a woman was pregnant. "Can we—?"

Casey laughed semihysterically. "For the holy love of crap, Joe, yes, we can go without the fucking condom!"

His laugh stopped when Joe took that sweet cock back into his mouth and tightened down, tugging on Casey's balls again, and Casey let out a breathless howl and shot down his throat.

Joe wrapped his arms around Casey's hips and pulled him close, tasting him full and still pumping in the back of his throat, feeling Casey's hands tangling in his hair and declaring irrevocably that their relationship was decidedly, perfectly changed.

Casey's shudders eased up, and Joe pulled back and wiped his face on his shoulders.

"Stand up so I can undress you," Casey murmured, and Joe did. Casey smiled up into his face and pulled the dress shirt off him one shoulder at a time. What was under it was a tank tee, and Casey spent a few moments running his hands over Joe's beefy, muscular upper arms. He paused for a moment at that long-ago scar from Rufus and moved to the side, where he placed a delicate benediction on the raised ridges left by Rufus's teeth.

"I was so scared," he confessed, rubbing his cheek against it.

"I'm fine," Joe said, smiling a little. "I'm fine, but I want to be naked with you, okay?"

Casey nodded. "I want nothing else on the planet ever," he said reverently. He pulled at Joe's tank, and Joe lowered his head so Casey could drag it off.

Joe toed off his shoes while Casey fumbled with his belt and then, in a flurry of impatience, shoved him down on the bed so he could pull off his pants.

The impatience ended, though, when Casey looked up and saw Joe looking at him, a little shyly, from the curtain of his straight black hair.

"Oh!" Casey said, blinking hard.

"Oh?"

Casey pushed a palm against his eyes. "Oh God, you're beautiful," he mumbled, and then he braced his weight on Joe's thighs so he could sink to his knees and bury his face in Joe's middle.

"I'm fat," Joe mumbled, stroking Casey's hair back from his face.

"You're perfect," Casey said, nipping at the skin on Joe's ribs. He stretched up and licked at a nipple playfully before pulling back and grinning. "Yeah, I know, you don't like that."

Joe flushed. "It's the pinching," he admitted. "I'm not sure about the licking—everyone just starts with the pinching."

Casey smoothed his hands over Joe's chest, which was hairy and broad, and then ran his fingers through the hair. "It's soft," he said with wonder. "I've always wondered. Guys my age don't have this."

Joe was lying flat on the comforter—he couldn't cover his hairy old body, so he covered his face. "Please stop," he muttered, and Casey kissed his stomach and then up between his pecs and then up to his neck, along his clavicle. He got to Joe's jaw, and Joe tilted his head to accommodate him and then heard Casey whispering in his ear.

"You are just as beautiful as I always knew you would be," he said, and then he punctuated it with a solid handshake on Joe's cock, which surged back to life after its brief bout of embarrassment.

"Nnng...."

Casey laughed softly. "And this thing is *huge*," he said, pulling back far enough that Joe could see his wicked smile. "I used to try to get a look at that, you know?"

Joe rolled his eyes—and then rocked his hips into Casey's sure grip. "I know—I had to lock your side of the bathroom—unh...."

Joe had his hand on Casey's back to feel the shudder that racked him as he held it tightly and squeezed.

Casey pulled back and looked at him soberly. "I know all about sex with men now," he said, nodding his head seriously. "And I really like receiving, but I want to stay just like this all night, okay?"

Joe felt something painful and precious behind his eyes. "Looking at you? Yeah. Yeah. Me too. Here." He reached into his end table and pulled out the Astroglide and gave it to Casey, who took it in his hand. First, though, he bent his head over Joe's cock and engulfed it all the way to the back of his throat in one smooth motion, and Joe almost came right there.

Casey pulled back and wrapped his fist around it and grinned. "I had to taste it first," he said wisely, and Joe grinned back.

"And?"

"It's awesome. I'm gonna be eating a lot of that in the future."

Joe grinned a little wider, and he and Casey both nodded their heads.

"There's a lot of it to eat!" Casey said, because there was. "God, you're huge!"

Joe shrugged modestly, and then Casey dumped a dollop of lube on him and he gasped.

"Lean back," Casey said, and just like Casey had done everything *he'd* asked, Joe complied. He'd long ago learned that sex was about trust, and he and Casey, they trusted each other from way back. Casey clambered up onto the bed and straddled his waist and then dumped some lube on his fingers and reached back.

Joe frowned and said, "I should—"

"Later!" Casey gasped, and Joe shivered and imagined what it looked like when he thrust a finger into himself and then—oh, he moaned!—another one. Casey moaned some more and then stopped stretching his own asshole and grabbed Joe's cock. It took a moment or two—he lowered himself just enough for Joe's heart to stop and then rose up on his knees, and then lowered himself and then raised himself, the whole time talking them through the process, like Joe didn't know what it was like to bury his cock in another man's ass.

"Oh God, yeah, that's it, a little... *ahhh*... and now back, and now down... *ooooohh*... a little further... a little further... oh... oh fuck... a little more... and now... oh, it's so good coming out... and... oh God... down more... oh Jesus, Joe, you're *huge*... oh God, feels so good... so good, so... oh, more... want more... oh *crap!* I want *more*, oh my *God*, Joe, *fuck! Fuck! Auuuughhhhhh*...." And there he was, sitting down flush with Joe's thighs, Joe's cock completely up inside him, and both of them just held still and shuddered for a moment while Casey got used to his size and his width and... just *him*. And then Casey started to wiggle, to squirm, to vibrate up and down, and it was time for Joe to take charge again.

He sat up abruptly and thrust deep, and Casey stopped talking and gasped, throwing his arms around Joe's shoulders and clutching him tightly while Joe wound his arms around Casey's back and held him so tight, he'd have to know he was safe. Casey trembled for a moment and then started moving again, squeaking when Joe bottomed out in his bottom and gasping as Joe slid out. He couldn't move that fast or that hard in this position, and there wasn't enough friction that way for either of them to come, but for a moment, it was just heaven to hold him, engulf him, wrap around him as he tangled himself around Joe, and they could keep each other safe, as close as they could possibly be.

But they couldn't last that long, and when Casey started moving frantically, Joe tightened his arms again and said, "Hey. Stop."

Casey grew abruptly still, and Joe stood up with him, still joined, and turned around, laying Casey on the bed still impaled on Joe's flesh.

"Auuuugghh... oh *yes!*" Casey gasped, because this position meant Joe was deeper now, and for a moment his hands scrabbled on the comforter until Joe leaned over and grabbed one hand and put it on Casey's prick, and then grabbed the other and put it over Casey's wonderfully responsive nipples.

"We good to go?" Joe asked, out of breath, and Casey begged.

"Please, Joe... oh please... just fuck me... oh God... it's so good... just—*ohmyGod, yes!* Faster! Harder! Oh holy crap, *don't stop!*"

And it was too much and too good and Joe couldn't have stopped if the floor had dropped out from under him. His hips pistoned faster and faster, and Casey shuddered and gasped and *screamed* in pleasure, and it was Casey's scream that did it. Joe roared and fell over, bracing his weight on his hands as he poured himself into Casey's body as he'd never poured himself into another human being, ever.

As he did so, Casey's hand jerking on his own cock became more and more frantic, and he gave another scream, this one higher pitched and shrill, and spurted between them, hot and thick white, as his body spasmed around Joe's. Joe managed to wait until he was done coming to collapse forward, crushing Casey into the mattress for one blissful, awesome moment before rolling over to his side and bringing Casey with him.

His cock was growing flaccid, and it fell out in a gush of come, but Joe was past caring about the mess. This was Casey, here in his arms, and he wasn't going to lose a precious second of it worrying about his jizz. It wasn't like he hadn't lain awake in this room over the past six months, imagining this moment and coming in his hand—the comforter would be okay.

He and Casey lay panting, looking into each other's eyes, for long moments, and although Joe wasn't sure what Casey saw, he knew what he saw.

Casey's almost-bushy eyebrows were arched, because Casey's eyes were open wide, and they were shiny and happy, fixed on Joe's face. His neck was still blotched—and now more razor burn than ever made it even blotchier. His mouth was wide and his lips were swollen and he looked truly, thoroughly marked and used, and the fact that Joe's seed was dripping out of his body and Casey's seed was coating Joe's stomach made that look just so much more arousing.

"That was… oh, God, Joe. That was… I honestly didn't know what the fuss was all about. God. We can do that again, right? Please *tell* me we can do that again!"

Joe's lips curved up into a slow smile. "Give me fifteen minutes and a washcloth and we can probably do it again tonight. Good enough for you?"

Casey smiled back, unbelievably sexy in the dark of the room. "Yeah, old man—I'll be impressed as hell if that's all it takes. But I wouldn't object."

Joe pushed Casey's sweaty hair from his eyes. "I love you, kid. There's not much I wouldn't do to make you happy."

Casey's grin turned serious. "I love you too, Joe. You know that, right?"

"I do," Joe said softly. "I do. And I believe it with everything, or we wouldn't be here."

The grin returned, but it was luminous and brighter this time. "Good."

I Just Died in Your Arms
~Casey

JOE must have gotten up sometime in the night to let the dogs in. When Casey woke up the next morning, achy and sore in a good way, and stumbled to Joe's big newly renovated bathroom to pee, they were there, sleeping on the floor at the foot of the bed, where Joe had put a big dog bed just for them. He must have added it after Casey left, and Casey approved. Sure, the house would smell more like dog this way, but Casey liked the smell of dog, and he'd always felt bad for them when they were exiled to the kitchen.

He looked around the bathroom appreciatively. Joe had let him choose the paint color, and it was cream, with black trim. Very manly, very understated. Very Joe. The place was big, with an oversized tub with a big showerhead—when Joe had been doing it up, Casey had gone for the big fittings, because he'd wanted Joe to spoil himself a little.

Casey stretched luxuriously like one of the inside cats (who were also asleep on the bed) and thought that Joe had certainly spoiled Casey.

Oh… oh Jesus and the saints above, last night had been… oh crap. Everything. Everything that had been promised about sex, from Dev's more and more confident adolescent fumblings to the few quickies he'd had between Dev and Robbie and hell, even Robbie— who was decent in bed—they'd all had the promise of that *thing*, that incredible, fantastic, wonderful *thing* that had happened between him and Joe the night before.

Twice.

Oh God. The second time had been slower, sweeter. Joe had rinsed them both off first with the washcloth after making sure it was warm, and he'd paid particular attention to Casey's nipples, and then his stomach, and then…. Casey shuddered. All points south. Oh yeah. *All* points south. Joe's tongue had followed the washcloth, and Casey had been unceremoniously flipped over onto his stomach and rimmed until he was squirming on the bed, pounding the mattress with that vague, unfocused, titillated arousal of having Joe's tongue caress that tender ring of muscle. He'd finally screamed, begging, and Joe had been inside him, his enormous erection so hard and rapacious Casey was pretty sure Joe had been stroking himself while he'd been rimming Casey, and the thought had made Casey's cock drool without even being touched.

And Joe had proceeded to literally fuck the come out of him, not just pounding into Casey's ass until Casey *howled* into the pillow in front of him, but manhandling him, making him sit up so Joe could reach around, holding his shoulder or placing a hand on the small of his back or his hips to position him just so. Every time Joe changed positions, held Casey's slighter body with those big hands and *made* him do what needed to be done, Casey's arousal ramped just a little bit higher. The second time, when he came, Casey's vision blacked, exploded into red-and-white stars, and he disappeared, shaking in orgasm for a good two minutes while Joe pushed him into the mattress with a big hand between his shoulder blades and fucked him through his climax, and then came himself.

The second time, Casey wouldn't let him go get a washcloth.

"No," he complained when Joe made to roll out of bed. "No. Let it stay."

"Casey…."

"Yeah, it's messy. I like it." He didn't have more words than that, as he'd lain on his stomach, Joe's come drying on his thighs and still trickling out of his body, but it had felt… pure. It was sex without fear—not just of disease but of worry. There was no worry about who Casey would be with this person in the morning. This person was Joe, and Joe loved him. Their bodies, slick and sweaty and spent? That was how they were supposed to be together. Casey didn't want that washed away. He wanted to feel deliciously used and slutty, marked on all parts of him by Josiah Daniels in a way that no one else could be.

Joe had wrapped his arms around Casey then, and they'd slept naked, warmly cocooned under the comforter and cuddled against the elements. Together, they were each other's world.

Casey woke up a little as he was washing his hands after taking a leak, and he found another washcloth in the rack above the sink. He hadn't gotten enough, hadn't had enough time. Joe had been too self-conscious of his own body and too ready to take over Casey's. Casey wanted to taste him, to suck him until he was crazy with it, until Joe's come was running down his chin too.

He padded back to the bedroom quietly, warm washcloth in hand, and wriggled under the covers. Before Joe could engulf him in that colossal hug again, Casey kissed his neck, and then his shoulder, and then down to his stomach. He regretted Joe's thing about the nipples, really, and wondered if maybe they weren't just hypersensitive. Maybe, when they'd been doing this awhile, Casey would spend some time licking them to see if loving them gently would do something that pinching them didn't. But right now, he wanted to nuzzle the hair between Joe's pecs and keep stroking the clearly demarcated path down to Joe's belly button. Joe started to shift, waking up a little, and Casey felt those big hands on his shoulders.

"Whereyagoin?" Joe's voice was slurred in sleep.

Casey pulled the warm washcloth out and very gently began cleaning Joe's flaccid cock—and kind of wished for a ruler. Any guy who claimed to have eight or nine inches had clearly never seen Joe, who really did. The thing was starting to grow in Casey's hand, emerging from the extravagant nest of black hair at its root, and Casey stopped washing and took the entire thing into his mouth, pretty sure that this was the only time he'd ever be able to accomplish this little feat.

And sure enough, it wasn't so little. In a moment it had filled his mouth and he had to pull back if he wanted to breathe. He held it in his hand, loving it. For one thing, it was oddly shaped, uncut, and thinner at the base than it was at the end—and the end was *truly* bulbous, but not the crown. The crown was small, like a baby's fedora perched on a watermelon. He experimented, pulling the foreskin tight around the bulbous end and wiggling his tongue on the ridge of the crown. Joe grunted, and he buried his hand in Casey's hair, massaging hard, so Casey knew he was doing okay. He popped that adorable little crown in his mouth and tightened his lips, getting the head wet and swirling with his tongue, and Joe's grunt turned into a full-out moan.

"Grab it," he muttered. "Hard at the base...."

Casey complied, comfortable with Joe at the wheel even when Casey had his hand on the stick. He stroked hard from the bottom to his mouth, and Joe moaned again. Casey pulled the covers back so there was room to spread out, and Joe did. He propped his feet up and spread his knees *really* wide, *suggestively* wide, and Casey had always been open to that sort of suggestion.

Casey rolled off the bed and repositioned himself at the apex of Joe's thighs, his washcloth in hand. He took that magnificent cock (oh God, it was so beautiful—he'd seen a few, and this one was *amazing*) in his hand and used the washcloth between Joe's furry ass-cheeks, making it ready for that thing Joe had done to him the night before and Casey really *wanted* to do now.

He kept stroking, and when he was done with the washcloth, he went to move his head into classic rimming position, only to have Joe stop him with a jerk in his hair.

"Kid, no one needs to floss *that* badly. You were doing just fine with that other thing!"

Casey blinked and laughed and got the joke, and then he dropped Joe's cock, spread Joe's cheeks, and dug in. The taste was musky (and a little soapy from the washcloth), but not overwhelming, and the *sounds* Joe made as Casey tongued the little pucker. He was hairy, yeah, but once it was wet, that was no big deal. What *was* the big deal was Joe's groan and the way his fist tightened on his own cock as Casey licked. Casey came up for air and grinned, and then he left his thumb rubbing circles over the little ring of muscle while he took Joe's erection in hand, scooting Joe's hand out of the way as he lowered his head and stretched his mouth over the end. Joe groaned again, and his hips bucked, and his hands clenched in Casey's hair again. Casey hollowed his cheeks and let some spit leak through to lube his hand so it slid easily on the shaft, and Joe started to pump his hips smoothly.

It worked *awesome!* Joe made the best noises, growls and grunts and groans. His hands in Casey's hair were tight and controlling but not cruel. Casey groaned, aroused, and kept sucking, kept stroking, feeling the hardness and the veins underneath his palms. Then Joe's hands weren't in his hair anymore, and muscles popped on that soft tummy as Joe leaned up and grabbed him by the arms, hauled him up easily, and draped Casey on top of his body. He leaned his head up, and Casey plundered his mouth for a kiss and then ground his erection up against Joe's, shuddering when the velvet skin of their cocks slid together.

Joe reached down with his big hand and grabbed the two of them together, and Casey braced himself with his knees on the bed to give Joe room. Their hips bucked as Joe let their skin slide together and it felt so good, and Joe was making those growls, grunts, and groans again, that foreskin giving extra slipperiness to everything involved. Suddenly, unbelievably, *Casey* was the one coming, and he buried his face in Joe's chest and ground out a howl as his come, slippery and hot, coated Joe's hand.

That must have been Joe's trigger, because his other hand, the one splayed on Casey's back, pulled up into Casey's hair and made a fist, and he closed his eyes, threw his head back, and growled as he came, their come mixing together in a *true* mess, all over their bodies.

Casey just lay on him and twitched for a few minutes, and Joe pulled his come-covered hand out from between them and smacked Casey lightly on the ass. Then he wrapped those great arms around Casey's shoulders and hugged him so tight, Casey thought he might feel safe for the rest of his life.

Their breathing finally evened out, and Joe laughed softly with what breath he had. "Casey?"

"Hm?"

"Can we shower *now?*"

Casey chuckled weakly. "I dunno. Can you carry me to the shower?"

"Probably—but I might throw my back out, and then where would we be?"

Casey pushed himself up and then scooted—slimy cock and all—so he could lower his mouth to Joe's for another kiss. "You're not that old, you know."

"I'm not today," Joe said seriously, and Casey realized that now that Lynnie was gone, he really had no one.

"You know, my lease is almost up. I told Alvin I wouldn't leave him in the lurch, but if we could give Alvin a place to stay, I could stay here."

The hope in Joe's eyes was hard to bear. "It's a long commute," he said, obviously trying hard to stomp on that plaintive note in his voice.

Casey shrugged. "There's restaurants up here. I'll get a job up here, go to school three days a week down there. It's no big." He remembered that arrogance he'd had six months ago and looked down, flushing. "That is, you know, if you don't mind Alvin here. And you want me."

That massive hand was in his hair again, pulling Casey gently back so they could look eye to eye. "Casey, I can not conceive of a world where I did not want you."

Casey wrinkled his nose. "Have the Mormons been knocking on the door again?"

Joe blushed. "Lynnie used to give them rides to the house—she got really bored before she found a job her ex-boyfriend didn't work at."

Casey laughed a little. "God. I feel bad. I feel like I kicked her out—and she lent you her *car*!"

Joe grimaced. "Shower," he said, because apparently there was no way to make that situation better. "Shower, and then breakfast."

One of the cats had taken off when the sex began and now she jumped up on the bed and put a delicate paw on Joe's shoulder and insinuated a wet pink nose between them to touch Casey's cheek.

"And then?" Casey asked, scratching Nick on the head. Nick, always the loudest, purred and fluffed her long orange fur.

Joe's hand came up and stroked the hair away from Casey's face. "And then us," he said. "Us. You and me. We can watch movies, we can talk. I've got some work on the house we can do together, like moving a phone line up here and other shit. We can make love. I'm sure the dogs will suck up some of your time. But we yelled at each other and then you left. If you're coming back, I want to make sure it's going to be for a while."

Casey nodded soberly. Yes. Forever.

He wanted to say it then—hell, he was dying to say it for the rest of the weekend and for the next two years. But he didn't. Joe may have said good-bye to Lynnie, but he hadn't said good-bye to the idea of children, and Casey hated the thought of Joe ever giving up a dream for him. As much as he would sally forth like forever was what was in his mind, as much as he would hope, he wasn't going to jinx this moment, this thing he was pretty sure they had, and tell Joe that he'd never be a father because Casey wasn't going to budge.

"You're going to have a hard time getting rid of me" was what he did say, and he said it lightly, and he said it to make Joe smile, because he didn't want to think of a time or a place where he might ever have to leave this place again. This was his home, and Joe had made it his home, and Joe might have been the one complaining about being old, but Casey was starting to think that he was too old in his heart to ever want to give up home again.

THE funeral had been on Thursday, and both of them had called in until Monday, so they really did have three days together.

Three easy days where nothing and everything happened. Three days where they fell asleep after having mind-blowing, achingly tender sex and woke up naked, tangled in each other's arms. Three days where their time in between was spent working on the property or watching movies that Joe hadn't wanted to see without Casey and Casey hadn't been able to watch without a VCR.

Their conversation wasn't always profound—but then, it hadn't been when Casey was living there, either. It was ordinary, just like Joe, which was why every minute of it felt perfect and more perfect.

On Saturday morning, the brand-new phone next to the bed rang, and Casey was closest to it. He rolled over reluctantly and got it on the third ring, giving a happy grunt when Joe followed him and grabbed him around the waist, pulling his body back to the warm center of the bed. (They were on their third set of sheets by Saturday morning. This set was olive green. Casey liked it very much, but he wanted to put some navy trim on it.)

"'Llo," he murmured, and he was actually relieved when he recognized the voice on the other end of the line.

"Casey? I'm sorry, honey, did I wake you?"

"No worries," Casey mumbled, thinking that was always the stupidest question on the planet. Of course someone woke you if you sounded mostly asleep.

"Well, I'm sorry. I didn't even know you were staying back with Joe. Good. I think he missed you."

Casey blinked hard. "Yeah, I'm back for a couple of nights. Maybe longer at the end of the semester. How are you, Mrs. Daniels?"

"Oh, I'm fine. Just haven't talked to Joe for a while. Wanted to know if he's finalized his Christmas plans."

Casey yawned. "I dunno." They hadn't talked about that yet. "Here, why don't you ask him?" Casey rolled over a little. "Joe," he muttered, "it's your mom."

He lay back down then, thinking he could probably fall asleep for another hour or so. They'd worked hard, clearing the foundation for the little mother-in-law cottage Joe was planning behind the chicken coop, and then they'd fucked solidly into the deep a.m. Casey figured they'd earned a nice lie-in this morning, as soon as Joe hung up the phone.

"Hey, Mom," Joe said sleepily. "Yeah, Casey's here. No, we're in bed, why do you ask?"

Casey's eyes shot open and his heart started pounding wonky in his ribs. He rolled over abruptly and saw Joe blinking, like he was maybe just now realizing what he'd said.

"Yeah, Mom," Joe said, catching Casey's eyes and grimacing. "Yeah, together." He pressed his lips together. "Because sometimes I swing that way." There was another pause, and Casey winced, because the squawking on the other end of the phone did *not* sound happy. "Yeah. I know he's not just a 'swing', Mom. Why do you think he moved out?"

Joe actually sat up in bed and clutched the covers to his chest like a virgin girl. "No, *not* because I wanted it and he didn't!"

Casey sat up in outrage and grabbed the phone before Joe could even protest again. "Mrs. Daniels? Yeah?"

"Casey?" Oh God, she was obviously upset. "Casey, you and Joe—"

"I've loved him since I've known him, Mrs. Daniels. He just finally stopped fighting."

There was an absolute silence on the phone, and Casey felt like every pore of his body was breaking out in a sweat. "Mrs. Daniels?" he said hesitantly, and Joe shook his head and rolled his eyes, grabbing the phone back with a muttered "Give me that!"

"Mom?" he said, pulling his hair out of his face with one hand and shaking it down his back. "Mom? You, uhm...."

Finally, a quiet question. "Yeah, Mom. I know. I know what this means. Yeah, I'll ask him. Bye."

Joe handed the phone to Casey, who put it in the cradle without a word. Then Joe lay back down on his side and gestured imperiously for Casey to scoot in back against him, and Casey did. There was no question here who got to be the little spoon—Casey wasn't going to argue. When he was tucked securely against Joe's naked body, clutching Joe's hand to his chest, he finally got up the courage to say something. "So?"

"So what?"

"What does it mean? That I'm here?"

"Well, Casey, I think it means we're gay."

Casey grunted and sat up again. "Well I know *I* am. God, Joe, don't be dense. You just came out to your *mom*! What did 'I know what this means' actually *mean*?"

Joe sighed and sat up next to him. "She gets 'gay', Casey. I know we think of California as the Left Coast, but there is actually a fair amount of liberalism back where I'm from. And my parents belong to that branch of Quakers that are usually, by definition, tolerant. Their lives are about kindness and service and seeking the truth of God's word." Joe sounded glum. "It got them burned as witches a lot back in the day—all the shit the Puritans said was the work of Satan, the Quakers simply accepted as human."

"So...," Casey said, his heart so high up in his throat it was hard to swallow. "Your mom...."

"She's happy for me because she knows I love you. If that love's changed, well, she knows me. She knows it's still love."

"But what does 'I know' mean?"

Joe sighed. "Are you really going to make me state the obvious?" His brown eyes were mild, and accepting, and sad.

Casey felt his mouth wobble, which went with the chin quiver, which went with the fact that all of his muscles seemed to be wrapped around his throat. "Say it," he whispered. "I want to hear you say it so it's not between us ever again." Of course it wasn't that easy. But for the moment, he'd pretend.

"Fine," Joe said, resting his face on his knees. His hair fell behind him, and not for the first time since Casey had seen this big, burly biker on a foothill back road, Casey saw past the mustache and the soul patch, saw beyond the hair, and saw a relatively young man, probably as vulnerable in his gentleness as Casey had been in his youth. "It means that you don't have a functioning uterus, so we're probably not going to have children." Yeah. This was not going away, whether they talked it to death right now or not.

Casey suddenly felt that loss almost as keenly as Joe. "I'm sorry," he whispered, his eyes burning with real, sudden, unanticipated pain.

"That you fell in love with me? That you made it stick until I loved you back the same way? Don't be."

Casey nodded and wiped his face with the back of his hand, and was reassured when Joe reached out and grabbed it and squeezed.

"Okay," he said, lying badly, "I'm not sorry at all. What are you supposed to ask me?"

"If you'll come with me back east for Christmas."

Casey scooted over close enough to lean on him as they both sat up in bed, carefully not looking at each other, the blankets in their laps. "You're going back east for Christmas?"

Joe shrugged and looked sheepish. "You weren't going to be here," he said gruffly. "And my mom could tell I was grieving. She actually just wired me the plane tickets and told me to make sure I had the time off work—that's what the phone call was about. I didn't really have a whole lot of choice in the matter."

Casey just looked at him. "I have no money," he said practically, "so it's all you. Am I going?"

Joe reached out and smoothed the hair from his face, then cupped his cheek. "Are you?"

Casey nodded. Yeah. Yeah. No bullshit, no letting Joe pretend (as if Joe would!) that this was something he did in California but not at home. "I want official. I want Mom and Dad and family. I want to meet your brothers and sister and play with their kids. I don't want a soul on the planet to doubt I'm yours. How's that?"

Joe smiled a little. "Yeah. That'll work."

"Good." Casey took his hand then and held it to his chest and tried to smile, but he couldn't. It was huge. It was an amazing gift, and he wasn't going to look it in the mouth. But he wasn't going to forget this cost, either.

SUNDAY evening, Casey put on his slacks and dress shirt (which he'd freshened in Joe's dryer) and a pair of underwear for the first time in three days. Joe put on his jeans and a button-up Hawaiian shirt, and Casey braided Joe's hair back and made sure his soul patch and mustache were trimmed, feeling intimate and privileged as he did so. They went out to dinner at The Black Angus, and although neither of them were up to the scrutiny of holding hands, Joe kept his knees pressed against Casey's the whole time.

They went to see *The Last of the Mohicans* next, and Casey ogled Hawkeye's chest, and Joe ogled *both* leads, and finally, finally, Joe took Casey back to his crappy little dump in Roseville.

"You'll ask him?" Joe said as they were parked outside the tiny duplex off Vernon Street, and Casey looked at him, sitting in the November dark.

"Alvin?"

"No, some other roommate!" Joe sounded unaccountably tense.

"About watching the house over Christmas, or about moving in after finals?"

"Both."

Casey looked at him, but Joe was carefully looking outside the truck into the moonlight. "Yeah," he promised, but something about Joe's urgency bothered him. He went to say something, ask, find out why, but Joe beat him to it.

"You know," Joe said, almost overly casual, "I lived alone in that house for almost a year before you came along. I had a few women there, a few men, parties every now and then—I was fine. I was. I loved the silence and the trees and the feeling of being all by myself. I actually thought of getting a dog of my own but thought that might be too much company, really. I liked it quiet. I liked being by myself."

Joe turned to him, and something about the way his hair fell out of his braid and forward into his face made Casey see that vulnerable mouth, those even cheekbones, and remember that Joe had only been twenty-seven when he'd picked Casey up off the side of the road, and that thirty-three was really not that old.

"But not anymore?"

"You left," Joe said softly, looking down at the steering wheel and picking at the vinyl cover with his fingers. "You left, and I thought I could hear my heartbeat in the house. If it wasn't for the dogs, I could have heard it echoing in our little valley. I missed you. I missed you so badly it was like I couldn't breathe. Like my heartbeat just expanded, squashed my lungs, stopped up my chest. I woke up in cold sweats, missing you. After Lynnie moved in, I woke her up four, five times, half-asleep, groggy as hell, asking her where you were, because you weren't in your room."

Casey swallowed hard. All those years of loving him, of caring for him—that didn't just go away because Casey got pissed off and moved out. Even if Casey and Robbie had stuck, it hadn't been right, just yanking himself out of Joe's life.

"I'm sorry." He mouthed the words, but his throat was so tight that he wasn't sure if Joe heard him.

"I mean, one fight and you just disappeared." Joe finally faced him, the one thing still unspoken between them making him as bare and as naked as a baby's powdered bottom. "God, Casey. I'd always thought that at the very first, you and me, we'd at least be friends. I—I want you home with me because if I leave you here, I'm not sure who we are."

"Friends," Casey said, swallowing hard. "We're friends. If I never go back home, if this weekend just disappears and never happened, I swear, Joe. I swear it. We'll still be friends."

Joe nodded. "Good," he said, and some of that nakedness disappeared. "Although it's probably pretty good we're gonna keep fucking—because that's sort of what we told my mother, right?"

Casey nodded. He was still a little blown away by that. A mother who still loved her son, because that was what mothers were supposed to do. He'd seen it work with Dev, but that had been different somehow. That had been Dev; Dev was spoiled in almost every way. Nothing about Joe had ever screamed "entitlement," but apparently that wasn't what you needed when you came out of the closet. Apparently all you really needed was someone who just loved you because that was who you were.

Someone like Joe.

"Either way," Casey said into the rainy darkness. Their breath was starting to steam up the windows of the pickup truck, and Casey sighed. His car's defroster had gone out two weeks ago. Joe was going to start the engine and all this fog was going to disappear. Tomorrow Casey would be driving to school and Alvin would be in constant motion, wiping the moisture off the windows as they went.

"Either way what?"

That pause had gone on a little long.

"Either way—friends or lovers. I won't just bail on you again, Joe. You'll always know I'm coming back, okay?"

Joe nodded, and then he looked up and smiled, a sudden heat in his eyes and the fullness of his mouth. "C'mere, kid, and prove it."

The words were all bravado, but the kiss? Was all sweetness, all tender touches of skin, gentle, tentative sweeps of tongue. It was a kiss that begged, and that said good-bye for now and not forever, and Casey sighed when Joe pulled back.

"I work a twelve tomorrow. Are you two going to be home in the evening?" he asked, and Casey shook his head no.

"I work tomorrow night."

"Spaghetti Factory?"

"Yeah."

"'Kay. I'll be by to switch keys with you. I have Tuesday off, and I'm going to work on your car."

Casey flushed. "I don't need you to fix my—"

"Casey, what do I do for a living?"

Trick question? "You're a nurse."

"Who do I see every day?"

"Are you still working in the NICU?"

"Sometimes. But sometimes I pick up shifts in the ER. Would you like to know who I see?"

Okay, so he knew where this had been going in the first place. "Crash victims," he sighed. "Yeah, Joe. Go ahead and fix my car. Alvin will be thrilled."

Joe pulled Casey close again and gave him a kiss on the cheek, a sweet, intimate gesture between two people who would see each other again. Casey turned to him and kissed him on the lips quickly and then wiggled out of the car before they ended up having sex on the first date. "Joe?"

"Yeah?"

"I love you. Drive safe."

"I love you too. You too."

Joe waited until Casey got to the foyer, and then roared off into the night, and Casey opened the door to their duplex without any ceremony at all.

"Hey, Alvin!" he cried, waiting for Alvin's muffled "Yeah?" from his room. Casey stayed outside and talked through the door. It was best not to go into Alvin's room without a lengthy introduction. They had no television, no computer, and very few books. Alvin had one diversion, and he was apparently going for some sort of world record in it, and although he was hung like a hippo, Casey didn't want to see it. Unfortunately, *that* ship had sailed. At least three times. "Alvin, how do you feel about living rent-free in Foresthill?"

Alvin's voice was strained and breathless. "Will there be free cable?"

"Yeah—all the Skinemax you can ask for."

There was a grunt and a faint groan, and when Alvin spoke through the door next, he was panting like a sprinter at the line. "Sounds… great! How're we getting to school?"

Casey smiled a little. "Give Joe time. He'll take care of that too."

And he would. Joe didn't talk about God a lot, but Casey was pretty sure he was out there, or Casey would never have met Joe.

I Still Haven't Found
What I'm Looking For
~Joe

THE look on Casey's face as the plane circled La Guardia was worth the cost of the plane ticket alone.

"Joe, look! That's New York! That's New York *City*!"

"Yeah, Casey, I know. It's been there for a while."

Joe looked over Casey's shoulder and tried not to shudder. Everyone knew that skyline. His parents had taken them into the city a lot when he'd been a kid—Statue of Liberty, with her close little double helix stairwell? Yeah, Joe had done that. Top of the Empire State Building? Joe had done that too. He'd stood at the base of the Twin Towers and looked breathlessly up, and, the summer he was thirteen, his mom had taken him into town to see a production of *Jesus Christ Superstar*. He'd come away with a greater appreciation of rock and roll but had still quietly refused to participate in the Sunday meetings.

"Are we going to get to go there?" Casey asked, looking at Joe with shining eyes, and Joe smiled back a little.

"Yeah—my mom got us tickets to go see *The Nutcracker* at Rockefeller Center. We'll probably spend a day or two in The City." (Funny how The City changed shape on the West Coast. Joe had always thought San Francisco was a lot more intimate than New York, but that didn't mean he wanted to drive there a lot now either.)

"Ballet?" Casey's wrinkled nose was very adolescent, and Joe chuckled a little and then swallowed again because they'd started their descent. He *really* hated air travel—he'd forgotten how the cabin's pressurization made your skin feel horrible and tight and your feet swell and just caused general discomfort. He was glad they'd abolished smoking on the plane—when he'd flown out to school in '78, the smell had almost made him sick, but not much else had changed in the intervening fourteen years. Besides, the airline had *just* gone smoke-free, and the smell still lingered.

"Don't knock it," Joe said, smiling a little. "*The Nutcracker* is the one ballet you've heard all the music to—you'll enjoy it."

"Will you?" Casey turned to him curiously, and Joe summoned a smile.

"Yeah. Yeah, I'll love it. Jeannie always loved it. It's sort of a sentimental favorite."

Casey's eyebrows—really dark, in spite of the sandy gold of his hair—furrowed, and he looked at Joe curiously. He and Alvin had moved all their stuff in the week before the plane took off, and Casey had been sleeping in Joe's bed for a week straight. It wasn't long enough to ease that deep terror Joe still harbored that he wasn't in the house, that somehow, Joe had lost him again when he hadn't been looking. Alvin was there now, enjoying having the place to himself, and watching the dogs, which was a plus. Joe had planned to have one of the neighbor kids—one of the ones he could hear playing basketball at night—come watch the animals, but Alvin was a hell of a lot more convenient.

"When was the last time you went home?" Casey asked, like it had just dawned on him.

"Nineteen eighty-six," Joe said promptly.

Casey frowned again. "So, the Christmas right before…."

"Right before we met, yes."

"Why haven't you gone back? I mean, if you didn't want to take me, I was old enough to stay alone?"

Joe looked at him and shook his head. "Like I was ever going to leave you alone," he muttered.

"I was a good kid!" Casey protested, and Joe nodded.

"You were! But you didn't deserve to be left alone. And I wasn't going to subject you to my family, either."

"Your mom sounds nice."

Joe sighed and tried to unpop his ears again. "My mom *is* nice. She could be one of the nicest, kindest, most tolerant human beings on the face of the planet."

"Then the problem is?"

"Kid, just look at the view, okay? You'll meet them soon enough."

Casey sighed. "Are you ever going to stop calling me 'kid'?"

Joe looked at him sideways and smiled. "Give it fifty years. Maybe."

Casey shrugged and watched that skyline grow nearer and nearer, and Joe watched Casey light up with the adventure of it all.

JOE'S brothers were there at the airport, all three of them. Peter, David, and Paul. They were all clean-cut men in their forties and late thirties, with Christmas sweaters and parkas and leather gloves, who shook Joe manfully by the hand and helped him pick up his luggage. Joe introduced Casey as his roommate, and Peter—the oldest—frowned a little, David rolled his eyes, and Paul winked. Paul was the youngest— apparently someone had filled him in on the roommate code of gay men, and he didn't give a ripe shit. Joe decided right then and there that he'd always loved Paul best.

Casey insisted on carrying his own suitcase—it was hard to miss. Joe had taken him out shopping for luggage right after finals, and he'd come back with purple.

"Really? Purple luggage, mustard trim?"

"I want people to know who I am."

"I know who you are, and who you are is not purple. Lime green on a black T-shirt, maybe, but not purple."

Casey had scowled at him. "They don't have lime green with black, Joe. I want your family to know us. For all I know, this is the last time you'll take me to see them!"

Joe looked at him in horror. "For shit's sake, why would you think that?"

Casey blushed, there in the luggage department of Montgomery Ward. "I'm assuming they're not going to want me back."

"Oh, fat chance. My mother's going to want to adopt you."

But Casey's blush didn't go away. "As long as no one assumes that's what you're *doing. And that's why I want the purple luggage."*

"Awesome, Casey. Seriously, seriously awesome. Bitchin'. Rad." *And then Joe went and plunked down four hundred dollars on what he would forever think of as "I'm having sex with Joe" luggage.*

And now Casey clutched his purple luggage suspiciously and waited for Joe's family to say something heinous, like his own family had. Joe could forgive him for that. Being called an abomination for bringing your boyfriend to your father's funeral wasn't going to fade fast, was it?

But Joe's family was who they always had been. Joe sent them letters, took their phone calls, sent them baby gifts—they may have never *thought* about the gay thing, and, well, it looked like Peter was going to have the grim big-brother talk with Joe when they were in *private*, but in spite of Joe's *personal* disappointment in God, his family continued to use their lives and their treatment of other people as an example of God's plan for the world.

Joe had never been so proud of them.

His brothers talked about kids and family and work. Peter was a cardiologist, David was a pediatrician, and Paul was a history teacher. They updated Joe on Mom and Dad, both of whom were aging nicely and staying incredibly active. They complained about their kids (Peter had four; David and Paul each had three) and praised their wives. (This, Joe thought, was why they were all still married.) They cracked the occasional dirty joke (and didn't look at Casey to blush even once) and picked on Cheryl unmercifully. The only thing that would have made that funnier was if she had actually been in the car.

"No, no, no!" Paul said enthusiastically, turning to Joe, Casey, and David in the backseat. "No. You had to hear her, little bro. So her kid has his finger up his nose—like, you know, every kid in the history of kids in the history of fucking history, and she turns to me and says, 'He's very tactile. We think he's gifted.'"

Casey, who had been enjoying their banter for most of the trip, hid his face in Joe's shoulder and guffawed, and Joe choked back a snicker.

"No!" David said on the other side of Casey. "That's not the best part! The *best* part is, Caleb pulls out like… like… I swear, I see sick kids every freakin' day, and I've never *seen* a booger this size. It was epic! It was the great wall of booger on this kid's finger—"

"David!" Peter winced, pained. "Do you talk to your patients like this?"

"Yes, Peter, yes I do, and they love me. So anyway, Joe, this kid pulls out this booger and Paul says, 'Oh my word, Cheryl. Is *that* a gift too?'"

"Yeah, yeah," Paul affirmed, keeping his body twisted around in the car. "And right at that moment, Cheryl pulls out a Kleenex, because, I don't know, she keeps them in her sleeve like Nana used to, and she goes after the thing, and suddenly Caleb realizes what she's doing, and lets out a shriek and says, 'It's *mine*!' and takes off through the house, the great wall of booger just dangling from his finger. Cheryl goes tearing after him, and by then, David and I are—"

"Oh God… Lisa too—that's Paul's wife, Casey—she was laughing so hard she literally sat down on the floor, and David sat down with her, and the whole time, we can hear Cheryl pounding around in the upstairs of Mom and Dad's house, screaming—"

And Paul and David chimed in for the finale, "Caleb, you come back here with that thing before you lose it!"

Joe lost it completely, and so did Casey, laughing until they couldn't breathe as Peter made his way—soberly and responsibly— through the snow-clogged roads.

They'd cleared La Guardia and The City by now and were up near Harriman State Park, and when they finally calmed down, Casey looked around him and gasped.

"Joe—Joe, there's no city. It's… it's all hills. And there's snow—I mean, not that shitty stuff they had on the ground at La Guardia but—"

"Yeah," Joe said, happy. It was pretty country here. The towns were crowded, but they were also intimate, and the country between them was often rural and rolling. "It's pretty."

"Not as pretty as Foresthill," Casey said loyally, and Joe put his hand on Casey's knee.

"No," he said quietly and squeezed. He felt it then, the thing he'd known when he'd given in to Casey so young. Casey would want to see the rest of the world. Joe might want to go sometimes, but Casey… Casey wanted to see it *all*. Joe had listened that night after he'd put Sunshine in Casey's care, and he'd heard Casey talk about the things he wanted to do or see. Being locked up in Foresthill with Joe was not part of those things.

"Hey," Peter said like he hadn't noticed they were having a moment, "since we're getting close, we actually do need to talk about Cheryl."

"What about her?" Paul rolled his eyes a lot when he talked. Joe wondered if it was a symptom of working with teenagers.

"You know!" Peter was shaking his head in the mirror and looking at Casey significantly, and it was David who let out the exasperated snort.

"Yeah, Joe? You know how Mom was all excited because Cheryl's husband is actually a Quaker too? Well it seems he's been going to the meetings of that branch with the stick up their asses, and she wants to talk you into screwing women instead of Casey."

Paul laughed and put his hand over his mouth, and Peter got that long-suffering look he used to get when he had to be in charge and the two of them wouldn't stop fighting—or putting things that moved in Cheryl's bed.

"Nice, David. Real nice. I can't believe people let you around children."

"I can't believe people let you *have* children," David sassed—as much as a thirty-eight-year-old man *could* sass. "There should be a law against being too boring for words."

"In high school it's called Social Darwinism." Paul snickered, and then, like they shared the same brain (which Joe had always suspected growing up), Paul and David stopped laughing and sobered.

"Just remember, Joe, we've got your back. Mom and Dad got your back. Cheryl and Chris, they're just two small voices, nattering away in a cave."

"Jesus, Paul," David said with admiration, "that was almost poetry."

"Well," Paul said, trying to look humble, "I do like to read."

The brothers busted up again, and the atmosphere in the car lightened, but Joe remembered Cheryl. They should have been best friends—she was only a few years older than he was—but Jeannie had loved him best, and Cheryl? Well, as an adult, he could figure that she'd probably felt left out, but that wasn't how she'd been as a kid. As a kid, she'd been an insufferable tattletale, like the entire focus of her identity was on being "the good one." He'd never really thought Cheryl *was* that good, but she sure did seem to know a lot about following rules. Joe had developed an antipathy toward rules after Jeannie died, and so whatever relationship he might have had with his remaining sister seemed to have been doomed from the time he turned seven.

But he put her out of his mind for the rest of the three-hour trip to their little suburb outside of Bethel. He wanted to hear from his brothers, share in their families, and reconnect. He wanted Casey to meet them, and know where he came from, and see that families didn't always have to mean pain.

And Casey was with him, hanging on their every word, especially when they told stories about their childhood. Joe squirmed a lot because the way his brothers remembered it, he was a hell-raiser, when it hadn't seemed that way at all.

"It was a perfectly logical thing to do," Joe said, blushing, and Casey leaned forward so he could look up into Joe's face.

"Oh my God, you're blushing!" Casey brought wondering fingertips to Joe's cheeks, and Joe snatched his hand—but not roughly.

"It wasn't the way they tell it at all," Joe protested, and even Peter egged him on.

"Yeah, Josiah, tell us how it really happened?"

"Okay, for starters, I did not *steal* Dad's car."

"No?" Paul arched his eyebrows, and Joe soldiered on.

"I told him Cheryl wanted to use it, and he said yes, so that's why I took it."

"You were twelve," Peter said grimly, and Joe turned to Casey a little desperately.

"This wasn't that big a deal back then—not out in the country," he said. "We knew kids who were driving all the time—it's not like California right now, okay?"

Casey laughed a little, indulgently. "I'm not going to go out and commit a crime, Joe. Finish the story!"

"Okay, what you didn't know was that they were going to use those rabbits for food—"

"Those rabbits belonged to the Wilsons!" Paul protested. "They could have used them for underwear! That still doesn't explain—"

"But their son, Barry—you remember him?"

"Yeah." Paul nodded. "I remember."

"Well, he'd raised them from hand. He'd *bottle*-fed them. So he comes to me, all upset about how his pet bunnies are going to end up on a spit that night, and I... well, I did lie to Dad, but I got use of the car, and *that's* why I stole the rabbits."

Casey looked at him curiously. "Okay, I get that. But the rest of it?"

Joe shrugged. "Well, I managed to get the hutch into the car and even managed to clean out the car, but I couldn't keep the hutch next to the house, because it was filthy. So I pulled the rabbits out and put them in the bathtub so I could hose off the hutch and put it down in the basement, where it's nice and warm, right?"

"And you put the rabbits in the bathtub," Casey giggled, "about ten minutes before—"

They finished together. "Cheryl took a bath."

Joe nodded. "The dumb thing was, she thought I'd done it on purpose—because that bathroom led straight to her room, and suddenly the little fuckers were *everywhere*, eating her clothes, shitting on her bed, eating her homework... oh God. She was *not* going to forgive me for that!"

Paul and David were still laughing, but they did sober enough for Paul to say, "She had it out for you from the very beginning. I swear, if Jeannie hadn't been there when you were born, she would have smothered you with a pillow."

Joe shrugged. "She was jealous. I mean, I loved that Jeannie loved me, but... it must have been pretty lonely, you know?"

"Not with a bed full of rabbits," Casey cracked gently, and the conversation went on.

When they finally arrived at the three-story, two-wing house that had been Joe's childhood home, Casey seemed... incredibly permanent, somehow. He was so very attached to Joe's family now. He knew their stories, he knew some of their secrets—Joe could almost believe that Casey would keep him forever and ever.

For the remainder of the trip, Joe managed to persuade himself that he could trust in this, trust in Casey, trust in the two of them. It was sort of a Christmas gift to himself.

JOE'S mother and father seemed to have shrunk in the last six years. They'd grown smaller and grayer, and Joe tried not to be dismayed when he had to hunch over to hug Celia Daniels. Her hair was cut short—had been since he was small—and very practically, above her ears, and it had grown a little sparser in the intervening years. But her arms were still strong around his shoulders, and her smile when she turned to Casey was nothing short of luminous.

His mother always glowed like that. He was relieved to see that, at least, hadn't changed. Griffin Daniels was a little shorter as well, but his chest was still broad; his shoulders might have hunched a little, but his eyes were still fine and brown and sharp under frightening eyebrows, ready to attack like vultures. Joe hugged him, and didn't feel any difference from his usual hug. There were no uncomfortable looks at Casey or back to Joe again. There was only the same steady, honest affection Joe had grown up with, and Casey's hand snaked into Joe's and clenched tight as Joe made introductions.

"Was your drive in all right?" Mom asked, and Casey suddenly spoke up.

"It was beautiful," he said reverently. "I can see why Joe sort of hides up in the hills in California. If he grew up used to all this, he probably needs it!"

Celia laughed, and Joe blushed a little. "I'm glad you love it," she said softly. "We were really sorry to see Josiah move, but it's nice that he's found something not too far from his roots."

"I like roots," Joe mumbled, and Casey slid that arm around his waist and squeezed.

"Good," Casey said dryly. "Because they seem to have grown you into a hella big tree!"

There was general laughter all around, and then Joe and Casey got to put their luggage in their room.

"We get our own room?" Casey asked excitedly as they tromped up the stairway.

Joe's expression grew pained. "Don't expect to be having sex in it," he warned. "My parents' house. I mean, uhm…."

Casey grimaced. "No, wasn't planning on it. I'm just glad we got it—it's like, official grown-up stuff!"

"Good. I'm glad you're feeling like an official grown-up, because Cheryl and her family should be back after dinner, and we're going to have to have our big boy panties on if we're going to make it through that without strangling her."

Casey raised his eyebrows. "Ooh… big boy panties. I didn't know that was your kink!"

Joe blushed, knowing it was visible on his cheeks and forehead and not able to contain it.

"Oh my God!" Casey laughed, putting the last of his underwear in the little dresser in the guest bedroom and then coming within touching distance to look at him closer. "What did I say?"

"No talking about kinky in my mother's guest room," Joe muttered, and Casey laughed harder.

"That's a deal!" he agreed, but then he sobered. "But I'll try to remember it when we get home."

Joe was blushing even more, but he was serious about not wanting to talk about kinks in Mom's house. "Good," Joe said decisively. "Because there are going to be enough complicated and uncomfortable conversations here as it is."

Casey cocked his head. "What's the deal with your sister? Your entire family is…." Casey floundered for words, waving his hands, and the gesture he settled on was the stroking motion of a boy petting a rabbit. "Incredibly gentle," he finished. "Your brothers—I mean, a pediatrician and a history teacher? It's like… *Leave it to Beaver* lives!"

Joe narrowed his eyes and chewed on his lower lip. "Yeah, if the Beav grew up and spent his college years up to his bong in dick, tits, and ass, it would be *exactly* like *Leave it to Beaver*."

Casey gave up all pretense of investigating the room and sat on the blue-and-beige striped comforter and just laughed. "God, you're an asshole. Are you going to tell me what's wrong with your sister? Besides the fact that she's a priss, I mean. Your brothers said something about… I dunno… a branch of your church or something?"

Joe nodded and sat down. "Yeah, it's a whole religious political thing. My folks try to stay out of it. Part of the whole reason the Quakers came to America back in the frickin' days of the Mayflower was to get away from the whole religious political bullshit thing. Except…." Joe grunted. "God. I hate this shit."

"Wait," Casey said, eyes narrowed. "I actually did get a high school education. Didn't the Puritans come over here to have freedom of religion?"

Joe rolled his eyes. "Yeah. Everyone was absolutely free to practice religion, as long as it was *their* religion." He let some of the tightness of travel seep out of his bones. He put his arm around Casey's shoulder, and between that wonderful, human warmth (the kid was like a radiator!) and the old-fashioned wrought iron furnace vent on the hardwood floor by the dresser, some of the feeling began to seep back into his toes after their frigid arrival here. God, he'd forgotten how badly the East Coast sucked in the winter. "The Quakers got persecuted a lot. It's why Philadelphia and Boston are near the ports and a lot of us are way the fuck up here. Anyway, old news. But the idea was simply a community of friends. No proselytizing—"

"What in the hell is that?" Casey was leaning on him heavily, his weight growing limp, and Joe toed off his shoes and bumped the back of Casey's new waffle-stomper so he could do the same. Casey grunted and bent down, untying the top part so he could kick off the bottom, and Joe answered him.

"Spreading the word. You know, those annoying people that *don't* show up on *our* doorstep because we live slightly south of Bumfuck, Egypt, and slightly north of Who the Fuck Cares?"

Casey had to laugh. "Yeah, Joe. We got missionaries when I lived in Bakersfield. Just because the Mormon's gave up on your house without Lynnie doesn't mean I'm a complete cultural desert." He started a yawn that went on as he unlaced his second shoe, straightened up, and toed it off, and Joe would have muttered a choice word about then, but the yawn had spread, and now Joe was having himself one too.

Joe gave up and wrapped an arm around Casey's shoulders, then drew him back on top of the blue-on-blue comforter. There was an afghan at the foot of the bed, handsome and in the same colors but made out of scratchy acrylic yarn. It didn't matter. Joe reached down and pulled it over both of them, and continued. "Well, the church had sort of a falling-out among itself in the seventies over things just like us."

"Us? God, that's so retarded."

"Isn't that word bad now?"

"What the hell ever. I don't get why people really have to give a shit what you and I do together, you know? Not planning to make anyone watch!"

"Thank God for small favors," Joe muttered. "Anyway, people like my folks are sort of taking the traditional route of 'leave people alone and treat them decently, and they'll find God all on their own.' People like my sister's husband, I guess—"

"Yeah, I get it. Fuckers."

"If only." Joe yawned. "Maybe if they spent more time fucking and less time getting up in our business, the world would be a better place." Casey started to giggle loopily, and Joe kept going. "Seriously, look at my brothers. They've each got a gazillion kids, and so do my parents, and they're happy to live and let live. Cheryl's got one kid—"

"Caleb of the giant booger?"

"Yeah, that's the one," Joe laughed. "Maybe if she was busy getting busy, she'd leave us the hell alone."

"You mean us in the universal sense of other gay people," Casey said grandly.

"Yeah," Joe mumbled. "Sure."

But he was thinking that Cheryl was going to make it a lot more personal than that.

JOE had gotten off of four twelves in a row, then gotten up at the ass-crack of dawn so Alvin could drive them down to San Francisco and they could board the plane. It was a good thing they didn't have security and gun checks, like they'd had when Joe had visited Europe right after school, or they wouldn't have made it. Casey had been too excited to let him sleep on the airplane, and laughing himself sick with his brothers pretty much finished the job.

By the time Cheryl tromped up the stairs, hollering, "Joe, get out here, it's dinner time, dammit!" Joe was in one of those tired fugue states where every breath between the thought *I have to wake up* and *Aren't I awake already?* seemed to last five years.

He felt the bed shift next to him, and fell back asleep for a second, and then he woke up in time to hear Casey's voice.

"Hey—how about we let him sleep. He's so out of it right now, he'll probably sleep 'til morning."

Cheryl's voice in response was hardly civil. "Are you the boyfriend?"

"You must be Cheryl," Casey said dryly. "Look, you can tell me I'm going to hell downstairs, okay? Right now, I want Joe to sleep."

"I don't know what my stupid brother told you about our religion—"

"Not a thing," Casey said bluntly. "But he's taught me about faith every day I've known him. And he hasn't slept in nearly forty hours, and I have faith he'll be a better person in the morning. Let's go downstairs so I can help your mom in the kitchen. She loves me, you know."

A part of Joe wanted to laugh, but that was too much effort. Instead, he was comforted. Casey was strong and good, truly good. Casey would fit right in.

HE WOKE up after a few hours because he had to pee, and he stumbled around in the frigid dark for a few minutes before he remembered where he was and how to find the tiny little bathroom attached to this particular guest room. It had a shower cubicle and a toilet and not much else, but it served its purpose, and Joe was able to strip off his sweater and jeans when he came back, which made him much more comfortable.

He slid back into bed next to Casey and wrapped his arm around Casey's middle, absolutely glorying in the strength of his wiry little body, and snuggled him tightly.

"Jesus, your hands are cold," Casey mumbled, and Joe growled back. They had gotten the hang of sleeping in the same bed almost immediately—it had been almost supernatural how easy it was to get used to having Casey right there, where Joe could touch him and know he'd be there as Joe slept. It had made those six months during which Joe had stumbled out of bed, frantically searching for him while half-conscious, fade to nothing in just a few weeks. Even nights when Casey had stayed at the duplex so he and Alvin could clean it up and move out, Joe had slept better. Some part of him had known, simply known in a rock-steady way, that Casey would be back.

"I'm sorry," Joe mumbled, a little bit awake now where he hadn't been when Cheryl had come to roust him. "I didn't mean to leave you to the wolves."

"You didn't," Casey said sleepily back. "You left me to the lambs." Then he giggled. "Get it? Lambs of God?"

"Oh hell, I didn't know you'd taken a literature class yet!" Joe said in disgust, and Casey snuggled backward.

"I didn't have to. Peter read some of your... whatever. The society's books that they rewrite every five years—"

"Books of Discipline?" Joe muttered, trying to remember when the last meeting in Philadelphia had been.

"Yeah. Anyway, they distinctly said that the Friends—right? Friends?"

"Yeah. Friends."

"Anyway, they're very supportive of us. I thought that was awesome. And then your sister's husband—what's his name again?"

"I keep forgetting," Joe confessed. "Matt? Mark? Charles/Tom/Steve?"

"Yeah, something like that. Anyway, he started talking about politics, and your dad just stood up and smiled and said, 'We practice in our home, Chris.'"

"That's it! Chris!"

"And you practice in yours. Good hearts seeking the true word would not reject family because they do not practice according to your wishes." Casey had been trying to imitate Joe's father, but he couldn't. Joe's voice—which he thought must be pretty deep and resonant, given the way the babies in the NICU settled when he spoke—was practically a soprano compared to Griffin Daniels's voice. And he was always so mild. Joe had gotten his sudden flashes of temper from his mother, he was almost positive.

"My dad's good people," Joe said softly.

"Your whole family's good people," Casey told him softly. "It's why you came out so damned good."

Joe smiled and wanted to ask Casey how *he* had come out so good, all family evidence to the contrary, but he fell asleep instead.

HE WOKE up early—heinously early for California, where it was four in the morning—and still pretty early for New York, where even the children were sleeping off travel and fun in the snow.

Joe desperately wanted to shower—he felt grimy—but he wanted to go somewhere first, somewhere he liked to be private, where no one would see him. He compromised and took a quick cold shower and didn't wash his hair, and then he dressed even more quickly in his warmest clothes. Someone had turned on the thermostat maybe a half an hour before, so it was a good sixty degrees in the house, and that still was warmer than it had been all night. There was a reason every bed had three wool blankets and a down comforter on it.

Joe shivered into his jeans and his boots and his sweater, then went downstairs, where his fleece-lined leather jacket, hat, gloves, and scarf were hanging on the line of pegs in the hallway. He heard his mother moving about in the kitchen and smelled coffee brewing, so he moved extra quietly so as not to disturb her. She would know where he'd gone, but these visits—private was the only word.

It was a good half mile to the tiny family cemetery in the far corner of his parents' property, but it felt good to tramp it in the dark-edged cold of a lonely a.m. Joe saw the last of the stars fade away from the graying sky, and saw the sky turn a frigid magenta before merging to the blue of a steel blade in a freezer.

He loved it, every last color change, every subtle, muted shift of heliotropic mood. He couldn't see the horizon on his property in Foresthill—too many tall trees, too many hills and valleys in too small a space. But here, the pastureland was wide and rolling, and Joe felt the freedom of horse country. The horses were bedded down in the barn, though, warm and happy and tended by Joe's oldest nephew, Eli, and it was quiet enough to hear Joe's boots as they broke through a foot of snow with every step.

At last he was there, a cemetery with barely two hundred plots, his relatives back to the early 1700s. Not all of them, of course—many had married and moved away, and he was sure there were other cemeteries dotted throughout New England with his kin housed in there, eternal inhabitants of the world's most humble hostel. Until Casey's father's funeral, this was the only cemetery he'd ever been to. It housed his grandmother and grandfather, who had both died when he'd been in his early teens, and it housed Jeannie.

Someone had been to her grave, he noticed, and swept away the snow. One of the last things he'd remembered to grab as he and Casey were running out the door was rattling dryly in his jacket pocket. He reached in, grateful for the cleaned grave to make this easier, and pulled out a packet of seeds.

"Hey, big sister," he said quietly, squatting on the frozen ground. "I hate to give these to you like this, but I'm hoping they'll be dormant for a while and then grow. It's been known to happen, right? All those plants people call 'volunteers'? I just feel bad, because the last time I was here in the summer I was nineteen, and all those rosebushes I planted died off. I'm sorry, sweetheart. This is just not good flower country unless it's wildflowers. So the seeds, maybe. You always loved daisies. I'll sprinkle daisies around the stone here, and maybe they'll grow."

He did that and then patted the headstone affectionately as he got heavily onto his knees.

"It's been a while," he said, still apologizing, "but I should tell you I have someone in my life now. It's a boy, but I don't think you'd mind. I like to think that *you* of all people would appreciate why I wouldn't give a fuck what anyone else thought. Casey doesn't either. You should meet him. I had a hard time seeing him, though. You always told me how smart I was, Jeannie, but I think that's just because we were tight, you know?" Joe thought of Casey climbing into his bed and trying desperately to make Joe commit. "I kept thinking of him as a little kid. He's not. Truly. Cheryl might come by and tell you that he's half my age—he's not. He's two-thirds my age, but it's not half." Joe had to laugh at that, because it was embarrassing and true.

"But sometimes, I think he's older than me. He's certainly tougher. I don't think I could have kept my good heart the way he has. Not with what the world threw at him. I mean, all the world threw at me was losing you, and look how far from our faith I've strayed."

Joe sighed and stood up from his knees—which were freezing on the ground anyway—and sank to his haunches, feeling silly, stupid tears of exhaustion and cold sneaking up on him. "You used to believe so strongly, Jeannie. I swear, I looked at you when you were singing, and practically saw God in your eyes. For so long—so damned long—I thought God had died with you, because I didn't see him anymore. But…." Joe closed his eyes and saw the way Casey had looked at him that first morning he'd shown up at the crappy little duplex, when Joe's hands had been shaking because Joe had been so glad to see him. "But I see God in his eyes, Jeannie. I don't pay much attention to doctrine, but I do remember what you taught me. It's all about the seeking, right? That's what we used to be called? Seekers? Well, I've found him. I've found God when I listen to him breathe next to me at night. There are other things I'd like to seek, eventually, but right now, I've found something, and I want you to be happy for me."

Joe wiped his cheek without self-consciousness and without trying to hold it back. It was why he came out here alone, and it had been why he'd come out here alone within days after they'd first lowered his sister's body into the cold ground and told him it was heaven.

He stood up a few moments later and shook himself off. "I'll be back, Jeanette. I'll bring Casey out here in the spring one year. He'll like that. He wants to travel. I'm not a fan, honestly, but I'll leave home for him. I'll come back again before we fly home, okay? I need to say good-bye."

He turned then and wiped his face one more time, pulling his T-shirt from under his sweater, jacket, and scarf to wipe it on. He was so busy with the mechanics of crying that he didn't notice Casey until he practically walked right over him.

"Steady there," Casey said dryly, but he pulled a pad of tissues out of his pocket and reached up and wiped Joe's face carefully. "You can wake up to sneak out of the house at the filthy ass crack of dawn, but you can't remember Kleenex? What's wrong with you?"

"I didn't count on my young lover being here to watch me fall apart," Joe growled, looking carefully away.

"Well, you should have," Casey said, keeping his voice surly, maybe just to keep Joe from feeling self-conscious.

"Yeah, and why's that?" Joe asked, actually managing to make eye contact.

"Because I love you, Josiah. I may be two-thirds your age"—Joe winced as he said it—"but I'm also 'older and tougher' than you." Casey sighed, and the asperity faded, replaced by sadness and a little bit of hurt. "Why'd you want to do this alone?" he asked after a moment that had the low tone of a sleeping cathedral bell. "Why'd you think I wouldn't want to hold you up?"

Joe smiled a little and bent his head, thinking how small this man looked, how young he sounded—but how truly old his heart was when it counted.

"Because I just found you," he said, and he kissed Casey softly on the forehead. "I'm going to be finding out how great you are for a good long time."

"Well, like you told Jeannie, isn't that what seeking's all about?" Casey said back, and he threw his arms around Joe's shoulders so tightly that when Joe straightened up, Casey hung on and climbed him like a tree, wrapping his legs around Joe's waist and resting his snowy shoes on Joe's ass. Joe helped him out, wrapping his arms around Casey's body and holding him tight, holding him close, holding on for dear life.

"What are you going to be seeking?" Joe asked, wanting to be doing this somewhere where there was more skin available to him.

"Me?" Casey asked, grinning. "I'm going to be seeking a career, and a degree, and I'm going to be seeking a way for you to have that other thing you want that you won't admit you gave up for me, and I'm going to be seeking a girlfriend for Alvin before he breaks himself beating off so much—"

"That's quite a list!" Joe laughed, loving him so much it hurt. He started walking, not sure if he could hold Casey for that long but willing to try.

"Yeah, but you didn't hear the best part!" Casey told him, exuberance cracking his voice in the end of the last word.

"What's that?" Joe asked, letting Casey's body slide down until his feet could touch the snow, and then he let go and crunched through that last twelve inches.

"I'm going to be seeking the parts in me that are good enough for you, Joe," Casey said softly, his gray eyes growing bright. "If those parts are in there, then I'm pretty sure you and your parents are right, and there is a God. And you showed him to me. Does that make you a good Quaker?"

Oh God… he was so short, and so young, and Joe loved him so much. "Yeah, I think so, maybe."

Casey laughed. "Good. Because I told Cheryl to kiss my naked gay ass last night, and I wanted to make sure I had a platform to stand on."

Now Joe did laugh and wrap his arm around Casey's shoulders, walking back in the shadowed blue trench he'd worn through the snow on his way through the yard the first time.

"What did she say that prompted *that*?" he asked, because Cheryl could be abrasive, but she usually tried not to piss people off quite that badly.

Casey shrugged, and Joe looked sideways at him, liking the way the rising sun turned his hair to fire and gold. "She cornered me in the kitchen," Casey confessed, "and tried to tell me that the way you and I were living was counter to her faith."

"Her words?" They didn't sound like Casey's, and Casey nodded.

"Yeah, dumbass—who do you *think* would say that?"

"Well, what did you say?"

Casey snaked an arm around his waist as tight as he could probably make it, and Joe caught his breath for form. "I told her that if she wanted something to give her faith, she should talk to you, because the only reason I had any faith at all was because I met you."

Joe's breath caught again, this time for real, and he pulled Casey in and dropped a kiss on his hair. "Me too," Joe murmured, and Casey turned his head and caught Joe's lips for a kiss.

"Yeah, but I didn't know that at the time." Casey scowled. "She started talking about doctrines and the book of what the hell ever, and *that's* when I told her—"

"To kiss your gay white ass," Joe finished for him.

"Yeah. Sorry about that, Joe."

"I'm not," Joe said, his heart beating so rightly in his chest that he almost felt warm. "Because you're right. Whatever else I'll be seeking, Casey, I've found my faith with you."

Something So Strong
~Casey

CASEY sat on the little stone ledge in front of the iron woodstove and leaned carefully on the wrought iron cage that surrounded it. It nestled in the corner of the Daniels family room and was used to supplement the gas heater, but the farmhouse was old, and it was large, and no number of those little crocheted dolls with the obscenely splayed legs was going to stop the minus ten degree draft that crept in during the winter.

Of course the number of people in the room—sitting on couches, love seats, chairs dragged in from the dining room, and standing in corners—tended to warm the room up, and a lot of those people were kids, and their metabolisms heated up the room just when they breathed. On the whole, the last time Casey had seen this many people crammed into a room for a purely social occasion had been for his continuation school graduation, and since most of those folks were either juvenile delinquents or teen moms with kids in the audience, the "stay and chat" factor had been decidedly reduced.

This was... overwhelming. Fun, of course—everyone here loved each other, even Cheryl, who tended to make her siblings scatter like leaves in the wind. The fact that not one of the brothers ever turned around to her and said, "Fuck off, you bitch-stinking cow!" was proof that the family really did hang together from the sheer honoring of affection.

But that didn't mean Casey was enjoying being an audience—even one in a child's seat in front of the fire—to this particular conversation, either.

She'd carefully avoided Casey after the "kiss my gay white ass" incident, and that was fine with everyone involved, including Joe's parents, who seemed to make an effort to corral Casey in another room whenever Cheryl was on a rampage.

And she *was* on a rampage. No, not always about the gay thing, but that was one of her favorite songs. Her entire playlist seemed to consist of things that other people were doing wrong: Peter worked too many hours and wasn't spending enough time with his teenage son, otherwise Elijah would have better manners. David didn't take his position at the hospital seriously enough, or he would have been chief resident by now. Paul was wasting his life as a history teacher, and didn't he want to get his administrator's credential and move up? And Josiah? Joe, Joe, Joe, Joe, Joe... a *nurse* and not a doctor? A house in the *foothills* and not the suburbs? Seeing a *man* and not a woman? From his mustache to his ponytail to his motorcycle; from his career to his residence to his quiet devotion to Casey—holy Christ on a shit-eating cracker, what was he *not* doing wrong?

And this was when Casey got to watch Joe and that quiet, steady patience of his truly shine.

They were standing, at the moment, in front of the stove, and if Casey had wanted, he could have reached out and slid his hand under Joe's jeans and palmed the hairy skin of his calf. He was tempted, because the press of people having conversation this New Year's Eve, 1992, seemed overwhelming, and he would have loved a little bit of contact, just to reassure himself that Joe was still there and still his.

He didn't, though. For one thing, he didn't want to see Cheryl's half-frightened sneer, which was the expression on her face when she'd walked down the hallway Christmas Eve and found the two of them necking under the stairs. They'd gotten a furiously whispered earful about having some respect for the other people in the house. Joe's reply of "Well, of course we do, Cheryl. That's why we weren't making out in the living room!" only served to make her more leery of seeing the two of them together.

Joe had gritted his teeth and borne it, though—as long as she didn't say anything bad about Casey or to him, that is. Casey had forgotten the whole "take your boots off in the mudroom" rule of the house and had stomped snow in the kitchen one evening before supper, and Cheryl had snapped that he may use street-trash manners in Joe's house, but she expected more. That had resulted in *Cheryl* getting hauled out of the kitchen by *her mother*, and Casey had only heard a little bit of that conversation from the bottom of the stairwell, but Celia's staunch support of him and Joe had made Casey as determined as Joe to keep the peace. It was funny. Casey had never backed down from a fight, had never backed down from flaunting his sexuality in someone's face. In fact, he wasn't known for backing down *period.* But he understood now why Joe both loved and feared his family. This many people, this many personalities, and you could love a person with all your heart and not stand to be in the same room with them either.

So no. Casey didn't slide his hand down the back of Joe's calf, and he didn't stand up, wrap his arms around Joe's waist, and stand on tip-top-toe so he could dig his chin into Joe's shoulder. He contented himself with curling up like a cat in front of the fire and completely corrupting Cheryl's one and only child.

"I'm surprised they let you into the nursery with that mustache, Joe. I mean, I'm surprised they let you work there at all. You're a grown man, what are they thinking?"

"They're thinking that I'm a grown man," Joe said, keeping a straight face. "I think they're also thinking that I can hold the little shits in one hand, test their blood gasses with the other, and that I make them feel incredibly safe."

Casey looked up from the face-making contest he was having with Caleb and smiled.

"Does he really?" Caleb asked seriously, and Casey looked back at him.

"Really what?"

"Really make kids feel safe?"

Casey thought about it. "He's the nicest person I know," he said thoughtfully, even though he was only talking to a four-year-old. "He could be the only person *I've* felt safe with, so I think I'm going to call that a yes."

Casey smiled and patted Joe absently on the thigh, in spite of his terrifying height. Joe looked down and smiled and sank to his haunches, and Caleb regarded his mustache with a singular terror.

"Do you want to yank on it?" Joe asked seriously, and the little boy's eyes grew wide.

"Can I?"

"Yeah, sure—but be nice. It's attached."

So Caleb wrapped his pudgy little fingers around the long beard/mustache hairs next to Joe's mouth and pulled.

"Ouch!" Joe said theatrically, and Caleb giggled and let go, put his hand in front of his mouth, and laughed even louder. Joe ruffled his straight sand-colored hair and stood up to talk to Cheryl again, and Casey looked at him in admiration. God, he was like that with *all* the kids, not just Caleb, and Casey started to hunger for him to have that baby that he would never admit he wanted.

"You're right," Caleb said, digging his finger inside his nose since his mother wasn't paying attention to him. "He's nice."

Casey hid a smile and waited to see how big this booger was going to be. Ever since Paul and David's story, he'd been looking for a record-breaker. So far, the kid had only managed garden-variety snot, and Casey was much disappointed.

"Joe, isn't he going to want to go out and see the world when he graduates? What's he getting his degree in, anyway?"

"Engineering, so far," Joe said, surprising Casey. He was right, but Casey had never gone through the whole "soul searching" thing that some people (Alvin!) went through to declare a major. Casey just knew it had to be a living with math that didn't include children, because while this one was nice and he liked Peter's oldest, Elijah, *very* much (partly because he wrote Joe letters on a regular basis, and partly because, when Cheryl had gotten upset about this, the boy had replied, "You gave me underwear for Christmas last year, Aunt Cheryl. Joe sent me a radio-controlled monster truck. Of *course* I'm going to want to keep in touch!"), Casey was pretty sure he couldn't handle a big batch of kids at the same time without killing one. Or many. Which meant teaching was right out.

But Josiah (which Casey was liking the sound of more and more as he heard Joe's family use the long version of his name on an almost constant basis) was great with them. He taught them how to groom the horses and how to hook up the harness on the old-fashioned, honest-to-God sleigh in the garage for sleigh rides, and when the kids were "out playing," there was a 70 percent chance that Joe was the supervising adult. (There was a 30 percent chance that it was Paul and David, in which case there was a 100 percent chance that *someone* would come in crying because the brothers had gotten too competitive.)

Casey got to see the driving engine that made Josiah Daniels, the man he'd loved and had been in love with forever, tick.

It didn't change his mind in the least. In fact, it made him want to be a part of this engine with even more of his soul. But that didn't mean he had any more patience for a woman like Cheryl, who was just *dying* to tell the world how it should be run.

"And look at him! He's more comfortable talking to the kids than he is with the adults!"

Joe met Casey's eyes in grim appreciation that "he" was still close enough to be heard.

"So am I," he said mildly, and he met Caleb's eyes and winked, then winced. Caleb had, at last, struck gold.

Casey turned and looked at the child and then felt his eyes bulge out like a cartoon character's. Really? Really. And there the kid was, looking for a place to put it, that work of art just dangling off his finger. And there was his mother's backside, replete in winter-white slacks, just a couple of feet away.

"Kid," Casey said, catching Caleb's eye, "do this." He made the time-honored wipe-the-finger gesture while looking at Cheryl's full and replete ass.

Caleb was not necessarily the brightest kid Casey had ever met. Forget that he was four; he tended to stand around with his mouth open a lot. Anyway, he walked right up to his mother and wiped that thing on her back pocket. Cheryl barely broke stride as she looked down and said, "Not now, sweetheart, Mommy's talking," and Casey gave the kid a toothy grin and a thumbs-up.

Joe's face turned red with the effort to not laugh.

"But Joe, don't you want him to have the same sort of things *you* had when you were that age?"

Joe looked affronted. "It wasn't that long ago, Cheryl—and yes. Yes, I want him to backpack around Europe for a summer. Yes, I want him to open every door that looks pretty. But no. I'm not going to kick him out of my life because you or anyone else thinks it's a wonderful idea!"

Cheryl opened her mouth to say something, but Joe looked down and offered Casey a hand up. "Casey, am I taking advantage of you and keeping you from doing the things you want with your life?" Joe asked, and he was, to Casey's horror, partly serious.

"If you try to send me out of your life again, I'll geld you," Casey said, and he was *completely* serious.

Joe winced. "Gelding? Seriously? Like I'm going to play around on you?"

Casey reconsidered. "I'll superglue your hands to your hair. We'll have to shave you bald. It'll be heinous."

Joe laughed a little and wrapped his arm securely around Casey's shoulders. Casey snuggled into him, more relieved than he could put words to that he wasn't at the children's hearth anymore. "I wouldn't dream of it," Joe said softly. "You can go traveling anywhere you want, Casey, but you'll always have a home with me."

Casey looked at Cheryl from the sanctuary of Joe's arms. "You should see our home," he said seriously. "Joe doesn't talk about it, but it was a mess five years ago. The carport was a death trap, the upstairs was down to bare boards—hell, I think Joe had even ripped out most of the drywall—"

"It was rotted," Joe confirmed. He nodded at Paul and David, who had come to join the conversation. "The first thing I did, before Casey came to stay, was take care of the roof, because the upstairs had rotted out from all the leaks."

"Yeah—I never saw it. He wouldn't let me up there until he'd stripped it to the floorboards and we saw how much of it was sound, because he said it was too dangerous—"

"You had to see him when we fixed the carport," Joe interrupted. "He was fu—" He stopped, because he didn't swear at his parents' house. "—frickin' fearless. Scared the rabbit raisins out of me the whole week we were working on it."

"He yelled a lot," Casey affirmed. "First time he ever lost his temper on me, I lost a few raisins myself. Anyway, we've repainted the entire place, refurbished the bathrooms, Joe replaced the carpet up the stairs and in our room—"

"You share a room?" Cheryl asked, and Joe raised his eyebrows at her.

"You share a room with your husband, Cheryl, what did you think? Never mind. Forget I said that. Give it a rest, okay?"

"What does Joe's room look like, Casey?" David asked. He and Paul were barely fourteen months apart, but they were seven and eight years older than Joe. "Does he still have rockets in it?"

"No," Casey said, and then he remembered something he'd seen after he'd been waking up in Joe's bed for a few days. The few weeks after that had been so hectic—taking finals, moving out of the duplex, getting ready for the trip. And them. They'd talked about them, as much as Joe would talk about a relationship, but they'd talked. But they hadn't had a chance to talk about *this*.

"But he does have a telescope set up by the window. I wouldn't be surprised if his next project's not a stargazing platform on the roof." He looked at Joe half questioningly. "Are you sure *you're* not the one who wants to travel?" he asked.

"I traveled," Joe replied, his voice as mild as it always was. "I traveled, I learned, I expanded my horizons, and then found the exact place I belonged."

"Well, I may expand my horizons," Casey said definitively, "but I've always known where I belong."

Paul broke the quiet between them with an "Awwww… God, you two are adorable. I may vomit."

"Really, Paul? Really?" Cheryl turned on him. "You're going to bring that up now, right before dessert? God, you've got the maturity of a third grader, do you know that?"

Paul smirked. "Big words for a woman with two inches of booger on her ass!"

Cheryl's shriek silenced the entire room full of people and continued as she turned around, sighted the offending stain, and then charged upstairs to change.

Joe looked at Casey in the ensuing chaos. "Well done!"

Casey preened. "I didn't do anything. It was all Caleb."

Paul, David, and even Peter were convulsing with laughter, keeping each other from collapsing on the floor. "Please," David gasped, "please, Casey, tell us you had something to do with that."

Casey smirked at him. "Well, it might have been my suggestion. Why?"

"God, Joe, if you ever let him move out, I'm adopting him!"

Joe grimaced. "Thanks, David. That's good to know."

"Well," Casey said, doing the math, "at least *he's* old enough to be my father. *You* aren't."

And that set them off again.

CASEY never did make friends with Cheryl—not that trip, and not the trips they took in all the years that followed. Joe said it was because they had fundamentally different approaches to life, and even though he eventually started writing his sister a little more often, he never forced Casey to like her any more than it took to be civil to the woman.

It was yet another thing that Casey loved Joe for. Like he needed one, but still.

The trip was wonderful as a whole, but they got home and Joe had maybe seven hours of sleep and then had to report to work. Casey barely remembered his good-bye kiss—long, lingering, sweet—before Joe disappeared through the door.

Casey just lay there in bed, letting consciousness come slowly, and thought about shit for a good hour after Joe left.

He had some idea of how Joe worked now, he thought. Casey was starting to understand why Joe did the things he did. He loved his family—warmly and with all his heart—but he seemed to be fully aware that he'd never really belonged there. Casey found himself picturing Joe, a little boy with rockets in his room, dreaming of being somewhere peaceful, somewhere the world didn't intrude. It wasn't that he was antisocial—he still had friends, he still had work parties, and he'd dragged Casey to his friends' houses so they could work as well.

It was just that a part of his soul was solitary, and self-contained, and happy that way, and the one exception—the *only* exception he seemed to have ever made—was Casey.

Casey opened his eyes and looked around the room some more. Joe had taken down the Steve Hanks prints and put up a big photo print, a picture, taken at sunset, of a couple of children playing on a beach. The color caught Casey's attention first, because it was sunset orange and gold, with the silhouettes of the children standing out in stark relief, but he couldn't hide from the subject matter, either.

Jeannie had come up a lot over vacation. Josiah's visit to her grave had been private, but the Daniels family wasn't the type to whisper the name of the dead as though they had done something shameful. No. Jeannie's name was brought up as much as Joe's when the family visited memory lane, and it was always with a sort of reverence and sorrow. Jeannie, everyone seemed to agree, had been the purest heart of them all. She'd been the gentlest, the one with the most instinctive hand in caring for animals and small children, and she had turned much of that gift, that quiet purity, on Joe. Maybe she had recognized the same things in him—the goodness, but the need for privacy too. The desire for intimacy rather than the desire for company. The desire to share what goodness you'd found in the world with your family, but only select members.

Casey sighed. He wasn't that good a person. He wasn't horrible, he was pretty sure, but he wasn't good enough to leave Joe for the sake of Joe's desire to have children. He wasn't. But as Casey sat up in bed and contemplated that beautiful, lonely picture, he remembered Joe playing with his nieces and nephews, and the way they'd all seemed to adore him with an unfettered joy.

Suddenly, he wanted this thing for Josiah as badly as Josiah wanted it for himself. It was the thing that filled his soul, the dream he didn't know he had, the thing he would be seeking for the two of them until, all probability to the contrary, it was something they could have.

HE GOT up eventually, thoughtful and still tired, and wondered how Joe was doing on his shift. He went downstairs to visit Alvin and found Alvin set up on the kitchen table with a big monitor sitting on top of a disc drive, and a cord connecting it to the wall. Casey blinked, thinking he might have seen something like that when he'd walked in the door the night before, but he and Joe had been too busy fending off overjoyed dogs and cats hell-bent on fatally tripping them.

"You got a computer?" Casey asked, squinting at the giant thing on the table.

"No, no!" Alvin said excitedly, tapping on the keyboard. "I've got a state-of-the-art IBM 386—man, it's the be-all end-all of technology! You gotta see it here. Look—I'm connected!"

Casey turned his head. "To what?"

"The Internet. I've got a provider and everything! I'll pay for it— the bill is in my name!"

"A provider for what? Because Joe and I don't smoke weed anymore."

"A service provider—I can send electronic mail and everything! Look. Look here!"

Casey drew up a chair and blinked. He looked at the screen at a bunch of clunky white letters on a black background and tried to figure out what the big deal was.

"Watch!" Alvin said. "I'm gonna find me some porn!"

And with that, he clicked a few nonsense letters and numbers with a line under it. There was a pause of about a minute when a bar appeared on the screen, and Alvin bounced eagerly on the chair. His hair looked like he'd cut it himself, his skin had broken out recently, and he didn't look like he'd slept in *ages*, but suddenly Casey was getting the feeling that what they were waiting for was the best Christmas *ever!*

"*See!*" Alvin burst out, and Casey stood up so fast he knocked the chair over.

"*Oh my God!* Those are tits! And that's a... a... oh *God!* Oh, Jesus, Alvin, I'm *gay!* I don't want to see that shit!"

"There's a guy in that picture too," Alvin said plaintively, and Casey looked down. Yeah, yeah there was, and he was fairly well endowed too.

"Well, lucky her," Casey said. "Next time warn a guy before you flash something like that. Jesus, Alvin—how in the hell did you find tits and poontang on a computer! I thought those were for typing up papers and shit!"

Alvin looked up at him and grinned. "Well, we're getting it through this."

He pointed to a small box that was plugged into their phone jack, and Casey looked at it curiously. "A modem, right?"

"You were just dicking with me with the other stuff, weren't you?"

Casey twisted his mouth, annoyed. "No. I'm still stupid tired from the trip. I remember, sort of—I had a computer class at Sierra, but I was fighting a lot with my boyfriend—I blew it off and got a C."

"So I have to suffer because you were fighting with... God. Who was it?"

Casey grimaced. "Oh, it was Robbie. He wanted me to move in, and I didn't want to yet because I knew I had unfinished business with Joe." Casey sat down and shook his head. "Feels stupid now. I don't think he's ever going to let me go again."

Alvin grunted. "He's going to have to if you're going to go on that trip."

Casey glared at him. "It's a graduation trip, Alvin. What year is it? I've got at least another four semesters. You do too. I mean, I know we're supposed to make it in four years, but I still haven't gotten some of my lower division."

Alvin nodded, his eyes still on the monitor screen. He'd pushed another link and was watching the bar in the middle of the computer tell him how long he had before it popped up. "I know. But I talked to my folks. They said that whenever I graduate, they're ready to send me to Europe. Since I live here, they can send me enough money so I don't have to work that much, and I want to go."

Casey thought about it. Two months traveling through Europe—it was everything he thought Joe might want for him. He told himself firmly that he didn't want it without Joe.

But he really did want to see the world.

He wasn't sure how Joe had known so accurately. Maybe he'd recognized Casey's drive when he graduated from high school and wanted so badly to go to college. Maybe it was the way Casey had inhaled every book Joe had ever given him, or his avid attention to the movies they'd watched over the last five years. Maybe it was just that Joe knew him, knew what he talked about, knew what he dreamed about—it didn't matter how Joe knew, but he knew.

Until Casey had been kicked out of his own home, he'd thought that four walls and a roof were the be-all and end-all of his existence. But it had taken him two months to fuck and blow his way to Foresthill, and he'd gotten this idea that the world was a much bigger place than he'd ever suspected. That moment as he'd been walking across the bridge and had thought of falling, falling through infinite space into the great beyond, the one thing that had really been attractive about that idea had been the great beyond. *Finally*, he'd get to see the world as maybe it really was.

When Robbie had left and Casey and Alvin had been struggling to find Top Ramen money, the idea of backpacking through Europe had been the Holy Grail. He couldn't think about Joe then. Thinking about Joe made him want to curl up and not eat and not sleep and just mourn. So he'd thought about a bigger world, maybe one where not having Joe wouldn't hurt so much.

He couldn't contemplate that sort of world now. He could want to go off into the great beyond, but he'd always, always need Joe and this home to come back to.

And that picture, that lonely, lovely picture of children playing in a sunset ocean, to ache dully in his heart.

"We'll see," he said. "We'll see. I just got back here again. I missed it. I've got two years to think about Europe. Hell, I've got two weeks before I think about *school*. Right now, I just want to think about home.

So that was what he did.

Joe came home only a couple of hours later, exhausted and a little giddy from it. "Yeah," he mumbled, "they sent me home. Apparently I wasn't worth a good goddamn, and that bitch at the NICU was going to write me up, but Janey just broke up with her boyfriend, so she took the rest of my shift." Joe yawned, and Casey stood up from the computer—because he and Alvin had been playing all day, in spite of the fact that Alvin never did stop calling up poontang and tits—and wrapped his arms around that great tree of a man and hugged him.

"I was going to make dinner," he apologized. "Since I'm home. Go shower. I'll have food when you get out. Then I'll put you to bed."

Joe yawned and, without even making an innuendo, went up the stairs like a good boy. Casey waited until he heard the water running (because it still made that horrid moan in the pipes) before he pulled out some Top Ramen (because that was what Alvin had bought while they were gone) and started the world's most basic dinner. He threw in some canned peas and corn and found some tofu that didn't look too bad in the refrigerator, and threw that in for protein, and then put it in a bowl and grabbed a placemat, and he was walking it up the stairs when Joe got out of the shower.

"I was going to dress," Joe complained, and Casey rolled his eyes.

"Put on your underwear, big man, and sit and eat. I'll brush your hair, bore you to death with Alvin's new toy, and you can fall asleep on your face as soon as you're done eating."

"Got things planned, do ya?" Joe grimaced, yawned, and swore. "Fuck." He eyed Casey glumly. "We haven't had sex in two weeks."

Casey nodded. "Well, if that thing wakes up in the middle of the night, feel free to poke me with it, 'kay? I'm still down with that—the novelty ain't worn off."

Joe reached into his drawers and pulled out a pair of flannel boxer shorts. He sighed as he pulled them on. "God, we haven't even done laundry," he muttered, looking at the stack of luggage in the corner. "I'm going to be living in scrubs for a week!"

"I'll do laundry when you go to sleep. Did I mention you took me by surprise?"

Joe eyed him suspiciously. "You know, kid, I just left my mother's house. I don't expect you to take over."

Casey grunted. "Sit down. Are you sitting down? Good. Awesome. Glad to see it. Here's your soup, now eat it like a good boy."

Joe glared at him and took a bite.

Casey smiled evilly. "You *are* a good boy. Awesome, kid, keep it up and I'll buy you some ice cream. I'm going to brush your hair now, and—"

"Are you enjoying yourself?"

Casey pursed his lips, pretending to think. "Yeah. Yeah, I think it's safe to say I *am* enjoying myself." He went to the bathroom and came out with a brush, the kind with the hard individual bristles, and then he clambered up on the bed behind Joe and began to work carefully on that long hair.

Joe grunted and Casey said, "Don't pay any attention to me. Just eat, okay? Did you see that thing on the table? Alvin got that as a present, and at first I thought it sort of sucked."

"Why's that?" Joe asked through a full mouth.

"Because the first thing he did with it was show me a picture of a girl with her whositz stretched about six miles wide."

Joe struggled with his food for a minute, and it was touch and go whether he was going to spew it back into the bowl. Finally he swallowed it, and Casey sat and let him and then resumed combing out that long, straight hair. He found a strand of gray there at the temple and thought about plucking it out, but he decided to let Joe keep it. He deserved it for spending two weeks with his family and not once bitchslapping his annoying sister.

"So how do you feel about it now?" Joe asked gruffly, wiping at his streaming eyes.

"I like it," Casey said as he took another section of hair and worked it gently. "I think I'm going to take a programming class next semester—I sign up for classes next week."

Joe grunted and took another bite of food. "I'll tinker with your car some more." Joe had actually given up on Casey's car in those few frantic weeks between reconciliation and leaving for New York. Casey and Alvin had gone to school in the pickup truck, and Joe had come to visit on the motorcycle. A couple of times Joe had driven Casey back and forth to Roseville on the back of it again, and Casey had clutched his waist and shivered in the cold December sleet. It would be nice to get the car back—and Casey had a moment to privately wonder how far he would have gotten without Joe. He didn't want to think that way—plenty of other working students managed—but still. Family was good. Support was good. He shouldn't have needed two weeks in New York to figure that out, but there you go.

"Well, that's nice of you and I appreciate it," Casey said, working on the last section of hair. It was drying a little in his hands, straight and coarse but smooth from the crown to the ends. Joe kept it meticulously trimmed. It never got ratty or split; he never let it get greasy or hang in his face. He was maybe a little vain about it, but in a quiet way, a way that told Casey that, for all it made him look like a nonconforming hippie, he was actually deeply rooted in his family's spiritual past.

It was funny that Joe had worried that Casey was too young to fall in love with him, because every day Casey knew him seemed to be another day to find a reason to fall deeper in love.

"Not a problem," Joe mumbled, and Casey laughed a little. Joe's hair was all done, and his mostly finished bowl of noodles was tipping dangerously. Casey rescued the bowl and set it on the end table, then laid Joe down on the bed and started rubbing his back—just skin on skin, no kneading—and Joe was asleep in moments.

Casey went back downstairs to get laundry started and pet the dogs and send Alvin to the grocery store, and the whole time he felt a sort of deep contentment in his bones. He really was home. He could leave and come back, and home was still here. Every time he went back up into their room, he bent and kissed a sleeping Joe on his temple or his lips. Joe was far too tired to respond, but Casey knew he'd done it.

"Welcome home, Joe," he whispered once, and he could swear the man smiled in his sleep.

Don't You Want Me
~Joe

1995

THE baby was only three pounds, but that was a damned sight better than the two and a half it had been two weeks ago at birth, and Joe sat in the rocking chair next to the Isolette and held the child to his chest, talking softly.

"Hullo, Levi, how you doin'? Yeah, me too. Kinda sleepy. Yeah, I know—I was gone for a couple of days. Sorry about that—two days off. Casey and I went down to Santa Cruz and played on the beach. It's pretty down there, my man. I don't know what to tell you. Just is. Yeah, I know, I should tell him I bought him the tickets. Stop grunting at me like that—you're three pounds, I don't think you get to be my conscience just yet. He's going to take it wrong. You know he is. I just don't want him to take it wrong. And, you know. I want him to come back."

There was a tiny sound next to him, and Joe figured he'd spent about enough time with Levi—it was Seth's turn now.

He stood up carefully, because Levi was still attached to the respirator, the heart monitor, the shunt that let them give him antibiotics, the feeding tube, and the pulse-ox monitor. It was a whole lot of tiny insults to a much tinier body, and the volunteer baby rockers who came to hold the drug-addicted bodies with the horrible knife-edged screams often stayed away from the preemies. It was too frightening, and there was too much chance of doing something wrong.

But Joe had been there when Seth and Levi had been born, and he felt a sense of ownership where they were concerned. He'd been spending his lunch hours and time after work coming in to talk to them, to hold them, to give them the sort of human contact that they needed to thrive.

It was hard to thrive when the person who should have loved you most didn't want a fucking thing to do with you.

Joe had been there when the mother had given birth—pediatric nurses were always present during a birth, and this was no exception, but there was also a pediatric doc who specialized in preemies there, and that was Joe's second clue that this was going to be a fucking circus.

His third clue was the social worker standing grimly by the fifteen-year-old girl with the yellow complexion and dirty brown and cracked lips, screaming that somebody had better get this fucking thing out of her because she needed another fucking hit.

Yeah. She'd been his first clue.

She'd shrieked so loud that the social worker consented to gag her—she was freaking out the other birthing mothers, and that was a bad thing. She was too violent to sit still for an epidural—the anesthesiologist would have shoved a needle through her spine and crippled her for life—and she was too hyped up on God knows what to put anything in her IV but fluids.

Joe remembered when Casey had first showed up on his doorstep, and smoking a little weed was no big deal, and only the rich kids snorted coke, and then, hey, it wasn't addictive, right?

God, the country had embraced one hell of a learning curve as far as drugs were concerned, and all the lessons were hard, and the cost of that education…

God.

They were the two tiny bodies that had issued, screaming silently because their lungs had barely developed, out onto the birthing table as Joe had watched.

The first one, Seth, had weighed in at two pounds, four and three-quarters of an ounce, and his twin brother, Levi, had been the bruiser at two pounds, five and a half.

They were born at twenty-five weeks, their little persons racked with the hard edge of addiction, their underdeveloped lungs not even capable of supporting their screams of pain. Joe had worked furiously on Levi until a second peds doctor showed up to help him, while the original doc had worked on Seth until he got a nurse in support as well. The girl had barely been dragged in at all, and the fact that she was carrying twins was a definite surprise.

Finally, finally, the babies were stabilized, their portable NICU Isolettes ready to be transported to the neonatal intensive care unit, and Joe heard Seth's doctor ask the girl if she wanted to see her babies before they took them away.

"I don't have no babies," the girl said, turning her face away. "Them things ain't a part of me."

In the end, Joe named them, because after three days the girl had relinquished her parenting rights in one scrawl of the pen and had hauled herself back on the streets, probably to die early somewhere Joe didn't want to think of. After three days of "Baby Gresham 1" and "Baby Gresham 2," Joe had quietly changed the placards to "Seth" and "Levi" and asked the social worker for their birth certificate paperwork as well. He'd given them his last name. When they grew up, he just wanted them to believe that someone had welcomed them into the world.

Joe sighed. It wasn't the first time he'd heard of a woman doing that, not by a long shot, but now that Casey was about to graduate from college and that slightly temporary feeling that all college students carried with them was fading into permanency, the knowledge that he was giving something up, something important, was starting to etch its way into Joe's heart.

The population of the foothills was growing, and with it the number of strays Joe and Casey (and even Alvin, once) wrangled to social services had seemed to increase. With every child abandoned, or who had run away or been kicked out of the house, a small wail had started up somewhere in his vitals.

That's not fair. I would have loved that child with all that was in me.

Casey knew. Casey didn't talk about it because Joe knew he felt guilty, no matter how often Joe told him that everyone made sacrifices for things they really wanted. Casey gave up going to parties for Joe, and Joe gave up this idea, this picture in his head, for Casey.

The one time they *had* talked about it, Casey had gotten pissed, screaming (and they *never* screamed, much like they never fought):

"Oh. My. *God!* I'm not giving up a fucking thing, you asshole! Not a fucking thing! There's *nothing* in this life that I want more than being with you. *Nothing.* Coming home and watching movies with you and sleeping in your bed is *everything* I've *ever* dreamed about. Don't compare what you're missing to what I'm missing. It's like I missed dessert and you're fucking starving to death. And don't think I don't know the horrible fucking injustice, right? A woman can go out and buy some dude's jizz, and *boom*, she's a parent. I looked adoption up, Joe. I know what you make, and I know what I'll make, and *maybe* we'll be able to afford it in five years, but even if we can, there's no guarantee anyone will even give us a baby. None. So don't tell me you're not sad, and don't tell me there's not a little part of you that isn't just *pissed* because you see these women who are given this wonderful fucking miracle, and they just throw it away." Casey gasped out a sob. "I'm pissed," he muttered. "I'm so pissed. It's not fair. Because look at you. You're... God, Josiah, if anyone deserves to have a child to love, man, it's you."

And an interesting thing had happened then. Joe had looked at Casey, who had been furious and hurt to the point of being in tears, and Joe had experienced a surge of faith. It was all he could call it—it was the only name he had.

"Our child will come," he said simply, believing it. "Casey, you want this for me—I can see it—and you want it for us, and that makes me so incredibly proud. I'm going to believe that if you're not giving up a thing for me, and you feel that in your heart, then our baby will come."

Casey had stood there for a moment, wiping his hand in front of his eyes, and then he had launched himself into Joe's arms. "I'll believe with you," he said, wiping his face on Joe's shoulder. "I believe *in* you, so I'll believe because you do. How's that?"

It was all Joe could ask for. It was all he needed to sustain him. He just hoped that Casey had the same faith in Joe's decision to send him backpacking over Europe, because that was going to be a tough sell.

He did the delicate hand dance around all of Seth's attached wires and tucked the baby against his chest before placing his own hand on the baby's chest and expecting the cries, shrill and painful, at any moment. It had been proven that holding babies like this helped them thrive, but it was hard to hear, hard to see the pain that any sort of sensory input caused the little guys, even human touch. It had also been proven that the cry of a drug-addicted infant raised human blood pressure, and Joe knew it took his commute home before his eyelid stopped throbbing with the increase of his heartbeat.

But Seth didn't cry, not this time. Joe looked at him, talking to him softly. "What's wrong, little man?" He scanned the monitors quickly, taking in heartbeat, blood-gas levels, temperature—uh-oh.

It was elevated by two-tenths of a degree. Maybe the nurse who had just checked the vitals had missed it. Hell, maybe it had happened in the last ten minutes, because these guys were so little, their metabolism moved just that fast. An alarm would sound in another tenth of a degree, but Joe looked at the little face—sallow, because Seth and Levi's father had been African-American, and they weren't quite healthy enough to be light brown yet—and saw the truth, and the peace, and he swallowed.

One of the NICU nurses came in. There was one more baby in the unit, and she needed to be fed.

"Jan?" he said softly, and the woman—a comfortable woman in her fifties who had seen too many changes in her life to have much sympathy for babies like Seth and Levi—turned.

"Yeah?"

"He's getting a fever," Joe said softly. "He's coming down with an infection."

Jan sighed. "Well, it's about time. I didn't think both of them were going to survive."

She walked away wearily to alert the doctor, and Joe looked down at the unusually still, spider-limbed infant, struggling life in his arms. "You can make it, little man," Joe said softly. "You gotta fight, okay? I mean, your first couple of days here have sucked, but you've got to believe me, it'll get better."

He held Seth for another five minutes, and then the temperature alarm went off because he'd increased another tenth of a degree. Joe gave his baby a brief kiss before the doctor came in and took the tiny form out of his arms.

HE GOT home late—about four hours late—and Casey was literally pacing the floor as he walked in. Casey's computer—truly *his* computer, since he'd changed his major to computer engineering and Joe had bought him a new one just on general principle—was backlit behind him. Alvin was living in the mother-in-law cottage they'd completed the summer before, and now, in March of '95, was planning on staying there and paying a comfortable rent until he found a reason to move on. He'd actually graduated midyear, but Casey's change in concentration had come with extra units—he was set to graduate in May.

"Jesus, Joe," Casey said as he walked in. "You didn't even call! I know you think I'm kidding when I talk about putting a car phone on the bike, but those things are getting smaller every day! I was worried shitless!"

Rufus and Hi both paced at Joe's feet, a little creakier than they had been, but still good dogs.

"I'm sorry," he said quietly, patting them on the head and then heading for the fridge to get some milk. He hadn't eaten during his lunch break—he'd been with the babies. He stopped with the milk carton midway to his mouth and put it back, screwing on the lid as he went.

"Joe?"

"I've got to shower," he said, looking sightlessly into the refrigerator. This was stupid. How long had he been on this job? He'd held babies most every day. He'd stopped floating to ER as soon as the miserable supervisor in the NICU who thought all male nurses were gay (and who hated them regardless) had quit, and he'd been allowed to tend his babies unmolested. The babies loved him. They loved his rumbly voice, and the way he didn't get excited about things, and his big hands that made them feel safe.

And he loved them.

"Joe... Josiah? What's wrong?"

"Shower," he said, his vision blurring. He'd been off shift. He'd stood back and watched as the doctor had assessed and done the ultrasound and said, "Necrotizing bowel. We're not going to be able to fix this, folks. Does the baby have any family?"

"Me," Joe said, and Doc Walters had turned to him, her round, wrinkled face kind.

"Are you family enough to hold him while he dies, Daniels?"

Joe had shrugged. "I named him."

She'd nodded and left, and Jan started to disconnect the baby from all of the monitors, from the shunt, even from the respirator, because anything that would make this happen faster would be a kindness. Joe had sat in the same chair he'd occupied when he'd talked to Levi, and told Seth about all the good things his twin would do, all of the beautiful days at the shore, and walking through the woods, or reading a book that made his heart break, and how Seth would always be with him, even if Levi didn't know.

Seth's last breath had been so quiet, Joe wasn't sure how long he'd been there, talking aimlessly to a dead baby, pretending he wasn't a father.

Casey's arms crept around his waist, and he tried hard to be in the here and now. He let the refrigerator close, and Casey whispered, "Come on, Joe, let's go take a shower."

Casey grabbed his hands and pulled him up the stairs and undressed him, even took his shoes off, and turned on the shower, all in silence.

Joe went docilely and thought, *Good. Crying in the shower. Time-honored male tradition when a man can't keep his objective distance. It'll be fine.* He leaned his hands on the tile, let the water hit his back, and prepared to let go.

Then Casey stepped in behind him. Joe shored himself up again, and Casey started a slow, simple seduction. He started with a washcloth and soap and very matter-of-factly hit all of the pits, creases, and wide spaces. There was a reason Joe hit the shower before and after work—bacteria wasn't something you wanted to transport either to or from a hospital, and the longer he worked and saw infection gnaw its deadly course when no one was ready for it, the more wary he was of doing his part not to make it worse.

"Tilt your head back," Casey said softly, and Joe did, an unexpected grunt of pleasure escaping his throat as Casey soaped his hair. His body shuddered, enjoying the attention, and suddenly all of the tension on his inside turned into sensitization on the outside.

Casey finished with his hair and then turned him around. "Lean back," he said, and Joe looked at him, blinking hard in emotional exhaustion and turmoil.

"What?"

"Just lean back," Casey said, kissing his neck, kissing his chest, licking his nipple with a flat tongue (which Joe had discovered he actually liked very much), and Joe didn't have anything in him to resist. He simply leaned back and allowed the water, Casey's touch, everything, to wash over him. When Casey's mouth found his semierect cock, his groan, echoing around the shower chamber, surprised him.

Casey was good at this. He liked to use his fist and play with Joe's foreskin, pulling it over the crown and back. In their first few months, he'd peppered Joe with questions about what it was like to still have a foreskin, and how things felt and what you could do with one that you couldn't do with a circumcised cock like his own. All those questions had led to an unquestionable expertise, and all their practice hadn't hurt. Joe grunted as Casey lowered his head until Joe was bottomed out in his throat, and then pulled back, and again and again. His hands cupped and tugged on Joe's testicles, and just that fast, Joe found himself at orgasm. His vision went dark and he came, confused and heartbroken and grateful to surrender everything for just this one moment of climax in Casey's skilful mouth.

He stayed back there against the wall, thinking that the water was going to get cold in a minute, when Casey stood up and turned it off. Joe opened his eyes and found that Casey had given him a clean towel—one of the newer, fluffier ones—and Joe stepped out after him dumbly. He hadn't said a word from the moment Casey had taken his hand.

He still didn't have any words as Casey brushed his hair quickly, helped him into boxers and then pulled on his own briefs, and the two of them slid into bed.

"Josiah?" Casey said softly, and Joe turned toward him in the dark.

"Yeah?"

"How are your babies?"

"Baby," Joe said, his voice breaking. "Baby. There's only one now."

"Which one died?"

"Seth."

Casey sniffed once. "The oldest. Maybe we can make a little monument for him out in the woods."

Joe broke completely. "That's a real nice idea," he said, and then he folded Casey into his arms and cried.

CASEY didn't have school the next day, so he rode on the back of Joe's motorcycle to the hospital, face tucked into that perfect space between Joe's shoulder blades, arms wound tightly around his waist, as Joe went to his shift. When they'd woken up that morning, Casey had asked to come in and meet Levi. Alvin was going to drive into town a little later and pick him up, but in the meantime, Joe appreciated Casey's warmth at his back as he negotiated the curves of Hwy 49 to Auburn. Casey's clasp tightened considerably when they went over the

Foresthill Bridge—Joe didn't know why, but for some reason the bridge disturbed his boy in ways he would never fully articulate. Joe kept both hands on the grips to reassure him that they weren't playing around up there, and then kept going.

The babies were allowed only one visitor at a time per room, so Casey put on a sterile gown and a mask before going into the NICU, and Joe looked at him through the Plexiglas. Casey just sat there, holding the tiny tube-riddled body gingerly and talking softly.

"That your man?" Doc Walters asked, and Joe looked at her. He didn't really socialize with the doctors. A lot of them treated the nurses like hired help, which was funny, because the nurses were often the only ones who actually knew the patients' names.

"Yeah," Joe said quietly.

"He want that baby as much as you?"

"Yeah," Joe said, because he was pretty sure it was true.

"That baby's got another six months in here, you know."

Joe nodded. "At the very least."

"There's going to be things wrong with him, learning disabilities, emotional disabilities—all sorts of bullshit. You know that, right, Joe?"

"I'm not stupid."

She sighed, looking at Casey, who apparently had told the baby a joke and was laughing at it himself. He'd cut his hair the year before, and it was crisp on his neck. If he held to form, he'd let it grow for another two months, until it was silky over his collar, and then cut it again. Joe liked the system—it was a good one.

"It's not easy for two gay men in the world right now. But it's becoming more common than you think."

Joe looked at her curiously. She was older—in her late fifties—with no-nonsense gray hair and a reputation for fairness among the nurses that was hard to maintain in the age-old enmity that existed there. "Is it?" he asked.

"I'll talk to their social worker," she said decisively, and Joe grimaced. He and social workers were sort of fifty-fifty.

"Roy Petty, out in Chana?" he asked hopefully, and she looked at him, surprised.

"You know him?"

Joe thought of the bald guy with the curly gray fringe and really large red nose. "More or less. We sort of pick up strays now and then. He's my contact."

"He like you?"

Joe thought about their limited exchanges, both when he'd been Casey's supervisor and with the other kids who had come and gone since then. "Yeah, I think so. He's not really a demonstrative guy. But he knows Casey pretty well."

Walters smiled. "I think if he doesn't have to worry about you, you're in. Would you like me to make this happen?"

Joe looked at her with sudden hope. "Yeah. Why?"

The woman shook her head. "Because we see them go into social services all the time, and we're pretty sure they're doomed. I'd like to see one make it, that's all."

"Yeah. Me too."

"I'll make that call." She didn't shake his hand or smile or anything else, just stumped away, a little woman with a purpose. Joe wouldn't even get to thank her before she retired, without fanfare, to private practice, probably one that wouldn't break her heart on a regular basis. At least Joe hoped so. Her passing kindness turned out to be one of the most important ones in his and Casey's life.

But at the moment, taking that baby home with them was just a hope, a hint, a maybe. If Casey hadn't cried in his arms for Seth, a baby he hadn't even met, the night before, Joe wouldn't even burden him with it, but Casey *had* cried, so Joe *would* tell him.

And eventually, he'd come clean about the graduation present that he was pretty sure Casey was gonna hate.

The One I Love
~Casey

JOE took him out to dinner and very bluntly rearranged his world.

"I'm going where?"

They were in the middle of Cattleman's, South Placer's most well-known and high-priced steakhouse, and Casey was sitting there in his best chinos and sport jacket, looking at Joe, who was dressed the same. Casey was wondering if his lover had lost his fucking mind.

"Europe, with Alvin," Joe said, then bit into his very rare steak and closed his eyes in bliss. "Happy graduation. Oh God. That's good."

"I'm sure it's fucking manna from heaven. Why am I leaving you right before we're about to bring a baby home?" He very thoughtfully did not add the "or lose him forever" part of that statement, because Levi was by no means out of the woods health-wise, even with four more weeks since his brother's death and another pound under his bracelet-size belt. And even if Levi made it, their adoption was by no means guaranteed. It was iffy, up in the air, like a big gay juggling show of paperwork and affidavits and interviews with the social worker and Casey and silent judgment whenever they walked into the office with a new piece of paperwork. Casey's identification was under question until Casey finally drove down to Bakersfield and got a new birth certificate from the hospital. He refused to call his mother. That would just fuck up the whole works—it would be like a voodoo whammy, Casey was damned positive. Casey refused to show the birth certificate to Joe too. The only name he wanted on his ID was Daniels, and the only reason he'd revisit that other name was so Levi could come home with them, where their baby belonged.

Yeah, Casey was a wee bit possessive, why do you ask?

Josiah finished chewing and swallowed blissfully, then sighed and opened his eyes. "Because. Alvin's going, you guys are best friends, and we can afford it. Because after this, you're going to have to decide on a job. Yes, I know about the job fair and how your whole concentration is in San Jose, so don't pretend I don't. I know about the offers from Intel, and yeah, of course I'd rather you go to Folsom because that way we can live together like married people, and my life would be real fuckin' easy," Joe said, not even once looking at the steak cooling on his plate, so he must have meant it. "Because if you come home, where everything in me is screaming that you belong, and we do get custody of one very small, one *very* needy child, you are going to be a grown-up for real and for fucking keeps, and before all that happens to you, I would like to give you two months in Europe to see the world, screw around, and maybe get a perspective that our— *my*—"

"Our," Casey said flatly, pleased that this wasn't easy for him.

"*The* house in Foresthill and the dogs and the cats are not the be-all and end-all of civilization, is that so goddamned wrong?" He took his next bite vengefully, and Casey watched with narrowed eyes as he remembered to stop and savor as he was chewing. "Yeah," Joe said through a full mouth. "Still good."

"When you say 'screw around', you mean...?"

Joe swallowed, but it didn't look easy. "Whatever you want it to mean," he said tonelessly.

Casey started to growl. "If you touched another man—or woman—I'd—"

"Geld me," Joe said, grimacing. "Yeah, Casey. I'm fully aware."

"So you want me to….." Casey couldn't even say it. The thought made him sick.

"You're missing the point here!" Joe said a little desperately.

"So explain it to me!"

"The point is, I want you to see the world—without any more baggage than you can carry with you, okay? I don't want to be the man who holds you back from anything, who keeps you from having or experiencing anything, just because—"

"Because I love you so much I'm stupid with it?" Casey snapped. The red was starting to fade from his vision a little. He got the concept. He did. He got what Joe was saying. He did. But that didn't mean that his visceral gut reaction wasn't a strong desire to take any man or woman who had the potential to sleep with Joe and nail them to a wall and gut them with a bowie knife. Yeah, yeah, he got that it wasn't *Joe* who was supposed to be getting some on the side, but that didn't matter. What mattered was—"Wouldn't you be the least bit jealous?"

Joe glared at him and then glared at his steak. "Goddammit. I knew I should have left this conversation for dessert."

Casey saw that his hands were shaking on his utensils, so he sighed, still mad but not seeing red in his vision. "Put the knife and fork down, Joe, so you don't shed any of my blood in here. Good. Well done. Now look me in the eyes and tell me it wouldn't kill you."

Joe looked off to the side. "Wouldn't kill me. I'd be too busy killing *him.*"

"Who?"

"Whoever."

Casey smiled and let a little more of his anger fade. "Which is why you're telling me to go to Europe and do this, I assume."

Joe looked woefully at his steak. "I'm not actually telling you to go out and do it, Casey. I think your trip could be plenty complete without it. I just want you to go... go out and have fun. Don't you see how badly I want you to have this before our world shrinks to just the baby and us?"

"I'll think about it," Casey said at last, and Joe relaxed enough to take another bite. "Still good?" Something about steak—Joe couldn't cook one to save his life, but he loved to eat them. They went out to a steakhouse about once a month, and it was always the same: Joe would about sell his soul for a properly cooked piece of rare meat.

Joe chewed blissfully. "Oh yeah," he sighed, and Casey turned his attention to his chicken and asparagus, feeling marginally better.

BUT that didn't stop him from stripping out of his good clothes when they got home that night like a rabbit on speed and diving for the end table with the lube.

After they'd returned from New York two years before, Casey had let his curiosity drive him. Joe had professed to have a kinky streak, and Casey had *needed* that explained. Rather than ask the man himself—well, at first, anyway—Casey had investigated the most holy of holy hotbeds of kink: Joe's lube drawer.

What he'd found there had blown his mind.

Dildos. Medium to large rubberized dildos and plugs inside the drawer—almost every one made as lifelike as possible. There were condoms (probably to make cleanup easier) and lubricant—even the kind that warmed and the kind that was good in water—and, well.

Dildos.

Joe liked to bottom—or, probably more accurately, Joe *dreamed* of bottoming.

Casey couldn't imagine any scenario in which someone would try to top him. He was a barrel-chested giant of a man. He wore the leather biking pants and jacket, and, well… he was everything a boy dreamed a bear-daddy leather-man would turn out to be.

But apparently in the quiet of his own bedroom, without anyone to judge him or expect him to be something, Joe liked a good hard fuck in the ass as much as the next tush-wiggling bottom, and Casey had tried to wrap his head around that in a big way.

It had taken him a while. The first time he'd mentioned the drawer and what was in it, Joe had made a game try at offering it to Casey, like that was what it was there for—other people.

The second time he'd mentioned it—that summer when Alvin was back at home, visiting his parents (and apparently trying to explain that he was still straight, even though his roommates were gay, which was why he got the mother-in-law cottage with its one bedroom, bathroom, and kitchenette pretty much as soon as it was done)—Joe had looked a little uncomfortable and walked away. That was it. Just walked away, no explanation or anything.

That had been over a year ago.

Casey had explored that drawer intimately since then—mostly in his own ass. He knew the feel of each toy, how it was best used, the mood he had to be in for each one. Joe would be away on shift, and Casey would be home alone, and if he had no homework, he'd be up in their bedroom, stark naked, masturbating his heart out and imagining Joe *was* home, and what he'd *really* like up his ass…

And what he thought he'd really like to do to Joe.

And Joe had just bought him a vacation package to Europe and pretty much told him he was going whether he wanted to or not.

Casey thought it was time for the jack-offs to come out of the box.

So Joe walked up the stairs behind him, and Casey jumped off the bed as Joe shed his shirt, and wrapped an arm around his waist.

"Josiah?"

"Yeah?" Joe grunted, and Casey breathed him in deeply. God, so male, so honest, so very Joe.

"I want you to do me a favor."

"What's that?" He half turned, an indulgent smile on his face, and Casey met his eyes squarely.

"I want you to get into bed and close your eyes, and don't open them until I say to, okay?"

Joe grimaced. "I thought we were gonna, you know…." He made helpless gestures with his hands and tilted his head. "Sex?"

Casey nodded enthusiastically. "Yes, Joe, we are going to do that. I promise. Just… just let me… let me surprise you."

Joe frowned. "Casey, a man doesn't always like surprises in his bed. Of all people, *you* should know that by now."

Casey tilted his head and gave an evil little smile. "Yeah, but Joe, sometimes a guy just likes to be trusted. Of *all* people, you should know that by now."

Joe sighed and shook his head, then toed off his shoes and stripped down to his boxers. He was preparing to throw his clothes in the hamper when Casey—who was pulling down the blankets and putting a towel on the bed, because neither of them were going to feel like changing sheets after what he had in mind—looked up and said, "Boxers too, big man."

Joe looked at him and grimaced. "With my eyes closed?"

"I *have* seen you naked before, Josiah," Casey said drolly, and Joe didn't take the bait and blush. Instead, he curled his surprisingly red lips into a droll smile of his own, the kind with heavy eyes and a full appreciation of everything Casey's body had to offer.

"I'm fully aware of it, Casey. In fact, I sort of appreciate that about you."

Casey's full-wattage grin flashed, and he gestured imperiously with his chin. "Boxers. Now."

Joe sighed and then laid himself out on the bed with his hands behind his head, gloriously, magnificently naked, his uncut cock starting to peek out of his wealth of black hair, his chest as wide and as furry as it always looked when Casey was in his arms, his hair pulled to the side so he wasn't lying on it, and his eyes closed.

Casey stripped so quickly he tripped getting out of his underwear and almost fell on the bed. "Here," he said hurriedly, "keep the eyes closed. I'm going to get a bandana, okay?" Joe had a lot of them from riding the bike. He swore he'd never used them for the twinkie code, and he definitely wasn't buying into any of the gang bullshit down in the cities; they just came in handy when you were trying to cool your face off or bind your hair back or any one of a half a dozen things that came up when you'd just ridden twenty miles on a souped-up Harley. Casey grabbed one of those—well laundered, soft, and faded navy blue—from Joe's clean underwear drawer and stretched out over the man he'd loved for... God. Ever. Casey had loved Joe forever. And then he tied it gently around Joe's eyes.

"Are you going to tell me what this is for?" Joe asked, and Casey sighed in frustration.

"Well, I'm sort of playing out a hunch, and if I'm right, you're going to be very happy. If I'm wrong, we're both going to be horribly embarrassed, and I figure the blindfold will help." Casey said this while opening the lube drawer, and as he turned around, he saw that Joe's cock—which had been looking pretty handsome at half-mast—was now fully engorged. Stiff, proud, the hood fully retracted, it flexed on Joe's belly with what looked like Joe's unconscious clenching of his ass.

Casey shivered. Oh yeah. Oh yes, oh yes, oh yes. Joe was going to get the rewards of having a kink drawer and a boyfriend who loved him, oh yes he was!

And Casey would get to, maybe, prove to Joe that sometimes, Casey really did know what he was talking about. That would be nice too.

He pulled out what he wanted—the lube, of course, and the toy he most wanted to see in his lover's body.

It was unprepossessing, at first.

An average size (because Casey was pretty sure Joe hadn't been in the drawer for a while) and a bright pink (because it amused him), it was realistically shaped, with a set of pretend balls at the base and a decent curve that *should* hit Joe right in the sweet spot. (Casey knew it hit him there when *he* used it.)

It was perfect for a guy who hadn't ridden for a while, and for the other thing Casey had planned.

So Casey set up, rolled the condom on the toy, and got to work.

He wasn't subtle in bed—never had been. He liked licking Joe's nipples, and now that Joe was lying in the cool of their upstairs, he knew his warm mouth would give Joe the shivers, so that was where he started. Joe started to quiver on contact, and Casey chuckled.

"Didn't know where I was gonna start, didja?" He punctuated that with a little lick, and Joe shuddered again, so Casey licked it one more time, at the same time he moved his hand—and he knew his fingers were a little bit cold—down to his favorite place and got a good grip.

He shuddered as Joe's cock filled his hand, and he played the game of trying to touch his thumb to his fingers when he wrapped hard and squeezed. He succeeded—barely—and Joe groaned, a little bit of fluid leaking out the end already.

Oh no—going too quickly! Casey scooted down and took Joe in his mouth, thinking that he felt enormous tonight, and wondering if it was the excitement of the blindfold or of being spread out to the air, or maybe that he'd heard Casey in the drawer and knew what was coming next. Something, because Casey knew this cock almost better than his own, and it was definitely more engorged than usual, and more sensitive (because Joe moaned with just the feel of his breath on the end), and Casey felt guilty for ducking under Joe's leg and ending the blowjob so soon. His sounds were so needy! But Casey parted Joe's thighs and then parted his cheeks and delved his tongue in between, doing it quickly enough that Joe wouldn't guess what he was up to and the touch of his tongue on the little pucker would come as a surprise.

Joe's hips arched off the bed, and Casey followed him desperately, grabbing his thighs with both hands and forcing him down before licking more and harder on Joe's least-used erogenous zone. Joe groaned, and he lowered his hands to Casey's short-cut hair and pushed, but since he didn't tell Casey to stop, Casey assumed that meant more instead.

"God... God, Casey!"

Casey pulled back and said, "You like that, huh?" He licked again while his hand reached for the toy and the lube.

Joe rumbled, "Yes, dammit, but... oh God... my cock, dammit...." Joe reached for his cock, and Casey stopped him with a little slap.

"Don't you dare!" Casey said, pushing up off the bed. While he was talking, he busied his hands, pouring lube on the toy and moving it into position.

"But, kid!" Joe sounded reassuringly young. Of course, whining did that to a man, but Casey didn't care. He was being surprised, and he was desperate, which meant he wouldn't protest when—

"Ooooooooooohhhhh *Keeerrrrriiiiiisssstttt!*" Joe's breath exploded all in a burst, and he pushed against the head of the dildo, forcing it deep inside.

Casey waited a moment while Joe's body got used to the thing, and then pushed it in a little more. And a little more. And a little more. And the whole time Joe was shouting (oh God, *shouting!*) and begging and pleading and finally, finally, Casey felt enough glide to push that thing home.

Joe's whole body shook and his hips arched off the bed, and his hands clenched in the sheets, and the whole time he was muttering to himself, "Oh God... oh God... oh God... damn... oh... Casey... holy crap, that feels good... oh geez... *Casey, would you fuck me with that thing?*"

Casey was happy to oblige. He started out slow, pulling it out gently until the shaped cockhead caught on its way out, and then he pushed in again while Joe writhed above him. He was being careful not to crush Casey by anchoring his legs, but every other part of his powerful body was trembling and wire-taut.

Finally, Casey couldn't handle anymore—*he* needed some satisfaction, and he wanted Joe to just totally lose his goddamned mind. He thrust the toy in to the balls and wiggled under Joe's leg to kneel at the side of his body, where Casey paused to lube up his own sphincter, his fingers shaking, he was so needy. God... watching Joe, wanting, at his mercy, so incredibly turned on—Casey could have come on the covers if he'd ground a little harder, and he *so* wasn't wasting that erection or Joe's frenzy on another round of laundry!

He rose up and swung his leg over Joe's hips, straddling him, and then grasped Joe's hard, weeping cock in his hand and lowered himself on top of it. Now *he* wanted to cry, it felt so good, and Joe? Joe went completely still.

"Kid?" he asked, his voice gruff and pleading.

"Yeah, Joe?"

"Can I grab you and fuck you now?"

"'Til I'm blind," Casey said cheerfully, and Joe dug his fingers into Casey's thighs and held him just high enough for Joe to piston his hips upward in a frenzied rabbit fuck that had Casey *howling*, throwing his weight a little forward and holding himself on the bed so Joe could *really* cock his hips and hammer him.

"*Oh God, Joe... keep it up... oh God... don't stop... don't stop, don't stop, don't stop, oh fuck don't ever stop fucking me!*" And his voice must have done it, or the first contraction of his orgasm. Casey's entire body froze in a clench around that giant thing in his ass, and he grabbed his cock hard and shot across Joe's chest, and again and again. For his part, Joe held on tight and buried himself in Casey's body, howling, coming, hot and hard, until Casey could feel it sliding out of his body and lubricating Joe's still-erect cock some more as he fucked through both their orgasms, until Casey was slumped on Joe's chest in a puddle of his own come. His hips could barely twitch anymore, he was so incredibly replete.

"So," Casey panted as Joe's hands came up and rested comfortingly on his shoulders, "do you trust me *now*?" He reached up and pulled off the bandana so he could see those wonderful, placid, warm brown eyes while they had this conversation.

Joe nodded, and Casey stretched a little more, letting Joe fall out of his ass in a gush of come, and thought dimly of a shower.

"Good," he said after their mouths met, and Joe's tongue swept between his lips, and they retreated. "Because I'll tell you something."

"What?"

"I'll go to Europe, and I'm damned grateful, but I'm not screwing around. Okay?"

Very slowly, Joe's lips turned up in a smile.

THREE months later, Casey and Alvin were in Europe, having the time of their lives. They were going with a tourist group, the kind that moved from hotel to hotel and then split up with the understanding that if you didn't make it back to the group, your people at home would be contacted immediately. It was typical of Joe to send Casey in a situation that was so safe and that gave him so much freedom at the same time.

They were in Pisa when Alvin got sunstroke. Poor Alvin—the hot Mediterranean sun had not been good to him. Casey had tanned, his hair turning gold like it did in the summer, but Alvin had spent most of his time burning or trying to keep from being burnt or getting sick because he'd had too much sun.

At Pisa, Alvin—who was great at not whining—had finally had enough. "God, Casey—don't hate me. I know everyone's going out to a club tonight, but… Jesus. I just want to sleep. I'm sorry."

Casey patted him on the shoulder (gingerly—he'd burnt through his shirt) and went downstairs, planning to have a dinner at the hotel and then go back to the room to keep Alvin company. Instead, he met Paolo.

Paolo was a sloe-eyed con man if Casey had ever seen one, and that first twitch of the full lips and slow assessment of the half-lidded, liquid brown eyes made Casey remember his street days, so very long ago, and he had to grin back.

Paolo sauntered up to where Casey was seated, and said, "You look lonely. Would you like some company? My name is Paolo, and I seem to have lost my group."

Casey looked at him wryly and glanced around the restaurant. Paolo must be exclusively a man's man, Casey figured, because there were two pretty girls at a table nearby who were looking at him excitedly, and at Casey too, and Casey didn't want to think about their heartbreak if they figured out what was going on at their little table.

"I'll tell ya what," Casey said, feeling generous. Paolo's white shirt looked a little threadbare, and it may have been a few days since he had showered with a mark. "You sit down, I'll treat you to dinner, and you skip the song and dance where you try to seduce me and roll me for my wallet."

Paolo spent a whole thirty seconds trying to look wounded, but apparently the weight of Casey's skeptical eyebrow was too much. "You are too kind," he said, seating himself and deferring to Casey as the waiter stopped by.

Casey ordered wine for Paolo and mineral water for himself—he was wearing a new white linen shirt, the kind that opened up almost to the navel, and he didn't want to spill wine on it before Joe got to see it. Levi had not been doing well when Casey left; Casey wanted Joe to be as happy as possible that Casey was home when he returned, in case things went south.

Casey frowned in thought, knowing that Joe's voice had sounded funny at their last phone call, in Rome, and wishing he knew what was going on. He'd asked repeatedly about Levi, and Joe had reassured him that their boy was fine. The whole social work thing was still up in the air, but since they had visited the boy damned near every day—hell, even *Alvin* had taken up visiting him at odd hours of the day—that had to count for something, right? The hospital staff knew them, and Alvin had started dating a nurse who worked in labor and delivery, and basically? That tiny child with all the tubes in his battling body had become the one point of purpose in the world of three grown men. The system might not recognize Joe and Casey as parents yet, but Levi was their boy in everyone's eyes but the law's.

"Might I ask what is the matter?" Paolo asked, and Casey figured what the hell? He was paying for dinner, right? May as well get a shrink service on the side.

So he started talking about Joe, and about Levi, and about the family and the promise and how he and Joe were in reaching distance of everything they'd ever wanted, and if Levi fought his last cold and the powers that be finally signed their paperwork, it would be within their grasp.

While he was talking, dinner arrived, and they ate—Paolo voraciously and Casey a little more carefully. He was never going to be able to compete with Joe, and his metabolism was going to slow down any day. When he was done, Paolo looked at him and shook his head.

"You would never think," he said after a moment. "Rich Americans come in all the time. Students whose parents will wire them more money, rich businessmen who are trying to escape their wives. I walked up to a pretty man and thought, 'He can afford to lose some money. He will probably even enjoy the lay.' You never think that you are walking up to a man with a lover and a good heart."

Casey winked. "Well, the good heart is mostly Joe," he said frankly. "But as for the lover… hey. Could you do me a favor?"

So after dinner, they went up to the concierge, and Casey asked to make a phone call to the States. He used his phone card and gave a sigh of relief when Joe picked up the phone on the fourth ring. Even though it was morning in Foresthill, Joe had put himself on the schedule for nights when Casey was gone. Casey was pretty sure he'd be waking Joe up out of a sound sleep.

"Joe?" he said, winking at Paolo. "How's Levi?"

"Out of the woods," Joe said, and Casey gave a sigh of relief. "Weren't you going to call me tomorrow?"

"Yeah, baby. I just wanted to tell you something."

"Okay." Joe yawned. "You know. Fire away."

"I'm standing here with a beautiful… oh God, *amazing*-looking guy. He's hot. Just… fuckworthy in the extreme."

"And you're telling me this because…?"

"Because he's about to leave the hotel to find someplace to stay, and we will *not* have sex. Isn't that right, Paolo?"

He gestured at Paolo, who bent down and spoke into the phone. "Is true," he said winsomely, winking at Casey.

"Is that okay?" Casey asked and was rewarded by Joe's dry chuckle, echoing darkly in his ear. Something about the sound reminded Casey of their room in the moonlight and Joe moving slowly and powerfully in Casey's body, like he had the night before Casey left.

"Yeah, kid. It's absolutely fine with me if you don't have sex with a handsome stranger. I love you, Casey."

"I love you too, Josiah. I really miss home."

"Four more weeks."

"Too long."

"You're telling me. Enjoy yourself, okay?"

"I promise."

And with that, Casey rang off. Paolo bent and kissed his cheek and only made a halfhearted grab at Casey's wallet before he left, and Casey went upstairs so he could bring a bottle of fruit juice and sparkling water to Alvin.

We'll Be Together
~Joe

CASEY'S call *had* woken Joe up at nine in the morning after a swing shift—but he didn't go back to sleep.

The first thing he did was go to the social services office in Auburn and sign what he'd been told was the final round of paperwork. He'd believe that eventually, but as it was, he and Roy Petty were practically old friends now. Petty had investigated the house, which turned out to be an excuse to stay for dinner, because Petty was newly divorced and not really a bad guy. Really, really *busy*, and not inclined to socialize when there was a kid present, but not a bad guy. They'd rented a movie—Roy asked him if he'd seen *Philadelphia* yet, and Joe said no, he and Casey wouldn't watch it. They'd seen too much of it in the last eight years, and it just hurt too damned much. Instead, they rented *Four Weddings and a Funeral*, which had come out the year before as well, and Joe had liked it very much. In fact, he liked it enough to buy it used, because he wanted Casey to see it with him.

So this visit in, Roy shook his hand and said, "When Levi is released from the hospital, Mr. Daniels, call me. I'll be there to sign you out and to check on you for the first two years. If there are no challenges after two years in your home, then he should—barring anything unforeseen—be yours to keep." Roy smiled kindly, looking tired, and anxiously glanced at his clock for the next appointment. "He's already yours, Joe. You and Casey made a real nice home."

Joe had smiled, pleased, bashful, and not quite believing that it was true, and gone on to his next errand.

He was driving the pickup truck with a dolly and a ramp in the back, because he was going to need them. He went to Rocklin, to Ruhkala Monument and picked up two basic headstones. One read "Seth Joshua Daniels, b. Feb. 22, 1995, d. March 7, 1995, Son to Casey and Joe." The other one read, quite simply, "Rufus."

Joe hadn't had the heart to tell Casey about Rufus. He'd had no idea how old the dog was—they'd had him for eight years, but old Ira had probably had him for six before that. One morning, Joe got up to let the dogs out only to find them curled up in the kitchen instead of by his bed where they'd been sleeping. That morning, Rufus hadn't gotten up. Hi had lingered, sniffing the cold body where his friend had once been, and Joe had been heartbroken, particularly because Casey hadn't been there.

If it had been Levi, well, Joe's passport was still in order—he would have flown to wherethehellever and given Casey the news himself. But it was Rufus, and Casey couldn't do anything about it, so Joe hadn't told him, and he hoped it was the right decision.

He'd buried Rufus where he'd buried Seth's ashes (because he'd been given custody of them and had applied for a permit to do that on his own property)—out in the back stretch, where you only went if you were looking for a lonely walk in the woods.

Hi had taken to wandering over there and sleeping in the impression made by the displaced dirt, and Joe thought that after Casey got home, they'd go pick out another puppy from the nearby shelter to keep him company, if he looked to last that long. Poor thing was like to grieve himself to death without his buddy. Joe might have to get that puppy alone.

So his second stop was to the headstone place. It was family owned and had been in the area for over a hundred years. There was even a street in Rocklin named after the family, and a little house rumored to sit on a foundation made entirely of broken headstones.

His third stop was to the pick-and-pull places in Rocklin and Roseville. There were a couple of them in the area, back to back, big junkyards out by the railroad, acres of cars stretching out to be sold as parts. Joe had sat down with a pad and pencil during breakfast, doing the math so he could get his first round of parts. By the time he was finished with that, it was five o'clock on a blistering afternoon. The temperatures were in the low hundreds, and the dust was so bad he could barely breathe. He rolled the windows down in the truck on his way up to his place, because the truck still didn't have air-conditioning. He left the truck parked when he got home, hopped on the bike in cut-off jeans and a T-shirt, and rode it down to Lake Sugar Pine, which was less than twenty minutes away. He swam in the lake for an hour and dried off as he rode the bike home in the green/red twilight of the foothills, planning his next move.

JOE waited anxiously at the gate of Casey's return flight at Sacramento's newly "international" airport, so called because it had a flight to Mexico. (It was big news—there was a sculpture of piled suitcases and everything!) Casey and Alvin should be coming up the ramp at any time—the arrivals/departures board said they'd arrived half an hour ago. Casey was, in all but his actual physical presence in Joe's arms, home.

Alvin's girlfriend, Wendy, was there waiting with him, casting surreptitious and shy looks Joe's way until he said something friendly. She smiled and replied, and together they talked about when they'd heard from the boys and what they'd been doing and how much they'd enjoyed the trip. It wasn't long before he was thinking Alvin should have Wendy for dinner more often, but odds were good Alvin probably wasn't going to let her out of the bedroom for at least another week.

Then Casey shouted, and everything else left his brain.

For a moment, Joe just looked at him hungrily as Casey dodged through the crowd coming from the plane, hauling Joe's old duffel bag over his shoulder as a carry-on. He was brown, which he usually was in the summer, and his hair had grown over his collar and was shiny gold from the sun. His face was a little bit rounder than it had been when he'd left—he'd complained about the rich food during the whole trip—but his deep-set eyes were squinting as he smiled, and he was *galloping* in an ecstasy of delight that Joe should be standing right there.

Joe turned and ran toward him and then stood still while Casey dropped his duffel mid-run and climbed Joe like a tree, throwing himself into Joe's arms, where Joe had needed him for the past two months.

Casey lowered his mouth to Joe's, and the kiss went on—could have gone on forever, but Joe caught some nasty comments from the people around them. He and Casey were usually pretty low-key in public, but not now. Now, the whole rest of the world could go fuck itself—Joe had Casey back. The world was perfect.

Alvin and Wendy were having a similar reunion, and then Casey and Alvin babbled over each other as they walked downstairs to the carousels to retrieve their luggage. Then they took that surprising step out into the sultry Sacramento night, crossed the throughway at the crosswalk, and headed for short-term parking.

When they got to the parking lot, Casey and Alvin stopped babbling about the crazy thing that had happened to them at a London pub, and looked at each other, sort of at a loss.

"God," Alvin said, smiling, "that was fuckin' real!"

The two of them hugged fiercely, in spite of Alvin's *really* uncomfortable-looking sunburn, and Alvin said he'd probably be back up in his little cottage in two days, and then he and Wendy disappeared, giggling, into the parking lot space while Joe took Casey toward the car.

Which was not the car Casey remembered.

"This isn't my Taurus!"

"No, Casey, a Volvo is not a Taurus," Joe said dryly, and Casey looked at him.

"A Volvo! How am I supposed to pay for a Volvo!"

Joe shrugged. "Well, I assumed you were going to get one of those job offers lying on the kitchen table."

"I've got job offers?" Casey looked dazed.

"Yeah. It seems all that college fair stuff you did before you left paid off."

"From Hewlett-Packard? From Intel? From Silicon Valley?"

"Yes." Joe smiled. So much to tell, so very few words.

"*All* of them?" Casey asked, flabbergasted, and Joe grinned widely.

"Yes!"

"But why a Volvo?"

Joe had used the little door-clicker to unlock the thing, and he and Casey swung their stuff into the trunk. Joe slammed the trunk and looked at him, his smile so real it hurt. "Because it's got one of the highest safety ratings of any car out there, and Levi's coming home in less than a month, and it matters."

Casey didn't climb him like a tree this time. He cuddled into his Joe's arms and cried until he hiccupped. Joe just held him, eyes closed, in the parking lot of Sacramento International, and let him. There was nothing else to do, no one else to be but the man who held Casey and let him be relieved and overjoyed.

Casey and Alvin had been flying for nearly thirty-six hours. Casey might have wanted to talk all night, but he got into the car and promptly fell asleep. Joe was able to wake him up when they'd gotten home, and he managed to stumble into the house and into the shower while Joe was bringing the luggage up, but Joe put the dogs to bed. Hi really had been grieving himself to death, so Joe had gone out and bought a big mongrel mix puppy that he'd been calling Jonesy because he'd liked *The Hunt For Red October*, and for no other reason. When they were sleeping (Jonesy chewing on Hi's ear and Hi patiently letting him) he started the first load of laundry from Casey's big suitcase. While that was working, he went upstairs to climb into bed and hold him, sweeping his hand in slow strokes down Casey's bare back as he slept.

For the first time, Joe contemplated their age difference and was grateful. Casey might have to endure some hellish years after Joe passed on, but Joe would *never* have to be separated from Casey again. It was okay; Casey was tough. Casey would survive, watch Levi raise a family, play with grandkids. Joe didn't think he'd make it if he couldn't see Casey for another two months. He'd be like Hi, fit to grieve himself to death, except it would take more than a puppy and patrolling the property against evil rabbits and squirrels to make him start eating again.

So Joe just lay there and held him and quietly, sincerely, thanked God.

THE next morning, Joe was up and showered and doing things like washing the laundry and feeding the cats when Casey apparently popped up like a jack-in-the-box and came scrambling down the stairs.

"Where's Rufus?" he asked, looking adorable with his hair sticking out all over his head and his briefs twisted around his body.

"What?"

Casey squinted at him, opened and closed his eyes, and said, "Where's Rufus? I… I don't remember seeing him last night. Where is he?"

Joe sighed. He'd been hoping to put some of this off at least until Casey'd had breakfast. "Go put some clothes on, baby," he said quietly. "I've got something to show you."

It was warm, even in the morning, so Casey came back down in his old cut-off jeans and a T-shirt and a pair of flip-flops, none of which would have made the cut to travel. He looked almost exactly like he had when Joe had taken him to Sugar Pine when he'd been in high school, and Joe quirked up a corner of his mouth under his mustache. He wasn't that boy anymore, never would be again, and as grateful as Joe was for knowing that boy, he was even more grateful for having the man in his life.

"C'mon," he said quietly, standing at the doorway and holding out his hand. "C'mon. There's something I need you to see."

It was a little chilly in the shadow of the pines and cedars, and Joe's house was in a valley, which meant they were almost always in shade. Joe liked his little valley, this hole in an increasingly busy world. Yeah, he'd gotten the satellite so they could have decent television, and he was going to subscribe to DSL as soon as the station got up this way because Casey needed it if he was going to stay up on technology, but mostly? He was content here, and some of his nicest, most peaceful moments came when he was standing on the red earth and looking up past the tree spires to the blue sky. If he were a man of words, he could have written poetry for that, but as it was, he just liked to raise his face to the heavens and let his heart fly.

Maybe he'd do that today, but for the moment, he kept his eyes on the ground as he and Casey picked their way back toward the heart of the property, to a place where Casey had once brought a sleeping bag so he could lay out under the stars to sleep because it was too hot in the house. Joe had cleared out the brush and leveled it a little, but mostly, it was the same forest clutter underfoot—slivers of wood, twigs, and fallen leaves from the oak trees and needles from the pine.

At the base of a truly spectacular Joshua pine, the fragrant kind with the bark that looked like round-ended puzzle pieces, were the two small monuments. Joe paused for a second and heard Casey go, "Aww," as he saw Seth's to the left, and then "No. No. Geez, Joe, why didn't you tell me?"

Joe shook his head and looked down into those familiar gray eyes, which were growing bright and shiny and almost spilling over. "If he'd been sick, that would've been one thing," he said truthfully. "But one morning, Hi got up and he didn't."

Hi, who had followed them out there, heard his name and woofed, pushing his head under Casey's hand for some long-overdue affection. Casey turned and squatted, gave the dog a hug, and got his face licked, and then Jonesy, the motley puppy with his mismatched coat of black, brown, and gray blotches in medium-length hair, came and licked Casey's face too.

"I was going to wait for you to get back to get another dog," Joe explained guiltily, "but he wasn't going to make it, Casey. He was going to grieve himself to death, and I thought that would be worse."

Casey kept petting, getting to know the puppy, reacquainting himself with the dog, but the bend of his neck, the curve of his shoulders, were studies in hurt. "You could have told me," he muttered.

"Yeah," Joe said, "I could have. But I already knew what it felt like to grieve all alone, Casey. I thought I'd wait until you got home and let you grieve with company."

Casey stood up and launched himself into Joe's arms, bitching the whole time. "That's a real shitty philosophy, you know that? Because

that left you here alone with no one to cry on, and it was so pointless—
"

"Was not," grumbled Joe. "Man, that phone call? The one from Pisa? With Paolo? That was fuckin' awesome. I'd have sent you twice to get one of those."

"You didn't have to send me once!" Casey accused, glaring up at him with a face blotchy and stained with tears.

"No," Joe admitted. "I didn't. But you need to be glad you went, because it's the last place you go somewhere without me, that's for damned sure."

"Promise?"

Joe nodded.

"I need to hear you say it, Josiah, because the thought of you here alone, doing this, fucking kills me. You've got to promise—it's the two of us, right? We're gonna be a fuckin' team. If you think I'm not scared of bringing a baby home, you're dead wrong. I can't do it if you're going to be all 'Joe is an island.' I've got to be a partner, Josiah. It just can't work the other way."

Joe nodded, swallowing hard. "I promise," he said, his voice gruff and nearly broken. "I promise. There's some shit a man shouldn't do alone. This place right here, that's one of 'em."

"What's another?" Casey asked, still suspicious, and Joe managed a little smile.

"Go through life, period, the end. Are you done here, or do you need some more time?"

"I'll come back later," Casey said regretfully. "I'm too pissed at you still to do this place justice."

"Fair enough. C'mon. There's something else I want to show you." Joe grabbed his hand again, and they turned back around.

"Did you change the furniture?" Casey asked suspiciously. "Because that would be okay with me. That couch is getting old and fucking ratty."

"We can get a new one when we get the baby stuff and turn your old room into a nursery," Joe said. "But no."

"The bathroom looked the same." Casey pondered. "Did you finally get DSL?"

"No, I told you there's no station in the foothills, okay? Wait a few years; we'll get it when it gets here! It's not in the house!"

"Okay, so why are we going back to the house?"

"We're not. We're going back to the garage, and you're being a punk, so stop it."

"Yeah, well, I haven't had sex for two months. It's starting to grate on me."

Joe turned around and glared at him. "Well neither have I, and I'm about to rip your fool head off. Give it a rest, will ya? We're almost there."

The carport still held Casey's car (the green Volvo now, not the white Taurus—it was still strange seeing it there, and probably stranger still for Casey), but the garage had been cleared out of all the building supplies since the mother-in-law cottage was built. Nothing but space, free and clear. Joe let the feral cats sleep there, and kept all of his tools and camping equipment, but there was still room for the motorcycle, so he'd been parking the thing there for the last couple of years.

But he'd had to clear a space for the thing next to it.

"Oh. My. *God!*" Casey looked at the attachment to the motorcycle, and then turned to Joe, and then looked at it again. "Joe! What did you do to the Harley?"

Joe looked at the sidecar with justifiable pride. "I made it a motorcycle built for two."

He'd never let Casey learn to ride. They were too dangerous, he'd worry too much, and that was that. But the Volvo was a family car, and the motorcycle was built for one. He needed his man by his side.

Casey ran his hand over the sturdy metal frame. The thing was homemade—it had a modified chassis from a Yugo and the single wheel from a smaller motorcycle. Joe had cut down the interior from a Volkswagen Rabbit for the shell and installed the back bench seat from the same car. In general, the thing was a hodgepodge of various vehicles, but it was welded, soldered, and electrically connected to Joe's Harley—it could be disconnected or connected with about five minutes' worth of work with a horizontal tow bar arrangement and a plug in so the lights would run off the motorcycle's battery. It was as safe as such a thing could be—and it even had a seatbelt and a roll bar.

"I had to modify the Harley," Joe said, trying to explain. "It was giving out too much noise and exhaust—I changed up the carburetor and replaced the exhaust manifold so the exhaust comes out on the other side, and it's not so loud. There's even a Plexiglas shield between you and the bike—no heat, no exhaust, or at least less of it. It should be okay."

Casey turned to him, his eyes shiny again but all of the recrimination gone. "But why?"

"Because a man shouldn't go through life alone," Joe said simply. "And you're too big to be riding on the bitch seat all the time."

And there it was, another armload of Casey, this one warm and wonderful and not angry at all. "I'll still ride the bitch seat sometimes, you know that, right?" he whispered, and Joe shuddered and held him closer, because he wasn't just talking about the back seat of a motorcycle. He was talking about being Casey—challenging, feisty, smart, and strong, and not letting Joe get away with jack shit and not settling for anything less than full partnership, even in this big scary thing they were about to do.

"I wouldn't love you any other way."

Epilogue

Paradise
~Casey

2011

AUSTIN was almost asleep by the time Joe pulled up into the garage. He'd wolfed down the sandwich and the leftover hamburger—sleep was only natural, and Casey knew from experience that the vibrations from the sidecar, that low to the ground, could be incredibly peaceful. Unless you were Levi, because every time Joe took *him* in the sidecar, he threw up.

Casey went into the guest room and got sweats and a T-shirt out of the drawers. After Levi had thrived so well in his first few years, Roy Petty had pulled some strings. They were certified emergency foster parents now—there were all sorts of sizes of things in there for just such an emergency.

On his way out, he heard Levi turn down the TV in his room. He was supposed to be studying, which was why he hadn't gone out to dinner with them, but Casey wasn't going to chew him out unless he saw a failed test. The kid did good—worked hard, harder than the other kids, because the insults to his little noggin when he'd been born didn't just go away with love.

"Casey?" Levi came to his doorway, and Casey looked up at him and smiled. He'd hit six feet tall that summer, and his body was all arms and legs and oversized feet. He'd said often that he wanted to be as tall as Joe. It could happen.

"Heya, Levi. How's the studying?"

Levi grimaced and ran his hand over his shaved head and the blond-brown kinky stubble that remained. For a while, it had been cornrows and beads and Casey rebraiding it a different way every week because Joe was at a loss for that one. Thank *God* Levi had decided he liked it better short. They'd bought a set of clippers and told him to knock himself out. "Algebra II. You wouldn't... you know. Want to come help me with it?"

God, it was hard to ask for things at seventeen, wasn't it?

"I'd love to," Casey said, standing on his toes and running his hand over that shaved head. God, he'd held this kid when he was a bald, screaming baby; he surely had the right to palm that big goofy teenager's head now, right?

Levi grinned, his teeth big and even (braces!) and white in his latte-colored, high cheek-boned face. He had a long jaw and a slightly flattened nose. No beauty contests in his future, probably, but that smile—God. Melted Casey, and had Joe wrapped around the kid's little finger, ever since his very first one.

"We brought home a stray, though," Casey said, looking at Levi meaningfully, and Levi nodded. This wasn't their first one, and Levi knew the drill. "We've got to get him showered and deloused before he goes to bed."

Levi grimaced. "Oh God. Doesn't Roy take care of that when we get them?" Lice. They'd all had 'em.

"Yeah, but we found this one. Your dad's calling Roy right now."

Levi nodded. "How bad?" One thing he'd learned growing up in Joe's house was that as hard as it was working through the ADHD, the dyslexia, the communication handicaps and slight hearing loss that his hellific infancy had bestowed on him, there was always someone out there who was worse off than he was. Casey had often thought that Levi could have been another statistic. He'd been an angry middle schooler, a screaming mess of a grade-schooler, and a walking teacher's meeting through much of his freshman year. But difficult or easy, he was Joe and Casey's kid. They took him to programs, monitored his homework, remembered his medication, and worked on his behavior modification with his full participation. And sometime in his freshmen year, they'd taken in yet another stray—a girl about his age who had cried nonstop for three weeks, and who had confided in Levi like she had confided in nobody since she'd first been placed in the Daniels home.

Casey was never sure what her story was. She'd been gone within a month to a halfway house with a shrink in residence, because Joe and Casey were afraid for her, and Levi was afraid she'd hurt herself, and that was enough for them. What he did know was that shortly after Cynthia left, Levi had walked up the stairs to their bedroom one night, when they'd both been up reading, and said, "I really love you guys. Dad, Casey? All the shit... I mean, I know I'm not a great student, but you know I love being with you, right?"

Casey and Joe had nodded dumbly, and Levi had turned around and gone down to his room, and they hadn't had one call to the principal's office or to meet a teacher or *anything* besides his yearly IEP meeting for his disability plan since.

Levi had grown up, and grown up fast, and Casey and Joe were beyond grateful.

They'd made sacrifices for this—neither of them regretted it, but they were there. Casey had only worked at Intel for a year. For a year, Joe worked nights and Casey worked days, and they played tag-team to watch Levi, because they did *not* jump through all those hoops to put him in childcare. But the commute—and the time away from Joe—was too damned hard. Casey had quit Intel and become an independent consultant as soon as Joe got DSL. He did okay that way—well enough to pay off the Volvo and for the family to go on some good vacations (lots of trips to that place in Los Angeles to see the mouse with the big ears—Levi *still* would rather go to Disneyland with them than anywhere else on the planet), and well enough to save for Levi's college so he wouldn't have to work. So decent, yes, but they weren't rich. Casey wasn't going to set the world on fire as an engineer; Joe wasn't going to have a cushy retirement until much later than he'd planned. But it didn't matter, because now, when Casey told Levi they had a new stranger, a new kid his age, who was going to share their home and their table and their dogs and their cats (a new generation of each, because time marched on) and, yes, Joe and Casey's time, Levi would say exactly what he was saying now.

"Okay. You want me to show him the ropes?"

And Casey smiled. "God, Levi—you're an awesome kid. You know that, right? I love you so much it's gross."

Levi smiled again. "Well, hell, Casey, I hope so. I've been practicing my suck-up for *years!*"

Casey smiled, stood on tiptoe, and kissed his son on the cheek. "Let's go check on Austin, okay? Joe's giving his info to Roy."

Joe was hanging up as Casey and Levi rounded the corner, and Austin looked up to see them and seemed relieved.

"Roy says you're good to stay for a week or two," Joe said. "Maybe longer, if you fit."

"Anyone ever stay forever?" Austin asked, looking around their little home. There were pictures on the walls—lots of them. Levi as a baby, asleep on Joe's chest; Levi as a five-year-old at Disneyland, hugging Mickey Mouse; the three of them standing at Lake Tahoe on a camping trip, taken by Joe's nephew, Eli. There were pictures of Alvin and Wendy and their three kids, and Eli and his girlfriend, and even one of Joe, Casey, and Levi with Joe's parents, taken shortly before their deaths in 2005. They'd died within a week of each other, and the whole family had gathered to mourn. There were pictures of Levi with fosterlings, camping, playing with the dogs, swimming in Sugar Pine, and pictures taken by Levi of the fosterlings with Joe and Casey at high school graduations and birthday parties. All of them—the entire collage of them down the hallway, behind the couch in the living room, around the big-screen plasma television—were framed, and beautiful, and them.

"Yeah," Joe said gently. "But if you fit, we'll probably only keep you until you're ready to go away to college."

"I'll be eighteen before I graduate," Austin said, looking wistfully at all those pictures, and Joe shrugged.

"Means you age out of foster care, not out of Casey and Joe's radar. Austin, this is Levi, our son. He's going to show you to the bathroom and help you make yourself at home in the guest room. We'll try and get you some clothes that fit in the morning, okay?"

Levi stuck out his hand, and Austin followed him down the hall, the two of them talking quietly about pop singers as they disappeared. Levi liked Miguel, Lil Wayne, and Usher and Casey and Joe let him have them. Joe liked to say that he didn't have to get Levi's taste in music as long as Levi didn't give Joe and Casey crap for theirs. It was a deal—but that didn't mean they didn't give some of Levi's songs a play on family trips, because that was only fair.

So Levi liked R&B, and Austin liked country, and they disappeared down the hallway, hammering out a code for being in each other's lives for an indefinite length of time, leaving Joe and Casey alone.

Casey watched them with a lump in his throat, and then he wrapped his arms around Joe's middle. It was a little harder to do each year, but it was always worth it.

"You think he'll be okay?" Casey asked gruffly, and Joe kissed him on his short graying hair.

"I think he'll be great," Joe said, and then his other arm came around and Casey was engulfed in that familiar, all-encompassing hug. "He's just like you, baby. He's a fighter."

"And I had you."

"And he's got both of us. And Levi. We're unbeatable."

Casey grinned a little. "Team Daniels. We're number one." He followed that up with a sniffle, because the last twenty-five years had been damned short.

"God, you're sweet," Joe said softly.

"Don't fuck with me, Josiah. I'm having a moment."

"So am I. Every moment I'm with you."

Casey gave it up and let a few tears come. "You suck."

"Not tonight. Tomorrow, when the kids are asleep. I promise."

Casey laughed through his tears, because he had to. Because that was the two of them, and that was how they would always be.

AMY LANE is a mother of four and a compulsive knitter who writes because she can't silence the voices in her head. She adores cats, knitting socks, and hawt menz, and she dislikes moths, cat boxes, and knuckle-headed macspazzmatrons. She is rarely found cooking, cleaning, or doing domestic chores, but she has been known to knit up an emergency hat/blanket/pair of socks for any occasion whatsoever or sometimes for no reason at all. She writes in the shower, while commuting, while taxiing children to soccer/dance/karate/oh my! and has learned from necessity to type like the wind. She lives in a spider-infested, crumbling house in a shoddy suburb and counts on her beloved Mate, Mack, to keep her tethered to reality—which he does while keeping her cell phone charged as a bonus. She's been married for twenty-plus years and still believes in Twu Wuv, with a capital Twu and a capital Wuv, and she doesn't see any reason at all for that to change.

Visit Amy's website at http://www.greenshill.com. You can e-mail her at amylane@greenshill.com.

Also from AMY LANE

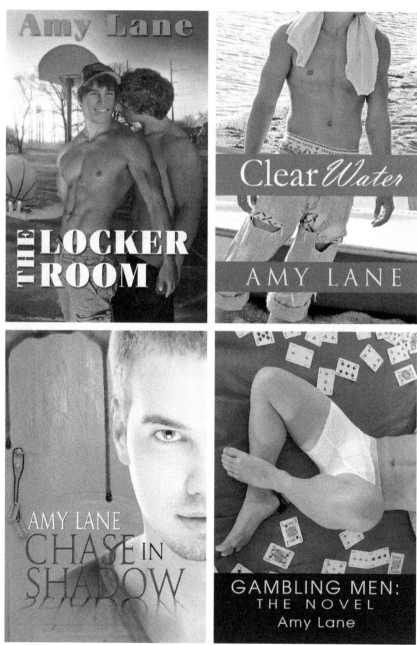

http://www.dreamspinnerpress.com

Also from AMY LANE

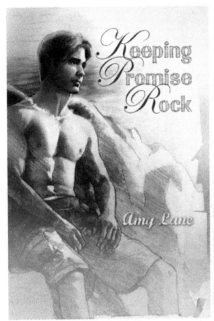

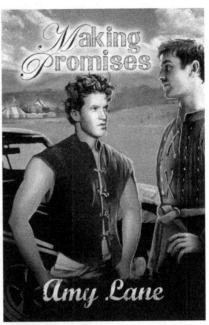

http://www.dreamspinnerpress.com

Also from AMY LANE

Bewitched by Bella's Brother — AMY LANE

the winter courtship rituals of fur-bearing critters — amy lane

Super Sock Man — Amy Lane

If I Must — AMY LANE

http://www.dreamspinnerpress.com

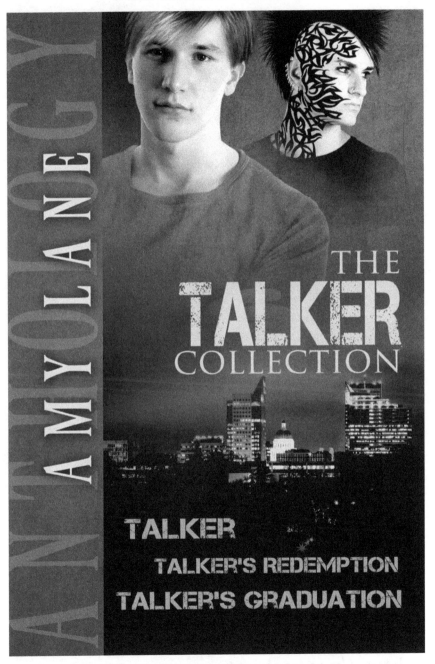

Also from AMY LANE

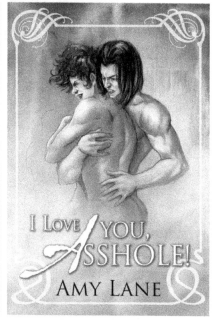

http://www.dreamspinnerpress.com

Now Available in SPANISH

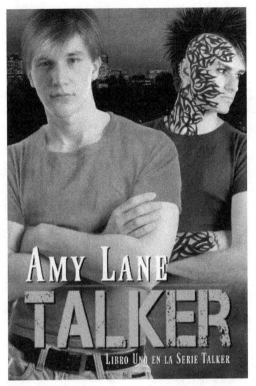

Reseña: Libro Uno en la Serie Talker

Tate "Talker" Walker ha pasado la mayor parte de su vida ocultando sus cicatrices debajo de una fachada punk y no fue hasta que se sentó al lado de Brian Cooper en un autobús, que esa fachada dejó de funcionar.

Brian ha pasado toda su vida siendo el hombre invisible y está acostumbrado a ver más allá de la superficie. Ve en Talker a un ser humano frágil y carente de afecto.

Brian es heterosexual, pero Talker está desesperado por amor y cuando su comportamiento tiene consecuencias dolorosas, se ve forzado a salir del armario… de una forma dramática. Hará lo que sea para que Talker vea que él es el Príncipe Azul que siempre ha necesitado.

http://www.dreamspinnerpress.com

CPSIA information can be obtained
at www.ICGtesting.com
Printed in the USA
BVHW052022181218
535925BV00016B/544/P